Are you the one?

INSIDE A KILLER'S LAIR

Without hesitation, Pescoli walked to the huge cabinet and opened the double doors. Inside were papers. Books on astronomy and astrology were slid into slots. Along with boxes neatly stacked and drawings . . . It was too dark to see, but . . .

Her stomach dropped as she recognized the pages. Notes that had been left on the trees above the victims' heads and more . . . Oh God, so many more.

Telling herself that she was running out of time, shivering with the cold, she surveyed the room for a weapon, or phone, or computer, anything so that she could protect herself and get word to the outside world, but no luck.

She did uncover a flashlight, though, and when she cast its beam over the contents of the armoire one last time, she nearly jumped out of her skin. There, along with the neatly drawn notes with their cryptic messages and stars, were pictures. Of the women he'd captured. Each one naked, bound to a tree, still very much alive, terror in their eyes.

Pescoli's stomach quivered.

She had no choice but to leave the evidence where it was, and find a way of escape. For herself. For Elyssa. For the others he'd alluded to.

Where are they?

Where is Elyssa?

Is she here somewhere?

Or is she already being forced through the forest to a lone tree where she is certain to die a lonely, brutal death . . .

Books by Lisa Jackson

SEE HOW SHE DIES
FINAL SCREAM
WISHES
WHISPERS
TWICE KISSED
UNSPOKEN
IF SHE ONLY KNEW
HOT BLOODED
COLD BLOODED
THE NIGHT BEFORE
THE MORNING AFTER
DEEP FREEZE
FATAL BURN
SHIVER
MOST LIKELY TO DIE
ABSOLUTE FEAR
ALMOST DEAD
LOST SOULS
LEFT TO DIE
WICKED GAME
MALICE
CHOSEN TO DIE

Published by Zebra Books

Chosen To Die

LISA JACKSON

ZEBRA BOOKS
KENSINGTON PUBLISHING CORP.
http://www.kensingtonbooks.com

ZEBRA BOOKS are published by

Kensington Publishing Corp.
119 West 40th Street
New York, NY 10018

All Kensington titles, imprints and distributed lines are
available at special quantity discounts for bulk purchases
for sales promotion, premiums, fund-raising, educational
or institutional use.

Special book excerpts or customized printings can also be
created to fit specific needs. For details, write or phone the
office of the Kensington Special Sales Manager: Attn.: Special Sales Department. Kensington Publishing Corp., 119
West 40th Street, New York, NY 10018. Phone: 1-800-221-
2647.

Zebra and the Z logo Reg. U.S. Pat. & TM Off.

ISBN-13: 978-1-4201-0277-2
ISBN-10: 1-4201-0277-X

First Printing: August 2009

10 9 8 7 6 5 4 3 2 1

Printed in the United States of America

ACKNOWLEDGMENTS

As always there are many people who helped me while I wrote this book. It's a case of the usual suspects, for the most part, and they're great: Nancy Bush, Alex Craft, Matthew Crose, Niki Crose, Michael Crose, Kelly Foster, Marilyn Katcher, Ken Melum, Robin Rue, John Scognamiglio, Larry Sparks, and more. As always, there may be some errors in the book, and they are all mine.

Chapter One

Regan Pescoli was hot.

Not in the sexual sense.

Hot as in furious. As in consumed with rage. As in pissed as hell.

Her hands gripped the wheel of her Jeep so tightly her knuckles bleached white, her jaw was set, and she glared through the windshield as if she could conjure up the image of the soulless bastard who'd sent her into this stratosphere of rage.

"Bastard," she muttered as the county-issued Jeep's tires slid a bit on the icy incline. Her heart was racing and her cheeks were flushed despite the subfreezing temperature outside her vehicle.

No one, not one person on this planet, could make her see red the way her ex-husband

Luke "Lucky" Pescoli could. And today was no exception. In fact, today, he'd crossed the invisible line Regan had drawn and he'd heretofore avoided. Damn, he was a loser. In all the years she'd been married to him, the only "luck" he'd brought her was bad.

Now, out of the blue, the son of a bitch was set on taking her kids away from her.

As the notes of a familiar Christmas tune played through the radio of her Jeep, Regan drove like a madwoman through the steep, snow-covered hills and canyons of this part of the Bitterroot Mountain range. The Jeep, windows fogging, responded, engine growling through the pass, tires spinning over the snowy county road that crossed this particular ridge, the backbone of a mountain that separated her home from that of Lucky and his new wife, a Barbie doll of a woman named Michelle.

Usually Regan loved this barrier.

Today, with worsening weather conditions, it was a pain.

Her last phone conversation with Lucky replayed like a bad record:ng on an unending loop through her mind. He'd called and confirmed that *her* children, the son and daughter she'd raised nearly alone, were with him. Lucky, in that supercilious tone of his, had said, "The kids, Michelle, and I have been talking, and we all agree that Jeremy and Bianca should live with us."

The argument had escalated from that point and just before she'd slammed down the receiver, her parting words to her ex had been firm: "Pack up the kids, Lucky, because I'm coming to get them. And that includes Cisco. I want my son. I want my daughter. I want my dog. And I'm coming to get them."

She'd locked the house and taken off, determined to set things straight and get her kids back. Or kill Lucky. Maybe both.

The Jeep's engine whined in protest on the snowy terrain as she slowed to an irritating crawl. She searched for her hidden, "only in a situation of extreme stress" pack of cigarettes in the glove box and found that it was empty. "Great." She crushed the useless pack and tossed it on the floor in front of the passenger seat. She'd been meaning to quit . . . completely and absolutely quit again for a while. Today, it seemed, was the start.

"Oh, the weather outside is frightful," some female country singer warbled and Pescoli snapped off the radio.

"You got that right," she muttered fiercely and gunned the Jeep around a corner. The tires slid a bit, then held.

She barely noticed.

Nor did she see the tall spruce, fir, and pine trees, their branches drooping under the pressure of snow and ice as they rose like majestic sentinels in the crisp, frigid air and snowflakes poured from invisible clouds. The wipers were slapping away the flakes while the heater thrust out BTUs. Despite the fan, the warmed air flow couldn't keep up with the steam on the inside of the windows.

Pescoli squinted and longed for a single blast of nicotine as she braced herself for the confrontation that was about to ensue. It promised to be epic. So much for "Merry Christmas," "Happy Holidays," and "Peace and goodwill to men." Not in Lucky's case. Not ever. All those platitudes about making nice for the kids, keeping the peace, and reining in her emotions were out the window.

He could not, could *not*, take her kids from her.

Sure, she worked a lot of overtime with the Pinewood County Sheriff's Department and lately, with the winter storms causing widespread electrical outages, road closures, and icy conditions everywhere, the department had been stretched thin. Then there was the Star-Crossed Killer still at large, the first serial killer ever to hunt in this part of Montana.

This guy was bad news. A patient, organized, and skilled killer who somehow shot out the tires of unsuspecting victims, then "rescued" the injured women before squirreling them to some private lair where he nurtured them back to health, gaining their trust and dependence before marching them naked into the storm-ravaged wilderness and strapping them to a tree where he left them to die a slow, agonizing death in the frigid, unforgiving forests.

God, she'd love to nail his ass.

So far the cruel bastard had killed five women, the last one, Hannah Estes, having survived long enough to be found and life-flighted to a hospital where she had died before regaining consciousness and identifying the sick son of a bitch. There was other evidence found at the scenes, of course, the crashed vehicles found far from where the victims were located and even notes left at each killing arena by the slayer, nailed over the victims' heads. But not one shred of evidence so far could be tied to any suspect. Not that they had any real person of interest. At this point, with the victims unrelated, no would-be killer had popped onto the radar.

Yet.

That would change. It had to.

In the meantime, while Pescoli and the whole damned department were logging in extra hours trying to nail the sick son of a bitch, Lucky had the audacity, the unmitigated gall to kidnap her kids and let her know he planned on seeking full custody.

Miserable prick.

She'd hung up from him less than half an hour earlier, called her partner to cover for her, and was now within fifteen minutes of the bastard's place. Popping in a Tim McGraw CD, she realized it belonged to Lucky and ejected it. She tossed the damned thing onto the floor of the passenger seat next to her empty, crumpled pack of Marlboro Lights. She thought fleetingly of Nate Santana, a man with whom she was involved. He had a way of turning her inside out, but she knew he was wrong for her. Way wrong. A good-looking cowboy; the type to avoid. And one she couldn't think about now. Not when she had more important things on her mind.

Damn Lucky!

The Jeep's tires slid a bit and she corrected carefully. She'd been driving these hills in blizzards for years, but she was furious and probably pushing through a bit too aggressively.

Tough.

Outrage guided her.

Her sense of justice fueled her.

She hit the corner a little too fast and started to slide, only to work her way out of it before the Jeep hit the shoulder and careened into the abyss that was Cougar Canyon.

She shifted down. The wheels slid again, as if the

road was covered in a sheet of ice, here near the crest of the final hill. A few more feet and she'd start her way down the hill . . .

Again the rig slipped.

"Losin' your touch," she chided as she reached the corner.

Crack!

The forest echoed with the sound of a high-powered rifle blast.

By instinct Regan ducked and with one hand on the wheel scrabbled for her sidearm.

The Jeep shuddered and she realized what was happening. In the middle of the friggin' blizzard, someone was taking potshots at her vehicle.

Not potshots. It's the Star-Crossed Killer! This is how he initially gets his victims!

Fear knifed her heart.

Her rig spun, tires skidded, her seat belt clutched, and behind the wheel she was useless.

Faster and faster the Jeep spiraled, sliding over the edge of the cliff. Frantically, she grabbed her cell phone, touched it, but it fell from her hand as the Jeep bumped and crashed through trees, lurching over rocks, metal crunching and screaming, glass and cold air spraying inside, the air bag slamming her.

Bam! The Jeep landed on its side, metal shrieking, sharp rocks and debris tearing through the door. Pain screamed up her neck and shoulder and she knew she was hurt.

Warm blood oozed from the side of her head as the Jeep tore through the brush as if on rails, then began to roll.

Oh, God . . .

She clung to the wheel with one hand, still holding tight to her pistol with the other, her world spinning, teeth slamming together and chattering. In her mind's eye she saw the victims of the killer. Rapid-fire images, naked women, dead, their skin blue, ice and snow encrusted to their hair, their bodies lashed so tightly to the trunks of the trees that their skin had broken and bruised, blood running down before freezing.

Oh, Jesus, no.

Blam!

The front end crunched on impact, jarring Pescoli to her bones. Her shoulder felt as if it were on fire, and she was pressed tight by the air bag, the grit from its release in her eyes.

With a scream of twisting metal, the Jeep spiraled off a tree, spinning down the slope, front panels crumpling, a tire popping as it rolled ever faster down the hillside.

Pescoli could barely think past the kaleidoscope of agony and fought to stay conscious. She held fast to her pistol, fumbling for the dash to push the button that would release the magnetic lock on her shotgun, if she could get hold of it.

But she had to. Because if she survived the crash and some son of a bitch carrying a rifle came to rescue her, she'd nail him. No questions asked. Fleetingly she thought of her life and the mess she'd made of it: her children and dead first husband; her second husband, Lucky; and finally Nate Santana, a drifter and sexy son of a bitch she should never have gotten involved with.

So many regrets.

Don't think like that. Stay awake. Stay alive. Be ready

for this twisted maniac and blow his balls straight to hell.

Gritting her teeth, she popped the magnetic lock on the shotgun release but nothing happened. It wouldn't budge. Despair welled but she still had her pistol. Her fingers closed over it now, and she took comfort in knowing it was there.

Shoot first, ask questions later.

She heard another grinding metallic groan as the roof around the roll bars crumpled, crushing down on her.

In a blinding second of understanding, she knew she was about to die.

Perfect!

I watch in satisfaction as the Jeep spins and rolls over the edge of the cliff and into the ravine. Trees shake, great piles of snow fall from limbs, and the sounds of shrieking metal and shattering glass are muted by the storm.

But I cannot rest on my laurels or pat myself on the back, for there is much work to do. And this one, Regan Elizabeth Pescoli . . . no, make that *Detective* Pescoli is different from the others.

She might recognize me.

If she's alive.

If she's conscious.

I must be careful.

Quickly, I roll up the plastic tarp which I laid on the spot where I had such a perfect and clear shot of the road. I lash it onto my pack, then make certain my ski goggles are covering my eyes and that my ski mask, cap, and hood disguise my face. Once assured my identity is obscured, I haul my rifle and begin trudging through the thick snow, grateful that the blowing snow will cover my tracks.

My vehicle is parked in an abandoned logging camp two miles from the spot where the Jeep has landed. Two miles of steep and difficult terrain that will take me hours to cross. Pescoli is not a petite woman and she might fight me.

But I have ways to deal with that.

I start hiking down the back side of the hill that overlooks the road and through a culvert to cover my tracks. It's tight and dark, no water trickling, and it takes a lot longer, but the extra half mile is worth it. Not only will it be harder for the imbecile cops to track, but also it leaves Detective Pescoli in the frigid air a while longer, lets the cold seep deep into her bones so that she'll welcome help from anyone. Even though she'll be wary.

I don't believe she could have survived the crash and gotten out of the car or escaped, not with the damage that I saw and heard as the Jeep spiraled over the edge of the cliff. But even if by some miracle she did survive well enough to extract herself and crawl away from the wreckage, I'll be ready.

A tiny jolt of adrenaline surges through my bloodstream at the thought. I've always loved to hunt, to stalk prey, to test my skills against the most worthy of opponents.

Smiling beneath the neoprene of my ski mask, I realize Regan Pescoli is certain to be one.

Run, I think, the gloved fingers of my right hand tightening over my rifle. *Run like the devil, you stupid cop-bitch!*

But you'll never get away.

* * *

Pescoli could barely breathe.

Her lungs were tight, so damned tight. And the pain . . . God, the pain.

She felt as if all the weight of the crumpled Jeep was compressing on her body, grinding against her muscles, squeezing the air from her lungs, the life from her body.

Don't be a melodramatic idiot.

Get out!

Get out now!

Save yourself!

You know what's happening and it's not good. In fact, it's very, very bad.

Desperately, adrenaline spurring her, she tried to release her seat belt, to thrust the damned air bag away from her face as pain splintered up her shoulder and she let out a wounded yowl.

Jesus!

Where once her body responded to her every command, now she was helpless.

Come on, come on! You don't have much time!

Even now she knew he was out there.

Felt his presence.

Realized he was coming for her with deadly and sure intent.

God in heaven, move, Pescoli, get the hell out of here!

Sucking in her breath, gritting against the pain, she forced her fingers into the space between the seats and pushed hard on the seat belt release button.

Click.

Finally!

Now if she could force the crumpled door or

somehow try to get through the windshield . . . But nothing happened, the belt didn't so much as budge.

What? No!

She tried again.

She heard the same metallic sound of release, but the damned thing was jammed. Like the shotgun catch.

Panic-stricken, she tried over and over again, grimacing against the pain, fearing that any second the killer would appear and that would be the end of it. Of her.

Don't give up! There's still time!

The blood that was oozing from a cut near her temple was freezing on her skin and she was shivering, her teeth chattering as the wind and snow raged through the shattered windshield, yet a nervous sweat ran down her spine.

Any second she expected the sick son of a bitch to appear.

Damn it, you're a sitting duck! Get the hell out of this rig!

If she could just reach the police band radio or her cell phone or . . .

Again she tried to release her seat belt and realized it was no use, the damned buckle was jammed tight. Hell! She was going to have to cut the seat belt . . . but with what? Grabbing at the console, she tried to open the lid, but it, too, was mangled. "Oh, for God's sake," she muttered, forcing one finger through the opening . . . while in her left hand, she still held her gun. There was a knife in her pocket. If she could just reach it . . . or the radio . . . or her cell phone . . . or her safety pack. If she were just wearing her safety pack—but she'd been off duty, so the small radio she sometimes wore at her shoulder was lost in the backseat. She hadn't thought she'd need it in confronting Lucky.

Jaw tight, she tried to reach into her pocket where she kept a pocketknife with a serrated blade, one that could saw through the seat belt.

She struggled to push her right hand into her pants and tried vainly to tamp down her panic, the feeling that any second she might go into shock and render herself useless.

Don't even think that way. Just keep working. You can do this, you can.

Swallowing back terror, she felt the knife with her fingertips. *Come on, come on.* She eased her hand farther into the pocket, all the while listening above the pounding of her heart and the wintry rush of the wind for footsteps or snapped twigs or any noise that didn't fit in this frigid wilderness, any human sound that would warn her of the predator who stalked her.

She would be found by her colleagues; she knew that. Eventually. Given enough time, the sheriff's department would locate her vehicle. Though not equipped with a computer, there were devices within the vehicle that would send out signals and the Jeep would be located. By the good guys.

But with the department stretched thin, and her own request that she needed some time alone, she would either be captured or freeze to death before anyone came looking.

Fear and fury swept through her just as her fingers clenched around the knife.

Finally!

She concentrated on pulling the small weapon up her leg, out of the pocket, away from the pain.

Hands shaking, she finally extracted the knife. Painstakingly, she opened the blade, then madly slashed at the air bag, which hissed and slowly collapsed. She pushed it aside and then began to saw at the seat belt. Her cheeks were numb, her fingers unresponsive as they began to freeze.

If she were uninjured she could have sliced through the belt quickly. As it was, it took all of her strength. She began sawing and *felt* rather than saw that she wasn't alone.

Holy shit.

She froze. The fingers of her left hand were clenched around her semi-automatic Glock. Cramped as she was, she needed the flexibility of the pistol. Once she was free of the wreckage, she could try for the shotgun again, see if she could get the catch to release.

She heard nothing save the scream of the wind and her own panicked heartbeat. She saw nothing but white on white, millions of furious snowflakes falling from the sky, creating a shifting curtain where only shadows and her own imagination created images. Her heart was racing wildly.

I know you're out there, you prick. Show yourself.

Nothing.

She licked her cracked lips, told herself that she was imagining things. She usually didn't take much stock in "gut feelings" or "women's intuition" or "cop's instincts." But now, in this lonely frozen canyon . . .

Was that movement? In the thicket only ten feet from the vehicle?

Heart drumming, she squinted as ice crystals peppered her face.

Nothing.

No! Yes, something was definitely moving . . . She dropped the knife and put both hands on the pistol, training it through the shattered windshield. Another shadow.

She pulled the trigger as the image leaped.

Bam!

The bullet hit the bole of a snow-blanketed pine. Bark and chunks of ice and snow exploded.

A great buck leaped out from behind the trees and sprang up the hill, a frightened gray shadow disappearing into the whiteout.

"Oh, God," she whispered, adrenaline spiking through her bloodstream. *A deer. Only a damned deer.*

She let her breath out slowly, started sawing again, and had convinced herself she was overreacting when she saw something move in the fragments of her rearview mirror.

She looked again and it was gone.

Get over yourself.

One last swipe with the knife and the seat belt released just as she felt a sharp sting against her nape.

What?

She slapped the back of her neck, felt something cold and metallic, a small missile lodged near her spine. Her heart turned to stone as she yanked a dart free.

Her insides liquified.

She nearly dropped the damned thing. Someone had shot her with what? Any kind of drug or poison could be inside the slim silver canister with its short needle and hidden charge that forced the foreign substance into her body.

She wanted to throw up.

Don't! Keep your wits! The bastard's near . . .

Again there was movement in the reflective shards of what remained of the mirror—a blurry shifting.

She blinked hard, brought up her pistol as she turned toward the window, but it was too late. Her fingers were already not responding to her brain's commands, the images in her mind scrambled, a tingling spreading through her.

The drug . . .

Another movement in the shattered, crumpled mirror.

The shotgun. She needed the shot . . . gun . . .

She tried to respond, to look for her assailant, but she was feeling numb all over. Her head lolled to one side, the pistol slipped from her fingers, and the world began to spin in eerie slow motion, images becoming dim and foggy.

"No!" she said, her tongue thick as she tried and failed to find her sidearm again.

And then she saw him, his features distorted by the broken mirror, a tall figure in white, ski mask obscuring his face, huge dark goggles shielding his eyes.

She was beginning to fade, to slip beneath the surface of consciousness as he said, "Detective Pescoli," in a warm voice that indicated he knew her. He was only a few feet away . . . if she could just aim her weapon . . . "Looks like you've had yourself an accident."

She rolled her eyes up at him and with one last great effort snarled, "Go to hell."

"Already there, Detective, but at least now I won't be alone. You're going to join me."

Not if I can help it, she thought with a sudden

burst of clarity. She scrabbled for her pistol, her hands sluggish as she brought it up and fired.

A series of blasts echoed through the canyon.

But the shots missed. Her aim was off.

As close as he was, she'd missed him, hitting only trees and rocks and God knew what else.

He sighed and clucked his tongue. "You're going to regret that."

She wanted to squeeze off another round but her fingers refused to respond and the best she could do as he came closer was to swipe at him with her hand, her fingernails catching in his ski mask, then tearing down his skin. He let out a surprised yelp.

"You bitch!"

That's me, jerk-wad, and I've got your epithelials and DNA under my fingernails. If I'm ever found, you're as good as dead.

She noticed blood welling on his skin and he reached into some kind of pack and pulled out something . . . an apron? God, she just couldn't focus . . . everything was so distorted . . . but she should recognize the piece of clothing dangling from his hand . . .

A straitjacket?

A chilling, mind-numbing fear sliced through her.

She realized he wasn't going to let her die easily or quickly, he was going to keep her alive, torture her, nurture her, but inevitably kill her, just like the others.

But a straitjacket? Being bound and rendered completely helpless . . . it was as if he understood her worst, most terrifying fears.

The white blizzard swam before her eyes, his image and that of the straitjacket clouding in the swirling, dancing, icy flakes.

As she sank into unconsciousness she felt no fear;

just a hard-edged determination that if she ever woke up again she was going to take this son of a bitch down. Way down. To a place so dark he would never, ever see the light again.

She only prayed she'd someday get the chance.

Chapter Two

Where the hell is she?

As a brutal storm shrieked through the surrounding canyons, Nate Santana paced in the stable, his cell phone pressed hard to his ear, no sound emanating from the slim, useless device. "Come on, come on," he encouraged but he knew it was no good.

Regan, damn her, was MIA.

No service appeared on the phone's small screen.

Frustrated, Santana jammed his cell into the pocket of his worn jeans and told himself to remain calm. He was just keyed up from everything that had gone on in the sleepy town of Grizzly Falls in the last few weeks. No big deal.

And yet, he felt worry eating at his gut, reminding him that everything that had been good in his life always disappeared and that Pescoli, damned her sexy ass, was the best thing that had happened to him in a long, long while . . . probably since Santa Lucia . . .

His thoughts took a dark twist as he considered the last woman who had changed the course of his life, then pushed her beautiful image from his mind. Shannon Flannery was past history.

Right now, he had to deal with the fact that Regan was ducking his calls.

Or was she?

He shoved a hand through his hair and glared at the indoor arena where a particularly stubborn and nervous colt was staring back at him, challenging him.

Usually Santana could be easily distracted by animals. In his experience they were a helluva lot easier to deal with than people. More trustworthy. More constant. But this frigid morning, he couldn't concentrate, his thoughts creeping ever to Regan.

Hell, he had it bad. And he hated it that she'd somehow gotten under his skin. *You let her. You allowed a quick, no-strings-attached fling to develop into a full-fledged affair starting to border on a relationship.*

His jaw tightened at the thought.

She was the worst woman he could have chosen to get involved with. The absolute *worst*!

He mentally castigated himself, calling himself a long list of names that grew progressively more derogatory. No woman in a long time had infiltrated his brain, or caused him to think about finding ways to get her into bed at all hours of the day. And Regan was a damned detective with the Pinewood County Sheriff's Department, for crying out loud.

What did *that* tell you?

Avoid. Avoid. Avoid!

But he'd been drawn to her like a dying man in the desert to an oasis.

A glance through the window confirmed that the mother of a storm wasn't letting up. Sub-zero wind howled through the deep ravines of this part of Montana. Ice glazed the outside of the panes and the snow was falling so thick and fast, he couldn't see the lights glowing in his cabin only a hundred feet away.

Inside, the huge stable with its indoor exercise arena was warm, the heating system wheezing and stirring up the dust of last summer, while the familiar smells of saddle soap and horse dung, scents he'd known all his life, filled his nostrils. Horses shuffled in their stalls; one, the nervous mare, sent out a quiet whinny. Sounds and odors that usually calmed him. Truth be known, he felt far more akin to animals than he did to most men. Or women, for that matter.

Until damned Regan Pescoli.

With her two children.

Two finished marriages.

Their relationship, basically all sex, wasn't the least bit romantic or conventional.

No vows.

No promises.

No strings.

No big deal.

Right?

So why was he edgy and restless? What was it to him that he couldn't reach her? They'd gone days without speaking before, even, upon occasion, a week. Though not lately. In the past few months, they had been in contact nearly daily. Or nightly. And he wasn't complaining.

He reminded himself that up here cell phone service was notoriously lousy, and that getting the NO SIGNAL message was nothing new. Even Brady Long, Santana's pain-in-the-ass employer, heir to a copper fortune and not afraid to throw his money around, couldn't get a cell tower built anywhere nearby. Which was usually just fine by Santana. A loner by nature, he didn't have a lot of interest or faith in technology.

Except for this morning.

So what if you can't get in touch with her? You know she's got to be up to her eyeballs in police business. The damned Star-Crossed Killer is still on the loose and there has to be emergency after emergency in this blizzard, homes without electricity, cars sliding off the road, people freezing to death. She's busy. That's all. Don't push the panic button.

Still, he felt it. That little premonition of dread that caused the hairs on the back of his neck to bristle and stomach acid to crawl up his throat whenever trouble was brewing. Not that he hadn't caused his own share of heartache and misery, but nonetheless, he sensed bad things coming; had since he was a kid.

"It's that damned native blood in ya," his father had always muttered under his breath when Nate had mentioned the feeling. "On your mother's side. Her great grandfather—or was it great-great?—was some kind of Indian shaman or some such crap. Could heal people with his touch. Cursed 'em, too. Well, according to yer mother. He was an Arapaho,

I think, or was it Cheyenne? Don't matter. He seen him a rattler or somethin' in a dream once and that did it. He became the medicine man. Prob'ly had the same damned tingling sensation you do, boy."

After these tarnished bits of insight, his old man had usually bitten at a plug of tobacco and chewed with great satisfaction, only to spit and wipe his mouth with the back of his sleeve. "All horseshit, in my book."

Not that Santana had ever thought for a second his gut instincts had anything to do with his ancestry. But tonight he sensed something outside. Something dark and intimately evil. Something threatening. To Regan.

Clenching his jaw, he told himself to ignore it. He didn't like the premonitions and didn't admit to them, wasn't going to take the kind of ridicule leveled at Ivor Hicks for his supposed alien abduction or Grace Perchant, a woman who bred wolf dogs and confessed to speaking with the dead, or Henry Johansen, a farmer who had fallen off his tractor fifteen years earlier, hit his head, and claimed he could "hear" other people's thoughts. Nope, Santana would keep his mouth shut about his sensations rather than suffer the ridicule of the townspeople.

As for Regan, he'd catch up with her later, one way or another. He always did. Besides, it wasn't as if they were married or even an item; that's the way they both wanted it.

He walked to the indoor arena where Lucifer, still glaring at him, pawed the soft dirt. A big black colt with a crooked blaze and one white stocking, he had a nasty streak that some would call independence; others referred to it as just being ornery.

Nate figured it was one and the same. Now the rangy colt's nostrils were flared, his eyes white around the rims, a nervous sweat and flecks of lather visible on his sleek hide.

"It's okay," he said softly, when he knew deep in his gut it wasn't. And the horse knew it, too. That was Santana's talent, or "gift," as it were. He understood animals, especially horses and dogs. He respected them for the animals they were, didn't put any human traits on them and, from years of observation and experience, learned to work with them.

Some people called him "weird"; others compared him to a snake charmer or blamed it on his mixed heritage when the truth of the matter was he used common sense, determination, and kindness. He just knew how to work with them. Maybe it was part of the Arapaho in him, but probably not.

He grabbed the coil of rope from a hook on the wall, slipped through the gate of the arena, then walked slowly toward the beast as the gate clicked behind him. Another blast of wind shrieked through the canyons, rattling the windowpanes and causing a twitch to come alive in the big colt's shoulder.

"Shh." Santana kept coming. Steady. Calm. Even though deep inside he felt the same tension that the horse was exuding, a fear akin to the panic visible in Lucifer's wild eyes. At any second the colt would bolt.

Thud!

The door to the stables banged open.

Santana froze.

And Lucifer took off like a shot. Zero to thirty in three short strides, hooves flashing and thundering, kicking up dirt as he galloped close enough to Santana that he could hear the colt's breath, feel his heat as a gust of frigid Montana wind whistled and swirled into the room.

His dog, a large Siberian husky, sent up a howl loud enough to wake the dead in the next county, and all the horses in the stable snorted and neighed, fidgeting restlessly.

"Nakita, hush!" Santana commanded and the big dog reluctantly lay down, blue eyes still focused on Santana.

Lucifer, tail up, eyes rimmed in white, ran back and forth along the penned area. If he could have, the big colt would have jumped the top rail of the enclosure and galloped as far and fast as his strong legs would carry him, clear through the door and across Brady Long's two thousand acres.

"Great," Santana muttered, knowing whatever confidence he'd gained with the anxious colt had been shattered. "Just . . . damned great."

He turned his attention to the open doorway, searching for whoever had been foolish enough to let the door slam. "Hey!" he called out as he climbed over the fence separating the exercise ring from the rest of the stable, vaulting the top rail and landing lightly on his booted feet.

No idiot stomping off snow and shaking away the cold appeared in the doorway. Only Nakita whining and staring outside to the dark night.

Frost-laden air screamed inside, but no one appeared.

Nate yanked the door closed, double-checked the latch as a drip of ominous worry slithered down his spine. The door had been closed tight, the latch secure. He was certain. He'd pulled it shut himself.

Or had he been so distracted by his missing woman that he had been careless and a stiff gust of wind had pushed the old door open? The latch had always been dicey. He'd been meaning to fix it; it just hadn't been high on his priority list.

Again, he had the uncanny sensation that someone was with him; that he wasn't alone. But all he heard was the sound of restless hooves in the surrounding stalls and the snorts of horses disturbed from their normal routines. He trained his eyes on the boxes, noting that the roan mare and bay gelding in abutting stalls were staring at the corner near the feed bins. Lucifer had stopped galloping wildly, but held his head high, his nostrils flared. As he slowed, his dark coat quivered and his gaze was centered dead-on Santana.

Nate grabbed a pitchfork from its hook on the wall and took two steps toward the shadowy corner near the oat bin.

Brrriiing!

The stable phone shrieked.

He nearly jumped from his skin.

Gloved hand holding the handle of the pitchfork in a death grip, he retraced his steps and snagged the receiver of the phone mounted near the door.

"Santana," he barked, receiver pressed to his ear as he scoured the interior of the stable with his gaze.

"This is Detective Selena Alvarez, Pinewood County Sheriff's Department."

He felt every muscle in his body tense. "Yeah."

"I'm Detective Regan Pescoli's partner."

He already knew that much. What he didn't know was whether Regan had confided to Alvarez that she and he were involved.

"Uh-huh."

"Pescoli didn't show up for work today. I thought you might know where she is."

So the cat was out of the bag about their affair. Good. "I haven't seen her."

"How about last night?"

His jaw tightened. "No."

"Look, I know you and she have a thing going. She never really talks about it, but I pieced it together, so if you know where she is—"

"I don't," he cut her off. "We were together a couple of nights ago. Haven't seen her since," he admitted, his jaw setting. "I've been calling her cell and the house phone. No answer."

"I was afraid of that." The woman swore softly and frustration was in her voice. Santana felt a chill colder than the bowels of hell. "If you hear from her, will you have her call in?"

"Yeah." He sensed Alvarez was about to hang up and asked, "Where do you think she is?"

"If we knew that, I wouldn't be calling you." She hung up and the word *we* reverberated through his mind. As in *we: the Pinewood County Sheriff's Department*. He replaced the phone, his guts twisting, the sensation that something was wrong validated. If the damned police department didn't know where she was, things were worse than he'd feared.

Boom!

Grace Perchant's eyes flew open.

Although, she thought, they'd never been closed.

She blinked. Tried to clear her mind when the sound of the blast, like the clap of nearby thunder, ricocheted through her brain again.

Snow was falling around her and she was standing in the middle of the road, in boots, her flannel nightgown, and a long coat flapping around her legs, her skin ice cold. Her dog, Sheena, was nearby, ever vigilant, ever loyal. With intelligent eyes and a black coat that belied her wolf lineage, Sheena waited patiently.

As she always did.

Even when Grace suffered one of her spells.

"Lord," Grace whispered, shivering, her fingers and toes nearly numb, her breath a cloud.

Images from her dream slid through her mind. Visceral. Raw. Real. Like shards of glass that cut through her brain.

She caught a flash, a quick, horrifying glimpse of a woman in a mangled Jeep, her body racked with pain. And a stalker. The evil one tracking her down.

Grace's heart rate accelerated as the image changed to a vision of that same woman now laced in a straitjacket and being hauled out of a wintry canyon. By a man in white, a man with evil intent.

Quickly the scene changed and the female victim was now naked, lashed to a frozen hemlock tree, her red hair stiff with ice and snow, her gold eyes round with fear, her skin turning blue.

Regan Pescoli.

The cop.

With heart-stopping certainty Grace knew that the monster had found her. Attacked her. Planned to kill her. If he hadn't already.

This wasn't the first time she'd had a vision; once before she'd caught a glimpse of the monster's innate and relentless evil purpose.

At that time, only a few days earlier, Grace had

tried to warn Pescoli, had told her of her imminent danger, but the detective had dismissed her.

As they all did.

So now the visions were more graphic. Closer. She looked up at the dark sky, felt the film of icy flakes melt against her skin. Her teeth were chattering. How long had she been out here? How far had she trudged like a sleepwalker along this winding, lonely road?

"Come, Sheena," she said, wrapping her arms around her waist as the wind keened through the hills. "Home."

The big dog, nearly 150 pounds, started trotting briskly along the fresh tracks that were beginning to fill with snow, her own footsteps, the wolf dog's paw prints, leading back the way from which they'd come, the way she couldn't remember having traveled.

Had she walked a couple of a hundred miles or one mile? The landscape at night, frozen and white, looked all the same. And her mind, usually clearer than ever after waking from her visions, couldn't discern any landmarks. But the tracks were fresh and she didn't think she was suffering from frostbite.

But she had to be close.

She half ran to keep up with the dog.

She hated the visions, for that's what they were, and wished they would stop, but they wouldn't. Not until she died, she thought morosely as she held her coat tight around her, the coat she didn't remember donning, and her boots crunched in the soft snow.

The visions had started when she was thirteen, at

the time of the accident that had taken the lives of her parents and older sister, Cleo. It had been a winter night much like this one. She and Cleo had been arguing in the backseat while their father squinted into the coming blizzard. Their old Volvo was straining uphill, the four-cylinder engine humming loudly, the tires sliding a bit, the radio filled with static.

"Goddamned snow," Father muttered. "I swear, next spring we're moving to Florida!"

"No!" Cleo overheard this. "We can't move! All my friends are here."

"Doesn't matter," he insisted and snapped off the radio. His jaw was set, same as it always was when he'd made up his mind. Headlights from an oncoming vehicle washed his face in stark relief. From the backseat, behind Mother, Grace had thought he'd looked suddenly old, the lines in his face seeming craggy and harsh.

Cleo pouted and ordered Mother, "Tell him we can't move!"

She turned to make eye contact with Cleo and said quietly, "Of course we won't."

"I'm serious." Father squinted, the headlights looming as they approached the curving bridge that spanned Boxer Creek as it cut through the canyon some fifty feet below.

"You can't be!" Cleo unbuckled her seat belt and leaned forward, pleading, touching his tense shoulder gently. "Don't even joke about it. I won't move."

"Honey, we aren't moving anywhere. Your father's a foreman at the mine. Now, come on, let's not worry about this."

Then, "What the hell?" Panic tightened their father's voice as the oncoming vehicle drew closer. "Dim those lights, you son of a bitch." He flashed his own lights.

"Hank," their mother reproved. Headlights, two blinding orbs, flooded the interior with harsh white light. "Hank! Watch out!"

Too late!

Trying to avoid the imminent collision, Father cranked on the steering wheel, and the car began to slide. Out of control. The passing truck hit their rear end and sent the Volvo spinning crazily.

Cleo screamed and was flung across Grace.

Grace's head hit the side window. Pain exploded in her skull.

Mother was yelling, "Watch out, watch out, oh, God!" as the wagon hit the rail, bounced back onto the slick pavement, and skidded ever faster to the other side of the bridge.

The reeling Volvo crashed through the guardrail in a horrifying groan of twisting metal, popping tires, and splintering glass.

Oh, God, oh, God, oh, God . . .

Down the car plunged!

Cleo was screaming.

Mother prayed.

And Father cursed as Grace lost consciousness.

She didn't feel the crash that snapped her mother's neck and caused broken ribs to puncture her father's lungs. She hadn't been awake to witness Cleo being flung from the car and pinned beneath it, crushed to death.

Eighteen days later, Grace awoke in a hospital to learn that the rest of her family was gone. Dead. She'd managed to live, though she'd been half frozen in the creek waters, her body temperature dangerously low, only a few bruises from the seat belt and a concussion to indicate she'd been in the deadly wreck. No other driver or damaged vehicle had ever been located and when she was advised that her family was dead, she'd simply answered "No."

Because she saw them.

Talked to them.

All of them: Father, Mother, and Cleo.

Even now. Forty-some years later.

Of course, the hospital staff were sure she was crazy, hallucinating, her brain conjuring up images.

If only, she thought now as the dog rounded a corner and she saw her small house, flanked by snowdrifts and dark as sin, sitting on a small hillock just off the road. Rubbing her arms, Grace picked up her pace and told herself that even if she told someone about her latest vision, she'd be disregarded. Sneered at.

Before the accident, as a child, she'd sometimes been lost in daydreams. Had been left on the playground more than once, never hearing the bell or the hoots and laughter of the other children.

Then, she'd been teased and had often run home crying, only to hear her mother say she was "special," while Cleo cringed at "the weirdo" who was her sister. Those days her dreams had been labeled as nothing more than the fantasies of a "gifted" child. There had been no medical reason that she sometimes blanked out. And though her IQ tests and exams had placed her right in the center of normal, her mother had always whispered to her that she was smarter than the others who cruelly taunted her, that they, the ones who called her "retard," were to be pitied.

But the playground barbs cut deep and after the

accident, when Grace still spoke to her dead parents and sister on a regular basis, worrying her aunt Barbara, and after she adopted her first puppies— two wolves who had lost their mother to a poacher— her visions had increased. Become more real, more definitive.

Those school bullies were right. Her condition *was* weird.

Now she made her way up the path to her door and found it ajar. Inside the house was cold, the ancient furnace unable to keep up with the frigid arctic temperature swept inside by the howling wind. Locking the door behind her, she turned on the lights and kicked off her boots.

She was keyed up. Edgy. Nerves strung tight.

After hanging her coat in the closet, she found her robe and cinched it tight about her waist. She lit a fire from kindling she'd stacked near the grate, then rocked back on her heels and watched the eager flames devour the paper and dry wood. As the flames ignited, crackling and hissing, promising warmth, Sheena curled up on a thick bed that Grace had sewn.

"Good girl," she said, warming her hands as she spied the clock on the mantel, near the fading, framed photograph of her family. It was morning, a few hours before dawn, and the images of Regan Pescoli were still with her.

The fire burned bright, golden shadows shifting through the small living area in the house where she'd resided all her life.

"An onus," she confided in Sheena, who was lying down, great head on her paws, eyes focused on Grace. No wonder she took the heat she did.

Rod Larimer, owner of the Bull and Bear, an inn of sorts in town, had referred to her as "our resident looney." And Bob Simms, the hunter who had killed the she-wolf twenty years earlier, had been known to say, "Crazy as a fruitcake. A real nutso. Should be locked up, if you ask me." Manny Douglas, a writer for the *Mountain Reporter,* had once described her as one of "Grizzly Falls's local color." Manny had kindly lumped her in with the likes of Ivor Hicks, who'd thought he'd been abducted by aliens in the seventies, and Henry Johansen, a farmer who fell off his tractor and hit his head only to claim he could read other people's minds.

Like you? she asked herself while staring at the flames.

Not all of the townspeople thought she was crazy. A few actually liked the whole clairvoyant thing, found it, and her, fascinating. Sandi Aldridge, the owner of Wild Will's, was always kind, and Aunt Barbara, though disgruntled at having to move here to take care of her brother's only surviving child, had always told her to accept the gift God had given her.

Hah. Now Grace grabbed a poker and jabbed at the fire, causing sparks to dance and red embers to glow a little more brightly. Going to the Pinewood County Sheriff's Department wouldn't be pleasant. Not at all. Sheriff Dan Grayson wasn't a fan and Pescoli's partner, Selena Alvarez, seemed icy and remote. But then that woman had secrets, held them close. Grace was certain of it. And she didn't like the idea of trying to convince Grayson, or Alvarez, or anyone associated with the police about her vision. She didn't want to suffer the ridicule that was certain to be thrust her way.

"What should I do?" she asked the dog and in that moment Grace heard her father's voice, clear as a bell. "Be smart," he advised gruffly. "Keep your damned mouth shut."

But her mother, as she had in life, disagreed with her husband. "Don't worry about what anyone says about you. A woman's life is at stake. You owe it to her to tell what you know."

"I don't *know* anything," Grace argued, feeling some warmth return to her toes.

"Don't you?" Her mother seemed close enough to touch, but, of course, Grace saw no one, not even a transparent ghostly outline. Just heard voices. As ever.

Straightening, she picked up the picture from the mantel. Staring at the photograph of her family clustered on the front porch pulled at her heartstrings. But she quickly pushed aside any maudlin sense of nostalgia or self-pity.

Images of Regan Pescoli's tortured face appeared again, and Grace drew in a deep, steadying breath. It was only a matter of time before she bucked up and faced the ridicule that was sure to be a part of confiding in the police.

"You know," she said to the now sleeping dog, "Sometimes gift is just another word for curse."

Strike three.

Seated at her desk in her cubicle at the department, Selena Alvarez swiped at her nose with a tissue and glowered at her computer monitor. She'd called Pescoli on her cell, gotten no response, tried to reach her partner's ex-husband, Luke "Lucky"

Pescoli, but the guy wasn't answering. Finally, she'd dialed Nate Santana again with no luck. Though Pescoli hadn't confided the name of her most recent in a string of loser lovers, Alvarez was certain Santana was the man she'd been seeing. The guy was just Pescoli's type: a good-looking drifter who'd rolled into town a few years back and had recently caught Selena's partner's eye.

When it came to men, Pescoli never seemed to learn.

Her first husband, Joe Strand, had been a cop who had taken a bullet in the line of duty, but there had been questions about his ethics. Pescoli had admitted to Alvarez that she'd married Strand, her college sweetheart, after learning she was pregnant and that there had been cracks in their marriage, affairs when they'd separated a while. Luke Pescoli, her sexy-as-hell but useless second husband, now owed her thousands in back child support.

That was the problem with Pescoli, she picked men for their looks rather than their brains or moral character. Nate Santana was a case in point. The guy was the quiet type, with black hair, razor-sharp features, and piercing dark eyes that never reflected any of his thoughts. An athletic cowboy type with a whip-tough body and cutting sense of humor, he appeared as ready to ride a bareback bronc as he was to spend all night making love.

Good for a fling, maybe. Definitely not suitable for a husband, which Pescoli had claimed she didn't want anyway.

Alvarez blew her nose and told herself not to worry. After all, Pescoli had called in. Again Alvarez replayed the message:

"It's me. Hey, I've got a personal issue to deal with. Lucky and the kids. It might take a while, so cover for me, will ya?" Pescoli's voice had been firm. Determined. Borderline angry.

So what else was new?

But that call had been made yesterday.

No word from her today.

Something was off. Definitely wrong. Pescoli was nothing if not a dedicated cop. Surely she would have called again, especially since there had been an arrest in the Star-Crossed Killer murders. No way would Detective Regan Pescoli have missed out on the action, not after months of trying to track down the whack job.

Sniffing, Alvarez tossed the tissue into her overflowing trash basket tucked under her desk. This cold—flu—she'd contracted was starting to really piss her off.

She doubted that she was overreacting. Even though Pescoli had indicated whatever issue she was dealing with would take some time, this was all wrong.

Alvarez glanced at the clock mounted high on the wall. Pescoli's message had come in late yesterday afternoon and since that time the Spokane Police Department in Washington state thought they'd arrested the killer.

Alvarez wasn't so sure.

Nothing seemed right today. But soon Sheriff Dan Grayson would be on his way to verify that the person who had been captured by the Spokane Police Department, and was now accused of being the serial killer who had terrorized this part of Montana, was their sick doer.

But Alvarez doubted the suspect arrested would prove to be the Star-Crossed Killer. The person in custody was definitely a would-be murderer, but so far, Alvarez hadn't been able to tie the suspect to any of the previous crimes. She glanced at the pictures of the victims lying upon her desk. Five women. Different races and ages with no connection to each other. She bit her lip and tapped her fingers as she thought about how hard Regan Pescoli had worked the case.

She would have moved heaven and earth to be a part of the suspect's arrest, no matter what her personal issues were. And she would have known about it. The stand-off and arrest had been splashed all over the news. Though most of the members of the press had swooped down on Spokane, a few reporters had stayed on in Grizzly Falls, still camped out in the surrounding streets, hoping for a new angle on the biggest story to hit Grizzly Falls since Ivor Hicks had claimed he'd been transported to a mothership by aliens.

She slid a glance to the clock on the wall. Nearly five P.M. . . . no way would Pescoli miss this kind of action.

Something was definitely wrong.

Alvarez scooted her chair back and tried not to think of the warning Pescoli had received from Grace Perchant, no less. Grace was an odd sort, cursed with some sort of psychic ability, if you believed her. Alvarez didn't. All she really knew about the odd woman was that Grace raised wolf dogs and talked to ghosts and never made much trouble. But recently, while Pescoli and Alvarez were having lunch at Wild Will's, Grace had approached the table. Her voice had been low, her pale green eyes troubled.

"He knows about you," Grace had said to Pescoli, her gaze lost in a middle distance only she could see.

"Who?" Pescoli had asked, playing along.

"The predator."

Alvarez had felt it then, that dip in the temperature that accompanies fear.

"The one you seek," Grace had clarified. "The one who is evil. He's relentless. A hunter."

Pescoli had been angry and had taken it out on the clairvoyant, but she, too, had been scared. They'd both known that Grace was talking about the maniac the media had dubbed the Star-Crossed Killer.

He's relentless. A hunter.

That much was true.

And an ace marksman.

He, Grace had said distinctly. Not *she*. Not the woman demanding to talk to her attorney in Spokane, the one everyone wanted to confront about the killings.

Sniffing some more, Alvarez leaned back in her desk chair. She wasn't one to scare easy, but today she felt a stark fear she tried like hell to deny.

The horror was spread around her in glossy, colored photographs of the victims. Five in all. Or, she thought as she picked up a picture of Theresa Charleton, the first victim, five that they knew of.

There could be others.

Innocent women naked and bound to trees in the wilderness, abandoned to die a long and painful death in the frigid temperatures of the icy landscape.

"Sicko." Selena's jaw hardened as she glanced

through a nearby ice-crusted window to the gloomy day beyond. Steely gray clouds huddled over the mountains, dumping snow, threatening a blizzard. Already parts of the county were experiencing downed lines and no power as the temperatures plummeted far below freezing.

"Merry Christmas," she told herself, as the holiday was just around the corner.

She tossed the picture of the first victim onto her desk with the rest and gazed at the grouping. Alvarez felt as if she knew all the victims intimately:

Theresa Charleton, married, no children, a schoolteacher from Boise, Idaho, who had been visiting her parents in Whitefish, Montana. Her nude body had been found lashed to the bole of a hemlock tree, her initials and a star cut into the bark, a note nailed above her head with the same information from the killer, the man whom they suspected shot out the tire of her green Ford, then, after the car had spun out of control and been totaled, extricated Charleton from the wreckage and took her somewhere to nurture her back to health. This before cruelly and savagely hauling her to a remote spot in the forest, tying her to a tree, and leaving her to die with her initials carved into the bark of the tree. A note had been left, her initials printed in bold block letters: **T C**

Now Alvarez stared at the picture of Theresa's face taken at the crime scene far from where her car had been located. The other victims had each suffered a similar fate: Nina Salvadore, a single mother from Redding, California, whose crushed red Focus had been discovered miles from her body. The note left at that scene had read:

T SC   N

No one, not even cryptologists nor agents with the FBI with cryptogram-busting computer programs, had understood the meaning of the notes. Afterward, in rapid succession, the bodies of Wendy Ito and Rona Anders had been located. Then Hannah Estes had been found alive near an abandoned hunting lodge by a news crew and taken to a hospital, only to die later as the disguised killer had boldly entered the hospital, yanking her life support and making certain she expired. Hannah hadn't been able to tell what she knew, or identify her killer, nor had any of the hospital cameras taken a decent photo of his image.

Bad damned luck.

All of the women had been driving alone through this area of the Bitterroot Mountains when their cars had been assaulted and they'd been taken from the original crime scene to be nurtured, then, like Charleton and Salvadore before them, had been strapped to a tree in a remote location and left to die an icy, brutal death. The notes and carvings at the scenes had only been different because of the positions of the stars and initials, but the result had been the same: Five women dead, the final note now reading:

WAR THE SC IN

With each victim's initials added into the text, the sheriff's department and FBI had come up with different ideas for the meaning of the letters, thinking perhaps that they could be jumbled, or that the killer was just screwing with them, that there was no meaning at all.

But deep down, they all knew that the killer, a very organized and clever person, was not only trying to tell them something, he was lording it over them that he was smarter than they. If his note was to make any sense, then he'd obviously picked out his victims before they'd been put through his personal emotional gauntlet of wrecking their vehicles, "saving" them, nursing them back to health somewhere, and then ruthlessly and cruelly leaving them to die in the wilderness.

He hadn't sexually molested any of them.

That seemed out of place.

His dominance wasn't physical, so much as emotional.

As far as they could tell, he set the women up, could just as easily have killed them, shot them in the head, or left them to die in their vehicles, but he rescued them, then abandoned them, assured they would die.

So far, he'd been right.

Except that now, if the Spokane Police and press were to be believed, the killer had supposedly been unmasked and captured . . . and *he* had turned out to be a *she*.

No way.

Alvarez took a sip of her cooling tea, then found a cough drop and sucked on it as she read over her notes for the dozenth time. As she did she was more certain than ever that Regan Pescoli was in trouble.

She tried Lucky Pescoli's house phone one more time and heard a cheery little voice, that of his wife Michelle, nearly giggling as she said, "You've reached

Lucky and Michelle. We're out right now, but leave a message and maybe . . . you'll get Lucky!"

Puke. Alvarez hated those pathetically cutesy voice-mail greetings. She didn't bother leaving a message. Just sucked on her menthol drop and flipped through copies of the notes the killer had left.

Craig Halden, one of the FBI field agents working the case, had carefully mapped out the stars left on the notes and chiseled into the bark of the trees where the women had been found. Using tracing paper he had overlapped the notes to show the position of the stars and in so doing decided the killer had chosen the constellation of Orion focusing on Orion's belt. Alvarez had done her own research on the subject and found that in mythology Orion was stung by a scorpion, then flung high into the sky.

If her theory was right and the last word of the note was scorpion as in **WAR OF THE SCORPION**, or, the phrase she was partial to, due to the spacing of the letters: **BEWARE THE SCORPION**, then theoretically, Regan Pescoli, with her initials of R and P, could be in real trouble.

As Grace Perchant had predicted.

"Damn." Selena's heart contracted as she took one last glance at the photographs of the Star-Crossed Killer's victims and plucked another tissue from her rapidly dwindling box.

Was Pescoli to be the next victim?

Alvarez's eyes narrowed. If so, then her car would be disabled somewhere, a shot through a front tire, a perfect shot from an expert sniper.

And if that were the case, sooner or later, Pescoli's Jeep would be found.

Or could she have had it out with her ex? A confrontation that had turned violent?

Either way it was bad.

She sniffed a third time and popped a couple of DayQuil tablets, hoping to hell she was wrong.

Chapter Three

Pescoli felt as if she'd been hit over and over again with a sledgehammer. Every muscle in her body ached, and just to move caused pain to sizzle up her spine and pound in a mother of a headache.

She let out a low moan as she tried to look around.

Lying on her back, feeling cold seep into her body, she opened an eye and tried to see in the darkness. Where was she? Though it was too dark to see clearly, the only light filtering through an ice-glazed window, she recognized nothing.

Groaning, she attempted to roll over. Her head thundered in pain, her ribs ached, and her muscles were stiff and cold, so damned cold she could barely think. And her shoulder . . . Dear Jesus, had someone tried to rip it from its socket?

She blinked, her eyes focusing, and she saw that she was in a tiny room with an unlit wood stove in one corner. Above her was a single, high window, and the only piece of furniture was this cot with its thin sleeping bag.

What the hell?

There was a door, probably less than ten feet away, but in her current condition, it might as well have been a thousand. She must've cracked her ribs somehow . . . been injured . . . hurt her shoulder.

Her mind was foggy, memories shuttered behind a wall of pain. Her left arm throbbed from shoulder to wrist and she hoped to hell she'd only bruised a muscle, that nothing was broken.

Instinctively she reached for her service weapon, but of course, it wasn't in her shoulder holster; in fact, she was naked, not a stitch of clothes on.

And her right wrist was handcuffed to the cot on which she lay.

Hell.

She was probably trapped by her own damned cuffs. Feeling even more the part of the moron, she tried to move her hand, to slip the cuff over her palm, but she knew better and, of course, she couldn't extract herself.

"Damn it," she whispered, trying to collect her wits.

Study your surroundings. Try to see where you are, what's in the room, if there is anything that will help free you. The son of a bitch could have been cocky enough to leave the key to the handcuffs or your phone or even your pistol nearby.

Squinting in the darkness, Pescoli found nothing that might help her.

There was a cover of sorts, like an army blanket that had worked its way down her body. With an effort, she reached down and tugged, pulling the itchy wool to her chin and noticing for the first time that her teeth were chattering. But nothing else.

Not even a glass of water. Just the cot. As far as she could discern.

Someone had brought her here.

Someone could be behind the door.

She started to cry out, but thought better of it.

Think, Regan, think.

She squeezed her eyes closed and concentrated, past the pain, to the memories that lurked in the dark corners of her mind. She'd been driving . . . Yes. Hell-bent to get to her loser of an ex-husband's place. He had the kids and Cisco, her dog . . . right? It was just before Christmas and she'd been in a white-hot fury . . . driving to her stupid ex-husband's house. And then?

She couldn't remember.

Closing her eyes, she tried to recall something, anything . . . Was there the crack of a rifle? Loud. Echoing. Reverberating through the icy canyons?

Oh, God . . . Her car . . . spinning out of control, metal groaning, the windshield shattering . . . She relived those terrifying moments when her Jeep had plunged over the steep side of a ravine, turning crazily as it propelled its way into the dark canyon.

Shivering, she refused to call out. She concentrated on the memory. The twisted metal, the flying glass, the air bag, the snow falling, and blood . . . Her hands had been bloody, her face cut, her weapon drawn as she'd waited, crushed within the confines of the Jeep's mangled interior.

And then . . . and then . . . and then *what*?

She squeezed her eyes tighter, trying to recall how she'd ended up here lying naked and broken on a cot in a shadowy room. The memory teased at her mind and then she heard it, a sound from the other side of the door.

Her heart jolted and she swallowed back a cry as she recognized the noise: a chair scraping back. Wood against stone. Then she heard the pad of heavy footsteps, like bare skin against rock.

She could barely breathe.

Someone was coming for her.

She felt a moment's relief and then a darker emotion filled her soul. Dread oozed through her blood. A gut instinct told her that whoever was beyond the thick oak planks of the door wasn't her savior.

Though she didn't know why, couldn't remember the reason for her distrust, she sensed instinctively that the person who had brought her here wasn't someone upon whom she could rely.

He's not your savior, but your jailor.

She swallowed back her fear and tried to think. She believed that the person who had brought her here was consumed with a horrifying and malicious intent.

She braced herself.

Waited.

But the footsteps passed by her door.

For the moment, she'd gotten a reprieve.

But she knew deep in her gut, it wouldn't last long.

Then in a blinding second of realization, she remembered.

Everything.

Her heart froze and she stared at the door as if her gaze could burn through the thick oak panels of an ancient, scarred door to the room beyond where the goddamned Star-Crossed Killer waited.

* * *

"You get hold of her?" the sheriff asked as he passed by Alvarez's cubicle. Dressed in a sheepskin jacket, boots, and gloves, Grayson was headed outside, his black Lab·Sturgis in tow, the brim of his battered Stetson in the fingers of one hand. He paused at Alvarez's desk.

"Not yet."

"Aw . . . shit." His jaw slid to the side and his eyes sparked in frustration. She supposed that once he would have been described as tall, dark, and handsome. And probably not that long ago. But these days, with winter raging and disabling the county and a serial killer hunting on his watch, Grayson was borderline gaunt, his face craggy, his hair shot with silver, his expression hard-set and grim.

And still, she thought, the most interesting man she'd met in a long, long while.

Grayson, like Alvarez, wasn't satisfied that the woman being held in the Spokane jail really was the serial killer who had been terrorizing Grizzly Falls. Only when he and the rest of the officers of the sheriff's department were convinced that the murderer was no longer on the loose, raining terror on the community in the middle of the worst damned blizzard Pinewood County had seen in half a century, would any of them rest easy. Especially with one of the lead detectives on the case gone missing. "This isn't good," he said in his low drawl. "Try again."

"I will, but trust me, Pescoli's not picking up. I told you the last call I got from her she asked me to cover for her, that she had a personal issue."

"Family problems, you said."

"With her ex. About the kids. She didn't elaborate." His eyes darkened. "That was yesterday," he said,

echoing her own thoughts. "Find her. Send someone to check her place. There should be a deputy
out in that direction. Rule, maybe. Or Watershed.
Check with them." Kayan Rule was a road deputy
for the department who looked more like a power
forward for the NBA than a cop. She had no bone
to pick with him. Watershed, on the other hand,
was a real pain in the ass. A good cop, but a jerk
who liked crude jokes and considered himself some
kind of lady killer.

"I'll handle it." She was already shutting down
her computer. "I'll run by her place. I was gonna
head out anyway," she said, wanting, no, *needing* to
do something, *anything* other than sit in this office
another minute while staring at photographs of
Star-Crossed's victims or trying to decipher the notes
that had been found at each of the crime scenes and
attempting to mentally connect them to the suspect
who had been apprehended.

"You sure?"

"Yeah." Rolling her chair away from her desk, she
reached for her service weapon, shoulder holster,
and jacket.

"Good." Grayson glanced at the clock. "And have
someone go out and talk with Lucky Pescoli." He
rubbed a hand over his face. "People get crazy this
time of year. It's supposed to be all love and peace
on earth, but there's always a spike in suicides and
murders. Domestic violence." His gaze was steady as
it held Alvarez's. "Detective Pescoli isn't known for
her long fuse."

Alvarez couldn't argue with that.

Grayson squared his hat on his head. "Let me
know what you find out. Has anyone checked with
dispatch? Seen if an alarm has come in?"

"They haven't heard from her either. No officer in distress came in."

Rubbing a hand around the back of his neck, Grayson shook his head. "This isn't like her. See what you can find out." He glanced out the windows to the snow-covered landscape. "As soon as the weather breaks, I'm flying with Chandler and Halden to Spokane today," he said, mentioning the two FBI agents who had been assigned to the case.

"The woman the Spokane cops arrested is not our guy," Alvarez stated flatly.

A muscle tightened in Grayson's jaw. "I hope to hell you're wrong."

She glanced to the notes strewn across her desk. "The person who's been arrested; she doesn't fit the pattern. I'll bet she's got an alibi for all the homicides."

"The Feds are checking."

"So am I." Alvarez wasn't trusting anyone else in dealing with the Star-Crossed Killer. Not even the FBI.

"In the meantime, find Pescoli."

"I will," she promised, sliding her arm through her shoulder holster and strapping it on. Grayson slapped the top of her cubicle wall and started toward the door, only to be roadblocked by Joelle Fisher, the receptionist and resident busybody for the department. Pushing sixty, she looked a good ten years younger than her age, and was forever dressed in spiky high heels and short, tight dresses with prim little jackets. Her platinum hair was piled as near a 1950s beehive as she dared and never was a single hair out of place.

It was an odd look, a step out of time, but somehow Joelle pulled it off.

Now, all in red, she was chattering on about a holiday party as if the horror of the last few months were the last thing on her mind.

"Cort's wife has promised to bring in her prize-winning crown jewel cookies. They took second at the church bazaar, you know, and only because Pearl Hennessy decided to enter her gingersnaps, the ones that have a hint of orange. Well, who would beat those, I ask you?"

Alvarez didn't stop to find out. The less she knew about the family of Cort Brewster, the undersheriff, the better. Alvarez didn't really like the man, though she couldn't put her finger on why. Brewster was a stand-up guy, been with the department for years, married to the same woman for nearly a quarter of a century. A devoted father of four, he was deacon in the local Methodist church and all that, but there was something about him that made her edgy, something that didn't seem to ring true.

That's because you're always suspicious, have been since your early teens, but you know why, don't you? Just your little secret that you don't dare share.

Ignoring that nasty little voice in her mind, she decided it was okay not to like Brewster. Just recently there had been an incident that reaffirmed Alvarez's opinion of the undersheriff: Pescoli's son, Jeremy, was found to be dating Heidi Brewster, Cort's pistol of a fifteen-year-old daughter. The kids had been busted for underage drinking and the tension inside Brewster had been palpable.

Merry Christmas.

All of Joelle's talk was falling on the sheriff's deaf ears.

"Fine, fine, whatever you think," Grayson muttered as his cell phone blasted and he picked up.

Alvarez hustled past the Christmas cookie discussion before Joelle could turn her attention her way. Tucking her scarf into her jacket, she headed outside where the wind whistled and the air seemed to crackle. She yanked on her gloves as she passed the flagpole where Old Glory was snapping and shivering in the stiff wind.

From the corner of her eye she noticed a news van, the last remaining one parked across the street, the driver cradling a cup of coffee that was so hot steam nearly obliterated the window. Most of the other members of the media had taken off, chasing the story in Spokane. Except for this lone newsperson, a die-hard still camped near the sheriff's department. An orange slash and the call letters of KBTR were scripted across the side of the dirty white van.

Alvarez avoided the KBTR van like the plague. Her dealings with the media had been few and she preferred it that way. Better to keep her private life just that. Her boots crunched across the snow as she found her Jeep. Scraping an inch of snow and a layer of ice off the windshield, she spied Ivor Hicks's truck rolling up the street. *Great,* she thought, watching Hicks as he huddled over the steering wheel of his wheezing truck. A hunter's cap complete with orange earmuffs was pulled low over his head and his eyes seemed twice their size behind thick glasses.

Owlish.

And a nutcase that made Grace Perchant, Pinewood County's resident ghost whisperer, look sane.

Ivor parked on the street and slid out, his heavy boots sinking into the snow that had been plowed into a dingy, deep drift near the curb.

"The sheriff in?" he asked, his glasses starting to fog.

"Just leaving, I think."

"Maybe I can catch him . . ." Wincing against arthritis, he hitched himself toward the building. Alvarez was glad to see him go before he started talking about alien abductions and the like, his favorite topic since his own "abduction." He still claimed to talk to Crytor, the general of the Reptilian alien forces or some such nonsense, and was forever reporting his conversations, all exacerbated by his affinity for Jack Daniel's, to the police.

Today, Ivor was Grayson's problem.

Alvarez settled behind the wheel of her county-issued Jeep and was out of the lot in seconds, her wipers cutting away any residual ice on the windshield, the heater blasting full force. She melded into the traffic winding its way down the steep streets that sloped down the face of Boxer Bluff. The upper tier of the town, including the sheriff's department and jail, sat high on the hill overlooking the five-hundred-foot drop to the heart of the original town of Grizzly Falls, or "Old Grizzly" as it was called by the locals. Shops, restaurants, offices, and even the courthouse lined the main street that ran parallel to the river and offered views of the raging falls for which the town was named.

Her police band crackled as she drove through the outskirts of town. She tried the phone again, was directed to voicemail, and tried to tamp down the doubts that gnawed at her mind. There could be a dozen reasons Pescoli wasn't answering, any number of excuses why she hadn't shown up. She didn't necessarily have to be the next victim of a sick serial killer . . .

But her initials work, don't they? If you really think the killer's trying to issue a warning, then the **R** *and* **P** *of*

Pescoli's name fit perfectly into the theory that the killer is slowly, with each victim's initials, leaving the chilling note of: **BEWARE THE SCORPION** *or* **WARY OF THE SCORPION** *or even* **WAR OF THE SCORPION**.

"What does it mean?" she asked aloud. "Beware the scorpion? Wary of the scorpion? No way." She stepped on the accelerator as the Jeep angled upward and the houses became sparse, giving way to the icy forest.

Alvarez didn't expect Pescoli to be holed up in her cabin, not unless she was deathly ill. But even then the woman would have enough sense to call out. Unless she was injured, couldn't reach the phone.

Or had been abducted by a deranged human being.

Selena tucked in her shoulders, physically fending that idea off. Pescoli had sounded irritated on the message she'd left, ready to wring her ex-husband's neck. But that wasn't a news flash. Regan and Lucky had suffered a bad marriage and, as she'd always said, "a badder divorce."

Alvarez didn't leave a message, just kept driving along the plowed county road where the snow was covered in gravel and had packed hard over the pavement. To access the side roads, a vehicle had to burst through the icy berm that had been left in the wake of the plows.

Fir and pine trees, needles laden with ice and snow, stood guard as she located the private lane leading to Pescoli's cabin. Snow nearly obliterated the tire ruts; no car, truck, or SUV had come or gone in a long while.

She navigated the winding lane, laying fresh tracks through the trees and across a small bridge before the cabin came into view. Pescoli's son's truck was parked to one side, snow piled high, but the garage door was down and the only lights that glowed through the windows were the colored strands of a Christmas tree.

Alvarez parked near Jeremy's truck, grabbed a tissue and swiped at her nose, then climbed outside and broke a path in the snow to the front door. On the porch, she knocked and waited. But the house was quiet. No sounds of voices, or a television, or their yapping little terrier came from within. In fact, the place seemed ethereally silent as night slid through the surrounding thickets.

She hit the doorbell and knocked again, but got no response. "Pescoli?" she yelled. "It's Alvarez!" Her voice bounced back at her, echoing through the deep canyons surrounding this isolated little house. On the porch she walked from one window to the next, shading her eyes against the reflection on the glass, noting that the house was empty, not a light on aside from the soft glow of the Christmas tree. Even the television was dark. She spied dishes on the counter and an open pizza box on a small table, but no signs of life. Nor evidence of foul play.

She walked around all sides of the cabin that hung on the side of a hill. On the backside, where the hill sloped, she peered into a window to Jeremy's room, but it, too, was dark.

No one was inside.

Once she'd looked through all the windows of the house, she backtracked to the garage, found a small window, and standing on her tiptoes peered inside. Empty.

The whole family was gone.

A bad feeling followed Alvarez as she looked around for places someone would hide a key. Nothing under the mat or in the pots near the front door. She checked under the eaves and on the window casings.

Nada.

She's a cop. It wouldn't be near the door.

Alvarez retraced her steps to the garage and searched, but found nothing, then circumvented the house again and stopped at the far side near the back of the fireplace where she noticed a vent. Unlikely.

"Nothing ventured, nothing gained."

She pulled the glove off with her teeth, then searched the vent and felt a bit of metal hanging inside. "Eureka," she muttered. Within seconds, she'd taken it to the back door and walked into the kitchen where the smells of pepperoni and cheese still lingered.

"Pescoli?" she called, slowly making her way through the small house. A living room with an attached dining area and the kitchen were empty. The Christmas tree leaned precariously in the corner near the mantel, a few scattered packages beneath its decorated limbs. Magazines and yesterday's newspaper, with a bold headline about the Star-Crossed Killer, were scattered over a battered coffee table and well-used couch. The bathroom, choked with hair and skin products, was bone dry, no moisture clinging to the mirror or beads of water in the tub/shower combo. Regan's daughter's room was a mess. CDs, nail polish bottles, DVDs, and clothes strung over her twin bed and floor. The bookcase was filled to overflowing with stuffed animals and dolls that, Alvarez suspected, Bianca had just about outgrown.

Regan's bedroom, only slightly bigger and only slightly neater, was vacant.

Alvarez ventured down the squeaky stairs and

pushed open the door to Jeremy's room, a ten-by-ten space complete with a television, some kind of electronic game system, and desktop computer huddled at the foot of his bed. It was dark except for a lava lamp giving out a weird, shifting glow. Dirty dishes peeked out from beneath the bed and posters of pro ball players and rock bands covered the walls. Above it all was the lingering sweet, smoky scent of marijuana.

So Jeremy was a pothead.

Perfect, she thought. Just what Pescoli needed: a teenage daughter growing up too fast and a son who was using drugs and involved with the under-sheriff's spoiled daughter. She eyed Jeremy's room and wanted to kick the kid to kingdom come.

But of course, he wasn't around.

On the nightstand was a picture of Joe Strand, Jeremy's biological father, though Lucky Pescoli had basically raised the kid and was the main father figure in Jeremy's life.

Maybe I'd smoke dope, too, if that were the case, Alvarez thought. Then there was Pescoli's daughter, Bianca, whose self-involvement was awe-inspiring.

As a single mom, Pescoli had her hands full.

Nothing in Jeremy's room gave Alvarez a clue to Pescoli's whereabouts. She walked upstairs again and into the kitchen. Standing at the stove, where a frying pan showed remnants of hash browns, she felt like an intruder, a voyeur examining her partner's life. "So where are you?" she asked, walking to the desk where a few envelopes were displayed, a couple of bills marked Past Due in bold red letters.

There was no sign of a struggle. No indication of any kind of violence whatsoever, just scratches on the exterior doors near the bottom of the wood, no doubt from the little mutt of a dog that was missing, though there was still water in a dish on the floor.

Through the window, she stared at the snow in front of the garage. Slight depressions showed where the last vehicle had driven through. Four, maybe five inches of new snow had piled over the old. Meaning Pescoli had been gone—? At least twelve hours. Maybe longer.

Alvarez took the door into the garage and frowned as she ran the beam of her flashlight over the wet puddles where Pescoli's Jeep had been parked. How long ago?

Returning the key to its hiding place, she was left with a feeling of dread. Slow-growing but sure.

Something was definitely wrong.

Walking back to her Jeep, she studied the cabin and placed a call to Grayson. When he didn't pick up, she left a message on his voicemail, then headed to the road that would eventually lead her to Lucky Pescoli's house.

She only hoped the son of a bitch was home.

Chapter Four

"Oh, God, save me," a frightened female voice whispers through the darkened hallways as I am finishing my exercise routine.

Ninety-three. Ninety-four. Ninety-five.

I count off each of the push-ups as sweat runs into my eyes and my arms start to shake, my hands flat against the cold stone floor, the fire hissing and casting the room in shifting golden shadows. My face burns, the scratches not yet healed, sweat like salt into the shallow wounds.

Outside the night is raw, a storm howling through this solitary canyon, hard beads of snow adding to the accumulation of several feet of fine white powder. Icy crystals that help me with my mission.

"Please, help me . . ."

I hear the desperation in her cries and it's soothing to me even as it breaks my concentration.

Ninety-six. Ninety-seven.

My form is military perfect, my back level, my muscles gleaming with perspiration, my shoulders and arms screaming, but the pain feels good, the sweet torment of my muscles straining, of mind over matter.

Ninety-eight. Ninety-nine.

She's crying now. Mewling and whimpering in the small bedroom. Like a lost kitten whose eyes have not yet opened, searching in the darkness, calling out to the mother cat.

How perfect.

I pause, but only for a second as I savor the last push-up, slowly, painstakingly lowering my body until my chest nearly brushes the floor, then just as determinedly, inching my weight upward. I hold my body in the final, perfect, suspended position and study my reflection for a minute. Flawless, strident muscles, thick hair, a handsome face staring back at me, veins bulging with the effort.

One-fucking hundred.

"Someone, oh please . . . can anyone hear me?" she moans.

It's time.

I release the pressure on my muscles and silently roll to my feet. From the back of a chair I retrieve my towel and dab away at the sweat as I listen to her cry. The longer she waits and worries, the more quickly she'll learn to trust me.

I'm coming, I think, knowing I must respond, play my part, act as if I truly care. I'll give her comfort and painkillers, offer her hot tea and a kind embrace, so that she will want more, will turn to me for comfort, to save her. She will be difficult, I know, a stubborn, intelligent woman not easily turned, but

I'll find a way to break her, to make her trust me, to give herself body and soul to me.

Not that I'll accept it.

Still, she will beg for me to take her, to hold her, to whisper that I love her, when, of course, I will not. I imagine the hope in her eyes, the quiver of her full lips, the touch of her hand as it slides slowly down my body in seductive invitation.

But I'll resist.

As I always do.

I add another log to the fire, sparks spraying, hungry flames licking the dry wood, coals glowing blood red and giving this primitive cabin a warmth, a coziness. I head to the small bathroom, walk quickly through the shower to soap off the evidence of my workout, then slip into jeans and a sweater. The casual mountain man.

She's sobbing quietly in the other room as I walk barefoot to the tiny kitchen where hot water is already steaming on the wood stove.

Excellent.

I pour a cup, add a tea bag, and watch as the water turns the color of tobacco. A faint memory flits through my mind. It's a picture of a woman long ago. Carefully, with silent calculation she'd dunked a tea bag into a chipped cup. She'd been pretty with her pillowy breasts and lips always colored a shimmering peach, lips that had forever been turned down at the corners, the aura of dissatisfaction hanging over her like a cloud. She'd smelled of cigarettes and perfume and had pretended to be my mother.

But she, like so many others, had been a fraud.

My hands are shaking. Trembling.

I hear her taunts.

"Idiot."

"Moron."

"Most likely to fail."

The tea is nearly sloshing over the rim of the cup.

I let out my breath slowly. Then from practice, I quickly dispense with the ugly memory, and, calm once more, carry the cup through the living area where I've just finished my routine and down the hallway to my captive's door. She's quieter now, as if trying to disguise the fact that she's been crying. As if she's trying to pull herself together.

Which she never will.

I tap lightly on the panels and open the old door slowly, a crack of light cutting into the dark interior.

She's lying on the bed. Frightened. Her eyes wide. Tears visibly tracking down her cheeks.

Am I a sinner or saint?

Her knight in shining armor?

A good Samaritan?

Or the embodiment of evil?

Soon, she'll know.

Luke Pescoli answered the door himself.

All six feet of him, squarely blocking the entrance to his single-level home. In a long-sleeved T-shirt and sweatpants, his blond hair mussed, he looked as if he'd been logging in serious hours in front of the television that was flickering in the background. The local news was on, the top story being the arrest of a woman thought to be a serial killer, and Regan's feisty little terrier was tearing through the house, growling and barking as he raced, paws clicking madly on hardwood, to the door.

"Cisco, hush!" Pescoli ordered, blocking the doorway as the scrappy little terrier tried to scramble outside.

She'd already determined she would conduct this interview in her most professional manner. She and Lucky had met before, but only in passing. "Hello, Mr. Pescoli. I'm Detective Selena Alvarez from the—"

"Yeah, yeah. Old news," he interrupted. "What do you want?" he asked, trying to control the jumping dog.

"I'm looking for Regan."

"Regan?"

Behind him she caught a glimpse of a flocked Christmas tree, pink and gooey-looking, standing guard over the flat screen as the warm smell of cinnamon curled from the interior. "Your ex- wife."

"Yeah, I know. What's with all the protocol? Regan's not here. No way she would be."

"She's missing and she left me a message that said she had business with you and—"

"Missing?" he interrupted harshly. Wariness darkened his hazel eyes. "What do you mean, missing?"

"She didn't show up for work today and she's not at the house."

"Are you shittin' me?" he demanded, disbelieving.

"Lucky!" a female voice shrilled behind him. *Michelle*, his wife, a compact, curvy woman, was barreling through the living room toward the front door.

"Watch your language! Bianca's here."

"Oh, save me," a girl said as Regan's daughter pushed her way past her father and stared at Alvarez suspiciously. "What are you talking about? Mom can't be missing. What's that supposed to mean?" She looked up at her father. "This is a joke, right?" But she was concerned. Her eyes, so much like her father's, reflected his worry.

He waved off the question. To Alvarez he said, "Start at the beginning."

"That's what I was going to suggest you do."

"Well, for God's sake, come on in," Michelle said, glaring at her husband and giving him a little-girl pout. "It's freezing out there and our gas bill is already too high."

Reluctantly, Lucky stepped away from the door and Alvarez stomped snow off her boots before crossing the threshold and walking into a room filled with Christmas decor. Along with the pink flocked tree, there were lights strung over the mantel and candles taking precedence over the hunting and sports magazines strewn over the tables. Ceramic elves with big eyes, drooping hats, and, in Alvarez's opinion, wicked, leering smiles were tucked between table legs and on windowsills.

"So you haven't seen Regan since . . . ?"

"Last week sometime when we picked up the kids," Lucky said.

"Friday," Michelle chimed in as she waved Selena toward the cluster of chairs near an unlit fireplace where inside the firebox, dangling dangerously over the charred logs, a plastic Santa's boot was visible, as if Old St. Nick were actually climbing down the chimney. "In the afternoon."

"But you talked with her since." She caught a glimpse of the local news on the television where there was running footage of a woman being forced into a squad car. *Breaking news from Spokane, Washington,* the running caption read. *Suspect arrested in the Star-Crossed Serial Killer homicide investigation.*

She perched on the edge of a blue side chair while her partner's ex-husband took up what appeared to be his usual spot on the couch. Cisco, traitor that he was, hopped up beside Lucky and turned his beady eyes on Alvarez.

"Yeah. Yesterday. When she found out the kids were with me." His gaze wandered to the television. "Looks like you caught the guy, huh?"

"Remains to be seen."

"Maybe Regan took off for Spokane to be part of the bust."

"Then the sheriff's office would know where she was," Bianca sneered, though she chewed nervously on her lower lip.

"What did she say?" Alvarez asked, bringing Lucky back to the conversation.

"On the phone?"

Selena nodded.

He shrugged. "That she was on her way. I'd told her I . . . well, that Michelle and I wanted full custody of Jeremy and Bianca, and Regan went ballistic. Told me she was coming over, and to get the kids and the dog ready."

"Did she show up?"

"No." He looked away from Alvarez's steady gaze. "I figured she'd cooled off. Changed her mind."

"Really?"

"Yeah, really. She does that, y'know." He was irritated now, paying a little more attention. "It's not like she hasn't said one thing and done another before. It's kind of her M.O."

"Yeah," Michelle agreed.

"You're her partner. You must know what a hot-head she can be," Lucky said.

"Seems to me she's been pretty rock-steady where the kids are concerned." For the first time Selena noticed that Pescoli's son hadn't joined the party. "Is Jeremy here?"

"Nah, he went into town."

"In this?" she asked, hitching her chin toward the window and the storm raging outside.

"He's nearly eighteen, been driving in snow ever since he got his license. It's nothing. I loaned him my truck 'cuz we left his at her house." As if a sudden thought occurred to him, he said, "You said you checked there at her place?"

"She's not there and her Jeep is missing."

"And she's not answering her phone?" Leaning across the couch for the handheld, he dialed a number, as if he could reach his ex-wife when the entire sheriff's department couldn't. When that didn't work, he pounded out a new set of numbers, then as he listened, said, "You probably tried her cell?"

"Yes," Selena answered carefully.

Frowning, he waited, then, obviously hearing Pescoli's voicemail recording, hung up and stared at the phone.

"Dad?" Bianca asked, her voice quavering slightly. "Where's Mom?"

"Oh, probably with some loser guy she picked up—"

"Lucky, don't—" Michelle warned, her perfect, pink lips puckering into a knot of disapproval.

Maybe she isn't so bad after all.

"But you can find her, right?" Bianca said, glancing from her father to Alvarez.

"Of course," Selena said, though she didn't like her odds. "Why don't you tell me what happened when she called yesterday."

He glowered out the window, watching as the snowflakes fell relentlessly from the obscured heaven. "We had a fight on the phone. That's no news flash. I thought she'd come barging in here ready for bear, but when she never showed I figured she'd decided to take some time to cool off. It's almost Christmas. She was eyeball deep in all this crap about the serial killer, so I thought she'd just chilled. Believe it or not, that happens, too."

A timer went off in the kitchen.

Michelle, as if she'd been sitting on coiled springs, shot out of her chair and hotfooted it past a crowded dining room table and through an archway.

Bianca looked at her dad. "Mom's okay, right?"

" 'Course she is," Lucky said, flashing a smile that radiated confidence.

Alvarez's cell phone went off and she climbed to her feet and walked to the entryway, to give herself a little privacy. "Alvarez," she said, grabbing another tissue from her pocket, and heard Undersheriff Cort Brewster's voice on the other end.

"We got a signal off of Pescoli's vehicle coming from up on Horsebrier Ridge." Alvarez's stomach dropped. She'd driven over the ridge on her way from Regan's house to here. "Rule's already on the scene and spotted the vehicle. Wrecked, buried in the snow. We've got another unit headed that way, the towing company alerted."

Alvarez sneaked a glance over her shoulder. Bianca was staring at her wide-eyed while Lucky was tuned in to the news. *Oh, God, what a mess.*

"Anyone see the driver?" she asked, her voice low.

"Not yet." His voice was grim. "Rule claims at least twelve inches of snow over the vehicle. He can't tell how badly it's wrecked or if anyone's inside."

"I'm on my way," she said, digesting what the undersheriff had said as well as what he hadn't. The temperature in that wrecked car would have been far below freezing last night and if Regan hadn't gotten out . . .

She clicked off the phone and turned back to the living room where Bianca was still staring at her.

"I've got to go. If you think of anything else, call me."

"That was about Mom," Bianca guessed, her face ashen. "Wasn't it?"

"We don't know. We think we might have found her vehicle. Nothing's certain yet."

"Where?" Bianca demanded, getting up from her spot on the ottoman.

Now, finally, she had Lucky's attention. He clicked off the television with the remote. Michelle, snowman hot pads covering her hands, had walked into the archway near the dining room and, too, was waiting.

"I don't know anything, but I will soon," Alvarez said. "I'll call."

"No . . . I want to come." Bianca was already starting for the door, but Lucky reached out a long arm and stopped her, held his daughter fast. For the first time he seemed to really comprehend how dire the situation was.

"We can't interfere with police business, pumpkin. Detective Alvarez promised to call us and she will."

Alvarez's heart sank as she walked to the door and let herself out. Whatever had happened to Regan wasn't good.

She knew it.

Lucky Pescoli knew it.

Only Bianca was holding out childish hope.

Chapter Five

Alvarez stood on the icy road that cut across Horsebrier Ridge and watched nervously as the rescue workers ascended the face of the cliff using ropes. It was dark, the wind blowing through the canyon, but the blizzard had given it a rest, no new snow was falling from the dark heavens. At least for now.

Tired, hungry, her stomach in knots, the cold medication wearing off, she, along with several deputies and members of the rescue teams from both the fire and sheriff's departments, had responded to the scene. The road was blocked, flares lit and sizzling orange, adding to the eerie incandescence of beams from flashlights, headlights, taillights, and cigarette tips all reflecting against a deathly white panorama of wintry forest.

Far below, crumpled and half buried in snow, was the remains of what had once been Pescoli's Jeep. The rescue team, with the help of ropes and climbing gear, returned.

"No one inside," Randy, a ruddy-faced fireman, said as he approached. He was shaking his head and turned to another fireman, Gary Goodwin, a man Alvarez had only met a couple of times. "Got a smoke?"

Goodwin obliged, offering up an opened pack of Winstons and a Bic lighter.

"Purse?" Alvarez asked as Randy, thick gloves on his hands, fumbled with the bummed cigarette and a lighter.

"I didn't see one."

"Weapons? I'm sure she had her sidearm, a shotgun, and rifle with her."

"Nothing." He was shaking his head. "But it's damned dark, I looked real good with my flashlight, but I could have missed something." He lit up and tossed the lighter back to his buddy.

"You didn't," Goodwin said, glancing down the hill again. "There was some junk in there, sunglasses, empty cigarette pack, shopping bags, but the Jeep's pretty crumpled up. Maybe we'll find something tomorrow, when we've got daylight." He didn't sound convinced as he jammed a cigarette into his mouth.

Alvarez silently agreed. And she figured the rest of the crew from the sheriff's department would be on board with Randy's assessment. If Pescoli had been abducted by the Star-Crossed Killer, her assailant would have cleaned out the Jeep, wiped away or taken any evidence with him, as he had with all the others.

Alvarez felt sick inside. She coughed, and the men stepped away from her. She flapped a hand at them and said, "Not the cigarettes. A nasty cold."

They stayed back. Alvarez didn't blame them.

She cleared her throat and gazed out at the frigid landscape. Their only hope was that the killer's M.O. of nurturing his victims back to health before brutally leaving them to die in the frozen wilderness would buy Regan some time. If that was the case, then there was a good chance Pescoli was still alive and if she wasn't too injured, she might be able to escape. She, if she hadn't sustained a head injury, would know what she was dealing with. The other victims hadn't been so lucky.

Lucky. Yeah, right. God, what a mess.

She spent another half hour on the ridge before calling it a night. There was nothing more she could do. The crime scene guys would go over the vehicle and surrounding area with fine-toothed combs and sophisticated equipment, the Jeep would be towed to the garage where it would be examined again and again. If the killer messed up . . .

But so far he hasn't.

Now the clock was ticking down, vital seconds in Regan Pescoli's life slipping away.

She rubbed her gloved hands together, trying to get some feeling back in her fingers. Her toes, too, were beginning to tingle and go numb despite warm socks and boots. And the cold medication she'd taken hours before had worn off. Her nose was running and her ears were plugged.

Walking to the edge of the cliff, she looked far below to the area where Pescoli's car had landed.

How had Star-Crossed known Regan Pescoli would be traveling this road at that particular moment in time?

How could he know?

Frustrated, she turned and looked up at the hill

rising above the road. From the ridge he might have had an open shot. Still, the odds of pulling it off were against him.

In the morning if the weather held off, officers would scour the ridge and hill, searching for shell casings or a spot where an assassin could lay in wait. Maybe this time they'd find something.

She squinted up through the darkness. Had the bastard camped out here in the middle of a blizzard with near-whiteout conditions?

He had to know.

Alvarez pictured him waiting. Patiently. Silently. Finger on the trigger.

She felt a chill deeper than the coming night.

How had the killer learned that Pescoli would be driving hell-bent for leather over this pass? From Pescoli's ex-husband? Her kids? Or had Pescoli's assailant somehow tapped into her cell phone and was monitoring her calls?

Or had the sick son of a bitch just gotten lucky?

What were the odds of that?

And there was that word again. Lucky. Just like the nickname that Luke Pescoli wore so proudly. An odd, unsettling connection.

You're grasping at straws.

She sniffed hard but still continued to look up to the top of the ridge, though the crest of the hill was obscured by darkness. She tried to imagine him waiting in the near blizzard. Somehow he *had* to have known that she'd be driving on this road. No one, not even a real nut-job, would wait out here in sub-freezing temperatures for hours, maybe days, on end.

Remember: this one's a real *wacko. He's got a pur-*

pose; he's driven. He's had to have spent months, maybe years finding the right women for his victims. Lying in wait outside in these conditions might just turn him on.

In her mind's eye, she saw the killer stretched out on the snow, or on something to protect him from the cold, as he propped his rifle on a fallen log, or a stump or boulder, maybe a tripod, something to steady the barrel while he trained it with steely composure on the road below.

He was a hunter, an assassin with an ace marksman's deadly aim.

Jaw sliding to one side, eyes narrowing, she wondered how the hell Star-Crossed had managed to pull off such a perfect shot as to disable a car and send it careening off the roads and into the canyons.

She blew on her hands, watched her breath fog.

How intimately had he known his victims before the attack?

And what was his game? Not sexual gratification. At least not to the point of penetration. Not one body had shown signs of recent sexual abuse or intercourse. No semen was found in or on their bodies, nor had there been any wounds to their breasts or vaginal areas. Contrarily, autopsies proved that the victims' initial wounds had actually started to heal before he'd apparently had enough of the game and brutally, without conscience, had lashed the women to trees in remote areas and callously left them to die.

The Pinewood County Sheriff's Department had searched every database imaginable for skilled marksmen who could pull off such a feat, from ex-military aces and mercenaries, to the antigovernment extremists, hunters, cops, and winners of shooting competitions. Anyone with a history of incredible skills with a rifle. So far, no one suspect had come to the fore.

Until the woman in Spokane.

But there was just no damned way she could have been responsible for Pescoli's disappearance, because she couldn't be in two places at once. Pescoli had been seen and on the phone here in Grizzly Falls while the suspect was nearly two hundred miles away in Spokane, Washington. The panhandle of Idaho and mountainous terrain separated the cities.

So, who was the killer with the dead-eye aim?

Surely someone who lived around here, who knew the terrain well enough to pick just the right spots, someone who seemed to have a thing against women. Her jaw hardened as she thought of the men who had given her—a woman detective, no, make that a Hispanic woman detective—a rough time, as if she were an oddity, someone to be teased. Whoever was behind the assaults, though, had a deep-seated hatred for women. All women, apparently, as he certainly didn't discriminate by race. And he could shoot straight as an arrow under horrible conditions, then "rescue" a woman from the wreckage of her car and haul her to some unknown destination.

A big man, from the size of one footprint they'd taken.

A local who had knowledge and felt comfortable in this rugged, frigid terrain.

A marksman.

A smart individual who was organized enough to locate these women, track them, wound them, and eventually kill them.

A hater.

Several names came quickly to mind: Dell Blight, a big man with a belly as large as his disdain of the sheriff's department. He'd been hauled in several times, drunk, once waving a weapon around, but then, he wasn't exactly a candidate for a national think tank.

Rod Larimer, owner of the Bull and Bear, or B&B Bed and Breakfast, as it was locally known, was currently enjoying a brisk trade, all because of the sudden notoriety of the town. And Rod was a man who despised Sheriff Grayson. He'd been married a few times and his wives had always left him. But could he shoot?

Then there was Otis Kruger, a mean drunk who owned an arsenal of weaponry and who had bragged about killing a doe out of season from an incredible distance—shot her dead center. He'd been hauled in for poaching, but again, wasn't the brightest color in the crayon box. A crack shot with a low I.Q. Dangerous combination, but could he really be Star-Crossed?

Selena expelled a breath. The best and brightest marksmen in the county were some of the very men she worked with: hunters and lawmen. But she wouldn't go there, couldn't believe someone who'd sworn to uphold the law would get off on making a mockery of it.

The wind kicked up, bitter cold, and some of the firemen were gathering their gear and packing up.

There was nothing more to be done tonight.

A headache had formed at the base of Alvarez's skull, her eyes were scratchy, and her nose was now running like a faucet. She logged out of the scene and headed back to her apartment determined to get some rest, have a fresh view of the case in the morning. But as she drove along the eerily quiet mountain road, her headlights reflecting brightly off the packed snow and ice, huge trees laden with snow surrounding her, she felt the winter cold seep into her bones. Shivering, she experienced a deep-seated fear that she'd never see Pescoli alive again.

"How're you feeling?" a deep male voice whispered.

Pescoli's eyes flew open but the room was in total darkness aside from a single pinpoint of light. A penlight? Her heart thundered and adrenaline shot through her system.

For a second she didn't know where she was and then she remembered driving over the icy ridge, the reverberant crack of a rifle, her Jeep spinning out of control down a steep mountainside.

And her rescuer.

She remembered the man in shadowy goggles who had pried her from the wreckage to bring her here as his damned prisoner.

She tried to move, to roll away, but her muscles were sluggish, wouldn't respond. Pain jolted down her shoulder and her gaze was fastened on the bright spot of light.

"I asked you a question."

He sounded irritated. Good. So was she. "How do you think I feel?"

"Not your best."

"Like I was in a damned accident that could have been prevented if some jerk-wad hadn't shot out my tire." She was glaring up at him, trying to focus, unable to make out his features, the small light ruining her ability to focus. "Who the hell are you?"

"Don't you know?"

"Let me guess. Not St. Peter, right? We're not at the pearly gates. And where are my clothes?"

He snorted, but she caught a glimpse of white, a glint from his teeth as if he found her amusing. "Definitely not St. Peter. And no, I wouldn't think this was the way to salvation." There was a smile in his voice. "You'll get your clothes back."

"When?"

"When I decide."

His way of keeping her humble and vulnerable, to make her lie naked and alone in the dark, but she wasn't going to buckle to that kind of psychological blackmail. "Why did you bring me here?"

"To help you."

"You fired the damned shot! I wouldn't call that help." She was agitated, fear juicing up her aggression. He ran the penlight down the length of her body, again humiliating her, stopping at her breasts where her damned nipples were rock hard from the cold. She heard him suck in his breath and she thought she might be sick.

"You're a beautiful woman, Regan." He said it as if he meant it.

"And you're a damned freak!"

As if he didn't hear her, he said, "Well-sculpted face, high cheekbones, and a strong chin. And long legs . . . nice breasts with dark nipples . . . flat stomach despite bearing two babies."

He knew about her kids? Terror swept through her. She wanted to snap at him to leave her children out of it, but she didn't dare show her Achilles' heel, couldn't let him know that her entire life centered around her kids. Instinctively she knew that if she gave him even the tiniest bit of insight as to how to really terrorize her, Jeremy and Bianca would end up here, imprisoned by him. Fear turned her throat to dust.

"And that boyfriend of yours, the drifter."

What?

"Does Santana appreciate you? Treat you well?"

Her stomach dropped. How much about her did this animal know?

"Or is he just around for a quick roll in the hay, a hot fuck?" He said it all in a harsh, unrecognizable whisper. As if he thought she might be able to make out his identity. "I bet you're a hot one, aren't you? That you like it when some good-looking loser tries to get into your pants. Is that right? You enjoy the ride?"

"You're sick."

"Sick?" That seemed to bother him. "You won't think so for long."

What she wouldn't do for a weapon of some kind, a gun or knife or even a baseball bat or nightstick, anything. Weak as she was, she'd haul off and whack him and send his black soul straight to hell. But there was no weapon and she was in no shape to attack anyone, and the beam of his light slid lower on her body, like a laser, trailing a path to the juncture of her legs where the beam paused, illuminating the reddish hair that curled there and feeling as if it burned a hole through her skin.

She tried not to think of the embarrassment, for then he'd win. He was doing this on purpose. Nor would she rise to the bait of bringing up Santana or her sex life. "You get your rocks off by torturing women? Humiliating them? Holding them against their will?"

He didn't answer, just trailed the tiny beam of light down her legs.

"Why go to all this trouble? Why stage accidents and then pretend to help the victims? Why not just kill them and get it over with?"

"You just don't get it, do you?"

"Enlighten me," she challenged, keeping her eyes trained on his shadowy features.

"You're a cop, Regan. A detective. You figure it out." He stepped close enough so that were she not riddled with pain, one arm chained to the cot, she would have jumped up and rammed his arm backward until he was on his knees, or thrown a well-aimed punch at his throat to render him spitting and speechless, or shoved his nose into his cerebrum.

"Try me." If she could just keep him talking, she might learn something, figure out his identity.

"It would take much too long."

"What else do you have to do?"

He stepped closer and the penlight offered enough illumination that she noticed a glint, a slim little line of silver in his other hand.

What the hell?

What was it?

And then she knew with dead certainty that he held a hypodermic needle in his right hand. *Oh, God, no!*

Pescoli freaked. She had no idea what drug might be held in the syringe, but she couldn't let him inject her with it.

"Wait!" she said, trying to scoot away. Her legs were free. If she could kick him. Land a blow square in his crotch, or on his face.

"Don't even think about it," he whispered, his voice ragged, and rough, yet nearly seductive.

Pescoli's skin crawled. Fear sizzled through her bones. She had to find a way to—

He sprang!

Like a cougar onto the back of an unsuspecting deer, he leaped onto the cot. She tried to move, but couldn't get away. Pinning her with his knees, his legs straddling her torso, his weight pressing onto her bruised ribs, he held her fast.

Pain shrieked through her body and she cried out. Her chest felt as if it had been crushed, her lungs on fire, her ribs shattering. She tried to kick and squirm but pain crippled her and his well over two hundred pounds didn't budge.

"No!" she forced out, her breath a panicked hiss. "Don't!" She bucked upward, but to no avail.

It was too late. With his spread legs only inches from her nose, the scent of his sweat in the air, he shifted slightly. Dropped the penlight. Grabbed her tethered arm.

Though she pummeled him with her free hand, he fended off her blows with his shoulder and body, and his legs, his thick thighs covered in denim so close to her face wouldn't budge. If she could bite him . . .

She moved, but he anticipated the lift of her head, the baring of her teeth.

"Careful," he warned, staying away from her teeth, "or I'll give you something you can really work on, fill that hot little mouth of yours right up. And you'll love it."

She shuddered inside. Thought she might be sick and throw up all over him.

From astride her he laughed, a brittle sound as hollow as all the caverns of hell.

"We're going to get you," she warned. "If not me, then someone else. They'll never give up. They'll run you to the ground like a rabid dog."

He struck quickly. Plunged the needle into her arm.

She felt a sharp, cold sting against her skin, then the horrifying pressure of some unknown drug being forced into her flesh.

"You bastard!" she hissed and he laughed again, that low, sick growl, and he crawled slightly upward, forcing his crotch even closer to her head.

Her stomach roiled and still she swiped at him, her legs kicking upward.

Her attempts were futile, all her struggling in vain.

The penlight rolled noisily across the stone floor, stopping against the door, its tiny beam offering faint, narrow illumination. There wasn't enough light to see his features clearly, just a glimmer of thin luminance that threw his face into a shadowy, macabre relief. His eyes were shielded by dark glasses, a baseball cap covered his head, and a beard darkened his jaw, yet she caught a chilling glimpse of his features. Rugged. Rough. Scratches down one cheek where she'd scraped his skin with her fingernails.

I know you, she thought, her arm suddenly heavy,

the pain in her chest easing as she started to drift away. *I know you, you miserable whack job, and damn it, somehow, someway, I'm going to get out of here and when I do, I swear to God, I'm going to nail your sorry ass . . .*

Chapter Six

Nate Santana snapped open his pocketknife, then sliced the twine holding a bale of hay together. The horses were waiting patiently in their stalls, ears pricked forward, dark, liquid eyes assessing him, only Lucifer showing impatience by snorting and tossing his dark head.

Daylight was still a couple of hours away but Santana was up even earlier than usual. Restless. His elusive sleep interrupted with dreams of Regan Pescoli.

Either she'd been making love to him, staring up at him with a naughty smile and arched eyebrows as he'd stripped away her clothes and made love to her, or she'd been lost in the darkness and he'd been running through a dark, night-shrouded forest calling her name, catching glimpses of her as she vanished into a thicket of brittle, snow-covered trees.

He'd woken up in a cold sweat, that tingling sensation that warned him of danger, ever present.

Using a pitchfork, he spread hay into the waiting mangers of Brady Long's small herd. He'd already exercised the horses as much as the small arena would allow and now was finishing up with the feed, measuring oats, tossing hay, making sure the water was running into the troughs, that the pipes hadn't frozen in this last arctic blast that had left so much of the state crippled.

Sometimes he wondered why he'd come back to this part of Montana. It wasn't as if he had any family left.

You just had to get the hell out of California, that's why, and Brady Long offered you a job and a place to stay.

He opened another bale, smelling the fading scent of summer in the dry grass, then forked it into the next box where Lucifer waited patiently, as if he were the most well-mannered colt on the ranch.

"I'm not buying it," Santana said to the black devil-horse, but his mind wasn't really on the task at hand. He was just going through the motions, getting through his morning chores, waiting for daybreak and the phone to ring.

He finished up and walked into the predawn darkness. Usually this was his favorite time of day, just before the sun rose, when the stars lit up the sky, the air was clear, and there was a calm to the universe, a quietude and peace that disappeared with daylight.

This morning, however, the stars were obscured and a bitter wind swept through the cluster of buildings that made up the heart of the Lazy L, the sprawling ranch owned by Brady Long.

A single security lamp shed an eerie light onto the snow-covered landscape and for the first time in days no snowflakes danced and swirled in its bluish beam.

Thankfully, the snowstorm that had ripped through the heart of the Bitterroots had stopped. At least for a while. But he still hadn't heard from Regan Pescoli.

And he'd caught the news last night that the police in Spokane had taken a woman into custody, believing her to be responsible for the deaths of several women and possibly even the serial killer who had terrorized this section of the Bitterroots. His first thought was that Regan was in on the bust, but a second later he negated that idea, as Alvarez had phoned him after the arrest.

He locked the door of the stable and hiked across the parking lot, a hundred yards through the drifting snow to his cabin with Nakita at his heels. The husky, full of energy, romped through the drifts, disappearing beneath the mantle of white, his tail all that was visible of him, only to reappear, eager for another foray in a new direction.

"You're an idiot," Santana reminded him, but he did smile as Nakita bounded on the small porch, snow covering his nose, whiskers, and thick gray fur. Nakita's long tongue hung out of his mouth and he scratched at the door.

"I know, I know."

Santana stepped into the cabin, three rooms with a sleeping loft tucked under the eaves of a steep roof. This tiny home was the original house on the Long homestead and well over a hundred years old. That was before copper had been found and mined in some of the surrounding properties and the Long family had gained all their wealth and built the cedar and stone lodge tucked into thickets of pine and spruce and overlooking Milton Creek, homage to Brady's ancestor who first claimed these acres.

Though his cabin was drafty, insulated poorly, Santana preferred it to the suite of attic rooms in one wing of the main house, quarters that had been dedicated to the year-round staff. Living in the big house was fine for Clementine, the housekeeper, and her teenaged son, Ross, but not for Nate. When push came to shove he would pick privacy over grandeur any day of the week. Besides, he needed to be closer to the livestock. And farther away from Brady Long whenever his boss decided to show up.

Heat radiated from the wood stove crouched in a corner of the cabin's living area. Somewhere in the last fifty years the compact space had been equipped with electric baseboard heat, but Santana liked the old stove with its glass window to view the fire burning inside. He figured the exercise he got sawing up the fallen trees on the property each spring and splitting the rounds was worth it.

Never once had Regan Pescoli been here. Nor had he spent any time at her house. It was as if they'd had some unspoken pact to stay out of each other's private space. "Stupid," he muttered under his breath. They'd both tried so hard to deny what was becoming more evident with each passing hour: that he'd fallen for her.

He hung his hat and jacket on a peg near the front door as Nakita nosed at his food bowl and lapped water wildly from his dish. Santana skimmed himself out of the weatherproof pants and boots before propping them up on the rock floor in front of the fire. After adding more logs to the stove, he fed the dog, cut a thick slice of brown bread for himself, and, after slathering it with butter, bolted it down, then warmed himself up in a shower.

One thought circled his brain: Regan's missing.

Toweling off briskly, his face a mask of granite, Nate tried not to succumb to panic. But he couldn't quite convince himself that everything was fine, that she was just busy or even avoiding him.

He threw on his clothes and headed back to the stove, feeling like something sinister was at stake.

Like a gust of wind blowing the stable door open and freaking you out yesterday? Face it, Santana, you're on the edge of paranoia. Because of a woman. Something you swore to yourself you'd never do.

Settling onto the worn arm of his recliner, he found the remote for his television while his dog was already snoring softly on the rag rug in front of the fire. His muscles were tense as he turned on the morning news.

What was it Pescoli's partner had said when she'd called and he'd asked concerning Regan's whereabouts?

"If we knew that, I wouldn't be calling you."

Again that unsettling feeling crept through his guts.

Man, Santana, you've got it bad. You can't get Pescoli out of your mind. What was it she'd said that she wanted? A relationship with no strings attached? Sounded good, didn't it? Except now she's under your skin. You can't shake yourself free from her, and face it, you don't want to.

His jaw tightened. It hadn't been that long ago that he'd sworn no woman would ever get to him again. But Pescoli with her burnished hair that flamed red-gold in the sun and eyes that shimmered from green to gold had caught him off guard. She was athletic, smart as a whip, and had a wicked sense of humor that always surprised him.

And then there was the lovemaking.

Hard and fast.

Or sensual and slow.

But never enough, no matter how sated he'd felt after one of their sessions at a local motel. And never boring. He loved to stare down at her as they made love. It excited him to see her beautiful nipples harden and her eyes grow dark as her pupils dilated with desire.

He couldn't get enough of her.

She was one helluva woman, he'd decided long ago, but one he'd never thought he couldn't leave.

Now he wasn't so sure.

Now he was scared to death, and Nate Santana wasn't one to frighten easily. In fact, he'd sometimes wondered if there was something wrong with him. In a case of fight or flight, he always chose fight. And it had landed him in some tough spots. Hadn't always been his smartest option.

Nor was getting involved with Pescoli such a great idea.

Everything about her should have warned him to stay away. She'd been married twice. She had two hellions of teenagers. She was a damned homicide detective, for Christ's sake. Yep, he should never have gotten involved with her, and if it hadn't been for the fact that she'd actually challenged him in a bar one night, first to pool, then to arm wrestling, and then to shots of whiskey, he might not have noticed the smell of her, the fire in her eyes that matched the flame in her hair, or the fact that she seemed slightly amused by him. Being attracted to her, playing her game, had been his first mistake.

Ending up in bed had been his second.

And now, his third: actually giving a damn about her. Caring about her. Missing her.

"Damn it all to hell."

He drank two cups of black coffee, thought about carving himself a second piece of bread but decided he couldn't force down another bite. Watching the weather report, only half paying attention to "more of the same," he finally surfaced to learn another storm was on the horizon.

Great.

Time was inching by. He glanced at the clock mounted over the sink and scowled. Still an hour until daylight. "Oh, hell," he said under his breath. He couldn't stand not doing anything. He whistled to his dog and walked to the door where he began putting on the layers he'd so recently peeled off. "Come on, Nakita," he said, as the dog yawned and stretched. "Let's go into town."

It was well past time to track Pescoli down.

After a miserable night, Alvarez rolled out of bed, stumbled through the shower, and dispensing with makeup, dried her thick hair, snapped a rubber band around a high ponytail, and wound the whole mess into a tight knot on her crown. She checked her image in the mirror, saw her eyes were watery from the damned cold, her skin lacking luster, her nose red.

"No beauty pageant for you today," she told her image before she brushed her teeth and swilled some sharp-tasting antibacterial mouthwash inside her mouth.

She couldn't afford to be sick.

Not now.

After pulling on silky long johns, she dressed in a sweater and department-issued slacks. Soberly, she looked at her reflection in the mirror and wondered what had happened to her. As a teenager, she'd been proud of her good looks, flaunted her slim figure, applied more makeup than she needed to her large eyes, high cheekbones, and full lips.

But that was a lifetime ago.

When life had been filled with laughter and promise.

Frowning, dispelling the image, she found her shoulder holster and snapped it on.

She was no longer all those things that had been important to her in her youth. "Hot." Or "cool." Whichever was in vogue. Even "tight" or "sexy" or "naughty" didn't appeal to her. Probably would never again.

Which was fine.

Except that she was alone.

No husband or lover or boyfriend on the horizon.

"No big deal," she said to herself while warming water for tea in the microwave. After all, she'd been thinking about getting a pet. Why not? Something living to come home to.

A bird would be good . . . maybe a parakeet or macaw or . . . who was she kidding? A bird? In a cage? Spreading seeds and crapping on newspapers lining the cage floor? Or perching on the curtain rod with its wings clipped?

Fine for someone else.

Just not Selena's style.

She was fine. Alone. Matter of fact, that's just how she liked things.

She glanced at her desk where more images and

notes about the series of murders were strewn over the desk in the tiny apartment where she lived alone. No man had ever slept in her bed. She'd been in Grizzly Falls for over three years, ever since leaving San Bernadino. "A loner," she'd been called, or an "ice princess." She'd even heard Pete Watershed, a coworker, suggest to a group of officers that she "probably swings the other way." Even now, feeling rotten, she smiled at that one.

If they only knew.

Not that she gave a damn.

Besides, Watershed was a dolt.

Alvarez figured that the less her coworkers and acquaintances knew about her, the better she could do her job. And she was all about her job.

The microwave dinged and she pulled out the cup of near-boiling water, then dunked a bag of tea into it. Her grandmother had insisted that honey and lemon be added to the tea in order for the concoction to "shake the cold loose," but Alvarez had neither item in the small kitchen of her studio.

Orange pekoe would have to do.

"Citrus is citrus," she told herself, blowing over her cup and gingerly tasting the hot tea. It nearly burned her tongue, but did soothe her throat.

Her cell rang and it sounded dull, as her ears were still plugged. She scrounged it out of her pocket and flipped it open. "Alvarez."

"She's not our killer." Sheriff Grayson sounded disgusted. "Nothing adds up. A copycat, it looks like, though how she knew enough about the crimes to try and kill Jillian Rivers in the same manner, we haven't figured out yet." He let out a long, angry breath. "I was really hoping she would be the doer and we could close the case, but that's not gonna happen."

Alvarez wasn't surprised. Last night she'd spent hours double-checking dates, places, and the suspect's whereabouts before finally going to bed. Nothing had matched up. The woman in custody couldn't have committed the murders of Theresa Charleton, Nina Salvadore, Wendy Ito, Rona Anders, and Hannah Estes.

On top of all that, Alvarez was certain they should be looking for a guy. A big guy, one strong enough to carry women out of snow-covered canyons, one smart enough to hide them away without detection, a sharpshooter with incredible accuracy: under sixty, probably, big, athletic.

And then there was the fact of her missing partner.

She shivered as Grayson said, "It sure would have been nice to get the mutt behind bars."

"We will."

"Any word from Pescoli? Brewster said they found her car."

"Nothing."

"Shit."

Alvarez's sentiments precisely.

"Find her."

"We will."

"Jesus, what a mess."

"We'll get this guy and we'll get Pescoli back alive," she said, hearing the ring of conviction in her tone, wondering if she were lying.

"God, I hope so." He cleared his throat. "Look, I'm on my way back. Chandler and Halden are staying on a little longer, wrapping things up with the

Spokane Police, trying to find a link as to how the suspect knew so much about the other murders. I'll see you at the office and we'll have a meeting of the task force. I want anything the crime scene has got on Pescoli's vehicle and her place. Get a search warrant and talk to her kids and . . . Oh, hell, you know what we need to do."

"Already on it."

"Good. Later."

She hung up, finished drinking her cooling tea, then stepped outside where the sun was rising over the eastern hills and traffic was starting to move through this part of the town.

Pescoli had been missing two nights now.

Chapter Seven

That bitch needs to be taught a lesson!

I rake my fingers through my hair and try to calm down, but my hands are shaking, my muscles tight as bowstrings as I pace before the fire.

All because of her.

Don't let her get to you. You're in control here, remember? You're the one who's calling the shots. She's wounded. Handcuffed. Under lock and key. You're in charge. You. Not that miserable joke of a cop who doesn't know her place. Do not lose it now, not when you've come so far, not when you're so close.

Not when you have so much to do.

Not just here, with these women, with him. He'll be here soon. You must calm down. You have to be ready. Your aim can't be off even in the slightest. The shot has to be spot on.

I close my eyes. Count to ten. Then twenty. I feel the stiffness in my shoulders relax a bit and I listen for the sound of the storm, the shriek of the wind, the pounding of sleet, but there is nothing. Only silence over the crackle of the fire.

Peace.

And yet, despite my pep talk and the quietude of the winter day, it's all I can do to hang on to my temper, to focus on the bigger picture, the greater good.

My work is too important to allow myself the luxury of becoming overwhelmed. I must be rock steady. And yet I'm rattled. Deep down. The bitch got to me and I have trouble repressing my anger.

Me.

Who is usually so calm.

It's that bitch of a woman.

Detective.

Regan Pescoli is rattling me and I can't let that happen. Not now. Not until it's over.

To find some relief I pick up her pistol, feel the smooth steel in my palm. There's just something about a weapon that brings a feeling of calm. I run the barrel over my cheek and down my neck, closing my eyes and reveling in the feel of it. I can't let a pain in the ass like Pescoli unnerve or derail me; not now when I need all my concentration.

Slowly I breathe more easily and I walk to my bar and pour a cool glass of vodka. It steadies my nerves, takes the edge off. I have to forget about Pescoli for a while.

It seems I have bigger fish to fry.

I put down the pistol and grab the rifle.

It's time.

I know him.

The thought hit Pescoli hard as she lay on the cot, her arm still handcuffed to its leg.

I know him, and the whack job is smart enough to realize that I might recognize him.

Groggy and weak, she forced herself up on one elbow and noticed a bit of light coming through a high window. Morning? Dawn?

For a second she thought of Santana. His image seemed to be with her each time she awoke in this cold, dark room. Her dreams had been rife with images of him, and each time she'd awoken to find herself here, alone and trapped, she'd blinked hard to call him back. Did he miss her? Suspect that something had happened to her? That was the trouble with their damned no-strings relationship; neither knew what the other was doing. She'd told herself that was the way she'd wanted it. Now she knew it was all a lie.

The grim thought that she'd never see him again hit her viscerally.

Don't go there. You will. You have to. You're a mother, for God's sake, you can't just give up and lie here in a pool of self-pity. For God's sake, Pescoli, do something to save yourself!

Gritting her teeth, she ignored the throbbing in her head, the dull ache that was her shoulder, and the hurt of her ribs and tried to move. Pain seized her chest but it was bearable. She'd been certain her ribs were broken in the accident, then cracked further when the psycho who had abducted her had sat on her while injecting her with God only knew what. Some kind of sedative, she figured, something to keep her dull and lifeless and maybe even to deaden the pain as she somehow had slept, and now she hoped that her ribs were bruised, not broken. They still hurt like hell, but she could move a bit and each breath no longer killed her.

As near as she could remember, he'd been back once since the time he'd straddled her, to check on her, offering her water and soup, not feeding her, but leaving a spoon and a tin cup of something that smelled like chicken bouillon, and a hospital bedpan—the ultimate humiliation.

The bastard had poked and prodded her as she'd lain motionless, unable to lift herself up, her brain mush.

That's why he keeps the place dark, she thought now as her mind began to clear, her brain coming into sharper focus. *It's why he rarely enters, why when he does he wears dark glasses, a baseball cap, and a beard—probably a fake one at that. A disguise.*

The trouble was, she didn't have any real clue to his identity. At least not yet. She eyed the doorway and the crack of light coming from beneath it. Once in a while a shadow passed, then paused, as if he were on the other side, peering through a peephole she couldn't see, or pressing his ear against the wooden panels to listen to her.

It made her skin crawl to imagine that he could observe her. *Don't think about it. Concentrate on getting out of here. If he's afraid you'll recognize him, then he must fear that you'll expose him somehow.*

If that were the case, then he had to think she might escape. She didn't kid herself for a minute into believing that he planned to keep her alive indefinitely or release her, not after all the effort he'd spent in capturing her, not after the way he'd treated his other victims.

Still, he was uncertain.

Otherwise he wouldn't be afraid of letting her see his face.

Somehow, she decided, as the first splinters of

dawn cracked through the small window high overhead, she had to unmask him and make good her escape.

And she had to do it soon.

Before it was too late.

Finally! A damned break in the weather!

Brady Long eyed the clearing skies with satisfaction. After a week of this damn bleak, sub-zero forecast, he was finally able to climb into his JetRanger and make the trip between Denver and Grizzly Falls. The ride was a little rough, but Brady had always been up for a challenge, whether it was on the back of a particularly mean-tempered Brahma bull, or climbing the sheer face of a cliff thousands of miles above the valley floor, or helicopter and extreme skiing or skydiving or whatever it was that brought him the next big rush of adrenaline.

He lived for it. A daredevil by nature, he never had understood placidity or fear. Life was to be lived on the edge, and those who took the safe road in life, who kept to their boring, secure ruts, were just plain wusses or sissies or pussies. Take your pick.

Maybe he'd been born with too much testosterone running through his bloodstream, but he liked it that way. And so did most women; at least the ones who interested him had said so.

Or, he thought now, as he flew his chopper over an ice-encrusted river that ran through the ranch, the women who were attracted to him were really interested in the size of his wallet. The name Long had been associated with copper, then silver, and even gold mines for generations.

A woman could show interest because he was good-looking, or because he was a challenge, or because he was fearless or because he was "richer than God," as one particularly buxom young blonde had whispered into his ear early one hot summer night. He didn't care what turned them on, just as long as they got there.

Yeah, the Long wealth made some flock to him, like vultures on the trail of a dying lamb.

And he was the sole heir . . . well, not technically. There was Padgett, but she was in no condition to contest his claim to their father's fortune, a wealth that was legendary in this part of Montana. And, he knew, his father had sown more than his share of wild oats, so there was always the chance one of Hubert's bastards, or his and Padgett's mother's, might get wise and make a pitiful claim. But if that were the case, he, and a team of lawyers that he would hand-pick, would fight any and all would-be Longs either by exposing them for the frauds they were, or for whatever other demons they were hiding in their pasts, or by settling out of court. It was amazing what a few hundred thousand would do in an effort to make an uncomfortable situation disappear.

Flying low, the chopper's rotors whomping in the crisp morning air, he examined the barns, stable, and old homestead house, covered in snow and clustered apart from the main living quarters.

Eyeing the terrain surrounding the house, he eased the big bird over the tops of the spruce and fir trees before spying the landing pad, a wide, flat circle not a hundred yards from the main house. Yeah, there was plenty of snow, but his chopper had been built to handle winter conditions and he had no trouble putting her down in the thick, icy powder, the JetRanger's skids holding steady.

Perfect.

He loved flying.

Should have been in the military. A pilot.

But then he would have had to take orders, and being obedient, or a team player, just wasn't in Brady's nature.

He cut the engine and let the rotors slow before grabbing his computer and bag from the back.

He'd left Denver on the down-low, not letting anyone there, even Maya, know of his plans. Well, especially not Maya. Pushing open the helicopter door, he hopped to the ground and slogged his way toward the house. He didn't want to think too much about his fiancée, a beautiful model who refused to sign a prenup and not just any prenup, but a fair one.

Not that he was in any hurry to get married, he reminded himself as he followed a snow-covered path through a thicket of spruce and the house appeared.

Brady couldn't help but smile. He loved this old, creaky lodge, had spent some of the happiest times of his youth here in Montana. He'd bagged his first buck not five hundred yards from the barn, learned to ride horses on this ranch long before he made a name for himself on the rodeo circuit, and lost his virginity up in the old man's bedroom, to the younger sister of his second stepmother.

Yeah, he had some great memories in Montana, and though he'd been all over the globe, whenever he needed to think, he came back. "Home" was what he thought of the stone and cedar house that stood so close to the creek, now frozen, not so much as a bit of water visible beneath the snow and ice.

He was free here, he thought, fishing in the pockets of his insulated ski pants and withdrawing a key ring as he made his way to a carport big enough for an RV or boat and separating the quadruple garage from the main house.

In Denver there were pressures. First there was Maya and her petulant insistence that they get married in a cathedral with hundreds of guests. She wanted to walk down the aisle in a white dress with a long train and have over a dozen attendants. It didn't matter that this would be his third time saying "I do" and " 'til death do us part."

Secondly, there was the board of directors, old farts and pains in the butt each and every one.

Third, there was dear old Dad. Still clinging to life by a thread in the nursing home but looking as if he might kick the bucket at any minute. Brady was sick to his back teeth of answering questions about his father. Hubert Elmore Long was dying. Period. What more was there to say except what he didn't dare voice, that he hoped the old man kicked off and fast. What good was lying, barely conscious, unaware of the world, suffering, for God's sake, when there was no hope left?

Angry, Brady unlocked the back door and walked through a mud room where he started stripping off his outer layers. He knew a lot of people thought he wanted the old man to die so he could officially inherit his fortune. What was it now? Forty, maybe forty-five million? But he already had control of the money as it was. Yeah, it would be nice to actually be the head of Long International, but hell, unofficially, he was. He just didn't want his father to linger any longer in that near-vegetative state that Hubert would have hated. He wanted the old man hearty and hale, a man who could stalk a bull elk for hours on end, or pull a calf from a cow having trouble birthing. He wanted the hard-as-nails executive who could negotiate stubbornly with the Chinese or Saudis or anyone on God's green earth—language being no barrier to him getting his way. He wanted the six-foot-four man who would laugh at a ribald joke while having a few beers at the Spot Tavern, or sip cognac while sucking on an expensive cigar in a high-priced New York hotel.

That's the guy Brady would like to see again.

But it wasn't going to happen.

So the husk of a human lying in Regal Oaks Care Center with the iron constitution and will to cling to life at any cost, *that* guy should just give it up.

He unlaced his boots and left them in the expansive mud room, tucked on the tile floor under a bench above, which his jacket and pants were hung and dripping. He wondered if Clementine was in the house, and that pleasant thought teased one corner of his mouth upward.

Clementine DeGrazio, a petite, pretty woman pushing forty who could clean a stove until it sparkled with as much gusto as she would get on her knees for Brady if he asked, which he did each and every time he returned here and had since he was in his mid-twenties. Her touches were everywhere, he thought, as he padded through the kitchen in his stocking feet. Fresh fruit in a bowl on the counter, three newspapers spread neatly on the table in the nook, country music emanating from hidden speakers, and as he opened the refrigerator door, he discovered platters of cheeses and deli meats, spreads and dips, his favorite nacho that just needed reheating. He knew the cupboards would be stocked with his favorites. All because he'd called her less than eight hours earlier.

Clementine asked for nothing other than to keep her job. Not only was she paid well, she and her son lived in this big house rent free. Still, he did, as he aged, feel a twinge of conscience about the eager if submissive sex.

God, he was getting old.

Things that never bothered him had started to dig a bit into his conscience. His old man lying near death in the nursing home, his sister in a far-off institution, and Clementine with her full lips and quick tongue . . . Oh, hell. He shoved his hair from his eyes and realized he hadn't thought of Maya and the way that he refused to give into her demands. Probably because she was as hardheaded and probably hard-hearted as he.

"A match made in heaven," he said and flicked on the lights, then made his way to the thermostat in the front hallway where an open staircase climbed to the upper floors and leaded glass surrounded the massive front doors. As he adjusted the heat down a couple of degrees, he glanced across the stone floor of the foyer to a huge room where the ceiling soared twenty feet upward and a wall of glass offered an incredible view of the forest and creek that wound through the grounds. A river rock fireplace stretched to the beamed ceiling on the opposite wall and leather chairs, tufted couches, and metal wall art, all compliments of his last ex-wife, filled the wide expanse.

"A goddamned fishbowl," his father had com-

plained, preferring the den located down a wide
hallway where he was allowed to smoke his cigars
while surrounded by pine walls covered with the
heads and hides of creatures killed by generations
of Long huntsmen.

From one of the bank of windows, Brady took a
look down the lane to the spot where, through the
trees, he could just make out the house that had
been built as part of the original homestead. Sure
enough, he caught a glimpse of some light through
the trees and assumed that Santana was either in
the cabin, stable, barn, or other shed. The guy was a
hard worker. For all his faults.

What was the old axiom? Keep your friends close,
your enemies closer?

Brady subscribed to the theory. Big-time. He
wondered if Santana guessed, then discarded the
question. Didn't matter. They'd known each other
as kids and, both super competitive, had butted
heads and clashed fists. There had been a few black
eyes and a couple of bloody noses, but Brady had always wondered what made Santana tick. The man
never sucked up to him, never gave in; always, it
seemed, looking down his crooked nose at Brady.
But Santana was a helluva horseman, communi-
cated with animals in a way that Brady found both
uncomfortable and fascinating. The upshot was that
Santana was working for him, here, in No-Fucking-
Where Montana, which was just as it should be.

Brady carried his laptop case to his father's den
and dropped the computer on the desk. Then he
found the bar located near another massive rock
fireplace and poured himself a stiff drink. Three
fingers of bourbon. On the rocks, again compliments of Clementine, who had left a filled ice

bucket on the counter. Ice cubes clinked softly as he carried the drink to his desk. Reaching down, he pressed a hidden button and waited as a false wall decorated with the fading coat of a zebra slid to one side and a bank of cabinets was revealed. Flanked by an arsenal of rifles, shotguns, bows, and pistols was a safe where, he hoped, his father's most recent will would be found.

He could have just asked his father's attorney, Barton Tinneman, for a copy, he supposed, but truth to tell, he didn't trust Tinneman any more than he held faith in his father's friends, most of whom had already died. And that went double for the members of the damned board.

The safe had an old-fashioned combination lock. No electronics or bells and whistles of any sort. Brady had memorized the numbers as a kid of five and never, ever, let on that he knew. Well, his sister, too, had learned the secret sequence, but it wouldn't do her a whole helluva lot of good where she was, locked away in a sanitarium, barely able to function, now would it? He felt a bit of guilt about her condition, then shrugged it off. Padgett had been unable to care for herself for half her life, nearly fifteen years, and before that time, she'd been a raving bitch, so he rarely spent too much time worrying about how she'd ended up there or what his part in it had been.

It was all water under the bridge.

He heard the soft click of ancient tumblers as he turned the dial.

"Sorry, Dad," he said aloud with the final flick of his wrist, the dial stopping at just the right spot, the lock giving way. Smiling in satisfaction, Brady set down his drink and yanked open the door to the safe.

He was certain the will was inside.

All he had to do, once he retrieved it, was wait a few hours, maybe days, for the old man to die.

Chapter Eight

The media had returned.

In full force.

Swooping back to Grizzly Falls with a vengeance, as if the sheriff's department had intentionally duped them with what everyone hated to admit, but now knew, was a copycat killer.

The real deal was still on the loose, here in Montana.

Alvarez pulled into the department parking lot and noticed vans from two TV stations based out of Missoula and another one rolling down the street, with a logo she didn't recognize. *Great,* she thought, pulling her keys from the ignition. *The media circus is gearing up for another show.*

She managed to lock her Jeep and make it inside without being approached by any reporters. Counting herself lucky, she peeled off her jacket and threw it over the back of her chair, then continued toward the kitchen where she heated water in the microwave and located the only bag of tea: Chamomile Mist. No caffeine. No flavor. No morning jolt. In a word: useless.

"Oh, sorry!" Joelle said, flying into the room with a shopping bag filled with groceries. Dressed in a long red coat, black boots, and a white scarf, she was the female version of Santa Claus as she bustled into the kitchen in a cloud of perfume and propriety. "I thought I'd get in before the morning shift arrived," she said, boots clicking across the floor. "But I guess I was wrong." Skewering Alvarez with a motherly but irritated glance, she hurriedly placed cartons of milk and cream into the refrigerator, forced boxes of coffee filters and sugar substitute packets into a drawer, then finally found a variety pack of tea. "Your cold still bothering you?"

Alvarez shook her head. Refused to give in to the urge to sniff. Didn't want to get into it. The last thing she needed was Joelle Fisher trying to mother her. "I'm okay."

The look Joelle sent Alvarez suggested she appeared no better than death warmed over. "Have you been to the doctor?"

Alvarez didn't respond, just opened the wrapper of the variety pack of tea and plucked out a bag of Earl Grey.

"I didn't think so . . . oh . . . here . . ." Joelle reached into the bag one last time and brought out a boxed fruitcake that she immediately unwrapped. "I picked this up at the store." Dried candy and icing glistened under the fluorescent lights as she unboxed the cake and slid it onto a plate decorated with silver bells, obviously something she'd brought from home to help get everyone into the holiday spirit.

With a serial killer on the loose.

And Regan Pescoli missing.

And power outages and icy conditions across most of the state.

And the press camping outside the door and the public in a near state of panic.

Alvarez plunked the tea bag into her cup.

"Hey, what have we got here?" Watershed asked, ducking his head inside the room. He eyed the platter where Joelle was meticulously slicing the cake and stepped eagerly into the kitchen.

"Fruitcake. But don't get too excited. It's from the store. I didn't have time to make my aunt Nina's like I did last year."

"Looks good to me . . . no coffee?" he asked, reaching for the glass pot, the bottom of which was discolored but dry.

"I haven't got to it yet! Give a girl a minute, would ya?"

Alvarez started to make a quick exit.

"I heard they found Pescoli's Jeep up at Horsebrier Ridge," Watershed said to her. "They've already sent up choppers to search the area, right?"

"Fingers crossed that the weather holds," Selena said.

"What?" Joelle's perpetual smile fell from her face. "Horsebrier Ridge? What are you talking about?"

But she'd already put two and two together and come up with four. Her hand flew to her mouth. "No . . ."

"That's why the reporters are here," she said.

"Sweet Jesus, I swear I didn't know. Hadn't heard. I was up half the night wrapping presents and signing the rest of my cards and just, you know, getting ready for Christmas and . . ." Her voice trailed off, her hand over her chest. "You think it's him because the woman they captured isn't the Star-Crossed Killer." Frantically, she sketched the sign of the cross over her chest.

Alvarez nodded grimly and glanced out the window. There were clouds in the distance, but they were high. For the moment visibility was good enough for helicopters to search for signs of Pescoli. It was too early to think that the killer, if he held her, would release her, but still, the pilots might see something. Anything.

"I'll put her in my prayers and call the church. They have a prayer chain," Joelle said a little shakily.

Alvarez hadn't put a lot of stock in prayer for a long, long while. After years of kneeling in front of a looming crucifix, listening to sermons in English and Spanish, believing with all her heart that Jesus would save her soul, she'd had an abrupt loss of faith.

Now she figured prayers wouldn't hurt, though she didn't send one up herself. Too many times God had turned a deaf ear to her prayers, so she decided not to waste her time. Or His.

"Oh, and Ivor Hicks wants to talk to you. Well, not you, but since the sheriff is out of town . . ."

Selena stopped short in her bid to leave the room. "Why?"

"I don't know." Joelle lifted her shoulders.

Watershed snorted. "Who knows what that old nut-job wants? Probably got another call from the general of the Reptilians or something." He chuckled a little meanly.

"I'll call him later," Alvarez said. Though Ivor had located Wendy Ito, the third victim, he was usually more of a pest than a help. More often than not he landed in the drunk tank and had to be released to his son Billy, who dutifully, if unhappily, took responsibility for dear old Dad.

Watershed might have a bad attitude about the man, but for the moment, Alvarez didn't have time for any of Ivor Hicks's nonsense, either.

She left Joelle and Watershed and made her way to her cubicle but before she sat down she received two phone calls, one confirming that Pescoli's Jeep was going to be hauled into the garage and the other that Grayson had asked for, and gotten, a search warrant for Pescoli's house. "Time to rock and roll," she said, swallowing two gulps of the tea, leaving the bag to seep in the remaining cooling liquid, then heading outside again.

The place looked empty.

Regan's car was missing, but her kid's pickup was parked out front. Santana didn't have a key, but he knew where she hid one, had overheard her talking to her daughter once when the girl had locked herself out.

So he let himself inside and was careful not to touch or disturb anything. It was obvious the place was empty. Even the damned dog wasn't inside barking his little head off.

He felt a little odd walking through the rooms she called home. Pausing in the doorway to her bedroom, he imagined her lying back on the thick duvet, that wicked glint evident in her eyes as she slowly smiled and crooked a finger. "Since you're here already, you may as well make yourself useful." Or something similar.

He swore under his breath and realized just how much he missed her. "What the hell happened?" he asked, just as the sound of a truck's engine cut through the morning air. He strode outside and stood on the front porch, expecting her Jeep to roll through the trees and the door to the garage to start cranking open.

Sure enough, a vehicle from the Pinewood Sheriff's Department came into view, but the license plate was off and the woman behind the wheel wasn't Pescoli. His heart sank as he recognized Selena Alvarez. Behind her, in another department-issued vehicle, were a couple of deputies.

"Don't move!" Alvarez ordered. She was reaching for her sidearm as she climbed out of the vehicle. "Hands in the air!"

He didn't argue. "I'm here looking for Regan," he said. "She's not here."

Alvarez gave him a we-already-know-that glare. "You don't know where she is?"

"I told you that yesterday. Things haven't changed . . ." But they had. He saw it in her eyes, in the purse of her lips. "Why are you here?" he asked as the two deputies in the second car approached and a third vehicle, a van from the crime lab, nosed its way into the wide parking area in front of Pescoli's house. "What's going on?"

"You first. Why are you here now?"

"I haven't heard from her, so I thought I'd start looking."

The deputies exchanged glances.

"What?" Santana demanded, fear growing inside him. "You know something? Where is she?"

Alvarez scowled at him and shook her head. "We found her vehicle."

"Where?" he asked, dread starting to pound through him. He lowered his hands.

"Horsebrier Ridge. Well, really in the ravine."

"She had an accident?" Panic tore through him. "Is she all right?" he demanded and caught the tightening of Alvarez's already grim lips. "What is this?"

His first thought that Regan was dead. But then, why the whole posse here at her house? Why the crime lab techs, who, bundled against the cold, carried cases and cameras in their gloved hands and started toward the house? "Can we all back up, please," one of them, a tall man suggested. "You touch anything inside?"

Santana shook his head.

"Just walked all over the damned place," Alvarez charged.

"Where's Regan?" he asked.

She stonewalled him, motioned him to leave the porch, her pistol still aimed straight at his chest. "Move it. Get out of the way."

"Is she dead? In the hospital? What?" His gaze moved to the two deputies. "Why the hell is half the police force here?"

Alvarez said, "She wasn't in the vehicle. It was smashed all to hell, but she wasn't inside. We think it was forced off the road."

"What're you telling me?" he demanded, dread worming through his soul. "Horsebrier Ridge, so she was on her way to her ex's? Is that where her kids are?"

"How did you get in here? You have a key?"

"I knew where she hid one."

"That could be construed as breaking and entering."

"I just need to find her."

She appeared as if she wanted to believe him but

her common sense wouldn't let her. "Let's go down to the sheriff's office and you can make an official statement there. You can handle this?" she asked one of the deputies.

"No problem." A woman deputy was stringing out crime scene tape, carefully walking around the yard.

But she was wrong. The way Santana saw it, they all had a problem. A big one.

"It's your turn to feed him," Bianca complained as she worked and worked to get her hair into a French braid, just like the one she'd seen in one of Michelle's glossy magazines. Sure it was retro, but Miley Cyrus had pulled it off on a recent red carpet and Bianca knew it would be perfect, P-E-R-F-E-C-T, for her date with Chris, if they could ever get together! Cisco was dancing at her feet, yipping and demanding food all the while giving Bianca fits and breaking her concentration. Her braid was a disaster!

"Jeremy!" she yelled, walking down the short hallway to the guest room/office where her brother was camping out. "Hey! Feed Cisco!"

Jeremy was flopped across the day bed that was way too short for him. Briefly he turned his attention away from the television where some army video game flickered—guys in camouflage with big rifles running around some burned-out Armageddon.

"Shit!" Jeremy yanked off his headset as the guy on the screen turned red with his own blood. "Look what you did. I just died! My whole company's under siege!"

"It's a game," she said in a withering tone. She was still working with her hair, her fingers winding strands together.

"So what's so damned important?"

"Feed the dog."

He pulled a face. "Oh, sure."

Cisco ran into the room and jumped on the bed.

"See, he wants some attention from you," Bianca declared.

"From anybody," Jeremy groused, but petted Cisco's little head anyway.

"Have you heard from Mom?" Bianca asked, trying not to worry.

"Nah, but she's pissed at me."

"That doesn't stop her from calling."

"Or bossing me around."

"Exactly." Bianca looked over her shoulder, then quickly shut the door. "Do you think Dad and Michelle know something and aren't telling us?"

"Like what?"

"Like, I don't know, she's hurt, got shot on the job, or had a wreck or . . . something really bad?"

"They'd have to tell us," he said, frowning.

Bianca gave up on her hair for the moment, let the unruly curls fall to her shoulders. "They're always trying to 'protect' us." She made air quotes to emphasize her point. "Mom's detective partner wouldn't have come out here unless it was really serious."

"I guess."

Jeremy scowled just as Bianca's phone dinged, indicating she'd received a text message. She clicked a button and found a picture of Chris on the screen. Chris and two of his friends, all wearing Santa hats and making goofy faces. She grinned and for a second, she wasn't worried about her mother. "Just take care of the dog," she ordered, hurrying from the room.

Jeremy, his video game ruined, watched her go. She didn't bother shutting the door, which really bugged him. But then everything and everyone was bugging him. Even Heidi Brewster, who kept texting him and trying to get together. He wanted to. Man, he wanted to. Heidi was hotter than hot and her mouth . . . holy crap, what she could do with that. He got hard just thinking about it. But she was trouble, and right now he didn't need any more of that. So he didn't respond to her texts and was probably really ticking her off.

Too bad.

Ever since he'd gotten busted for Minor in Possession of Alcohol with Heidi, he'd been in a bad mood. Mom had grounded him, Heidi's jerk of a father had warned Jeremy to never see his daughter again, and now they were stuck here with Michelle and Dad, which wasn't all that great.

In fact, he was getting sick of them. Lucky was either trying to buddy up to him or tell him what to do. Like he was his real dad or something. It was just stupid. Then there was Michelle. Jesus, she was hot, too. Always running around in high heels and tight jeans and tops that showed off her boobs. He'd even caught a glimpse of her coming out of the shower, her hair wet, no makeup, big breasts with tiny pink nipples standing at attention from the cold. He'd noticed, though, that she wasn't a natural blonde. The worst part was, he was pretty sure she'd seen him. Their eyes had met through the steam of the bathroom where the door was opened far enough to give him an eyeful. Since then he'd pretty much holed up in his room, and he was certain that when Michelle talked to him, she was thinking the same thing he was. There was something in her eyes, and the way her tongue was visible against her shiny lips, that told him she knew he'd seen her naked.

He couldn't help but wonder if she'd set him up, if maybe, she wanted him to make a pass at her. *She's your freakin' stepmom, butthead. Don't think like that!*

Rolling off the bed, he grabbed his boots. It was time to go and get his car, call a friend, and find out what the hell had happened to his mother. He didn't want to tell Bianca that he was worried, too, but in this case, she was right. Something was wrong. Mom would *never* have just let Lucky tell her he wanted custody. No way would she have rolled over on that. She would have fought him tooth and nail. Jeremy had figured it was a good deal. He'd decided that Mom would have been so petrified of losing Bianca and him that she would have done anything to keep them happy and this whole stupid grounding thing would disappear. Afraid of losing custody altogether, she would have let Jeremy do whatever he wanted.

Oh, come on, who are you kidding? Mom would never allow that. She'll ride your ass until the day she dies.

"Crap," he said under his breath, then texted his friend to come and get him. He needed to go home and look for himself, try to figure out where she was, then grab his truck so he had wheels, a way to get out of this overdecorated house with its gooey-looking pink Christmas tree and his stepfather's hottie wife.

Throwing on his oversized camo jacket, Jeremy jammed a stocking cap onto his head before walking into the kitchen. He found a bag of kiblets for Cisco, who had tagged after him and was so excited he was barking and making tight little circles near his dish.

"About time you woke up," Michelle drawled. Dressed in jeans, high-heeled boots, and a tight turtleneck sweater, she strolled into the kitchen. Today, her makeup was in place, her platinum hair framing her face.

Cisco wolfed down his food as Michelle snapped on the radio. Some Christmas carol started playing through the suddenly too-small kitchen. "Want some breakfast?" Was her voice breathy? Oh, God. She gave him that look again, the one that said I-know-what-you-saw, as she snagged an apron from a hook on the pantry and slid it over her head. It was a Mrs. Santa apron. Short, red, trimmed in fake white fur. She tied it around her slim waist and he couldn't help but imagine what she would look like without the jeans and sweater, just the apron and tall black boots.

"No breakfast," he managed as the dog finished. He automatically let Cisco outside, a breath of cold air racing into the stifling kitchen.

"You sure? I could make pancakes." She turned and faced him, one hand holding a spatula up, and for a second he caught an image of her spanking him with it. Or him spanking her. Lying across his lap, her rounded butt red as she squealed in pleasure/pain. Oh, shit.

"No," Jeremy croaked out. "Tyler's on his way over to pick me up."

"You're leaving?" Now she was pouting.

"Uh-huh." He *had* to get out of here and fast.

Cisco returned, bounding into the room, snow

covering his whiskers. Jeremy slid the slider door closed as the phone rang so loudly he nearly jumped.

Michelle pounced on it like a cougar onto an unsuspecting antelope. "Hello?" she said into the handheld receiver. "Yes, this is Mrs. Pescoli . . . Uh-huh. Wait a sec, I'll get him." Her smile had fallen from her face and her gaze when she looked at Jeremy again had lost all of its teasing glint. She headed toward the archway leading from the kitchen and with her hand over the receiver yelled, "Luke?" No response. "Luke! Telephone! It's the police!"

Jeremy's heart dropped like a stone. "The police?" he repeated as Bianca, cell phone in hand, appeared.

Her eyes were round. "Is it Mom? Is she on the phone?"

Of course not, you nitwit. Michelle would have said, "It's your ex-wife" or "Regan's calling again" or "The bitch is on the line," not "The police." He was about to say what he was thinking until he noticed the fear in Bianca's eyes. She knew. As well as he.

"What d'ya mean, it's the police?'" Lucky demanded, zipping up his fly and buckling his belt.

"The sheriff's department." Michelle was as serious as Jeremy had ever seen her as Lucky grabbed the receiver.

"Hello . . . yeah, this is Luke Pescoli . . ." He glanced at his kids in one quick sweep. "They're here. With me. What's going on?"

And then he listened. While Bianca bit her lip, her fingers curled over her cell in a death grip, Michelle standing like a statue in her stupid apron and holding the pancake flipper, even Cisco, for once, standing stock still, Jeremy held his breath.

"Yeah . . . I see . . . But she wasn't inside . . . ?"

Jeremy couldn't stop himself. "Who? Who wasn't inside? Mom?"

"Shut up!" Bianca hissed, but she was white as a sheet.

As if from a distance he heard a horn beep.

"Yeah, well, I'll keep them here with me until we know more," Luke said quietly. Sober as a judge, he hung up. The car's horn honked impatiently.

"What?" Bianca asked, tears welling.

Jeremy's ears started a dull ringing.

"They found your mom's Jeep," he said. "Down in the gully, off Horsebrier Ridge."

Bianca let out a little squeak.

"That's no 'gully.' It's a damned abyss," Michelle whispered.

"Is she okay?" Tears trickled down Bianca's cheeks.

Luke sighed. "I don't know."

Jeremy's heart was beating like a drum and a ringing filled his ears. "So where is she? In a hospital?"

"No," Luke said as Bianca flung herself at her father and he held her tight. "She wasn't in the Jeep. It was wrecked. Bad. But she wasn't inside."

"Oh, God," Michelle said and while Luke was shaking his head, trying to stop her, she blurted out, "He's got her! The damned Star-Crossed. He did this! Oh, for the love of God . . ."

Bianca let out a howl.

"Shut up, Michelle, we don't know that. We don't know anything!" Luke bit out.

The honking continued.

"Who the hell is that?" Luke demanded.

Jeremy snapped out of it. "My ride."

"Mommy!" Bianca sobbed brokenly.

"Shh, baby, it's gonna be all right," Luke said without enthusiasm. Without belief.

Jeremy knew better. Nothing was going to be right. Not if everyone stood around here doing nothing. No way was he going to stick around. Without a word, he ran out of the room while patting his pockets to make sure his keys and wallet were with him. His father finally woke up and started yelling his name, but Jeremy took off through the front door, across the path he'd shoveled yesterday and toward the driveway where Tyler McAllister's Chevy Blazer waited.

Chapter Nine

So maybe Santana wasn't as bad as she'd originally thought, Selena considered. At least he did seem to care for Pescoli. He sat at her desk, answered questions, glared at her, his square jaw tight, his razor-thin lips compressed to an unyielding line. He hadn't been able to offer her any further clues to Regan's accident or abduction, but he seemed genuinely worried.

"That all?" he asked as a phone rang down the hall.

"For now."

"You'll keep me in the loop."

She didn't bother to answer or even to smile.

"Then I'll check in."

"Do that," she said, her headache returning. Santana wasn't next of kin, he wasn't even related to Pescoli. And he wasn't a cop. "Remember that this is a police matter. The sheriff's department and the FBI."

"Meaning?"

"That sometimes when a person is involved with a victim, even a potential victim, they try to help and end up getting in the way."

"Are you warning me off?"

"If you're thinking of doing some investigating on your own? Yeah. Leave it to the professionals."

"I work with horses."

Her eyes narrowed. "Not always." She noticed that he didn't so much as flinch. "I checked. You were with the military. Army Ranger. Right?" She crossed her arms over her chest. "And Army Intelligence?"

Not a flicker.

"I'm serious, Santana. Stay out of this. Impeding an investigation, getting into trouble with the law, it's not worth it."

His gaze narrowed just a bit. "But she is," he said tersely as he climbed to his feet. He didn't so much as smile, just added, "Let's go, Nakita." With a whistle to his dog, a husky that had settled in under the chair he'd taken, he strode away. Alvarez watched him go. He was sexy all right and had that I-don't-give-a-damn attitude some women found fascinating down pat.

But he did give a damn.

About Regan.

"Pescoli's main squeeze?"

She turned and found Sage Zoller, an elfin-looking junior detective who was just a few years younger than Alvarez, standing at the opening of her cubicle. Tiny but tough, Zoller ran marathons and mentored at-risk teens.

"Main Squeeze?" Alvarez repeated.

"I know. Archaic, huh? It's what my parents call

each other." She was watching Santana as he strode around the corner. "Jesus, there's something about a rugged, good-looking guy with a big dog."

"Oh, give it up." Alvarez was not in the mood.

"Yeah . . . good idea. Besides, we've got other fish to fry. Another car's been spotted."

"Another car, other than Pescoli's Jeep?" Suddenly Zoller had all of Alvarez's attention.

"Just this morning. Van Droz caught the call. It's nose-down in Boxer Creek not far from Keegan's Corner . . ."

Which was also known by the locals as Dead Man's Curve.

"A red Saturn. Montana plates. Visible enough to determine that the car is registered to Elyssa O'Leary."

Alvarez's stomach nosedived. The name rang a bell. "She's one of the women who's been reported missing." She returned to her cubicle and sat at her desk. With a few quick keystrokes, she pulled up the file, including a driver's license and pictures of Elyssa Katherine O'Leary. Brown hair, brown eyes. Freckles. Twenty-six. Nursing student. Only child of Marlene and Brian O'Leary. Alvarez swallowed, thinking that the girl, even now, could be lashed to a tree somewhere in the rugged Montana wilderness, dragging cold air into her already-freezing lungs. "We have to find her."

"And Pescoli."

"Christ, yes!" she snapped. "Have you pinpointed this? Put it on the map?"

"Not yet."

"Let's go." With Alvarez leading the way, they cut through several banks of cubicles to the task force room where pictures of the crime scenes and victims were posted on one wall. Nearby an enlarged map of the area had been hung and pushpins indicated the crime scenes, not only where the mangled cars had been located, but also the position of the areas where the victims had been found.

"Do you have the exact location of O'Leary's vehicle?" Alvarez asked, stepping around a large table in the center of the room where the task force met. The chairs now were empty, pushed tight against the table by the cleaning crew. Nearby, a phone with a desk was stationed in one corner, an officer doing paperwork manning it. He looked up as they walked in, then turned back to his reports. All of the calls that came in with tips for the task force were routed here where Zoller, or whoever else was assigned the duty, answered the phones and coordinated the messages with the detectives and FBI agents.

So far, in the past few months, ever since the first victim, Theresa Charleton, had been found lashed to a hemlock tree in the wilderness, the department had logged over a thousand calls.

None of the tips had panned out.

"The Saturn was discovered"—Zoller looked at the note in her hand for confirmation—"uh, exactly 4.6 miles from the corner of Henrici and Durango."

Alvarez located the position, right at the sharp corner, and pushed another pin in place. "If the killer's M.O. remains the same, we should find her in a two-mile radius from the car . . ." She ran a finger around the area of rugged canyons and hills, forests, and stone outcroppings. "Let's get the choppers to take a look-see, get some pictures. I think they're already in the air for Pescoli, right?"

"Yep. No response yet."

"They won't find her," Alvarez predicted as she unwillingly stuck a pin into the map, indicating the location of Pescoli's Jeep. "It's not time. The son of a bitch waits. Helps them heal before . . ."

"Yeah, I know." Zoller was nodding, her mop of dark curls shining under the fluorescent tubes mounted in the ceiling.

Selena eyed the map critically, trying to come up with something, an area they'd overlooked where the bastard could be holed up, a spot where they would likely find his next victim.

She glanced to the blown-up copies of the notes found nailed to the trunks of the trees over the victims' heads. They were similar with their star pattern, each just slightly different. Star-Crossed was trying to tell them something, but what?

"Has anyone called O'Leary's parents?" she asked Zoller.

"Not yet."

"Let's hold off on that until we look through the car."

Disturbed, feeling as if she were missing something, Alvarez headed back to her desk and scanned the missing persons report again. In his statement, the father, Brian, swore that no one on earth would want to harm his child, except for her boyfriend, Cesar Pelton, a divorced father of two and "hoodlum who couldn't hold a job." Pelton, according to Elyssa's father, had "knocked her around" a couple of times, though no police reports had ever been filed. Elyssa's mother, a meek woman, had stayed silent, neither agreeing or disagreeing with her husband.

The nightmare just kept getting worse, Alvarez thought as she glanced outside and noticed the first few flakes of snow beginning to fall.

Dr. Jalicia Ramsby had seen it all in her fifteen years of practice: A full spectrum of psychological diseases. Everything from clinical depression to bipolar disorder to schizophrenia and dissociative identity disorder, more commonly known as multiple personality disorder, and post-traumatic stress syndrome, to name a few. She'd tried to help patients who were alcoholic, suicidal, manic depressive, autistic, you name it. She'd worked in clinics, in hospitals, in shelters, even in a prison.

And she could readily spot a fake.

Or so she thought.

However, the patient in room 126 gave her pause.

As she sat in her new office at Mountain View Hospital, a bright room with a breathtaking view of the Olympic Mountains in west Seattle, she drummed her fingers on her desk and ignored an unopened bottle of Diet Pepsi, her usual jolt of caffeine in the morning. Something was off. Something she couldn't quite define. Yet. She glanced at her tidy desk. Aside from the bottle of soda sitting on a woven coaster, there was a glass half filled with ice, a picture of her daughter at her eighth-grade graduation, a bud vase with a single white rose, and the open file. Fifteen years of notes, diagnoses, pictures, medical reports, and interviews.

Jalicia had read them over twice, trying to get a handle on Padgett Renee Long, and couldn't. The other patients in her care she understood. They didn't necessarily fit into neat little psychiatric boxes, but at least their conditions were consistent with other cases and gave her a frame of reference from which she could work.

Padgett was different.

She twirled her desk chair around and searched the bookcase, a virtual wall of tomes on every subject she'd found interesting. As she scanned the familiar titles, she thought of the quiet woman in 126. Not a word uttered other than prayers.

For fifteen years.

And yet there was intelligence behind Padgett's cornflower blue eyes; Jalicia sensed it.

Not finding a title that would help, she turned back to her desk, cracked open the soft drink, poured it carefully into a glass with ice cubes, and watched the foam rise then fall, little bubbles bursting and creating a soft, tiny spray. She carried her drink to the window and stared outside.

Rain was spitting from the gray sky, clouds obscuring her view. Christmas lights twinkled in the row of fir trees lining the drive, a cheery reminder that the holidays were near.

Sipping her soda, Jalicia watched a sedan roll up the drive and take a parking spot marked for handicapped drivers. A man in a thick coat and fedora climbed out of the car, stopped at the trunk, and pulled out a wheelchair. He opened the chair and eased it close to the passenger side, then helped a portly woman into it.

Jalicia's desk phone rang and she turned away from the window. "Dr. Ramsby," she said, glancing at the file, then the clock. One of her men's groups was scheduled to meet in ten minutes.

"Yes, Doctor, I just wanted to alert you that a

Mr. Barton Tinneman has been calling. He's the lawyer for Padgett Long."

Jalicia crossed to her desk and flipped open Padgett's file to the first page. Barton Tinneman's name was listed.

"Did you get his number?" she asked, glancing at the clock again.

"Of course."

"E-mail it to me and I'll call him back as soon as I can." She wanted to ring up the attorney right away, but decided she needed more than ten minutes for a conversation about Padgett Long.

"Will do."

Jalicia hung up and finished her soft drink. Maybe after talking to the attorney, she'd gain some insight into the mystery that was Padgett Long.

He was gone.

There wasn't a sound emanating from the other rooms and the firelight that usually glowed under the door was fading. If Regan was ever going to escape, now was the time.

Short of somehow sawing off her hand, however, she was screwed. There was no way to get the damned handcuff off her wrist.

Damn it, Pescoli, think. Don't give up. This is your opportunity.

She was hurting, her ribs aching painfully, her shoulder reminding her that she needed medical attention, but she'd always had a high tolerance for pain, which had helped her excel in high school and college sports. Once, she'd played basketball on a sprained ankle and still made the winning shot. But this pain was all-enveloping and she had to concentrate to think beyond it.

She couldn't get out unless she somehow extricated herself from the damned bed. Rolling slowly to her feet, still chained to the leg, she studied the makeup of the cot. The frame was steel and could be folded up, but the leg she was chained to was bolted down to the floor. Without a key to the handcuffs or bolt cutters, her situation appeared useless . . .

Where there's a will, there's a way. Her father's words echoed through her head.

She ran her fingers over the leg of the cot. It was welded to the piece screwed into the floor. The only possible weak place in the contraption was either the screw or the weld. Since she didn't have a screwdriver or a knife, she had to attack the weld. Examining it as best she could in the dim light, she took heart. It looked hastily done. A weak point if she ever saw one.

Maybe there was a chance.

Nothing ventured, nothing gained. Once again her dad was speaking to her. She tried kicking the leg free, but in her handcuffed position couldn't get any power. She decided it would work better if she flung herself onto the cot, hard, over and over again, hoping to weaken the weld. So she did. Throwing her weight onto the cot, jerking with her arm at the same time.

Pain rattled through her body.

She had to bite down to keep from yelping.

Five minutes later, exhausted, she collapsed on the cot. No . . . . this wasn't the way. She had to think of something else . . .

In her mind's eye she saw an image of Nate Santana, his smile twisted and devilish, his eyes twinkling as he lay across a bed. "You can do it, Detective," he said. "Once you set your mind to it, you can do just about anything."

Now, lying in the cold room, she felt tears begin to well. If only she had the same faith in herself as he had.

Try again.

Setting her teeth against what she knew would be blinding pain, she struggled up, threw herself onto the cot again, and yanked up with her arm.

Pain screamed through her body, rattling her ribs. Like knifes slicing through her muscles. No, this wouldn't work. Slowly she rolled off the cot again, swiped a kick at the leg with no results, took in a long, deep breath, then, holding on to the handcuffs with her free hand, she set her bare heels on the floor and heaved herself backward.

Nothing.

Oh, God. She had to do it again.

Setting her jaw, she threw herself backward with all her strength.

Was it her imagination, or had she felt something give?

Yeah, all the tendons and ligaments in your shoulder. That's what gave.

"One more time," she said under her breath, her forehead beading in sweat despite the cold temperature. Gathering herself, she counted to three, then gave it her all, trying to hurl her weight backward as the handcuff attached to the cot yanked hard against the weld.

There it was, that feeling that something would give.

She just had to keep trying.

No matter how painful it was.

Before the son of a bitch who'd trapped her here returned.

The wail on the other end of the line said it all.

Alvarez thought if she lived to be a hundred that shriek of horrified denial would be with her forever.

"Noooooo!" Marlene O'Leary had cried, sobbing, while her husband, on the extension, had been cold.

"But you just found the car, not Elyssa," he repeated, trying to squeeze a drop of hope out of the circumstances.

"That's true." Alvarez had explained the situation, knowing she was destroying these people's lives.

"Nooooo . . . Nooooo."

"Shh, Mother!" Brian O'Leary cautioned, though with a hint of compassion. "We don't know what's happened to Elyssa."

"But . . . But . . . oh . . . Oh, God . . . No, no, no." She sounded as if she were hyperventilating.

"Marlene. Calm down. Look, Detective, I'll call you back."

"My baby, no, no, no," the desolate woman cried. Alvarez heard the sound of O'Leary shushing his wife and imagined the burly, gruff man wrapping his beefy arms around his frail wife, holding her steady while his very world collapsed.

There was a final click as they hung up the phone.

"I'm sorry," Alvarez said and felt sick to her soul. She was supposed to be tough, to have a thick skin so that she could deal with the horror and tragedy of homicides, the taking of a life by another human being. Mostly, she could handle it, but dealing with grieving loved ones, giving them bad news, that was the part that ate at her and caused her to sometimes second-guess her career path.

She hung up the phone and sat at her desk, staring at the picture of Elyssa O'Leary smiling into the camera at some DMV office in Montana.

She might not be dead yet.

But there was no report from the crew of the helicopter that had gone searching earlier, and the snow was beginning to fall in earnest again.

Chapter Ten

"Hello, Mr. Tinneman, this is Dr. Ramsby at Mountain View Hospital in Seattle, returning your call. I'm Padgett Long's psychiatrist." Seated in the chair in her office, Jalicia had waited five minutes for Tinneman's secretary to roust the lawyer up, and now that he was finally on the other end of the line, she had trouble biting back her irritation.

"Oh, good, good. I was hoping you'd call," the man said in a rush. "I just wanted to let you know that Padgett's father's health has declined substantially in the last few weeks. He's been in a care facility, a great facility, Regal Oaks, the best in Denver, but he's failing and a few weeks ago hospice was called in. I'm afraid it looks like Mr. Long's failing and, unfortunately, probably won't last out the month, possibly the week."

"I'm sorry. Thank you for the information." Jalicia waited. There was more to the attorney's message, she was sure of it.

"You don't have to worry about Padgett's care; Hubert was very careful to see that she will be taken care of for the rest of her life. A trust has been established, so nothing should change. As always the bills can be sent or e-mailed here and we'll pay them promptly. But—"

Here it comes, Jalicia thought.

"Well, Padgett and her father were extremely close before her accident and . . . and I was wondering how exactly to break the news to her, or if it's a good idea."

"We don't lie here, Mr. Tinneman."

"Oh, no, no. Of course not. But, well, I haven't seen Padgett in a while."

That was the understatement of the year. Jalicia had pulled Padgett Long's records and Tinneman's name was not on any of the visitor lists. The only people who had seen Padgett in the last eighteen months were her brother, Brady, over a year earlier, and Liam Kress, a family friend whose visits had been fairly regular. No one from the firm of Sargent, McGill, and Tinneman had ever set foot here.

"What is it you're suggesting?" she asked, checking her watch.

"That Padgett might be upset if she learns about her father. That she might even want to come to the funeral, if that's possible."

Dr. Ramsby considered the patient in room 126. Would she even know? Register to the news that her father was dying? She flipped through the records. Padgett Long had come to Mountain View voluntarily. There was no court order. She could leave any time she wanted to, though it was doubtful she understood her rights.

"Would her brother or some other family member take her?"

"I don't know."

"A caretaker?"

"There is none. Unless we hire someone."

"Someone from your firm."

"Oh, well, I don't think so."

"What is it you want me to do, Mr. Tinneman?"

"I'm just informing you of the situation," he responded curtly.

"Okay."

They were at an impasse. There was clearly something more Tinneman was trying to impart, but he seemed to be dancing around the subject.

Finally, he said, rather coolly, "Do you *know* Padgett Long, Dr. Ramsby?"

Jalicia bristled. "I'm her doctor."

There was a long pause and the voice on the other end of the connection lost all its country-boy charm. "You're fairly new at Mountain View. Maybe you haven't had time to really get to know Padgett. I've worked with the Long family for years."

"She's my patient. If there's something you're trying to tell me . . ." Jalicia's own voice was cool. She struggled with people who were too cagey.

"She has her rights, too," he said, as if trying to convince himself. "I realize that. And she probably does, too. I don't know how she'll react to her father's condition or his death. As I said, they were extremely close. Good-bye."

Jalicia hung up and stared at the phone. What kind of a phone call was that? And what the hell was up with Padgett Long? She opened the thick file and decided to start at the beginning, fifteen years earlier, when sixteen-year-old Padgett Long, mute and skittish, the result of a head injury and near drowning, had become a resident at Mountain View. She'd spent half her life here, all of her adult years, behind the locked gates of this private psychiatric facility.

Her feeling that something wasn't right had just been compounded by Barton Tinneman's enigmatic call.

Pescoli's right wrist was raw. Bruised by the handcuff that was welded to the cot's leg. The skin was scraped and broken even though she'd used the corner of the blanket the bastard had left for her to give her some cushion as she flung her weight away from the cot, trying to weaken the weld. Her left wrist, at the other end of the handcuffs, was relatively unscathed.

Don't think about it. Keep trying. Time is running out. The son of a bitch will be back soon. You know it.

She was sweating. Salty drops running into her eyes and down her back despite the frigid temperatures.

But the leg of the cot was giving a bit. She was sure she felt it and if she could just keep at it, she would be able to get free. Right?

But how long?

Is there enough time?

Can you do it?

Setting her jaw, she threw herself back into her task. She hadn't come up with a better idea for escape and this would have to work. It *had* to!

Over and over again she stood up as much as her manacle would allow, hunched over since there was little play between her right wrist and the weld, then flung herself back on the cot, yanking the cuff, grinding her teeth to keep from crying out.

She had no idea how much time had passed, only the lightening of the sky gave her an inkling, but the tiny window cut into the wall high overhead didn't offer much illumination and the cloud-covered sky allowed her little measure of the minutes and hours slipping away.

She only knew that whatever time she had to escape, it wasn't enough.

Though whatever drug he'd given her had worn off and she was no longer groggy, that could change when he returned. If he came into her room she would have to act as if it were still in her system.

If she was still here when he got back.

Oh, God, she hoped not.

She prayed he was long gone, or better yet, that she could find a way to turn the tables on him, discover a weapon of her own and surprise him. Let the prick know how it felt to look down the barrel of a gun or feel the blade of a knife at his throat.

The problem was, even if she was able to somehow get the drop on him, she didn't know if she could restrain herself from blowing his sorry ass away.

She knew she should somehow arrest him.

Bring him in.

That way they could find any other victims.

Give him his day in court.

Let justice prevail.

"Bullshit," she muttered as she threw her weight against the handcuff again and felt the cold metal bite into her wrist, her arm feeling as if it would be pulled from its socket. Was this justice? Was what he was doing to her, to the others, in any way fair and equitable?

Squeezing her eyes shut, she dug in and was sure, oh, God, please, that the weld was starting to give way. "Come on, come on," she whispered through gritted teeth.

Yes! There was a shift. A little one.

Oh, Jesus, there had to be.

All this effort couldn't be in vain.

She leaned forward for a second, took in three long breaths, felt her muscles screaming, her ribs aching, but she ignored the seductive urge to give up, to roll back onto the cot and pull the blanket to her chin to shiver alone in the dark. Readying herself, making certain the cuff was over the weld, she threw herself backward onto the cot again.

She couldn't let the bastard win.

Not without a damned good fight.

In her mind's eye, she saw her children. Bianca, just starting to develop into a woman, a smart girl who'd recently discovered boys. Jeremy. Oh, God. He was headed down the wrong path. Smoking marijuana, dabbling in who knew what, drinking and getting into serious trouble with Heidi Brewster.

What would happen if they didn't have her?

Would Lucky and Michelle raise them?

What a disaster that would be.

Oh, Lord, give me strength.

She was gasping now, drawing in ragged breaths, still working at the weakening joint of welded metal. She had too much to live for to end up the victim of some sicko.

In a flash, she thought of Nate and her heart twisted. She'd never believed she loved him, hadn't admitted it for a second, but oh, God, she might have been wrong. His quick wit, His sexy smile. The way he could turn her inside out . . .

Stop it!

She had to concentrate.

Because of the kids.

Because of Nate.

Because there was no way she was going to let this twisted nutcase win!

Tyler McAllister was high.

And it wasn't even noon yet.

Not that it really mattered, but today, with his mom missing, Jeremy had no time for McAllister's crap. He sat on his side of the Blazer, tapping his fingers nervously on the window ledge of the door while Tyler lit a cigarette, then with the smoke dangling from his lips, gunned the engine on the empty road, hit the brakes, and sent the SUV skidding sideways. He laughed then, thinking it was hilarious.

Jeremy didn't.

"Cool it!" Jeremy yelled over the bass of some heavy-metal song he didn't recognize.

"What?" McAllister yelled back as the Blazer straightened and Tyler adjusted the wipers. Snow was falling again. Not big, heavy flakes, but tiny icy crystals that indicated the weather was gonna get worse. The fir trees were already heavy with snow and ice, their branches drooping. Traffic was light, thank God, because McAllister wasn't driving all that great.

McAllister gunned it up the hill that started the long straightaway to the crest of Horsebrier Ridge. On the other side of the mountain the road twisted, followed the creek, and turned like a sidewinder, but here, on the near side, at a higher elevation, the road cut like a knife through the surrounding hills.

"Check it out!" Tyler, grinning like a goon, hit the gas again and laughed as the Blazer fishtailed and the music blared. The windows were beginning to fog, but he didn't seem to notice. "Ha!" Another tromp on the accelerator.

It pissed Jeremy off. "Just . . . just . . ." Jeremy snapped off the iPod. The interior of the SUV was suddenly silent.

"What the hell do you think you're doing?"

"I don't have time for this shit! Just drive to my house, dickhead, and quit fuckin' around."

"It looks like somebody got up on the wrong side of bed this morning," Tyler mocked in a falsetto voice, as if he were someone's mother.

Which only bugged Jeremy all the more. "Don't! Okay? Just . . . don't! I asked you for a ride home. Nothing else."

"What the fuck's got into you?"

"My mom's missing."

"Lucky you." Tyler shrugged. "I'd *pay* to have my mom disappear. She is *such* a bitch."

Jeremy's fist balled and he nearly slammed it into McAllister's jaw. "Stop, would ya?"

Tyler pulled a face, like a little kid with an exaggerated frown, his Winston still dangling from his lips. He looked like an idiot. Hell, he *was* an idiot!

For the briefest of seconds Jeremy wondered if maybe his mother was right, that he should try to find some other friends. But that thought was gone in a flash, disappearing as quickly as it had come. "Just fuckin' drive."

Tyler snorted a stream of smoke and switched on

his iPod again, cranking it up until the bass was booming and the lead singer screeched at the top of his lungs. Maybe that's what Jeremy needed: to get lost and forget about all this. A sweet buzz that would dull his anxiety, lift him out of the funk into which he was quickly sinking.

"Hey . . . what's this?" Tyler said when he saw the detour sign a quarter of a mile from the crest of the ridge. The icy lanes were blocked, cones and a cruiser for the Highway Patrol blocking access. A tall policewoman was pointing to the side road, indicating that they should turn down the secondary road or turn around and go back the way they came. Tyler snorted again. "What the hell do we do now?"

Jeremy's stomach hit the floor. "Stop."

"What?"

"No, I mean it. Stop. Stop the car."

"But that's a cop!" Tyler said as if he were imparting some vast unknown knowledge.

"I know."

"Look, man, this is a bad idea—"

"My mom's a cop, too."

"I'm tellin' ya, stopping is a mistake."

"Just do it!"

"Shit!" As Tyler braked, Jeremy flung open the door and slid a bit as his boots landed on the icy road. He grabbed the handle of the door, righted himself, then used the idling Blazer for support as he walked around the rear through the falling snow. A cloud of exhaust followed him, as the SUV really needed a ring job.

"Hey!" he called to the policewoman.

She was watching his every move. "You can't go through here. Road's closed," she said, shaking her head and frowning. Along with what appeared to be a sour disposition, she wore the big-brimmed hat and dark uniform of the Montana Highway Patrol. Sunglasses covered her eyes.

"Why?"

"Accident." Her expression was stern, her mirrored glasses shielding her eyes as snow caught in the wide brim of her hat and collected on Jeremy's shoulders. The wind was kicking up, too, whistling softly through the canyon. "Now, move along."

He looked farther up the hill and stared at the tow truck, its engine almost pressed into the bank on the high side of the pass, its rear end poised near the ravine on the other. "I can't," he whispered, his voice failing, his guts twisting. "I think my mom was in that accident."

Her lips compressed. "What's your name?"

"Jeremy Strand," he said, shaking inside. "My mother's Regan Pescoli. She's a detective with the sheriff's department."

"Pinewood County?"

"Yeah." He swallowed hard. It was one thing to learn about the accident, another to come face-to-face with it. And for the first time he wondered if she could already be dead. If he'd been lied to. He felt sick inside. "Was she in the car?" When he noticed the stonewalling expression of the trooper, he added, "They said she wasn't. My stepdad got a call this morning. And they said that when they found the car, she wasn't in it."

"You should go home," the officer was saying. "To your stepdad. Can I call him for you?"

But Jeremy barely heard what she was saying as he looked past her shoulder and saw, through the thickening snow, the outline of a tow truck parked sideways across the road at the summit of the mountain. People in snow gear were standing nearby while the whine of a straining winch filled the canyon.

Jeremy stood transfixed, his eyes focused on the crest.

He was vaguely aware of Tyler revving the engine, hinting that they should leave, and the stern-faced trooper's disapproval, but he couldn't budge and as his mother's mutilated, wrecked vehicle slowly appeared, the metal wrenched, the windshield and tires blown, Jeremy thought he would throw up.

No one, not even his tough-as-nails mother, could have survived that wreck.

She had to be dead.

This will be an easy one, I think, parking my truck upstream from the property. A simple kill.

Different from the others.

Special.

One for which I've waited years.

One I will definitely savor.

What's the old saying? *Revenge is always best served up cold?* Something like that. Well, it couldn't get much colder than this with temperatures sliding below freezing and fifteen years of waiting.

But now the time is right.

I've checked.

Brady Long is alone.

I take my rifle from the back of the truck, then begin the long trek to the main house where, no doubt, he's already settled in. The prince in his castle.

The snow is beginning to fall again. Tiny flakes

that swirl and dance, quietly changing the landscape, distorting the view, muting the sounds of the day.

I follow the path of the stream easily, from memory, having run this course dozens of times in the past.

Quickly.

Moving through the thick pines and hemlock, I spy the house, a hundred yards away, the roof thick with snow, dormers protruding, windows dark. But on the main level there are lights, glowing warmly in the gray morning, inviting me inside.

It's all I can do not to smile, but I warn myself not to savor the kill until it has happened, until Brady Long has taken his last, rattling breath. Only then will I be able to relish my success, as justice will finally prevail.

Through a thicket of naked aspens, I move along a deer path and spy the helicopter sitting still as death, long rotors unmoving, the windows of the cockpit already showing a thin layer of snow.

Closer to the house, I turn and head toward the garage at the far end of the building, away from the windows in the den and living area. Though I'm dressed in white, I'm certain I blend with the landscape, I must be careful. The element of surprise is necessary.

At the door I listen.

Sure enough, music is emanating from the speakers inside the house. If nothing else, Brady Long is a creature of habit. Which makes my job so much easier.

The back door is unlocked, so I don't have to bother with a key. I walk softly and quickly through the kitchen to the main hallway. In the foyer, I peer into the living room.

Empty.

My heart is beating a little more quickly now. I'm sweating inside the house in my ski suit and I flip my goggles onto the top of my head as the amber lenses are starting to fog. I have to have complete visibility. It's necessary that I be accurate and deadly.

I make my way to the open door of the den.

Sure enough, Brady is there. Sitting in a big leather recliner, feet up, cigar in one hand, drink resting on the desk. Bourbon, I'm guessing. A fire is burning in the grate, and there are papers strewn over the desk. Of course. Hubert's will. Brady Long is so damned predictable.

His eyes are closed and he's singing along to some rock tune from the eighties, mouthing the words like he's some famous hard-rock band front-man.

Idiot.

My rifle is already at my shoulder. I take aim. But I want him to have a moment of fear, to see me and realize that justice, long overdue, is being served.

"Long!" I yell and his eyes fly open.

In a split second he recognizes me and forgets all about the song. "What the hell?"

But he knows.

His startled face says it all.

He starts to move, to leap from the chair.

Too late!

I pull the trigger.

Chapter Eleven

Using his walking stick, Ivor Hicks stole across the property line separating the federal land from that of Hubert Long, a miserable S.O.B. if there ever was one. From what Ivor had heard, Hubert wasn't long for this world and that was just fine by him.

And yet, he didn't like tromping across the government's land or into Long territory, for that matter, but he felt compelled this morning and he knew why.

The aliens. General Crytor, the damned Reptilian leader who had transported Ivor to the mothership back in the seventies, was still using him for experiments. To do his bidding. Like a goddamned slave. The invisible chip those alien bastards had implanted in Ivor's body forced him to do Crytor's bidding and was probably the reason his arthritis was so bad. Well, that and the damned cold. Even with his thick jacket and a stocking cap, boots, and gloves he felt the bone-piercing cold that his little nips of Jim Beam hadn't been able to ward off. Damned orange two-legged freaks with their lizard heads and snakelike eyes. Crytor, he was the worst of the lot, the leader, but there had been others, too, who had cocked their heads like vile orange crows as they poked and prodded him with their needles and probes. It was amazing he'd survived. Those lipless extraterrestrials had done experiments on him, examining everything ranging from his lungs to his testicles.

Ivor doubted, after the abduction, that he could father any more children.

"Reptilian sons of bitches!" he hissed into the cold winter air, and the wind seemed to laugh and shriek at him, as if it, too, thought him crazy. Maybe that was good. He wasn't sure how much Crytor knew of his thoughts, but the general surely could hear his words, and Ivor had felt the wrath of the Reptilian's punishment many times before—headaches that would take a grown man to his knees.

Crack!

The sound, like the blast from a rifle of a poacher hunting in these woods, or a car backfiring up on the country road, reverberated through the forest.

Damned idiots with their guns.

Now, those were the crazies.

He kept walking. Though no one in Grizzly Falls believed his alien story, not even Doc Norwood who treated him, Ivor knew what he knew. The fact that he'd been found, near naked, with an empty bottle of whiskey near him, had convinced everyone who knew his tale that he was just a drunk, that he'd been hallucinating.

"Hallucinating, my ass," he said and winced at a pain in his temple. Crytor again. The Reptilian seemed to have as much objection to swearing as his wife, Lila, had. Rest her soul. He made a quick sign of the cross over his old down jacket and kept on trudging. He wasn't Catholic, wasn't even certain about God, but he had his own brand of reverence and it had become a habit whenever he thought about his wife, or spoke her name, to make the sign of the cross over his chest. It made him feel better.

Sometimes those Catholics got things right.

The snow was coming down in heavy flurries and his glasses were beginning to steam. Where the hell was Crytor prodding him this time? It worried him because on his last trek into the mountains, when the damned aliens were forcing him into the wilderness, he'd run across a dead girl, stark naked, tied to a tree. Jesus, that was freaky. And about as bad as what he'd feared his fate was to be: that he would be transported to the mothership once again. At that thought his hands began to shake uncontrollably. Hell, he couldn't go back there. Couldn't! This time, he might not survive. Using his teeth, he tore off one glove, then reached into his jacket pocket and unscrewed the lid of his flask as the memory of the dead girl crossed his mind. Asian. Probably in life she'd been pretty. But when Ivor had found her, her lips had been purple, her skin blue, her eyes glassy, her black hair stiff and covered with snow.

Wendy Ito.

That had been her name.

He'd been interviewed by the cops, then the reporters. Of course, the whole alien abduction thing had come up, as it had before. In the seventies he'd sold his story to a magazine, but he wondered if he could write a book about his experiences.

Oh, hell, that would really piss old Crytor off. Ivor glanced around the frozen wilderness. Everything covered in white. The falling snow a veil that made it hard to distinguish anything farther than ten feet in front of him.

He took a couple of long pulls of whiskey, felt the warmth of the liquor slide down his throat. He was about to put the flask away, then took another swallow. Couldn't hurt. Not out here in this damned snow forest.

Winter wonderland, Lila had called the Montana wilderness. Just like the song. Ivor had never believed it and had kicked himself to hell and back for not taking that roughneck job in Texas he'd been offered thirty-five years before. Lila had pitched a fit. Wasn't about to leave her ailing mother or pull their son out of a school where he was "doin' just fine." So Ivor had stuck it out at the mine, Hubert Long's copper mine, as long as he could. Until Lila had up and died on him in '78 and goddamned Crytor had abducted him in '79. After that, Ivor had lost his free will. Had never been able to move to the Lone Star State or anywhere warm, for that matter.

Now, his skin crawled just being on Hubert's land.

Nothing ever good came from being close to the Longs; he was certain of it. Had told Lila years ago and she'd pooh-poohed him. "You don't know what you're talkin' about," she'd said as she'd climbed into their old Dodge on her way to work as a barkeep at the Spot, their favorite tavern. "Hubert's okay and he's not cheap. Always leaves a big tip."

Ivor hadn't been convinced. One more swallow of whiskey, then he capped the flask. It was damn near empty. He knew he'd filled it before he'd started on this mission to only God knew where and truth to tell, he felt a little wobbly.

Just Crytor and his damned prod.

Jamming his glove onto his hand again, Ivor crossed the creek, wondering why he let Crytor manipulate him, why he'd been the one chosen that day.

He didn't have much time to speculate as he spied the big house. Hell, it would take six or seven, maybe even eight of his little houses to make up the size of the mammoth structure. Pitched gable roofs, three stories, windows that sparkled from dormers. And this was just Hubert's hunting lodge, one of the homes he had sprinkled throughout the country.

Some people were just too rich.

He stopped, realized he was in the creek, and took a step. Nearly fell as he reached the opposite bank.

A few lights were on, he thought, though his glasses had begun to fog. Probably the housekeeper, Clementine, and her oddball of a son Russ . . . no, that wasn't right. Ross. Yeah, that was it. Ross. Though he was pushing twenty or so, he still lived with his mother. Somewhere inside Hubert Long's private estate.

Oh, hell, who could blame them?

Ivor struggled up the steep bank, his walking stick not much help. He had to grab onto a root ball from a fallen tree to climb closer to the house, though why he was here, he wasn't sure. Maybe Clementine would make him a sandwich, or offer him a drink—she had in the past when he'd done some handyman work around the place. He'd fixed a couple of broken drawers in the pantry, replaced some faucets, little jobs . . .

Now, he paused, caught his breath. Took off his steamed glasses to wipe them clean. Without them, because of his cataracts, he couldn't see five feet in front of him.

He fumbled the glasses, nearly popped out a lens, then dropped them into the snow.

Bending on one knee, he reached into the bank and stopped short.

Had he seen something?

A movement to his left?

His skin crawled and he squinted, patting the ground, looking for his damned specs.

Nothing.

Just his imagination.

He turned back to the snow, then saw movement again. A blur in the snowy curtain . . . like a ghost flitting through the quivering aspens.

Ivor froze.

He caught his breath.

Saw the wraith again.

Oh, hell no, not a wraith! Shit no! This huge white beast ran awkwardly across the open yard. A Yeti! That was what it was. Goddamned abominable snowman, running through the forest with a long club in its hand. Oh, God, oh, God. First the aliens and now this? Was this sighting of a bona fide Yeti why Crytor had forced him onto Hubert Long's property? To give him some validation?

Heart thudding, he watched as the beast, picking up speed, loped across to the helicopter pad where a chopper sat idle, collecting snow, then dashed through the trees, only to turn its massive head and eyes, amber and filled with pure evil, toward him, zeroing in on him.

On one knee, Ivor bit back a strangled cry. His damned ticker nearly stopped. This was it. The massive snow monster was sure to beat him to a pulp with that long dark club . . . oh, hell, was it a rifle? Had the snow creatures evolved to the point of firearms? He crawled backward, slid down the bank, and silently prayed like he'd never prayed before, a sudden convert.

As if God spoke to the monster, it turned and sped away, running through the snow, its black paws visible.

"God help me," Ivor whispered, clutching his chest, listening to the pounding of his heart and feeling snow fall onto his upturned face. He'd been spared. Because of the Lord? Crytor? Or just dumb luck?

Maybe Yetis were nearsighted.

Whatever the reason, he'd been saved.

Jesus H. Christ, could nothing go right?

Why the hell was the old man on the Long property?

After all the years of waiting, of planning, of being certain that no one was around, the old geezer had the nerve to go out for a wintry stroll to Brady Long's hunting lodge.

Calm down.

Don't lose it now.

No way could he recognize you.

And yet, there was always the chance.

I cast off my gloves, along with my white suit, when I arrive at my truck. Everything, along with my rifle, is tucked away, hidden in the false flooring, and I'm dressed as I usually do in jeans, a flannel shirt, down vest, and jacket. No one saw me change, no one would suspect a thing.

And yet the old man was there!

I should have popped him while I had the chance.

It would have saved me a whole lotta trouble.

But no . . . better to stay with the plan. The guy is half blind and probably stumbling drunk.

You're okay. It will be fine. Just drive into town, order the all-day breakfast as you usually do . . . Make certain you're seen.

As the miles pass under my tires, using the road that leads away from Grizzly Falls, I put distance between myself and Brady Long. Slowly, I feel the calm that always comes after the rush of the kill. This one is different, so different and yet there is still that deep-seated and tranquil feeling of a job well done.

"Mission accomplished," I tell myself, glancing in the rearview mirror just before I take a cut-off and double back around the Montana acres that belong to Hubert Long. I smile when I think of all the repercussions I've created with the single act of killing one man.

If the old man doesn't blow it for you.

I still hear that annoying voice in my head, the one that accuses me of not doing the deed perfectly. It follows me into town as I park in a spot where my truck is often seen. I waste no time, but am out of the truck and down an alley to the main street that runs along the river in this part of town—past the brick courthouse with its gigantic Christmas tree positioned not far from the flagpole. Along the icy sidewalk I smile at a nearly frozen bell ringer asking for donations for the needy.

"Merry Christmas," he says and I nod as if this is the brightest, most holy season ever. I even find a dollar bill in the front pocket of my jeans and stuff it into the red donation pot. "Bless you."

"Thanks." I look him squarely in the eye. *If you only knew.*

Hands in my pockets, I hurry through the narrow streets toward my destination: Wild Will's, a restaurant that serves breakfast all day and where the locals hang out. Through the doors and past the ridiculous long-dead stuffed grizzly bear dressed in some kind of angel get-up that stands guard. On its hind legs, dwarfing everyone who walks in, "Grizz" is a local attraction who "dresses" for the seasons.

Ridiculous.

Today, a fake halo made from wire and tinsel is lying crooked on his head, tilted over one ear. Equally fake-looking wings sprout from behind his massive shoulders and a string of colored lights surrounds his thick neck. Though his mouth is caught in a perpetual snarl, his glass eyes fierce, someone has tied a book of Christmas carols onto one of his huge, clawed paws.

Oh, right, the shaggy bear is getting off on "Silent Night."

Some of the locals think it's funny or cute. I find it vulgar.

But I grab a complimentary paper and follow

Sandi, the owner of the place, to a booth. A tall woman who wears too much makeup, she offers me coffee and a wink while I order a farmer's breakfast of eggs, bacon, hash browns, and biscuits with country gravy. Sandi, she likes me.

"We've got fresh trout, if you'd rather have that than the bacon," she says with a smile that shows off her oversized teeth.

"How about both?" I'm hungry and want her to take note that I'm there. To remember me.

"You got it!" She's pleased and doesn't bother writing down my order. "What happened to you?" she says suddenly and is staring at my cheek where that damned Pescoli slashed away some of the skin and my whiskers haven't quite covered the wounds.

I grin. "Stupid accident."

"With a bobcat?" she asks.

"That would make for a better story." I look sheepish as she fills my coffee cup. "I was playin' with a friend's dog. Got a little too close and got nailed by a paw." I pick up the now full cup and shake my head.

"Pretty big dog."

"Yeah . . ." I point to the menu to derail the conversation. "You have any pie today?"

She grins and looks over to the glass case. "Pumpkin, lemon meringue, Dutch apple, and huckleberry, of course."

"Huckleberry."

"Whipped or ice cream?"

"Ice cream." I give her the look that says, "Come on, who would want it any other way?" Breakfast with pie, not my usual, but again she'll take note and remember me.

"Hey, Sandi. How 'bout a refill?" a tinny male voice asks from a booth on the other side of a row of tables, over by the window.

"Right with ya, Manny," Sandi calls over her shoulder and I feel my insides tighten. Manny Douglas is a weasel-faced writer for the *Mountain Reporter,* a local two-bit rag. He first coined the phrase *Bitterroot Killer,* which was renamed by the national press as the *Star-Crossed Killer,* which is only slightly better.

I huddle over my coffee and open the complimentary paper, the very rag he works for, then ignore him as he chats up Sandi. God, would I love to give him a taste of what the "Bitterroot Killer" is really like. Manny's made it his personal quest to try and unmask me, not that he could. But he aggravates me just the same.

Loser, I think, perusing the paper as Manny's reed-thin voice reaches me.

"No, not yet," he's saying in that puffed-up braggart way of his. "But I've got some ideas. I knew all along that the cops were on a wild-goose chase to Spokane. The killer, he's from around here, knows these parts like the back of his hand. He won't be traveling too far."

You can bet on that, Weasel-Face, I think, but just sip my coffee and pretend interest in the sports page. I would love to shut him up permanently, but he's not part of the plan. So he's safe. If he had any idea how long I've worked, how I've planned to find just the right women . . .

". . . as a matter of fact, I think I'm on to him."

That pricks my attention. I flip the page.

"Is that so?" Sandi pretends interest as she refills the cups of Manny and some woman he's trying to impress, a brunette I don't recognize.

I take another swallow of my coffee, slide a glance in his direction and find him staring at me. Does he know? Can he guess? I tense, but hide it and manage a quick nod of acknowledgment, a friendly lifting of my chin, but his lips twist into a stoatlike sneer and he turns back to his breakfast partner, the unfamiliar brunette.

A blaze of embarrassment crawls up the back of my neck. Snubbed by the reporter. It's all I can do to control myself, pretend that his brush-off doesn't offend me.

By the time Sandi brings me the oval platter, I'm in control again. "Here ya go," she says grinning. "And I'll bring the pie when you're about done with this."

"Thanks."

"You're going to love that trout!" she predicts loudly as if she's trying to ply the fish on other customers.

She leaves and I dig in, but I barely taste the food. I'm too keyed up. As much as I've tried to calm down, the run-in with the old man up at Brady Long's place, Sandi's remarks about my cheek, and the cold shoulder from the reporter remind me that I have to be careful. Now more than ever.

Despite the fact that I left Brady Long bleeding to death and Regan Pescoli is now my captive, there's much to do. No time to sit back.

It's time, I decide, as Sandi, ever diligent, tops off my coffee, to ratchet things up a notch. Give old needle-nose something to write about.

The stars aren't in quite the right position, but I can't afford to wait.

I have to leave a message for the cops.

Soon.

Sandi deposits the slab of pie with its glob of melting ice cream. "Here ya go," she says before bouncing off to another table to refill a near-empty cup.

Yeah, I think, picking up my fork. Real soon.

Chapter Twelve

Something was off.

Out of synch.

Santana was about to drive past the main house on his way to his cabin when he noticed that the lights in the den were blazing and the back door, the one connecting the house to the carport, was wide open. Clementine's red Volkswagen Rabbit wasn't parked in its usual spot, though Ross's beat-up 4x4 was tucked by the garage, six inches or more of snow piling over the roof and hood.

That, in and of itself, wasn't unusual.

She could have left early, taking advantage of the break in the weather that now seemed to be changing.

Had he seen her car this morning when he'd left?

He thought so.

Then it wasn't a big deal . . .

But the door . . . and the den lights on, smoke rising from the chimney. Uh-uh.

He pulled his truck up to the garage and parked, then cut through the carport to the door, which was open, the screen door banging in the wind.

Odd.

Through the back he saw footprints, two sets coming toward the carport, one leaving, though all were beginning to fill with snow. He squinted through the curtain of falling snow and spied the helicopter, resting on its pad, rotors, cabin, and tail boom all collecting a thick layer of icy white crystals.

So Brady Long was back.

Hubert's black-sheep son.

Good. He needed to talk to Brady, his boss, and explain that he'd need some time off. Despite Alvarez's warning, Santana wasn't about to sit idle while Regan was missing. No way. He'd go nuts, and regardless of Alvarez's opinion, Santana could help. He'd been a tracker and hunting guide before and after his stint with the army, and he did have an innate ability to tell when things weren't right. Like now.

Long's return didn't explain the open door or double set of footprints. Clementine's son, Ross, was a big kid, but the footprints were all wrong. Too many leaving, not enough returning. Unless someone came with Long on the chopper, then went back outside.

Your imagination working overtime, he told himself.

Nonetheless he'd always relied on his gut instincts, and he had to check things out. Find out that everything was all right. He'd start with the house first and then, if his imagination got the better of him, follow the footsteps before they disappeared with the snowfall.

At the door, he heard music. Loud. Guns N' Roses. Axl Rose's voice screaming over Slash's familiar guitar riff.

And the scent of cigar smoke filtered down the long hallway off the foyer.

Yeah. Brady Long was back.

He saw the newspapers on the table, some snacks left out for the boss man. Clementine's work. Always afraid of losing her job, she went above and beyond for Hubert's only son.

So she'd known he was returning, but she hadn't mentioned it to Santana.

When have you seen her in the last couple of days?

Following the scent of one of Brady's Havanas, Santana walked to the double doors of the den and took one step inside. In a heartbeat he spied Brady in his desk chair, facing the door. His eyes were round and blood was blossoming through his shirt. His mouth moved, but it seemed almost convulsive.

"Jesus!" Santana was through the door like a shot. "Brady! Oh, hell!" He reached the desk chair. "Brady! Shit! Brady! What the hell happened?" Heart pounding, pulse racing, he yelled over the echoing music, "Clementine! Ross!" But, of course, there was no one to answer him. "Damn it!" With one hand he tried to staunch the flow of blood. With the other, he picked up the phone on the desk and punched out 911. The phone only rang once when he heard the dispatcher's voice. "Nine-one-one, what is the nature of—"

"I've got a man with a . . . a wound to his chest. Nearly dead. Looks like a gunshot. We need an ambulance here immediately. Out at Hubert Long's estate." Panicked, feeling the weak beat of Long's heart under his hand, Nate rattled off the address. All the while his eyes scanned the room for any sign of the attacker, or a handgun on the floor suggesting that Brady had tried to off himself. All he saw was the cigar slowly burning into the area rug— dropped to the floor, he supposed, during the attack—and a short glass of amber liquid, ice cubes half melted, still on the desk. "I need an ambulance now!"

"Sir, what is your name?"

God, how could she be so calm?

"Nate Santana, I work for Brady Long and I walked into the house and found him in the den, bleeding to death, now get someone here ASAP!" He looked around for anything to help staunch the blood. This was taking too long. "Should I get him to the hospital?"

"Do not move the victim! I'll connect you to an EMT and I've already dispatched a unit to your location. Stay on the phone."

"But there's a chopper out back and—"

"Do not move the victim. Do you hear me? Help is on the way."

"Oh, hell." He hit the speaker dial, then turned to his boss. But he knew it was already too late. Brady's eyes were fixed, his face drained and white, blood appearing on his lips. His mouth worked like a fish out of water. "Hang in there, Brady, for Christ's sake!" Santana urged, feeling warm, thick blood through his fingers as he pressed vainly on the man's chest. "You just hang in there!"

What the hell happened? Did someone come in the house and shoot Long while he was at his desk?

The operator was on the phone again, squawking, and he had to pick up and press it to his ears as the rock music was pounding so loudly he couldn't begin to hear the speakerphone.

"Mr. Santana, are you there?"

"Yes!" He shouted. They were running out of time! All the first aid he'd learned years before wasn't going to help.

"I'm patching you through to an EMT who's on the way."

Long took a gurgling, rattling breath.

"Damn it, they'd better get here fast!" He turned back to his boss. There was so much blood, so damned much blood. And Long's eyes had lost what little glimmer there had been in them. "Brady!" Santana yelled, trying to shock the dying man back to consciousness. "Brady! Stay with me!"

But already Santana knew it was too late.

As the final guitar chords of "Sweet Child o' Mine" died, so did Brady Long.

"What the fuck is this?" Tyler hissed.

"I don't know, but I don't like it." Jeremy was staring through the foggy windshield as McAllister's Blazer slid over the small bridge that spanned the creek, then nosed into the clearing where Jeremy's house stood.

In front of the snow-covered cottage was a four-wheel-drive police vehicle, parked right behind Jeremy's truck.

"Let's get out of here."

"No!"

"Hey, man, I've got my stash in here." Tyler was in a panic, worried like hell about being caught with a few ounces of weed or a vial of prescription painkillers he'd swiped from his uncle. "I'm not hanging out. These are cops, for fuck's sake."

"Fine. Go." Jeremy climbed out of the Blazer and slammed the door shut.

McAllister pulled a quick, sliding one-eighty and tore out, the back end of his Chevy fishtailing as he reached the bridge, then shot across.

Jeremy turned toward the house where a path had been beaten in the snow from all of the foot- and boot prints. A big black dude stood in the doorway, a guy with a weird name who worked for the sheriff's department.

"You're Jeremy Strand," he said, walking off the porch, his breath making a cloud in the air. "Deputy Rule."

Now he remembered. Kayan Rule. His mom had said good things about the guy. Like he was a smart cop.

"Where's my mom?"

"Don't know, son."

"Everyone says that, but I saw her Jeep. It was all messed up. Wrecked. Being pulled out of the canyon up on the ridge."

"She wasn't in it, if that's what you're asking." The deputy was still walking along the path, his frown hard-edged.

"Then where was she?"

"We don't know. That's why we're here."

"She's not here!"

"You're right."

"She was in her Jeep. On her way to see my step-dad, and then she wrecked."

"Appears that way."

"So what? Is she dead?" he demanded, fear

pounding in his temples, his stomach churning. His dad had died; Jeremy knew all about losing a parent. He thought he might pass out.

"As I said, we don't know."

"But she wouldn't loan the county vehicle to anyone. She never even let me drive it," Jeremy said, so frustrated and scared he was sweating. Mom had to be okay. She just had to. "So she was in her Jeep. And if she wasn't when you found her, then she's hurt somewhere or in a hospital or oh, God, dead . . . or . . ." The horrible thought that had been lurking just beneath the surface of his consciousness reared its evil head. His stomach turned instantly sour. His mouth was filled with saliva. "You're not telling me that . . . that what? That the damned killer who's been around here . . . I mean, they caught him in Spokane . . ." No, that wasn't right. He'd heard on the news that the killer they'd arrested in Washington probably wasn't responsible for all the deaths around here. "No way." He was shaking his head, glaring up at the cop, who looked like he belonged in an NBA uniform rather than county-issued jacket and slacks.

"As I said, Jeremy, we don't know anything yet. Now, what're you doing here? Looking for your mom?"

"Yeah, and getting my truck."

Rule glanced toward the lane down which Mc-Allister's SUV had vanished. "I guess that's okay."

"Damned straight. It's *my* truck."

He didn't say it, but Jeremy had been around his mom long enough to read the guy's thoughts, that this, his house, his mom and Bianca's home, could be a crime scene.

That evil fear, the one that had lifted its head,

loomed larger. Dark and sinister, it bit into his heart. "I . . . I need to go inside."

Rule hesitated, then shook his head. "Why don't you wait on that?"

"Do I have to?"

"We're trying like hell to find your mother, Jeremy, and we don't want to do anything that might compromise evidence. Take the truck and go back to your friend's house or maybe your stepdad's. You've got a little sister, don't you?"

Jeremy didn't answer.

"You might want to look after her."

Jeremy didn't want to show the guy just how scared he was. "Fine," he said with all the intent of coming back here as soon as the cop left. His stomach was threatening to lurch again, so he spat the extra saliva into the snow and walked to his truck. He climbed behind the wheel, flicked on the engine, and heard it sputter and cough before catching. Once he'd revved it a couple of times, he turned on the defrost, then grabbed his scraper and went to work on the snow and ice that had built up in the past few days.

His cell phone chirped and he checked it.

A text from Heidi. His heart did a stupid little leap.

Where R U? Grounded? Come C me.

Oh, yeah, right, and risk being killed by her father, the damned undersheriff, his mom's boss. No thanks. Not today. Not with Mom missing.

Heidi was hot. Though she was a tease, she was about to put out; he could tell. And Jeremy was always horny. Man, oh, man, could he use that kind of release.

But not now.

Not today.

He didn't text her back, just put his strength into scraping off his damned windshield so he could make tracks.

All of a sudden doing it with Heidi Brewster wasn't quite so appealing.

From far in the distance Santana heard the wail of sirens. The cavalry was on its way. Not that it would do much good. At least not for Brady. His soul was on its way straight to hell. It wasn't coming back.

Santana had turned off the music, put the cigar that had fallen to the floor from Brady's fingers into an ashtray where it still smoldered, and was sure he'd catch hell for disturbing the crime scene. Well, hell, he couldn't save Brady Long's life, but he could keep the place from burning down.

Holy Mother of Christ, what went on here?

His jacket and hands covered in blood, Santana sat on the long leather couch opposite the desk and thought morosely that this was the longest time he'd been in a room with Brady Long where they hadn't argued. It had taken the man's death to accomplish that feat. It was a wonder he'd stayed in Brady's employ.

He eyed the room. No sign of a struggle. But someone had killed him.

Who knew Brady Long would return today?

Clementine, obviously.

Her son, Ross, no doubt.

Neither one was capable of murder. Clementine was nothing if not subservient, to the point it almost made Santana sick, and Ross, he was a big, quiet kid who helped out around the ranch, oftentimes cleaning the tack, or mucking out the stalls, or feeding the stock.

Yeah, he was a hunter.

Yeah, he had a rifle with a scope.

But murder?

What if Ross walked into the room while Brady was trying to get Clementine into a compromising position? How would the kid react to his mother being treated like her boss's mistress?

No, it didn't wash.

But the kill was too neat.

Almost professional.

Not quite. The bullet went into his chest, not his head. A pro would go for a head shot.

As Santana reconstructed the scene, it appeared that Long had been at his desk, rocking out to Guns N' Roses and whatever else was in the CD changer, having himself a cigar and a drink, when someone got the drop on him.

Who?

Why?

Dozens of people, lots of reasons. Brady Long had made as many enemies as friends in his life. Still . . . murder?

"Who did you piss off so bad?" he asked the dead man as the sirens screamed louder and he heard Nakita barking from his truck.

Long's drink, ice cubes melting, was still on the desk. But then the man himself, dead and staring sightlessly, was still in his chair.

He heard something else.

A footstep?

Then a soft thud and another footstep, the unmistakable sound of leather scraping against the floor.

The hairs on the back of Nate's scalp prickled.

Could the killer still be in the house? Was he coming back to make certain the job was finished? Maybe Santana had interrupted him.

Don't jump to conclusions. It could be Clementine; her son could have taken her car. Or she might have left Ross inside when she drove off.

Neither scenario changed the fact that someone had killed Brady Long.

Stealthy as a cat, Santana climbed to his feet, then slipped silently to the side of the room to hide just inside the doors, out of view to anyone who passed. Someone would have to take a step or two inside the room before he would be visible. The only weapon he had on him was the jackknife he used to cut baling twine. Not much good against a pistol or revolver.

He waited.

Thunk.

Step.

Noiselessly he opened his knife. Hearing his own heartbeat, he tensed, ready to spring, his eyes glued on the open doors.

Closer and closer.

The sirens kept screaming and suddenly emergency vehicles, lights flashing, shot into view through the window, spraying snow from their tires in all directions.

"What the—?" a male voice asked, just on the other side of the door.

Santana's hand tightened over the hilt of his knife.

"Brady? Holy Mother of God!" The warbling voice rose an octave. "The Yeti, he did this to you?"

Yeti?

A second later, Ivor Hicks, using a cane, hobbled into the room.

Chapter Thirteen

"I don't care what you say, I'm not running this investigation using psychos, whack jobs, and/or nutcases!" Sheriff Dan Grayson was in a foul mood as he stalked down the hallway to his office. It didn't help that one of his best detectives was suggesting the irrational.

"Grace Perchant knows something," Alvarez, at his side, insisted.

"Trust me, she doesn't know up from sideways." He'd been in Spokane going over the notes and records of the copycat killer who'd been captured by the Spokane authorities and had been up most of the night. Early this morning he'd returned to find that not only had Pescoli's wrecked Jeep been located, but now there was another car impounded that could be part of a possible crime, a red Saturn registered to another missing woman. And Alvarez, one of his most down-to-earth detectives, was suggesting they take advice from Grace She-Who-Talks-to-Ghosts Perchant.

Christ, this was a mess.

"Grace called. She'd had a dream—"

"Oh, for the love of God, that's it? A dream. Look, I don't give a damn if she hung upside down by her toes like a sleeping, rabid bat! She's a nutcase. Everyone in town knows it! Maybe you can convince the FBI to talk to the local loonies, maybe they have some kind of pseudoparanormal division like you see on TV, but not here, not in my department!"

"Not exactly P. C.," Alvarez pointed out.

"I'm not interested in being politically correct," he said, irritated. "I'm just trying to hunt down a sick serial killer who has decided to use my jurisdiction as his personal playground."

"So we should use any means possible."

Is she really suggesting we talk to Grace Perchant? A self-proclaimed ghost whisperer or some such nonsense? In Grayson's estimation Grace was an odd duck, nothing more. Harmless, but an odd duck, all the same. "Next thing I know you'll be wanting to take statements from Ivor Hicks and Henry Johansen."

"If it would help the investigation." Fire in her dark eyes. "I just got a call from the deputy who supervised winching Pescoli's Jeep from the canyon. Looks like a bullet went through one of her tires."

Grayson's deepest fear was realized. "That son of a bitch!"

"Exactly." Selena was furious now, her cheeks flaming. "So I don't think we should discount any statement. I just want to see what Grace knows."

"She was already interviewed."

"Before Pescoli went missing."

They were at his office door now and stomach acid was burning a hole in his gut. His thoughts were on Pescoli, a woman he'd worked with for years. Who was he to tell Alvarez, one of his smartest detectives, what to do? It wasn't as if he had any better ideas. "Do whatever it is you think you should." He waved her off and knew he was being ornery, but he didn't care.

Her cell phone rang, and she picked it up, turning and heading toward her desk. Damn, he didn't need a fight.

Inside his office, he hung up his hat and jacket, glanced out the window to the view of the lower part of the town and the nearly frozen river, then dropped into the desk chair and scowled at the stack of messages awaiting him. Whether he liked it or not, it seemed that Pescoli and Elyssa O'Leary were the next intended victims of Star-Crossed.

There had to be a way to catch the bastard, Grayson thought as he cracked his knuckles. He just had to figure out how. And fast. In his mind's eye he saw Pescoli, a tall, strong woman with a wicked sense of humor who was tough enough to do a damned good job while raising two kids on her own. She was unconventional, bent the rules way too far for his liking, but she always got the job done. And now she was a victim? His jaw tightened as he remembered the other women who'd died naked in the elements, left to freeze to death.

Pushing aside his dark thoughts, he clicked on his computer, read his e-mail, then sent out an e-blast ad-

vising everyone working the Star-Crossed Killer case
of a meeting at four P.M. in the task room. Maybe by
then Agents Chandler and Halden from the FBI
would have tied things up in Spokane and be back in
Grizzly Falls. If not, he'd carry on without them.

He couldn't wait.

The weather, as always, was a problem, he thought,
sliding a glance out the window where snow was collecting and icicles hung from the eaves. It had been
a bitch of a winter. One of the coldest on record.
And it wasn't close to being over.

Rubbing his eyes, he heard the familiar sounds of
the department on the other side of the door: ringing phones, muted voices in conversation, a humming fax machine, the furnace rumbling, footsteps
clipping down the hallway.

God, he was tired. Bone weary. This job that he'd
once found so engrossing, that he'd thrown himself
into after his wife left him, was starting to wear him
down.

*Don't let it. This is your passion; your duty. You just
need a little rest.*

Leaning back in his chair and propping the heels
of his boots on the short filing cabinet, Grayson
fought a mother of a headache. It had started near
his temples when the chopper that had brought
him here from Spokane had landed, just before the
next storm had begun to shower this part of the
state with snow all over again. It was definitely exacerbated by the fact that a killer was still terrorizing
the county. The victims' families were clamoring for
justice, the townspeople were scared out of their
wits, the media was demanding more information for

the public while both constantly airing "updates" and trying to get exclusives from the husbands, mothers, fathers, and siblings of the dead women.

Not to mention it was the Christmas season.

And now Pescoli looks like she's the next victim.

No wonder his head throbbed.

But still, he shouldn't have snapped at Alvarez. She was a good cop. Doing a damned good job. And he knew that she would put science and evidence over theory and statements from the resident nut-jobs. So if she wanted to talk to Grace Perchant or even Eleanor Mackey, the woman who not only cut hair but also read palms and held seances or the like over on Corinthian Avenue, so be it.

He found a jar of aspirin in his desk drawer, unscrewed the cap, and popped a couple, swallowing them dry.

He hadn't eaten since last night—a burger, fries, and beer in a dive not far from the police station in Spokane—but he didn't really feel hungry.

His desk phone jangled and he saw it was a call from Joelle.

"What's up?"

"I've got bad news," she said solemnly.

Was there any other kind? His first thought was of Pescoli. His heart seized. If someone had found her frozen body tied to a tree . . . "Yeah?"

"Dispatch just called."

Grayson steeled himself. Set his jaw.

"Brady Long's been killed."

Grayson thought he'd heard wrong. "What?"

"Homicide."

"Brady Long?" he repeated, stunned. "Where? When?"

"The call just came in. Nate Santana phoned from the Long estate."

"Santana? Wasn't he just here?" Grayson was certain he'd seen the guy pull out of the station just as he was driving in.

"About an hour ago. Units are on the scene. Deputies Watershed and Connors are there. Ambulance as well."

"Good."

"And Ivor Hicks is there, too."

Grayson closed his eyes and sighed. Could things get any worse? His boots hit the floor. "Does anyone have any idea why Hicks and Santana are there?"

"I think Santana works for the Longs."

"And Ivor?"

"I don't know."

Grayson's bad day just took a nosedive.

"I'm on my way out there now." He hung up, slipped on his shoulder holster, checked his sidearm, and slid his arms into his jacket sleeves. He'd been back less than two hours, hadn't even had time to round up his dog yet, and all hell had broken loose. Again.

Sometimes he wondered why he didn't resign.

Because you love it, Grayson. Who the hell do you think you're kidding? Muttering under his breath, he grabbed his hat off the coatrack and walked down the hall to Alvarez's cubicle.

"You heard?"

She was at her desk examining copies of the notes taken from the crime scenes where the victims of the Star-Crossed Killer had been found. On her computer screen were anagrams using the initials of the women who had been abducted. He noted that she was already trying to add the initials of Elyssa O'Leary and Regan Pescoli into the cryptic message from Star-Crossed.

"About Brady Long?" She nodded.

If she was still pissed about their last conversation, she didn't show it. "I'm on my way there now."

"Wanna go together?"

"Sure. You can drive."

She shot him a look as she secured her pistol into her shoulder holster. "Even if I take a detour on the way back to interview Grace Perchant?"

He actually felt his lips twitch. "Not on a dare, Alvarez."

She didn't smile either, but her dark eyes weren't quite as hostile as they had been. "Then I guess you'll be walking back. Let's go."

She was dead tired, her wrist aching, her body spent. Regan flopped onto her cot and wondered if she'd ever break free. It felt as if she'd been working to break the damned weld for hours and all the while she'd been afraid that at any second she'd hear him return.

You can't give up, she told herself and began to shiver with the cold, the sweat on her body chilling. *Just a few minutes. I just need a few minutes to rest.*

She let out her breath slowly and gathered her strength.

What if the weld doesn't give?

What if it's stronger than you expect?

"It will," she whispered, refusing to allow in the doubts that plagued her. It was too easy to fall prey to fear in here. All alone. Cold. Totally dependent on the psycho.

She couldn't let the isolation get to her.

Letting out her breath, she heard the slap of wind against the high window, but nothing else. No rattling of timber, no shaking of walls.

Why was that?

And the small window, it was covered with snow, the view obliterated.

She'd looked around her gloomy room over and over again trying to get some clue, a little insight, as to where she was, but for the first time, she thought she understood. The window was high and alone because this room was underground. That would explain the dankness, the feeling of moisture that had made her skin crawl, the lack of sound from the outside.

She'd thought it was her imagination, but no . . . and that would explain, at least partially, why they, the police, had never found the creep.

She had no idea where she was. She barely remembered the ride in the back of a truck, a white truck with a matching camper, she thought. A big, full-sized truck. Domestic. Ford? Chevy? She'd caught a glimpse of it before he'd decided to tie a blindfold over her eyes, and damn it, she had only caught two letters of the license plate: 7 and 3, or had it been 8, with snow covering part of the numeral?

She couldn't remember. She'd been so out of it because of the drug he'd injected in her, and she hadn't been able to fight as he'd pinned her arms inside a straitjacket, then forced a gag over her mouth that smelled of vomit and chlorine bleach, as if he'd tried, and failed, to clean it. She'd almost retched, but had somehow kept the contents of her stomach down, knowing if she'd let go that she might drown in her own puke.

Would it have been a worse fate than this?

Of course!

She couldn't let her mind wander down any crooked and dark path that suggested death was better than this. Succumbing to the seduction of the Grim Reaper was only being a coward.

Don't go there.

At the moment of her abduction her mind had been addled, but she knew he'd strapped her to some kind of stretcher—or had it been a canoe?—that he'd dragged through the snow. Lying supine, unable to use her hands to brush away the snowflakes, she'd stared up at brittle, naked branches of trees, frozen and white. When he'd pulled her into a clearing, she'd spied the truck. And in a second he'd recognized his mistake and blindfolded her, yanking back her hair in the knot of the scarf, uncaring of any further pain he caused.

He hadn't said a word; just gone about his task of trussing her and tossing her into his truck. She was treated with all the skill and indifference of a hunter used to dressing a kill and hauling it out of the forest.

He'd smelled of sweat and some underlying soap or cologne, but she'd only caught a whiff of it before he'd tossed something in beside her—the stretcher? Had it been collapsible so that it would fit?

Before she could wrap her mind around whatever it was that was lying next to her on the cold metal bed, he'd snapped the tailgate shut, walked to the cab, and started the truck. The engine had caught immediately.

With the crunch of breaking snow and ice, the pickup had rumbled forward from the canyon somewhere beneath Horsebrier Ridge. She'd tried to concentrate, to listen to the sound of the tires, counting how many seconds it was until the feeling within the bed of the truck changed, when the tires either started to hum against bare pavement, or echo over a bridge, or reverberate with the crunch of gravel, but she was fuzzy and lost count, and the tenor of the grip of the tires against the snowy terrain never changed.

After a time she sensed that they'd gone from deep drifts of snow to more packed ice . . . there had been a shift, as if the driver had finally located a more traveled road, but even that was a blur in her muddled mind.

She hadn't even been sure about the distance or amount of time the trip had taken. Had the ride been twenty minutes? Thirty? Or more? She had no idea.

Though she'd felt the speed of the truck change for several curves, never did it come to a complete stop.

Not until he'd reached this destination.

Then, with dread pounding through her brain, he'd pulled her roughly from the truck and her thought that she might kick him was instantly gone with the pain that erupted through her ribs and shoulder. She'd nearly blacked out.

He'd slung her over his shoulder and carried her, weak as the proverbial lamb, inside . . . and now that she was thinking about it, she was certain there had been steps, that his boots had rung against stone or concrete as they'd entered, and yes, descended into this place.

Where the hell am I? she thought now, looking around. Had he, or someone before him, built an underground lair? In a cave? Or an old basement? Was there a house above?

Her eyes focused on the ceiling. Never had she heard anyone walk on it, but the window was above-ground, right? She looked at the window with its blurry glass, then across the ceiling to the top of the pipe that led from the wood stove near the door. Beside it was a stack of firewood and a poker—oh, God, what she wouldn't do to get her hands on that!—and there was an old bellows and some leather gloves as well, and even a barbecue lighter, probably complete with fingerprints.

She studied the stove. Even in the darkness she could see it was an antique, the kind her great-grandmother had cooked on around the turn of the last century. Its pipe didn't vent upward through the ceiling, but turned at a ninety-degree angle to disappear into the wall where the door to the next room, *his* room, opened.

Her eyes focused on the door. It was thick, but cut a little short, so that a slice of light would slip beneath it when he was there, when his own fire was glowing, when whatever he used for illumination was lit. She'd watched his shadow, seen when he'd come near to listen and maybe look through what she thought was a peephole in the heavy panels.

Pervert.

She let out her breath in disgust. She couldn't just lie here and wait, for God's sake. He could return at any moment. Her skin crawled at the thought.

She closed her eyes for a second, tried to find her strength, and thought about Santana. His fit form. His quirking lips. He had a way of making her laugh no matter how dire the situation, and on the rare occasions when he couldn't, all he had to do was touch the back of her neck with his fingers, or kiss her shoulder . . .

The back of her throat caught.

Oh, for the love of God, stop this! You're being a sniveling fool! The kind of woman you abhor! Come on, Detective, you've got to get up!

Keep working on the weld!

Gritting her teeth, she started to roll off the cot when she heard it.

An unfamiliar sound.

Soft and broken.

Pescoli froze and strained to listen.

Was she imagining things?

Then she heard it again. A moan. No, more than that, a woman's mewling, pitiful sobs.

And she wasn't making them.

Chapter Fourteen

In life, Brady Long had been big news.

In death, he might just be bigger, Alvarez thought, as she drove past the open gates to his estate and saw a news van from station KBTR already parked at the side of the road near the fence. A cameraman, dressed in a down jacket and insulated pants, was setting up, while the reporter waited nearby, stomping her feet. Another van was just arriving, flinging snow as it approached.

"How do they get the word before we do?" Grayson said as Deputy Connors, standing guard and blocking the drive from anyone but police, waved them through.

"Sixth sense," Alvarez said. Wipers losing ground against the ever-falling snow, she passed by thickets of pine, hemlock, and aspen, the vehicle lurching in the deep ruts from previous vehicles. Red and blue lights flashed through the trees, reflecting in the snow and the huge windows of the Long mansion.

An ambulance was idling in the snow on the parking area near the garage where a fire truck, two vehicles from the sheriff's department, and a beat-up truck with a dog inside were parked.

"Bad news travels fast," Grayson observed.

Especially if you're as prominent as Brady Long.

Alvarez cut the engine, pushed open the door, and stepped into over a foot of snow. She trudged behind Grayson toward an open door that was sheltered by the carport, signed into the scene, and walked inside where techs were already taking pictures and measurements.

Ivor Hicks was seated at the kitchen table. He looked up at Grayson and seemed relieved. "Sheriff! Thank God you're here."

"Ivor thinks he saw a Yeti," Deputy Watershed informed them.

"Like a Sasquatch?" Grayson responded distractedly.

"Not unless the son of a bitch is a friggin' albino. Everyone knows a Sasquatch is black or brown or gray. I saw a Yeti. Abominable snowman, you know," Ivor said, a little disgusted at the sheriff's ignorance. "A Yeti. He was here, I tell ya. A huge thing, maybe seven or eight feet tall. All white and hairy with yellow eyes like lasers!"

Watershed looked at Grayson. "He refuses a breathalyser."

"I told ya, I had a few drinks. So what? Nips to keep my blood flowin' in this effin' storm. I *know* what I saw!"

"What were you doing here? On Hubert Long's property?"

Ivor opened his mouth, then shut it firmly.

Watershed, one very skeptical eyebrow raised, said, "It's the aliens again. They forced him out in the cold to hike over here."

"I helped you with that Ito girl, didn't I?" Ivor snapped, glowering at Watershed as if he were the very embodiment of Satan.

"We'll talk about this in a minute." Grayson looked at the deputy. "Call his son, Bill. Tell him to pick up his father at the office."

"You leave my boy outta this!"

"It's either that or the drunk tank, Ivor," Grayson said on a sigh. "You choose." He and Alvarez walked past a dining room with a twenty-foot ceiling, double chandeliers of deer antlers and lights, and an oval table that could easily seat a dozen people and overlooked a breathtaking view of the backyard. At the table, a man and woman were huddled over a laptop computer and cell phone, examining Brady's electronics and making notes. On the floor around them were open cases of computer tools.

"No one lives here full-time, right?" Alvarez asked.

"Maybe the housekeeper?" Grayson suggested.

Careful not to get in the way of the techs working the scene, they cut through the foyer. Nate Santana was waiting in the vast living room. Rather than sitting on any of the leather couches or reading chairs, he'd chosen to stand at a bank of tall windows that looked onto the front of the house. Outside, instead of pristine snow and wilderness, a carnival of police and emergency vehicles were parked in all directions.

Santana's hands were in the back pockets of his jeans, blood visible at his wrists, his expression hard and set. Another deputy, Jan Spitzer, was with him.

She'd separated him from Ivor so that the department could get individual statements and find out if the two mens' stories gelled. Santana glanced over his shoulder as they passed, and it was obvious he was edgy, nervous, his features drawn.

"Give us a sec and we'll be right with you," Alvarez said before following Grayson down a wide hallway that ducked beneath the front stairs on its way to the den.

Double doors opened to a massive room that smelled faintly of cigars and the acrid, metallic scent of blood. Several officers were in the room, busy taking measurements and pictures and dusting the area for finger and shoe prints.

"Here's our victim." Virginia Johnson, a crime scene tech, was collecting evidence. She looked up when Grayson entered and motioned to a once-handsome, and now very dead, man who'd obviously been shot as he sat in his desk chair. His skin was white, his face ashen, his shirt slick and scarlet with blood. "Brady Long."

"Already had the pleasure. When he was alive." The sheriff walked closer to the body and examined the wound—bloody flesh visible through the stained shirt. "He sure as hell pissed someone off." He glanced up and ran his gaze around the room. "Robbery gone bad?"

Johnson frowned. "Doesn't look like it. And no forced entry. No signs of a fight. But we do have something. Take a look at this." She pressed a hidden button on the desk and the wall near the fireplace, one with a fading zebra hide stretched over it, moved to display a collection of firearms that would impress any member of the NRA. Beside the weapons was a safe.

"Anyone know the combination for the safe?" Grayson asked.

She shrugged. "We're looking for it. The computer geeks are already checking his laptop. They found it here in its case."

"He didn't even have time to fire it up?"

"Looks like he hadn't been here long. His outerwear was still wet and dripping in the mud room. No sign of him going upstairs or helping himself to anything to eat. There were things prepared, looks like for him, in the refrigerator. He didn't bother with it. Just grabbed a drink from the bar and came straight in here. We're already looking into any calls of interest to, or from, his cell phone, text messages, and the same with e-mail or notes in his computer."

Grayson frowned. "It's a start. Let's find out the name of his attorney, get a look at his will and figure out who benefits, and then talk to whoever's close to him. See what they know. And the housekeeper. She must've known he'd be showing up, so let's hear her story, how she knew he'd be back at the ranch, and if anyone else had any idea that Long was flying here. Someone he works with? What about where he keeps his helicopter, that's how he got here, right?"

Johnson nodded.

"And the door was unlocked when you arrived?"

"The back door, to the carport, yeah."

"Where do you think you're going?" Spitzer yelled from the hall as footsteps echoed on the stone floors. Alvarez and Grayson looked over as Nate Santana boldly entered the room.

"When Long was around he never locked his doors," he said, obviously overhearing part of the conversation. He stopped just inside the double doors, and Spitzer appeared behind him, eyes blazing.

Alvarez held up a hand to stop the confrontation. "You wanted to add something?"

"I'd like to know what the chances are that a thief shows up just after Brady lands his chopper around back? Even I didn't know he was going to be here, and I'm his damned foreman."

"You think someone was lying in wait?" Alvarez asked.

"Must've been, or else the killer's pretty damned lucky. That is, if you believe in coincidence."

"Unlikely," the sheriff said, scowling.

Spitzer, standing a pace behind Santana, was fit to be tied. Her face was flushed, her lips knifeblade thin in anger. "I'm sorry, Sheriff." She looked anything but apologetic. To Santana she added, "Let's go. Back to the living room."

"Wait." Alvarez wanted to hear what Santana had to say. "You think this was planned? Premeditated?"

"Looks that way to me. I think someone wanted Long dead and they made it happen. I think whoever did it knew he would be alone."

"How?"

"Beats me." Santana lifted a shoulder, stared at the dead man, then glanced away. "There's usually someone on the ranch, someone who could see or hear something."

"The housekeeper," Grayson said.

Santana nodded. "If she goes out, it's in the morning and not always."

Alvarez was taking mental notes. "And her son?"

"He's nineteen. Comes and goes. Works here

with me. Lives upstairs in one of the wings with his mother, Clementine, but goes to community college and hangs out with his friends, so he's not here all the time."

"School's out for the holidays," Alvarez pointed out.

Santana shrugged. "His car is parked near the garage, so he's either with his mom, or someone came and picked him up."

"The 4Runner," the sheriff guessed.

Santana grunted a "yeah" and Alvarez said, "We'll need to talk to both Clementine and the boy."

Santana said, "His name is Ross."

Grayson asked, "No dad in the picture?"

"Never seen or heard about him." Again Santana lifted one shoulder.

"But no one was here when you showed up," Alvarez clarified.

Santana shook his head slowly, then explained about noticing things were off, how he'd stopped at the main house, spied the open door and the unusual sets of footprints before he'd walked inside. ". . . I found Long, right there in his chair," he finished, motioning toward the victim. "He wasn't dead when I got here, but he was bleeding out. I called nine-one-one, tried to save him, and then heard someone in the house. I thought it was the killer. Turned out it was Ivor."

"Hicks was in the house?" Grayson's brows slammed together.

"Came in after me, I think. The same way I did," Santana explained.

Grayson thought that over, then turned to Johnson. "Someone's checking the tracks outside?"

She nodded. "Slatkin's taking measurements, too." Mikhail Slatkin was another crime scene tech.

Still disgruntled, Spitzer narrowed her eyes at Santana. "We've got dogs on the way. They'll be all over you."

He half-smiled and said nothing.

Alvarez had a mental "ping" and looked Santana over even more closely. "That's right. You're some kind of animal whisperer, aren't you?"

"I work with dogs, yeah, and I've got mine in the truck. He could track your guy. Get a head start."

"The dogs will be here in five minutes." She wasn't giving Santana an inch and Alvarez noticed the blood on his hands again.

"Anyone take samples?"

"Done," Johnson said.

Santana added, "The blood belongs to Long."

"From when you were trying to save him," Alvarez clarified.

His eyes glittered. "That's right, Detective."

As the tech took the sample of his blood away, Santana gave a concise rendition of how he'd spent the last hour and a half, first at the sheriff's office, then driving here to find Brady Long dying just before Ivor Hicks walked in.

"That gibes with what Hicks is saying," Spitzer admitted, though she was still angry that Santana had shown her up to her boss.

"Except I didn't see any Yeti or Reptilian general or anything out of the ordinary. Just the tracks and open door," Nate said calmly.

At that moment Bellasario, the deputy coroner, arrived. She was tall, nearly five-ten, with brown hair scraped away from her face and pulled into a thick, short ponytail. She dropped a body bag in the hallway, then worked efficiently, examining Brady Long carefully and scowling at the size of the wound. "Someone wasn't taking any chances that he would pull through."

"Then why not shoot him in the head?" Grayson said. "Or a second time?"

"Because the killer wanted him to suffer." Santana offered up his opinion flatly, as if it were a fact.

Grayson's eyes narrowed on Santana, studying him. "You have any idea about next of kin? Brady wasn't married, was he? Kids?"

"No kids that I know of. Married a couple of times but divorced the last I heard. Engaged to some model, but I didn't hear they ever tied the knot. But then," he said, his lips twisting a bit, "Long and I weren't exactly tight."

The sheriff scratched the back of his neck. "Okay, so no wives or kids. But the old man—Hubert—he's still with us?"

"Barely, I think, but I never heard he died. Brady had him in a nursing home, I think in Denver. But I could be wrong."

"What about siblings?" Alvarez asked.

"He's got a sister. Padgett." Santana glanced out the window, but Alvarez guessed he wasn't seeing the snow falling over the trees and vehicles parked in front of the house. It seemed as if he were looking inward. "I knew Padgett when we were kids, she's a little younger than Brady. A year? Maybe two, I can't really remember, but she's been in some kind of care facility since the accident."

"What kind of accident?" Alvarez asked. "When?"

"Boating. Maybe fifteen years ago?" Santana frowned. "Clementine will know."

"What happened?" she questioned.

It was Grayson's grim voice that answered, "A bunch of kids were out and hit some rocks, flew out of the boat. Padgett got trapped underwater for a while."

"Only two people on the boat," Santana corrected. "Padgett and Brady. He survived, ended up with some cuts and bruises, but he couldn't get his sister out from under the wreckage." His eyes darkened. "At least that's the way he told it. Padgett, she never spoke again, far as I know. Again, ask Clementine. She was working for Hubert at the time. Just started, I think."

"So where's Padgett's care facility?" Selena asked.

Santana shook his head. "Hell if I know. The Longs didn't talk about her much. Figured that's the way the family wanted it, you know? Out of sight, out of mind."

The deputy coroner straightened. "Okay, I've got all I need, you can move the body now," Bellasario said to the sheriff. "When you're done, we'll haul him outta here." Bellasario was already unzipping the body bag while an assistant rolled in a portable gurney.

As soon as Long's body was removed from the chair in which he died, Johnson went to work. Blood had stained the expensive chair's seat and back, and a small hole had been torn in the oxblood leather. "Here we go. I want to see . . . aha . . . think I found it." She was digging at the back of the chair. "Our boy was shot clean through. Entry wound in his chest, and exit a little lower, near his spine, like the killer was standing over him." Using a knife, she urged the bullet from the padding. "Come to Mama," she said, biting her lower lip. With her gloved fingers, she removed what appeared to be a bullet from the leather. "This," she held up the bullet for inspection, "probably would have blown through the chair, too, maybe lodged in the floor of the baseboard if it hadn't been for the steel reinforcement in the back cushion." She eyed the bullet critically and her eyebrows drew into a concerned knot. "Seen this before. .30 caliber."

Alvarez's heart went stone cold.

".30 at close range." The sheriff was eyeing the slug as Johnson dropped it into a plastic evidence bag. "Lotta firepower for a close-up job."

"And just like the bullets that tore holes in the tires of Star-Crossed's victim's vehicles." Alvarez's words seemed to hang in the air, hollow and cold. She didn't want to believe it. This brazen murder of one of the richest men in the country couldn't be related to the other homicides. And yet . . . Fear and incomprehension crawled through her.

"Star-Crossed?" Santana's jaw had tightened.

"Hey, get him out of here," Grayson said to Spitzer.

"Yes, sir." She snapped to attention.

Santana was having none of it. "The same son of a bitch who's got Regan?"

The sheriff glared at Santana. "We don't know where Detective Pescoli is."

"Don't give me the company line, Grayson!" He was agitated now. Cords on the back of his neck strident, his lips blade thin, he looked as if he were trying, and failing, to rein in his temper. "Everyone in this room, hell, in this whole damned house knows that her Jeep was shot and wrecked and she's missing. Now you're telling me that the same freak who's done who the hell knows what to her has walked in here and killed Long?"

Grayson barely held on to his temper. "Just because it's the same caliber bullet doesn't necessarily mean—"

Santana's eyes snapped fire. "Like hell."

"Let's go!" Spitzer was trying to grab Santana's arm and shepherd him out the door, but he yanked himself free of her grasp.

"Find her," he rasped to Grayson, pointing a long, bloody finger at the sheriff. "You damned well find her."

"We will." Grayson's voice was cold steel.

"I mean, before it's too late and some idiot like Ivor runs across her out in the woods, dead and naked against a goddamned tree!" He brushed off Spitzer's repeated attempts to corral him, then turned and headed out the back door. His shoulders were stiff, his jaw set, his boot heels ringing with determination.

Alvarez watched him go. No way was Santana going to sit tight and let the professionals do their jobs. She'd seen his rock-solid conviction to do things his own way in the angle of his chin, the glitter in his eyes, and the determination that flattened his lips over his teeth.

The loner was going to try and take justice into his own hands.

"He's a rogue," she said just as Grayson's cell rang, and he nodded as he took the call. She walked to the window and watched Santana climbing into the truck with the dog. If the rifle used this morning at his employer's house was the same as the one that had shot out the tire of Pescoli's Jeep, then Santana was in the thick of it. His boss. His girlfriend.

But you saw how upset he was about Pescoli.

He's not the killer.

"What . . . Who? . . . Yeah, but wait. I'll send Alvarez down, she can bring 'em up . . . What? Yeah, I know. Tell the press, I'll give them a statement today, at the department . . . Hell, no, not now. I've got a meeting at four with the task force. After that. Closer to six. Maybe later. Whenever I'm done." He snapped the phone off before whoever was on the other end of the connection could ask anything else, then he met the questions in Alvarez's eyes. "That was Connors at the gate. He's got Clementine and her son freaking out, demanding to be let in. The television cameras are rolling, so let's bring 'em up."

"I'm on my way."

"Are you sure she's unaware of what we're saying?" the African-American psychologist asked Martha, the big floor nurse who had been at Mountain View for as long as Padgett could remember.

"Near comatose," was the response. Martha had never been long on insight, just rolled in and did her job before clocking out, always leaving early.

Jalicia Ramsby PhD frowned at the response. Well, really, it wasn't very P.C. How did the fat slob of a nurse know anything about her? Padgett wondered, as she sat in the chair she'd claimed years before and rocked gently. Ostensibly she was staring out at the gray afternoon, her mind as blank as

Martha believed, but she could see them behind her. They appeared ghostlike and washed out, their cellophane images seeming to float over the darkening landscape of lawns, hedges, and leafless trees in the grounds that surrounded Mountain View.

Slowly fingering the rosary on her lap, as if she were praying, Padgett told herself she would have to be wary of the newcomer. Dr. Ramsby was slim, straightforward, and sharp, with close-cropped hair, coffee-colored skin, and big eyes that didn't seem to miss much.

Head turned toward the window, Padgett moved her lips, as if in prayer, and kept her eyes blank, for she was certain Ramsby was watching her image in the glass, just as she was watching the psychologists.

Oh what a devious game we play, Don't we, Doctor? she thought but kept mouthing the familiar prayer. "Our Father who art in heaven . . ." No sound escaped her lips and she noticed, in the sheer pane, Ramsby's arched eyebrows come together, small lines radiating over her nose, red-tinted lips pursed in disbelief.

Why? Why didn't this woman trust the diagnosis that had been with Padgett ever since she'd been helped over the threshold of this ancient and revered hospital?

Some of the best psychologists and psychiatrists had examined her. She remembered, though, the last one to show any true interest in her had been Dr. Maxwell, and his interest had dwindled quickly years before.

So why this new interloper?

Why now, when it was most important that she seem as dull as the bread pudding the unimaginative cooks served each Wednesday?

Change nothing. Remain the same. No one will ever know.

"Padgett?" she heard, her name said a little more loudly, the black doctor trying to get her attention.

Padgett never stopped rubbing the beads or moving her lips. "Hail Mary, full of grace . . ."

Chapter Fifteen

Nate Santana had never been one to sit idle. So today, while the police were swarming all over the main house, he was going to track down the bastard who'd shot Brady Long. Before the damned snowstorm covered the killer's tracks.

So thinking about it, he checked on the stock, then saddled Scout, a sturdy, paint gelding with pale blue eyes and a marking on his flank that looked like the state of Alaska. Strapping a pack and a bedroll behind the saddle, he then grabbed his Winchester and headed out. There was no reason to bring Nakita, though the dog whined miserably as he left; but the snow was deep and drifting and until he needed the husky's keen nose, he'd follow the tracks himself on horseback.

He cut across the back of the property, on a path that should intersect the boot prints he'd seen earlier. He'd spied the direction they were headed, and if Ivor's Yeti was the killer and not a hallucination, then the tracks should head due west, into the foothills and, he suspected, intersect with an old logging road that ran between Long's acres and those of the federal government.

As the gelding plodded through the drifts, Santana kept his eyes on the frigid landscape, searching for anything out of the ordinary.

Why had someone killed Brady Long? Not that the man didn't have his share of enemies, but why now? In the middle of the worst winter in Montana's history? And who would know Long was arriving? His current girlfriend, that model, Maya something-or-other? Someone he worked with? Friends he planned to meet? Or just Clementine?

Then there was the deeper question. The one that tore at his soul. Was Brady Long's murder connected to Regan Pescoli's disappearance and all the other killings committed by the Star-Crossed Killer?

A coincidence?

Or cold, hard truth?

There hadn't been a murder in these parts since Calvin O'Dell's wife shot him dead for sleeping with her grown daughter, and that had happened five or six years before; Santana hadn't even been in Grizzly Falls when the scandalous events had unfolded. But since then, no homicides. Not even gangs or drug busts or hunting accidents—nothing in Pinewood County. Now, not only had Star-Crossed decided to make the area his private playground, but a copycat had followed in his footsteps. Now, if Brady Long's killer proved to be someone else, then there would suddenly be three murderers on the prowl.

Awfully unlikely for these parts, but who knew?

Brady's could be a murder for hire.

He wanted to believe it. The man had made

more than his share of enemies, but his thoughts kept circling back to the fact that the same caliber weapon used in shooting out the tires of Star-Crossed's victims' vehicles had been used on Brady Long.

But Star-Crossed doesn't kill with a firearm. He leaves his prey to die in the wilderness. This isn't really Star-Crossed's M.O.

Nate tugged gently on the reins, guiding Scout across a meandering creek that wound through an outcropping of boulders and a few scraggly pines. Ice snapped under the gelding's hooves and a bit of water ran beneath the frozen surface of the brook.

He was north of the house now, far from the helicopter pad, the snow falling around him, the wind a brittle reminder that winter had settled in hard. Eyeing the ground, he searched for prints, any kind of depression in the white blanket that covered the ground.

"Where did you go, you son of a bitch?" he wondered aloud, his breath a cloud as he searched for any trace of the cold-blooded killer.

What if this maniac has Regan?

The back of his neck tightened at the thought and his eyes thinned as he scoured the ground. *I'll kill him,* he thought, *I'll kill the bastard and won't think twice.*

He felt as if steel bands had been coiled around his chest and they were growing tighter with each breath, with the knowledge that the woman he loved was in the madman's clutches. *The woman you love, think about it, Santana. That's a big leap from good times, hot sex, and no strings attached.*

He'd met Pescoli in a bar.

Hadn't known she was a cop.

Hit on her.

She, sipping whiskey, had been amused, one dark red eyebrow arching in interest.

"You want to buy me a drink?" she'd asked, shaking her head, burnished curls shining in the soft lighting of the Spot Tavern.

"Maybe," he'd responded and signaled to the bartender, who slid a second short glass of Jack Daniel's to clink against her first.

"That was easy," she said.

"Easy's my middle name."

"I doubt it." He'd smiled at her then and she'd returned the favor.

"What's your sign?"

"Oh, come on," he said, momentarily disappointed.

"The sign that you're wearing though you don't know it. DUI? Trespass? Failure to appear? Those are the signs I'm seeing."

"What?"

She gave him the once-over, her eyes moving from his face, down the length of him and back up again. In a quick scan she'd taken in his muddy boots, faded Levi's, clean but well-worn work shirt, and three days' growth of beard. "It takes more than a shot of Jack for me to dismiss the charges." She finished her drink, set the glass on the table, and eyed the second shot of whiskey. Then her lips slid into that sexy smile that took his breath away. "But just so you know, I don't roll that way. No bribes. You'll just have to take your chances with the judge."

"Don't know what you're talkin' about."

"Sure you do."

"You think I'm trying to bribe you?" he said, just

as it was beginning to dawn on him that she was a cop. A keep-your-distance, avoid-at-all-costs cop. "You're with the *police*?"

Her grin widened and she glanced at the barkeep. "Hey, Nadine, we got ourselves a Rhodes Scholar here. Buy the man a drink. On me."

Nadine's peach-colored lips tried, and failed, to hide a smile as she poured another and placed it on the bar. He'd raised his glass and touched the rim of hers. "Nate Santana."

Her eyebrows tugged together a bit, as if she'd heard the name, then she said, "Regan Pescoli. That's *Detective* Pescoli to you."

And so it went. From a game of pool, then laughable arm-wrestling, to throwing back shots. But he didn't need the trouble that came with getting involved with a cop, and not just a cop, but a detective with two half-grown kids and two marriages under her belt.

The kind of woman to keep away from at all costs.

But there had been something about her, right from the get-go, that had hooked him, and now, astride the paint, squinting beneath the brim of his hat, he was damned well going to find her. No matter what it took.

Was she crazy? Had she really heard a woman's cry? Pescoli had spent what seemed like hours alternately trying to free herself, to escape while the creep wasn't around, and lying on her cot, straining to listen, trying to determine if she wasn't alone.

It made sense, she thought.

Star-Crossed kept his victims a while, healing them before tying them to trees and leaving them in the wilderness. He collected them, kept them in rotation, held them here at his lair, wherever that was, in separate rooms, and then later on left them to die.

Her heart lay heavy as she thought there might be others as well. Who knew how many. She remembered sitting on the corner of Alvarez's desk, going through the women who had been reported missing in a five-state area, then culling out those who might have been passing through this area of Montana, women traveling alone, of any race or religion. There had been dozens . . . She looked at the door separating her room from the area from which he'd appeared, from where she instinctively knew he resided.

Or had she imagined the noise?

Had the howl of the wind sounded like a woman sobbing brokenly?

She had to find out.

"Hey!" she yelled, not for the first time. "Anyone here?"

Her voice echoed, seeming to mock her, making her feel more alone than ever.

"Hey!" Louder this time. "Who's there?"

Again no response.

You're goin' out of your flippin' mind! You're alone, Pescoli.

Once more. "Is anyone there?"

She waited.

She heard nothing but the rush of the wind and her own thudding heart. Still, she knew her ears had picked up something earlier. And she had to find out. No matter what.

If someone else was being held captive, Pescoli had to save that person as well.

She considered the case, going over the events that had brought her to this point. At first the authorities had believed that the killer had hunted his victims, then left them to die only at certain times of the month, predominately around the cusp of the Zodiac signs, but that pattern had altered as his lust for the kill had increased—or so it seemed.

Now there was no lull before the storm, no twenty-odd days of reprieve between the womens' deaths.

She strained to listen.

Heard nothing.

Maybe it was just her overactive imagination. Tired, she closed her eyes. Working at the damned weld had proved useless. And her body screamed for relief. To rest. To heal. She took in a deep breath and could almost hear Nate Santana's voice. "You're giving up? You, Detective?" A derisive snort. "Hell, I never would have figured you for a quitter."

"Bastard," she whispered, as if he could hear her. But, of course, no one could. Her throat closed as she thought of him.

She blinked against a rush of stupid tears, fought them back and told herself to quit thinking about the cowboy and concentrate on the task at hand. She had to fight through the pain and free herself.

Star-Crossed, that twisted son of a bitch, would be coming back, and soon.

Who knew when or if she'd get this same chance to save herself and whoever else was trapped with her here.

Setting her jaw, Regan threw herself into her task

again and was rewarded with more pain. Mind-numbing, bone-rattling pain. Her wrist ached where the cuffs had dug into her flesh and her ribs and shoulders were on fire. She hauled herself to the cold floor and tried to kick at the weld without twisting her wrist even worse.

She couldn't give up.

Not yet.

Not ever.

Where is Liam?

Trying to allay her fears, Elyssa shivered on her bed in the small room that Liam had so generously offered her. But he was gone, for much longer than usual, and she felt that uncertainty, the fear, began to gnaw at her again.

Don't be silly. He's been good to you. He'll be back. You know it.

But he could have had an accident . . .

He was going to try and get his truck started and if that failed, snowshoe into town for supplies. She was still too injured to go with him, but he would try to get help, he'd told her.

"Don't worry," he whispered, his big hands smoothing her hair. "I'll get you out of here. By hook or by crook." She'd looked into his eyes and trusted him—of course, she'd trusted him! She'd touched his cheek, the side where the scratches were so visible.

"That's what you get when you try and help a bear cub out of a tree," he told her. "I'm just lucky the mama bear didn't show up or I'd have a lot more than a few little scratches."

"I thought bears hibernated in winter," she responded and he chuckled.

"City girl. Don't trust what you read in textbooks. Wild animals do what they want when they want. Whatever nature tells them to. They're like people, you know. They can't be pigeonholed."

Was that true? Didn't bears mate in the summer and spend the winters in their dens with their young? Or did they sometimes come out of their lairs to feed . . . That's not what she remembered from her biology class in college. Before nursing school, she'd gotten her bachelor of science and had taken three terms of biology, but that had been a while back and she really wasn't thinking clearly. And it didn't really matter anyway. All that concerned her now was getting home safely.

"First, a hospital," Liam had corrected when she'd mentioned that she wanted to return to her family by Christmas. "I know first aid pretty well, I have to, you know, living up here and yeah, I had a few leftover pills to help you through the pain. But you'll need to see a doctor before you hightail it back to Missoula." He'd smiled then, a kind smile that made her feel a little guilty as she had a boyfriend already, a man who she hoped would surprise her with an engagement ring at Christmas, which, of course, wouldn't go over well with her father.

Dad just didn't understand Cesar, who, Elyssa had to admit, was a little rough around the edges. But he just needed a good woman to help him wrest his kids from that bitch of an ex-wife of his.

But here, with Liam, her feelings for Cesar had gotten a little confused. And he could be mean . . . but Liam, he was kind. Good. Had rescued her when he'd found her car at the bottom of the canyon after the Saturn's tire blew and she'd lost consciousness.

She'd woken up to Liam trying to help her from the vehicle. He'd been out snowshoeing when he'd found her.

At first she'd been fearful, but as Liam tended to her wounds—a sprained wrist, twisted knee, and cuts and abrasions, possible cracked rib or two—she'd begun to trust him. He was gentle and caring, and everything he'd done to help her get well was exactly right. She'd taken enough nursing classes to know. And he'd tried to call the police, but his cell phone didn't work all that well and hers had been lost in the wreckage . . . so she was here in this small room, tended to by a man who truly was a Good Samaritan. He had a crutch that was much too long but it allowed her to hobble through the three rooms of his cabin: the living area with its small wood-fired stove in the alcove, which served as kitchen, too; another bedroom, "his" room, on the far side; and a small bath. There was another door, too; one that was locked from its other side, which Liam had explained was a staircase that led to his work area. He "puttered around" in geology and it, along with astronomy, seemed to be his passions, though he made his living, he claimed, as a fishing and hunting guide, spring through autumn. Winters, he holed up here.

"I guess I'm a bit of a loner," he admitted and at first she'd been frightened. Hadn't she heard something about a serial killer in this part of the country? She hadn't paid much attention, just caught headlines online and while passing newsstands.

Some of the students had talked about it, but she hadn't been that interested, nor did she ever watch the news. It was all too depressing.

So the thought had crossed her mind.

But Liam had been too good to her.

And she thought he might be falling in love with her.

Not that he'd ever tried anything. He hadn't even kissed her, just touched her gently when he'd tended to her injuries. Nonetheless, she was thinking less of Cesar these days and more and more about what it would be like to kiss Liam, to run her hands down his long back, to feel the hard muscles of his buttocks.

"Oh for God's sake!" It was crazy. She barely knew him, and yet, the way he seemed to undress her with his eyes belied his feelings. The chemistry between them was palpable. And when she caught him staring at her, the back of her throat closed. She always looked away, afraid he might realize that she was fantasizing about him.

Stop it!

She couldn't think that way.

She was just experiencing a bad case of cabin fever.

And he was the only person she'd seen in weeks.

The person who touched her as he bathed her or checked her wounds, his fingers feather light on her skin. No wonder she had sexual thoughts.

She bit her lower lip, found it quivering.

Pull yourself together. He'll be back.

Yes, he was out, but it was because he was trying to make it into town to explain about her accident and get help, to let her parents know that she was okay.

But he'd been gone so long.
And she was scared.
Couldn't help the tears that ran down her face.
She prayed that he was safe.
That he would come back to her.
And that it would be soon.

Chapter Sixteen

Just shy of the logging road, Santana pulled up on the reins. So far he'd seen nothing other than a snowshoe hare peeking from beneath the needles of a icy hemlock tree, and he'd traveled nearly two miles.

He searched the ground for any sounds of footprints, but the blanket of white was undisturbed, the snow coming down faster than ever, tiny crystals stinging against his face.

He'd thought he could find the spot where the attacker had left his vehicle, a wide area in the old access road where it curved close to the back fence of the Lazy L.

It only made sense.

Santana knew the area and the fence line like the back of his hand, and if he were trying to sneak into the property, to gain access to the house without being seen, that would be the spot he would choose.

He kept his gaze on the ground as the horse steadily walked on and wondered what the connection was between the Star-Crossed Killer and whoever had blown Brady Long away.

He's someone familiar with the territory.

Someone you've met.

A loner who knows the hills as well as you do.

An ace marksman, who is agile and strong enough to walk miles carrying a hundred-and-twenty-pound woman, a survivalist type who has a hidden lair and knows the area well enough to stay off the cops' radar.

Maybe he's a cop. Someone on the inside staying one step ahead. Turning the investigation in the wrong direction.

He considered the deputies and detectives he'd met in the department, but he didn't know them well enough to start narrowing the field. Besides, that was reaching, wasn't it? Why would a cop go off his nut and start abducting and torturing women?

He suppressed an inner shudder.

Approaching the fence line, he rode along the taut strands of barbed wire, searching for any tracks in the abandoned logging road, but the snow was unbroken, no trail of footsteps visible, no tire tracks marring the surface.

"Damn it," he muttered under his breath.

What was he missing?

What?

He thought of Regan and wondered if she was even still alive.

Hell!

The thought hit him hard. A sucker punch to his gut.

He clenched his gloved fists and fought sudden

despair. She was too alive. Too vibrant. After their first meeting, he'd pursued her and she'd had nothing to do with him. In fact, her exact words had been, "Listen, cowboy, no offense, but take a flying leap."

Still, that hadn't stopped him. The more she'd played hard to get, the more interested he'd become, which, even at the time, had seemed damned foolish, but there it was. She'd taken the time to explain to him that she wasn't interested in any kind of a relationship and her reasons in refusing to date him were simple: she had kids to think about and a job that sucked up every ounce of her energy. She didn't need or want to give up the time, or exert the effort it would take to add a man to her life.

"Besides," she'd confided when he'd caught up with her at Wild Will's one night, "I'm not all that great a judge of character when it comes to men. Consider yourself lucky, okay?"

He hadn't, and eventually he'd worn her down. They'd met for a drink at the bar in a restored hundred-year-old hotel overlooking the falls. One drink and lots of conversation had led to another, then another. Eventually, on a dare, she'd challenged him to a wrestling match and he'd paid for a room upstairs where she, within seconds, had pinned him on the floor and lay breathing hard over him, the floorboards of the ancient hotel smooth against his back.

"Give?" she'd said, her breath smoky with the whiskey she'd consumed.

"Don't think so."

"But I've got you."

"Do you?"

"Oh, yeah, cowboy. If you haven't noticed, I'm on top."

"Maybe that's the way I like it. Maybe I let you get the drop on me."

"Sure," she'd laughed, tossing her red curls over one shoulder, perspiration visible on her flushed face in the dimmed lights. "You let me—"

In that second, he'd pushed up, flipped her over, and while she, surprised, lay beneath him, he'd trapped her hands over her head, holding them with one hand, then kissed her with all the pent-up emotion that had been building for six months. To his surprise she didn't resist, but closed her eyes and let out a long, sensual moan of pleasure.

"You're . . . relentless," she whispered.

"Yes."

She'd laughed then, a deep throaty chuckle, and he started tugging on the hem of her sweater. She, once he released her wrists, returned the favor.

Her body was long and lean, athletic and strong, her breasts full and tipped with pinkish nipples, her sinewy legs capped by a nest of curls that confirmed she was a natural redhead.

He reveled in the feel and taste of her, trying like hell to draw out every moment, to savor the experience, but it had been so long and he'd wanted her so much that he'd been a wild man, touching and tasting and kissing. Lips running over bodies, the smells of perfume and sweat ever present, arms tangling, his knees urging hers apart. He was hard as hell and when she hadn't resisted, he'd made love to her in a fury that had left them both gasping and wanting more.

He'd complied.

All night long.

So now, to think that she might be . . . no . . . she couldn't be. He looked a hundred yards ahead where the fence sagged a bit and he saw it. Tire tracks, now filling with snow, but definite lines of tread on the far side of the barbed wire, and on the Long estate, a trail of footsteps one leading toward the main house, a second returning. They were already covered by several inches of snow. The same with the tread, but there was still a chance that the police could find something.

He was about to put a call into Alvarez's cell phone when he heard the dogs. Looking through the curtain of snow he saw a dog handler and two bloodhounds following the unbroken trail.

"Hey!" the officer called. "Who the hell . . . Oh, God, Santana? I should have known."

He recognized the voice before he could make out the features of Jordan Eagle, the local veterinarian who also worked with rescue and tracking dogs. Behind her, looking as grim as ever, was Deputy Spitzer.

"I thought we told you to cease and desist," she called, her glasses fogging under the brim of her insulated cap. She was breathing hard, trying to keep up with the dogs straining on their leashes.

Santana shook his head. "I didn't hear that."

"Then hear it now. Cease and desist."

"You need to get your techs onto the logging road." He pointed a gloved finger at the tire marks still visible in the snow on the other side of the fence. "Looks like the killer drove through here, walked in, killed Long, then turned around and left the way he came in."

"Are you deaf? You need to back off of this investigation," she snapped but was already reaching for her cell phone.

As the dogs, two bloodhounds, sniffed at the ground, trotting near the fence line, Jordan observed, "Still getting into trouble, I see." She was a petite woman with coppery skin that hinted at her Native American heritage, a straight nose and near-black eyes that showed her emotions. She just happened to be one of the few people in Grizzly Falls whom Santana trusted.

"A habit I can't seem to break."

She looked over the fence and eyed the tracks as Spitzer talked on the phone, explaining the situation. "So what's your take on this?" she asked him.

"Nothin' good."

"You think this is the work of the Star-Crossed Killer?"

"I don't know." Spitzer threw a frown up at him as she carried on the conversation. "I'm just the dumb ranch hand who came in when Brady Long was dying."

"Yeah?" she said, then shook her head and snorted a laugh. "Not in my book, Santana. No way."

Spitzer hung up the phone. "The crime scene techs are on their way," she said. To Santana, she said tersely, "Now, why don't you tell me why it is you can't just mind your own business?"

"Brady Long made it my business," he said, but kept his thoughts about Regan Pescoli to himself. As yet, there was no connection between her abduction and Long's murder. Just speculation.

So far.

"You got that wrong," Spitzer said.

"We'll see." Rather than get into it with her further, Nate returned to the paint and turned the horse back around.

The police are idiots!

Morons!

I can't believe that they were fooled by an imbecilic copycat, and a poor one at that, and now they're running around chasing their own tails over Brady Long.

I should feel some satisfaction over this, but instead I'm frustrated as I make my way back to the cabin, the truck's engine whining as I take the final curve and pull into the lean-to where my snowmobile is hidden. There's just enough room for the two vehicles, and this shed is still half a mile away from the place I've hidden them—the next two women who will end up frozen. The discovery of their dead bodies will show the police just how inept they are.

In desperation the sheriff's department is even listening to the crazy old man now, about the "Yeti" he viewed on Brady Long's property.

Ha!

What the hell was Ivor doing up there?

He could have messed everything up.

Once again, I think I might just have to kill him.

In a way, it would be a blessing for him. Take him out of his unrealized misery. Shut him up permanently and save him the embarrassment of being the town looney.

I cut the engine and listen as it dies, ticking softly as it quickly begins to cool.

The police, of course, tried to keep him quiet, but, as always, and because the deputies on duty are inadequate, Ivor managed to get to one of the television reporters who had camped out in town. I saw the "breaking news" on the television over the bar when I stopped in for a drink and conversation with Nadine. There was Ivor Hicks in all his glory, eyes wide behind his oversized glasses, insisting that a huge white creature, a Yeti, with a long club had killed Brady Long.

"I was afraid fer my own life, let me tell you. I figured the creature might have X-ray vision or worse. Looked straight at me with gold eyes that seemed to glow."

Try as they might, the cops just hadn't been able to shut him up, and Talli Donahue, a blond reporter for KBTR, was always ready to interview the old man. It was almost as if she were making fun of him when she posed her questions, as if she wanted to wink at the camera. She'd had a twinkle in her eye, almost like "Watch this," as she and Ivor spoke. She'd caught him in town, trying to make his way into the Spot, his favorite tavern, a place I know he frequents.

Reporting!

All that tabloid trash.

It's getting as bad as the shoddy police work. I can't wait to step up my plan. I climb out of the truck and cover it with a large insulated tarp. I don't want to chance the engine freezing and not starting when I need it most. Then, strapping on my snowshoes, I start hiking back to the cabin with the sad news for Elyssa that I never made it to town, that for a few more days she'll be stuck inside the cabin.

But I promise, the storm is about to break and I'll be able to get her out soon.

And I will, I think, savoring this part of the plan.

Finally she's ready and so am I.

It's time for Elyssa to face her darkest fears.

Deep down, she's worried that I'm the Star-Crossed Killer. I saw it in her eyes when she first woke in the cabin. She was on painkillers then, and out of it, so I was able to allay her fears, to convince her to trust me, but in that part of her brain that's instinctive, she hasn't quite let go of her dread.

I walk across a small hill and deeper into the forest, avoiding the old mining road that has been closed for years. No reason to arouse suspicion, as surely the police will search it eventually, when they get their choppers airborne again. From the air the access road looks like nothing, but I can't risk driving my truck on it. The tracks of the snowshoes will be invisible, however, especially with the ever-falling snow.

Now Elyssa has crossed the line.

Yes, she's worried that I'm not who I say I am, but she is also so dependent on me that she is falling for me.

They all do.

In time.

I see her watching me as I prepare the food, or bathe her, or even walk into my "bedroom." Her eyes follow me and she's starting to fantasize.

As I care for her, I make sure that my head is close to hers and I feel her gaze on my mouth. She wonders what it would be like to kiss me. She imagines running her tongue down my skin, even what it would be like to make love to me with her mouth.

I tingle just thinking about it, my cock growing hard as I skim the surface of the snowdrifts and ease around a final outcropping of rock to the back entrance of my private cabin. It's been a good day already, what with the killing of that prick, Brady Long, and it would be a nice way to celebrate to fuck the hell out of Elyssa.

But that would be breaking my own rules.

These women are untouchable. If I want to get laid, Nadine with her smoky breath and sexy little tattoo over her buttocks would gladly raise her rump to me, offer herself up. I like it that way, to come in from behind, so that I don't have to see the whore's face. She's willing and wet and hot, but a whore just the same. I feel nothing for her.

These women, the ones I've spent so much time hunting down, they are worthy, but if I ever gave in and made love to them, the tide of power would turn. No . . . I cannot give in.

But my damned penis isn't paying attention. Stiff and anxious, it impedes me. So I stop at a snow-bank, grab a handful of icy crystals, unzip my ski pants, and jam the snowball into my crotch.

I have to bite my tongue to keep from gasping aloud as the ice instantly shrivels my hard-on and I'm able to think clearly again. I can't, *won't*, be impeded from my purpose by my erection.

I reach my destination, a shanty that appears to be falling down: graying wood siding that has withstood the test of nearly a hundred Montana winters; shingles on the roof that bubble and peel; and a window of thin, rattling panes, now completely iced over, painted black on the inside. Unlocking the door, I step into the shack and start peeling off the outer layer though it's still freezing within the thin walls. They aren't as bad as they appear from the outside, however, as I've insulated and nailed sheet-rock over the panels of fiberglass that help keep out the cold. I walk to a back door, which, too, is pad-

locked. It creaks as it opens and I light a lantern before descending the stairs to the underground tunnels, built during the silver-mining era.

I've spent years improving these tunnels and
rooms, updating them, making everything usable for
my special purpose. Long before any of the women
I've chosen were brought here. There are various
tunnels that sprout off these steps, some short, others
long and, eventually airless. Some have other exits,
others dead-end. I've explored most of them and
use them to store supplies. But today, I ignore them
as I traverse the memorized route, using a small
flashlight for illumination. The tunnel leads me to
my own quarters, barely underground, close enough
to the surface that a chimney draws upward, allowing me to keep the caverns warm. I worry about the
chimney and the smoke it brings to the surface, for
if it is seen by the authorities, my operation could
be discovered.

There is a log and stone cabin above my living
quarters, a fortress of sorts, where I also keep my
guests. If seen, the smoke could be construed as
coming from its chimney because the authorities
cannot find me.

Not until I'm finished.

Worried, I decide to hurry things along. I had
once had a plan, using the Zodiac signs, but it
proved too cumbersome and I had to wait too long
between the killings . . . stupid police . . . Now I'll have
to rush . . . but maybe that will work well and really
throw off the cops. It's not as if I don't have more
than one who will suffice . . . . And I could really shock
Sheriff Grayson and his band of incompetents if I
used more than one at a time. Why not up the game?

I smile to myself for all the planning I've done

here in the old mine. "Clever boy," I whisper, thinking again how Mother would have been impressed. And shocked. Here, there are so many tunnels, so many secret spots, so many places to hide a person and no one would ever be the wiser. Thank goodness I've been thinking ahead. Putting the plan into action. Finding those who are worthy to be left. Making certain I have enough . . . inventory. Again I smile. I really am far smarter than anyone would ever imagine, especially Mother.

If she could only see me now. And witness the women who have come to love me. To trust me.

Outside the door to my work space I peel off the next layer of clothes—my ski suit—and leave it on a hook, so that it will stay clean and drip on the landing. Then with my key, I let myself in.

Honey, I'm home, I think and smile at my little joke as I walk through my larger living space to the detective's door and peer through the peephole.

Somewhere a door creaked.

Damn!

Regan slid onto the cot and closed her eyes, as if she'd been sleeping. The hairs on the back of her arms lifted as she heard soft footsteps. *His* footsteps. Her wrist was bruised and swollen. Though she'd managed to work at the weld, saw that it was cracking, she hadn't yet broken through the soldered seam. If she just had a little more time, a little more strength.

Don't give up. You can beat this guy. You can.

But as she felt his gaze crawling up her body, she recoiled inside and she was certain she was in the presence of raw evil. She didn't care if he was men-

tally off or not. Depravity fed depravity and this
freak needed to be stopped.

It's up to you.

*If you can off him, you can save not only yourself but
all the others he has planned for his sick game.*

Her heart nearly stopped when she heard the
click of tumblers and sensed her door sweep open.
Bile rose up her throat as she thought of him watching her. Though the bodies of the women who had
been found in the forest had shown no evidence of
sexual molestation, surely they had endured some
kind of hellish torture at this maniac's hands.

"I know you're awake," he said in that oily
smooth voice of his, one that sounded familiar.
"You don't have to pretend with me."

Slowly, she opened her eyes. He was standing
over her, a big man, still disguised. The goggles covered his eyes, the beard had to be fake, but in the
darkness she saw the scrapes to his skin that hadn't
yet healed. Score one for the good guys.

"Good morning, Detective," he said softly. "Well,
it's really not morning anymore . . ."

"Who the hell cares?"

"Mmm. See, you *were* playing possum. And not
very convincingly." He dropped a fresh liter of
water onto the bedside table, along with some kind
of protein bars. "I thought you'd like to know that
the world has just been rid of some scum."

What the devil was he rambling about?

"You've heard of Brady Long?"

Hell, yes. Who hadn't? Brady Long was the only
child of one of the richest men, if not the richest
man—copper baron Hubert E. Long—in the county.
No . . . wait, that wasn't quite right. There was an-

other child, wasn't there? A girl? Had she died? Regan couldn't remember.

"I see he's familiar to you. Well, he's one less citizen the sheriff will have to worry about." He turned away then, and with his gloved hands, picked up several chunks of cut wood that had been stacked against the wall, shoving them into the front of the stove where the dying embers reacted, crackling and shooting out hungry flames.

"What happened to Brady?" Regan asked, her curiosity getting the better of her.

"He met an unfortunate end, I'm afraid."

"You killed him?"

He slammed the door of the wood stove shut, then turned to loom over her again. His teeth flashed in a satisfied leer beneath the fake beard. "The story goes that a Yeti took care of him."

She stared. For the love of God, this guy was really bats. Certifiably insane.

"That's what the news is reporting."

"Really?" *Don't engage him. He's getting off on it.*

"Isn't it interesting?"

"Not really."

He clucked his tongue at her naïveté, mocking her that she would try and fool him. "And the more interesting part is the Yeti, he kills with a rifle, a .30 to be exact."

"How do you know this?"

His horrid grin widened. "Because I was there, Red. Witnessed it all."

"You did kill him, you son of a bitch."

"I've done the world a favor, but that's the problem with doing good deeds, you know. They're always misunderstood." His smile faded a bit, and in the orange shadows of the fire, his face, with its disguising dark beard and the scratches running down one cheek, looked the very embodiment of malevolence. "But that will change . . . soon."

He gazed down at her with purpose and Pescoli felt as if snakes had slithered up her spine. He was planning to kill her, of course, but now she knew it would be soon.

Chapter Seventeen

Grace Perchant's home was something right out of a fairy tale. A cottage in the woods that looked like the Brothers Grimm had designed it, nestled in a cute little spot in the wintry landscape where, despite its charming and picturesque appeal, dark and deadly creatures lay within.

"Must be the cold medication," Alvarez said as she parked in the rutted lane outside the cabin and followed a broken path in the snow to the front door. It was just a house. Quaint, yes. But a house in the woods. In her three years with the department, she'd been to many a backwoods cabin in the forest. Grace Perchant's was no different. Not at all.

She'd left Grayson at Brady Long's estate as he'd elected to stay longer and planned to catch a ride back to the office with the undersheriff. Brewster had shown up just about the time Alvarez was leaving. She'd gotten all the information she could and had stuck around to interview Clementine De-

Grazio and her son, Ross. The housekeeper had said she'd received a call from Brady Long the night before, saying he was planning a "quick trip up" if there was a break in the storms. Clementine had made sure the house was stocked with his favorite foods and liquor, then, earlier in the morning, she'd driven with her son to her sister's house for a pre-Christmas gift exchange as the sister was planning to leave town until after New Year's. Ross, pretty much a silent, bored-looking teen in sunglasses and stocking cap, had sullenly agreed with his mother and a quick call to the sister had confirmed that Clementine and Ross had been gone all morning.

Though Ross seemed unaffected by Long's death, Clementine had been beside herself, alternately crying and shredding tissues as she wrung her hands and sniffed back tears. She appeared to be grieving for a man who had more enemies than friends, if most of their sources, including Grayson, and even Nate Santana, were to be believed.

But Clementine had been as grief-riddled as a mother.

Or a wife.

It occurred to Alvarez that Clementine DeGrazio might have been more than Brady Long's housekeeper. Something to check on.

Now, however, she had to deal with Grace Perchant.

On the tiny front porch, she rapped on the door just as she heard deep growls emanating from the other side of the door. Oh, right. Grace kept wolves or half-wolves, hybrids or something. Presumably, she would keep them at bay.

"Sheena, hush!" a woman's voice commanded

and the noise from within instantly subsided. A second later Grace herself opened the door. "Detective." Wearing a long cardigan sweater over thick tights and a black turtleneck, she offered the slightest of smiles. "I hoped you'd call or stop by." She stepped out of the doorway and inclined her head, a wisp of graying hair escaping its topknot. "Come in."

The dog, Sheena, lay on a padded bed near an antique-looking and dusty couch. A fire burned brightly in the hearth. Every window ledge and end table was covered with pots of small, trailing plants and softly burning candles, dripping wax. A tinderbox ready to ignite.

"You're here about your partner. Please sit." Grace waved Alvarez into her seat and the dog, watching every movement, didn't rouse.

"A few days ago, at Wild Will's, you warned me and Pescoli that she would be taken. I think your exact words were 'he's relentless. A hunter,' and you were speaking about the Star-Crossed Killer. You said you heard a voice and the voice said 'Regan Elizabeth Pescoli,' and you touched her and said she was in 'grave danger.' I think that was it."

"You have a good memory. Yes. And I was right," she pointed out as she sat on a chair near the fire and next to the dog's bed where Sheena had curled into a ball, her golden eyes slowly closing.

"How did you know?"

"The usual way. I saw parts of it. Kind of a dream."

"I always heard you talked to the dead," Alvarez said, picking her words carefully. "So, you have dreams, too?"

Grace stared out the window, where the tiny

flames of the candles reflected on the panes and ice outside. "No. Not usually, but the dead, when they talk to me, they allow me some insight . . ." She smiled a little sadly, as if she knew she sounded crazy. "I heard a voice a few days ago, a voice from a dead girl. The one who you found in Wildfire Canyon. The hairdresser."

A frisson of disbelief tickled the thin little hairs on Alvarez's nape. "Wendy Ito? She talked to you?"

"Yes."

"When?"

"A few days ago."

"How?"

Grace turned to face the detective again and her pale eyes cut straight to Alvarez's soul. "I heard her."

"How did you know who she was?"

"I saw her face. Blue and frozen. She spoke to me, but her eyes didn't move, nor did her lips. She warned me. Gave me your partner's name. When I asked how she knew, she explained that she'd seen things. Documents. Of different women. The only one she could tell me about was that of Regan Elizabeth Pescoli."

Alvarez held up a hand. "Now wait a minute—"

"That's all she said, but once she mentioned your partner, I had a dream and the images were scattered and sharp, didn't make any sense. But I think they were of Regan Pescoli."

"A dream? While you were sleeping."

"Yes . . . I found myself outside. With the dog."

"Has this happened to you before?"

Grace shook her head. "Never. Not until these killings," she said. "What's happening to me now is different. The dead want justice, I believe. They're reaching out to me with more insistence than ever before." She said it with a conviction that worried Alvarez. This woman really believed that the dead talked to her.

On the floor beside Grace, the wolf dog stretched and yawned, large teeth showing before Sheena closed her golden eyes and slept again, her breath whistling softly through her nostrils.

"In this dream did you see her killer? Did Wendy happen to mention his name? Describe him? You said 'he,' which we assume, but is there anything about him that you can tell me, something that would help us locate him?" As she heard the words pass her lips, Selena cringed a little inside. She was a woman who believed in science and evidence. She didn't trust psychics or visions or dreams or anything that couldn't be explained by fact. Yet here she was, hoping this woman who most of the townspeople thought was off her rocker could help.

"I only have a sensation. A man in white. He camouflages himself to blend in, I think. With the landscape. The snow."

"But Wendy saw him." As had all the victims. Alvarez was convinced that they had come to trust him, to believe in him, though she had no proof of that; it was only her theory.

"She saw him, but she didn't transfer his image or description to me. I'm sorry." And she looked it, seated on the corner of the dusty couch, her hands clasped in front of her, her eyes nearly luminescent.

Alvarez asked a few more questions and Grace answered quickly, honestly it seemed, but who knew? The woman could be as loco as everyone thought. But Alvarez urged Grace to tell her anything she could remember.

"There were some things that I was told about," Grace said, her silver hair catching the hearth light.

"By Wendy Ito?"

"Yes."

"What kind of things."

Almost as if she were in a self-imposed trance, Grace stared into the fire, then started talking about seeing a needle, a hypodermic. And a straitjacket, and a stretcher of some kind. Alvaez tried to press her when she trailed off, but Grace could give nothing concrete: no name, no description, no address.

Nothing to tie one person to the crimes.

Grace slowly surfaced and said, "You need to help her," which only fueled Alvarez's feelings of anxiety and inadequacy.

"I will," she promised, then headed back outside. Climbing into her Jeep, she was just turning around when her cell phone rang. She picked up as she drove onto the main road, her wipers fighting like hell to clear the windshield of the damned snow that showed no sign of letting up. "Alvarez."

"It's Joelle. Are you coming back here?"

"On my way."

"Good, good."

Alvarez got a bad feeling about the conversation. Joelle hadn't just called to suggest she be part of the Christmas cookie bake-off. "What's up?"

"It's Regan's son."

"Jeremy?" Alvarez whispered, her heart sinking. The kid was already in a helluva lot of trouble; he didn't need any more. "What about him?"

"He's down here at the station, demanding to know what's happening with his mother. I tried to calm him down and suggested he go home, even offered him some cookies and fruitcake."

Like always.

"But he's determined to talk to someone about Pescoli and considering how things are with Undersheriff Brewster, I thought you might be able to talk to him."

"I'm on my way," Alvarez promised and hung up. She didn't know what she'd say to the kid. She wasn't good with teenagers, but she'd give it her best shot.

"It's no big deal," Bianca said, miffed that Michelle would even try to deter her. Bianca was nervous, wanted to get out. Her worries about her mom ate at her and, as she flipped through the channels of her father's monstrous television, she couldn't concentrate on the reality shows that she usually loved. As many stations as the satellite dish provided, there wasn't one that caught her interest. So she'd texted her boyfriend and they'd made plans.

But Michelle, usually so cool, seemed to think she needed to suddenly assert her stepmotherly authority.

As if!

"Chris and I are just going down to the concert at the courthouse," Bianca said from the couch. She rolled her head around, so she could see into the dining room where Michelle was adjusting the strands of silvery tinsel that she'd looped through the chandelier that hung over a round glass and wrought-iron table.

"Is that right?" Obviously Michelle wasn't buying Bianca's admittedly lame excuse. "Why?"

"Duh! It's Christmas."

"I think you should stay home. Does your mom

let you go out on dates? Does Chris even drive?"
Michelle's neatly plucked eyebrows drew together
as she looped the tinsel through a curlicue of
wrought iron.

"His brother is taking us. He's got his license."

"And what time is the concert?"

Michelle sure wasn't the pushover Bianca had
thought she'd be. At least not since she'd lost her
job as a teller in a local bank that had shut its doors.
Now she was taking this whole stepmothering job a
little too far. "Around seven? I'm really not sure. We
were going to get something to eat and then go
there."

"In this?" Michelle looked through the window
to the falling snow. "I don't think so, honey."

"But—"

"Look." Michelle spread her fingers wide, red
fingernails decorated with tiny white snowflakes standing out like claws. "Your dad's got a lot to worry
about with the storms shutting down the interstate
so he can't make his usual run," she said. That
much was true. As a truck driver, Lucky was losing
money daily while the roads were impassable. He'd
planned to take some time off at Christmas, his first
ever that Bianca could remember, but the weather
had taken away his options. "And let's face it, he's
worried about your mom."

Maybe. Maybe not.

"Don't give me that look. He is. And then there's
Jeremy. Your brother blew out of here and we can't
get him on the cell phone. He's supposed to be
grounded."

"But I'm not," Bianca wheedled, reminding
Michelle that she was the "good kid" of the two.

"Just hear me out, Bianca." Michelle's voice had a

tone in it that Bianca didn't like, hadn't noticed before.

"You're not my mom." And at that Bianca felt tears bloom in her eyes. Hot, scared tears. She'd tried not to think about what might be happening to her mother, and she'd spent the last few hours texting and talking to Chris, but she couldn't just stay cooped up here.

The back door slammed shut and she looked up to see her father walk inside, the scent of cigarette smoke clinging to him as he hung up his jacket in the front closet. He caught the angry glare Michelle tossed his way.

"What?"

Michelle appeared about to snap back a hot retort, then thought better of it. "She's your daughter. You deal with her," she said, then turned and, pink high-heeled slippers clipping in a furious staccato rhythm, she hurried into the sanctity of "her" kitchen.

Bianca glared after the woman her father had married. An airhead, that's what Mom called her, but Bianca wasn't so sure.

"Okay, what's going on?" he demanded.

"I just want to go to hear a Christmas concert tonight," she complained, crossing her arms under her breasts and pouting.

"I don't think so."

"Why?"

Her father looked at her as if she'd lost her mind, then launched into the same tired arguments she'd already heard from Michelle. The weather was bad. She was too young. Jeremy was already MIA and in big trouble and blah, blah, blah. That was the trouble with being the second one, the first ruined everything.

". . . so if Chris wants to come over here and . . . hang out . . . play games or something . . . that would be okay."

"Play games?" She rolled her eyes. What did he think she was? Seven?

"Okay, then watch TV or . . ." He looked to the kitchen as if hoping Michelle would appear and offer up some kind of really cool idea to help him out of this, and Bianca realized her father didn't understand her at all. "Come on, honey. Give Chris a call and see if he'll come by. I should get to meet him. Maybe we can have pizza or . . . spaghetti . . . or . . ."

"Pizza. We can do pizza." Michelle stuck her head into the doorway. "I've got some in the freezer and extra pepperoni and olives in the pantry."

"Whoopee." Bianca twirled her finger beside her head.

Scowling, Michelle disappeared again.

Dad got all grumpy. "You're staying in. And so is Jeremy, when I track him down. Until we find out what's happened to your mom, I want you both to stick close. Got it?"

She fought a new spate of dumb tears.

"Got it, pumpkin?"

"Got it!" She only hoped that he never, *ever*, used that dumb nickname for her around Chris. It was just stupid and gross. She marched into her bedroom, slammed the door, and flopped down on the bed. Sniffing back tears, she found her cell phone and speed-dialed Jeremy. Maybe he could get her out of here.

She'd called him all day and he hadn't picked up, so she texted him:

Where R U? Get me outta here. NOW.

She thought about adding more info, then just sent the text and prayed that he would arrive. Jeremy bugged the crap out of her. He was just such a dipwad most of the time, but he was her brother and he knew what a pain Dad could be.

Bianca had always thought Michelle was okay, but she was changing her mind fast. What was this putting down rules and playing like she was Mom? What a bunch of garbage. Mom could be a real pain, but at least she was her mother. Michelle trying to act all parental and stuff, it was just wrong.

Bianca rolled onto her back and stared at the ceiling. She thought of her mother and her insides turned to ice at the thought that Mom was in real trouble.

Then she tried calling Chris.

Maybe he would come over . . . It was kinda lame, the whole pizza thing, but she needed him right now.

Really needed him.

At Mountain View Hospital, Dr. Jalicia Ramsby rotated the kinks from her neck as she walked down the hallway to her desk. It had been a morning of meetings, first with her women's group, which consisted of five women who had suffered through abusive relationships, and then an administrative meeting, where she was told that she'd have to cut costs in her department, probably losing at least one aide. "Times are tough," Hedgewick, the administrator, had told all the department heads. "The economic decline is taking a hefty toll."

"But people are still sick. They still have to get treatment for mental illness," Ramsby protested, a few of her peers rumbling agreement.

Hedgewick had appeared concerned, his lips pursing, his eyes behind his reading glasses darkening, his hands clasping over the smooth table top and his neatly typed pages. "That's what makes our job challenging," he said, placating her. "We have to offer the best services possible while staying within the constraints of the company budget."

She thought about the Mercedes he drove but held her tongue. His wife was rumored to be wealthy in her own right and it didn't matter. Hedgewick always kept his eye firmly on the bottom line.

Now reaching the door to her office, Jalicia looked down toward the far end of the hallway where a woman quickly slipped around the corner. For a heartbeat, Dr. Ramsby thought the petite woman with the dark hair was Padgett Long.

Which was ridiculous. Padgett never moved faster than a slow walk and she was in the secure wing.

Maybe someone who looked like the silent patient?

Ramsby walked swiftly enough that her lab coat billowed as she headed toward the corner. She had to have been wrong. As far as she knew Padgett had never been out of her wing and surrounding yard.

Which was sad, but true.

So why . . . ?

Within seconds she rounded the corner to the landing area where she could have sworn the woman had darted.

The corridor was a dead end to a wall of windows now splattered with rain from the ominous clouds scudding across the sky. On the right were two service elevators; on the left, restrooms. Ramsby noted that both elevator cars were heading downward, one at the second floor, the other stopping on ground level.

Had the woman gotten on one?

Had it been Padgett?

Jalicia had never been one to discount a person's feelings or gut instincts and she'd often felt that something was off around Mountain View. Curious, she stepped into the women's room and found it empty. The men's was locked.

Hmmm.

Telling herself she was imagining things, she waited near the elevators, her arms folded over her chest, her eyes on the restroom door, her hunger for a cigarette burning through her blood like fire, though she hadn't smoked in over eight months. Maybe it was time to try the damned patch.

Brrring! She nearly jumped out of her skin when her cell phone went off. Checking the screen, she saw that her secretary, the ever-impatient Annette, was calling. "Yes?"

"I've been trying to reach you," Annette said, obviously peeved. Again. Soon, Ramsby feared, it would be time to have an attitude adjustment talk with the woman.

"I was in a meeting."

"I know, but that lawyer Barton Tinneman's called again. I thought you'd want to know."

Hubert Long's, Padgett's father's, attorney. She wondered what he wanted now. "I'll have to call him back later."

As she snapped her phone shut, the door to the men's room clicked open and Dr. Langley, a frail-looking psychologist with a thin white beard and perpetual knit brow, was tucking his shirt into his pants as he walked out. He looked up and caught her eyeing him.

"Anyone else in there?" Ramsby asked, her gaze doing a quick once-over of the tiny room while the door was open. She caught a slice of her own worried reflection in the mirror over the sink before the door slowly closed.

"Pardon?" Scott said, coloring slightly. He cleared his throat and adjusted his tweed jacket.

"I thought one of my patients may have wandered . . . oh, never mind." Ramsby felt suddenly foolish. "I was mistaken."

"No one was with me in there, Dr. Ramsby, if that's what you're asking." Langley's white eyebrows inched up a notch.

"I wasn't asking anything," she said, then turned on her heel and headed toward her office again, the feeling that something wasn't right at Mountain View greater than ever.

Chapter Eighteen

Oh, great.

Now Mom's partner was going to try to give him some advice.

Jeremy saw it in the set of Selena Alvarez's jaw and the way she walked straight to the table where he'd been asked to wait in this tiny little windowless room, an interrogation room, he thought. It smelled of sweat and bleach. Bad. And he was uncomfortable, always had been when he was near a police station. His mom had said being a cop was in his blood because both she and his father had been on the force, but uh-uh, no way did he want anything to do with law enforcement. He didn't trust cops. Sometimes even his mom.

"Hi," Alvarez said. All friendly-like. Though she wasn't smiling. Mom had said she was intense.

Jeremy wasn't up for small talk. Just like he hadn't wanted any cookies from the woman with the fake smile and weird clothes. "Have you found my mom?"

"Not yet."

He'd thought he was ready for bad news, but he suddenly had trouble drawing a breath, as if someone were sitting on his chest. "I saw her car," he admitted. "Totaled. At Horsebrier Ridge. It was . . . A tow truck was winching it up from the canyon floor." His stomach twisted as he remembered the mangled wreckage. "Is she dead?" He was trying to appear in control of his rapidly eroding emotions.

"I don't think so."

God, this was freaky. Horrible. Jeremy felt his damned leg trembling and he wanted to scream. *Mom isn't dead, she isn't dead. Not like Dad . . . oh, dear God, no . . . Mom isn't dead.* "You don't know, though."

"No. But your being here isn't going to help. The best thing for you to do is to go home with your dad and sister—"

"He's *not* my dad and I can't go home. The cops are all over the place."

"I meant to your stepfather's house. Isn't that where Bianca is? With Luke? And his wife."

He lifted a shoulder. *No one ever calls Lucky, Luke. Well, except Michelle, especially when she's really pissed off.* "I don't keep track of my sister."

"Maybe you should. Until your mom gets back."

"What if she doesn't?" Jeremy blurted out, his worst fears right out in the open, all of his confidence stripped away. His throat was tight and his eyes burned. Oh, shit, he wasn't going to let himself cry. No way. But he was scared. Scared as hell. "What then?" he demanded, his voice cracking a little. Holy crap, would he be stuck living with Lucky and Michelle? Could there be anything worse? And what about Mom? Where the hell was she?

Alvarez was staring at him as if he was from outer space and he finally realized he was chewing his fingernail and spitting the bits onto the floor—something his mom hated and was always ragging on him about. From the looks the detective was shooting him, she wasn't keen on his nervous habit either. "I'm, um, I'm just worried." He forced his hand to his lap, but his damned leg was still shaking nervously.

"I don't blame you," she said, a bit more kindly, "but you can't do anything down here. Trust me."

He flinched. Whenever an adult started out saying those two words, "trust me," it meant they were about to try to force you into doing something you just knew in your gut was wrong. "We're doing everything we can to find her."

"It's not enough," he said flatly and for the first time noticed the little camera mounted near the ceiling. Oh, God, was he being filmed?

Footsteps rang behind her and over Alvarez's shoulder, through the open doorway Jeremy caught a glimpse of a tall man with thin, silvering hair heading their direction.

Undersheriff Brewster!

Heidi's prick of a father.

Shit!

"What's *he* doing here?" the big buffoon demanded, stepping around Alvarez and looming over Jeremy seated in the uncomfortable chair. In an instant, Jeremy was on his feet, almost standing eye to eye with the tall cop.

"He's worried about his mother."

Brewster gave him the evil eye. "You should be in lockup for what you did, Strand."

"I didn't do anything."

"Got my daughter drunk. God knows what else would have happened if you hadn't been picked up." He was mad all over again, his face turning red, his lips bloodless.

"Cool it," Alvarez said tautly.

Brewster hooked a thumb in Jeremy's direction. "All this little jerk-off wants to do is get high and drunk, then go out driving and try to get into my little girl's pants." He leveled a hate-filled glare at Jeremy. "You keep your filthy, horny hands off my daughter, you hear me, boy? You so much as call her, I'll have you arrested."

"For what?"

"Anything you can think of, only worse."

"Enough!" Alvarez snapped out. She stepped between Jeremy and Brewster. She was a full head shorter, but she held her ground even though Heidi's dad was her boss. "Let me handle this, sir," she said, trying to defuse the situation, but it was too far gone.

Jeremy smelled the fight before the first punch had been thrown. Though his brain warned him, *Don't let the old fart goad you into it. Don't try to take him down,* he felt that sizzle in his blood, the tension in his muscles, the tightness between his shoulders. God, he'd love to land one fist onto Cort Holier-Than-Thou Brewster's smug face.

The old man felt it, too. "Come on, punk. Hit me. You know that's what you want to do."

"Undersheriff Brewster!" Alvarez was still wedged between them. "Stand down! Both of you."

"But the punk thinks he can take me. Sick little perverted prick. He wants to screw my daughter and beat the crap out of me. Isn't that right, Strand? You're a loser, you know that. A dope-smoking, beer-sucking loser, and Heidi's too good for you, so you just stay away."

Jeremy's fist balled so hard it hurt.

Just one shot, that's all he wanted. To show this asshole what he was.

"Try it, sissy."

Oh, God.

His cell phone beeped. Another text message.

"What's that?"

"We've got more important things to worry about," Alvarez pointed out coldly.

In a second, Brewster lunged and had Jeremy up against the wall, one arm twisted painfully behind his back, his face turned sideways but smashed into the cinder blocks.

"Stop it!" Alvarez ordered.

But Brewster pinned him harder and started patting him down. Jeremy squirmed. He couldn't let Heidi's dad see the pictures she'd been sending him. Brewster would kill them both. "Let me go!"

"I think you've got some weed on you, punk!"

"No, I don't!"

"Stop it, Brewster," Alvarez warned.

"What is this . . . Oh, here we go." He reached into Jeremy's pocket and pulled out his wallet and cell phone.

"Give that back!" Jeremy said, panicked. Oh, God, the guy was going to look at his cell phone. "It's mine!"

"What's it got on it? Your dealer's number?"

"No, Mr. Brewster, please, don't—" The change

of tone was a mistake. Jeremy saw it in the flare of interest in Brewster's eyes.

"Then you've got nothing to hide."

"Isn't this an invasion of privacy or—?" Jeremy's voice dropped as Brewster opened the phone and dark red color climbed up his neck to burst into his face, so that his blue eyes looked about to pop from his head.

"What the hell is this?" he hissed. "What did you do to my daughter?"

"Nothing!"

"Are you trying to tell me that Heidi sent you these of her own free will, you little snot?" He was advancing on Jeremy again and this time Alvarez stood between them.

"Stand down, sir! If you don't stop harassing this boy, I'm going to arrest you." Alvarez was all business. Jeremy thought she might draw her damned weapon.

"Arrest *me*? Are you out of your mind, Detective?" Brewster snarled.

"You don't want the department to face assault charges. Sir." Her voice was like steel.

Brewster snorted, "This punk'll hide behind the law over my dead body."

"Fine!" Before he could think, Jeremy rounded on the man, his fist smashing into Brewster's jaw. The older man's head snapped back and he went reeling against the far wall, Jeremy's cell phone clattering to the floor. Jeremy looked down and saw the picture, the one of Heidi in the Santa hat and red panties, her beautiful tits with their dark nipples completely bare while she was sucking on a candy cane and winking at the camera.

Oh, Jesus.

"You little pervert!" Cort Brewster sputtered, back on the balls of his feet and rubbing his cheek, his eyes gleaming with satisfaction. "You're under arrest!" He glanced at Alvarez. "Read him his rights, Detective, and make sure he understands that he's in my custody now."

"Sir, his mother is—"

"Doesn't matter." Brewster pointed a shaking finger at Jeremy. "This kid's a troublemaker. Walkin' a thin line. Now put his butt in jail. He assaulted me. The way I figure it, we're doing his mother a favor." Brewster, looking like he would like to kill Jeremy, turned on his heel and strode out of the room.

"That was a dumb thing to do," she hissed to Jeremy once they were alone. "Real dumb."

"He's an asshole."

"And the undersheriff."

"He wanted to fight me."

"You took the first swing, so you have to go down to a holding tank for a while." She bent down, picked up the phone, and saw the picture of Heidi. Her lips twisted downward and she shook her head. "And you might want to remind your girlfriend to keep her clothes on when there are cameras or cell phones around." She pocketed his phone and led him through the department.

"You're not really going to arrest me."

"I don't really have a choice," she said tiredly. She didn't bother with cuffs, but did read him his rights as she walked him down to a room where he was to be booked. "I'll try to square it with Brewster. Talk to Sheriff Grayson, if I have to. Everything that happened is on camera, so I think we can work things out. We here at the department have a lot more to worry about than Heidi's attempts to pose for *Play-*

boy. But her dad has to cool off a while before that happens. It could take a little time."

"How much?" he asked, the thought of being locked up again starting to panic him. Why the hell had he let that son of a bitch spur him into hitting him?

"I don't know." He didn't say anything and she pushed a finger into his forearm. "Got it?"

He did, but he didn't like it. "Yeah," he mumbled.

"Good. Hang tough." She paused a moment and added, "I'm going to get myself a sandwich from the vending machine. Want one?"

"No, thanks."

"Sure? It's been a long day."

He shook his head. He had a feeling this long day was going to get longer.

The task force meeting brought everyone up to speed. Stephanie Chandler and Craig Halden, the two FBI agents, had returned and they sat at the table in the task force room with Sheriff Grayson, Undersheriff Brewster, Alvarez, Zoller, and a few others.

Alvarez didn't say a lot, just sipped her tea and hoped the half of a chicken-salad sandwich she'd choked down before the meeting would sustain her. She'd popped a couple of daytime cold capsules, too, working to keep her symptoms at bay. So far so good. She had yet to straighten out the mess with Regan's son, but she would. She owed her partner that much. And Brewster, just because he was the damned undersheriff, couldn't get away with being a bully, a cop who let his emotions get the best of his judgment.

She sent a look his way, but Brewster steadfastly avoided her gaze. Some of his anger had evaporated and he was feeling a little more like the jerk he was.

Good.

For now, Jeremy hadn't been booked. Alvarez would like to keep it that way.

The discussion moved from the copycat killer to Star-Crossed and then touched on Brady Long's death. The lab hadn't yet reported if the bullet found at the Lazy L proved to be a match for others they'd discovered at the scenes where the wrecked vehicles of the victims had been located. But everyone was edgy, wondering if Star-Crossed had changed his M.O.

"What would be the point?" Chandler asked. She was tall and slim, her blond hair scraped away from a face with high cheekbones that hinted at a Nordic heritage. A pair of sunglasses was propped on her head and Alvarez had never seen her without them. "I mean, he's gone through all the trouble of leaving notes, using the victims' initials, leaving his victims to die naked in the freezing weather. Now, out of the blue, he walks into Brady Long's house and just fires at the guy point-blank and leaves? Where's the organization, the planning, the attention to detail that our boy has shown? And why?"

Grayson said, "It took some planning and waiting for Long to show up."

"Not the usual victim," she argued. She held up fingers as she counted the ways this crime was different. "Not female. Not traveling across the state in a vehicle. Not injured. Not left to die in the wilderness . . . Oh, hell, I could go on and on."

Halden held up a calming hand. "We're just being cautious," he said. "We already got fooled once, by a real copycat."

"Anyone ever figure out how that killer knew so much about Star-Crossed?"

"There were clippings of all the killings, videotapes of the press conferences, and a lot of stories that the television and radio stations had run. She pieced together most of it, but there's a chance she had a mole."

"A mole? Like a spy? *Here?*" Grayson was on his feet and pointing at the floor as if to indicate the entire sheriff's department.

"As in *some*one with police ties. Not necessarily anyone from this department."

Grayson muttered under his breath. He was tired and it showed, the lines around his eyes deeper than normal, his usual slow-spreading smile nowhere to be found. His feathers ruffled, he sat down next to Alvarez and across the table from the federal agents. "Okay, so you guys will find out how the copycat got her information," he said to Halden. "But right now let's concentrate on the original. He's still at large, still using my county as his personal hunting ground, still got one of my detectives and at least one other woman, and he's *really* pissing me off.

"I've got a press conference in"—he checked his watch—"less than an hour, so let's get to it. Go over what we do know."

"I know that Ross DeGrazio, Brady Long's housekeeper's son, owns the same caliber weapon and he's a helluva shot," Brewster offered. "Saw him in a competition I entered. He almost beat me. Came in second."

"The college kid?" Grayson looked skeptical, then lifted a hand in acquiescence. Nothing made sense.

Halden said, "We'll check out his weapon and alibis."

Selena made a mental note to look into Clementine's kid herself. Was it possible?

"Any other ideas?" Grayson asked.

"The boyfriend of Elyssa O'Leary," Chandler put in, checking her notes. "Cesar Pelton. He was a marine. Dishonorable discharge. Spent some time as a security guard before he had domestic assault charges leveled against him by his ex-wife." She suddenly had everyone's attention. "But he has no connection to the other victims. As for an alibi? We're not even sure Elyssa's car was hit. He lives in Missoula, so it's close enough to be possible, but we have no corroborating evidence other than he's abusive."

"So . . . he's not a suspect?" Selena asked.

"It doesn't seem right. The ex-wife is a liar and Pelton's been pretty visible around Missoula this whole time. He's quick with his fists, but is he organized enough? He can barely hold down a job. Keeps overdrawing his accounts and gets into trouble with the law. Doesn't appear to be near as smart as our guy." The FBI agent seemed frustrated and tired. Alvarez had done some checking on Pelton as well and had nearly written him off, too. "We'll keep looking at him," Chandler said, but she sounded a little disinterested.

Brewster said, "My money's still on DeGrazio. Or someone who lives closer to Grizzly Falls."

Grayson checked his watch. "Anything else?"

The discussion went on, different theories bandied about, all tips that had come through the hotline discussed and doled out, the notes left at the crime and map of the area where the cars and bodies were found passed around.

They'd about wrapped up the meeting when there was a tap on the door and Joelle poked her head into the room. "Sorry," she said, and Alvarez half expected her to come clipping in with a tray of snickerdoodles, cranberry pinwheels, and Mexican wedding cakes, but instead she said, "I know you asked not to be disturbed, but Officer Slatkin is on the phone and he says he's got some information you're wanting."

Everyone went silent.

"Put him through on line one." Grayson motioned to Zoller, who was seated at the desk with the phones. "Put it on speaker." She did and in a few seconds the connection was made.

"This is Grayson. What've ya got, Mikhail?"

"First a confirmation. The bullet that was lodged in the back of Brady Long's chair is a match to those we found at two of the sites where the wrecked cars were located."

Alvarez's heart sank. So Star-Crossed had changed.

"Okay, what else?" Grayson asked.

"The tox screen came back on Wendy Ito. There were traces of Rohypnol in her blood."

"The bastard gave her a roofie," Chandler said coldly. "Date rape."

Alvarez frowned. "Except he didn't rape her. Never does."

"That's right. No sign of sexual molestation," Mikhail Slatkin agreed over the speakerphone. "We're doing deeper tox screens on all the victims, to see if there are traces of any other date rape drugs, but they pass through the body fairly quickly."

"Do what you can," the sheriff said. "Thanks."

Zoller hung up as Dan Grayson surveyed his team. "Looks like this investigation just changed course." He rubbed the back of his neck and scowled. "I want to know who benefits from Brady Long's death. Find his will. Dig up what you can on his ex-wives or anyone he screwed over. Who he's dating, who he dumped, who he cheated, anyone with a bone to pick." Tapping the table with his fingers, he added, "Could be a pretty long list. Then check out his father, see if he's alive or dead."

"Holding on by a thread. Hospice has already been called in; Hubert's tough, he could last another two months or two minutes," Brewster said. "I called the nursing home and that's all they would tell me, but he won't be long for this earth."

Eyes thinning, Grayson said, "Then what about the sister? Paige, is it?"

"Padgett," Alvarez corrected.

"That's right. I'm thinking she's about to become a very rich woman."

Stephanie Chandler said coolly, "Searching for Long's killer is all well and good. However, there are still five dead women as well as two missing, including one of your detectives."

A tic developed near Grayson's left eye, and it was evident that he was trying to keep his simmering anger under control. "Make no mistake, Agent Chandler, nothing has changed as far as the victims of the Star-Crossed Killer are concerned. The investigation is ongoing and intense. We aren't letting up an inch. We're going to use every resource of this department to find that son of a bitch, but now the investigation has widened, taken an unforeseen turn. We're not only looking for a killer who gets off on letting his victims freeze in the wilderness, we're searching for a murderer with another reason to kill as well. Maybe something deep and personal. A vendetta, perhaps. I'd say the psychological profile of Star-Crossed just changed, so we're going to adapt." He was standing now, leaning across the table, the tic intense and rapid. "But it's my intention, no, make that my personal mission, to find the twisted prick and throw his ass in jail before he takes another life!" He looked around the table. "Now, let's make it happen."

They all scooted back their chairs and picked up their papers and coffee cups, but as Alvarez made her way back to the desk, she glanced out the window at the steely clouds and blowing snow that caked against the windows.

The storm wasn't abating.

Nor was the Star-Crossed Killer.

He wasn't finished and he told them so in the notes he'd left at each killing ground.

There was no note near Brady Long's body.

In that respect, Alvarez felt, sliding into her desk chair, Grayson was right. Long was a departure. Maybe killed by an accomplice? Or because he knew something? There had to be a connection. One that wasn't yet obvious.

Another copycat? That seemed beyond coincidental.

Then what?

She picked up copies of other missing persons reports, of women who seemed to have disappeared in the last six weeks. Flipping through the pages,

reading the names as she looked at pictures from
driver's licenses, or graduation photos, or snapshots
taken by loved ones, Alvarez's heart sank.

Patricia Sorenson.

Alma Rae Dodge.

Holly Benjamin.

Tawilda Conrad.

Those were just a few, and every one was a possible victim of the Star-Crossed Killer. Alvarez tucked
the pictures aside and walked to Pescoli's desk.
Messy. Unkempt. Photos of her two kids tacked to a
bulletin board along with notes and reports and her
calendar.

Alvarez hoped to hell she was still alive.

"Hang in there," she whispered, touching the
desktop before sitting down at Pescoli's desk and
switching on her computer. Zoller and a computer
geek had gone through everything, but Alvarez
wanted to look for herself.

"Where the hell are you?" she wondered aloud,
her headache coming back with a vengeance as she
went through her partner's favorite bookmarked
Web sites, then searched her recent history, and finding nothing that would help.

Alvarez sighed, thought about Jeremy cooling his
heels in a jail cell, and wondered if anything would
ever go right. She hadn't had a chance to talk to
Grayson about the kid, and Brewster was still pissed
as hell, so for now, Jeremy would sit. Unless Lucky
Pescoli wanted to step up to the plate.

Unlikely.

And it didn't hurt Jeremy to think about his actions even though the fight really had been insti-
gated by Brewster, the second in command. *Great
role model, Cort. Way to be a good cop and a Christian.*

Alvarez closed her eyes and rubbed her temples. They needed a break in the case. In the weather. In anything. Learning nothing more, she headed back to her own cubicle and nearly tripped over the secretary.

"Press conference is starting!" Joelle announced as she flipped on a red cape decorated with felt Santa faces appliquéd onto the scarlet background. To Alvarez they seemed to be leering, and more creepy than cute. "Aren't you going to stand by the sheriff?" She tugged on a pair of black gloves and walked toward the front doors.

Of course, Alvarez thought, reaching for her jacket.

"I can't be there," Joelle added. "I promised my niece I'd take her to see Santa Claus. He'll be down at the courthouse tonight during the concert in the park."

"Tonight?" Alvarez glanced to the darkened, frozen window.

"Bad weather doesn't stop Santa," Joelle said. "He lives at the North Pole, you know."

"Does he?"

"Of course." Joelle flashed a bright smile, then pulled the hood of her cape up over her bouffant hairstyle. A white ball topped the hood, making it more, Alvarez assumed, festive. "You know, Selena, it wouldn't hurt you to believe just a little. I know that we're in a bad way here, a real pickle, but that doesn't mean you can't believe in the spirit of Christmas."

"Really?"

"Mm-hmm."

Alvarez zipped up her jacket and headed for the double doors that would lead outside to the spot on the porch where the press had gathered. Some of Joelle's advice she'd take to heart. When it came to Sheriff Grayson, Alvarez would stand by him until kingdom came and went again. Grayson was a good man. A smart, determined civil servant. He spoke with authority and conviction, he backed up his beliefs with action and took the duties and responsibilities of a sheriff to heart.

But tonight, she thought, as the winter wind whipped through her and rattled the chains on the flagpole, dumping more and more snow over the ground, Grayson was kidding himself. She hoped beyond hope that they would be able to stop Star-Crossed before he struck again. She wanted desperately to believe that no more bodies would be discovered.

But she was a realist.

Santa Claus didn't exist.

And Star-Crossed was going to kill again.

Chapter Nineteen

Soon, I think, as I sit at my table, my neat boxes of notes, pictures, IDs, and personal treasures spread around me, the fire burning soft and hissing snake-like, reminding me of my purpose.

Yes, Elyssa's time will be soon. The storm is supposed to slow a bit, which will make conditions perfect for a lesson in survival . . . just like my own. How many times did my mother take me into the snowy wilderness and advise me on the skills of survival and what it would take for me to "become a man"? She, the bitch, was right, of course, but I always thought my father should have been there to stop her from leaving me to find my way home in mid-winter. She encouraged me to live off the land and I learned to shoot small prey at an early age. I was good at it. Received her rare praise and found deep satisfaction in controlling the destiny of some other living thing. Should that jackrabbit live? Could I really kill a squirrel from a hundred feet?

Could I lie still and motionless long enough for the doe to leave her fawn?

Yes, my mother taught me much.

And my father . . . he left me to my own devices and my mother's authority.

Thanks a lot, Dad.

I pour myself a drink and push aside the fuzzy memories of my youth. I'm much too tired to take Elyssa out today, and I still want to relish the memory of the last seconds of Brady Long's life. I sip the cool drink, feel it slide down my throat and begin to warm my blood. Just one drink. No more. I still have much to do.

Elyssa, the twit, is able to walk again, and she's been here long enough to trust me, yet be anxious about leaving. Tomorrow is Christmas Eve. Maybe then I'll take her outside. I'll have to be extra attentive to her tonight, just in case. Ease her concerns and witness how far she's willing to go to bend to my will.

She's a pretty thing.

But dull.

Unlike Regan Pescoli.

I look at the door to Pescoli's room again, think about her lying on the cot. She'd kill me if she could, and that's interesting. A challenge. Makes my blood sing in my veins. I can't wait until it's her turn.

But not yet. There is a plan, remember? One you must stick to.

My gaze slides across the table to the neat stack of notes I've worked so painstakingly to create. Starting with the first, Theresa Charleton and her initials:

T   C

How exciting the schoolteacher had been! I spread my copy of that note—the one I left for the police to find—on the table, checking the position of the star over the letters. Did they have any idea that the position of that particular heavenly body was precise? That it changed with each of the notes as I left them with the women? Nina Salvadore, the computer programmer and mother, was the second, and Wendy Ito, the fiery Asian woman who mistakenly thought her martial arts training would save her, was third. *Think again, bitch. All those lessons didn't help!*

Rona Anders, a drab, drab woman, who had kept whining about her fiancé, was next, and finally it was Hannah Estes's turn—the bitch who had been found alive, rescued, and nearly survived. That had been close. She could have pointed me out in a lineup, but without her my message to the police would not be complete.

I eye my copies of the notes I left. So perfect. Even to the precise location of each different star in the sky. Could the police guess? Were they smart enough to figure out what I was telling them?

They now had five notes. Soon they would be studying the end message, trying to solve the puzzle of it, attempting to insert the initials of the two women they will find in the near future, wondering if there are more bodies stiff with the cold, dead and waiting in the vast forest.

I smile and take another drink, allowing a melting ice cube to slide slowly into my mouth.

WAR THESC I N

Will the cops be smart enough to figure out where the new initials will fit into the message? Will the FBI agents be able to help, with all their computer programmers and cryptographers? I doubt it. After all, they're led by that useless piece of flesh with a badge, good old Sheriff Dan Grayson.

I snort at the thought of him. What a poor excuse for the keeper of security for the county! I bet he's squirming now. Good. I love the fact that I get to deal with him and he, who has been touted as so smart, so clever . . . has no friggin' clue.

Maybe I should help Grayson and his pack of cretins out . . . even give them a little taste of what is to come. It would be nice to shake them up a little after their incredible gaffe of chasing after the wrong person . . . a woman, no less.

Desperate, that's what they are.

I spy the notes that I've planned to use in the future. Perfect copies waiting to be tacked to the trees over the heads of the appropriate women. Hmmm.

It's taken years of planning—*years*—because the time has to be right; the potential women with the right initials to be driving through the Bitterroots. I have backup plans, of course. Groupings of women with the same initials who are potential targets, because it's a damned hard trick to make the message work. That, too, can change, as I have several potential notes that will spell out essentially the same warning. So my bases are covered.

The tidy boxes I've kept, dozens of them with notes and files on all the women, prospective candidates for my work. They're alphabetized by name, have pictures attached, usually taken discreetly by my cell phone, or even with the woman's permission. I have cards on each one with information about where they work, where they're from, what they like to do, and most *importantly,* their travel plans.

Many, hundreds, have been discarded. Their names weren't right, they had no plans to drive through the mountains in this part of Pinewood County. Those are mostly the ones I met years before, when my plan was first forming.

I sip the vodka while the fire burns brightly and Pescoli plots her escape on the other side of the door. I don't yet know how she plans to do it, but it will be done, I'm sure. I wish now that I'd hidden a small camera in the room and make a note to myself to do so in the future.

It's one detail I hadn't thought of when drawing up my plan. I replace several boxes, slide them into their individual slots in a cupboard I built years before. Oh, yes, this has been a long time in the making.

Mother, I think, would be proud.

At my attention to detail.

I mentally pat myself on the back for my patience. It has served me well over time—while waiting for the perfect shot, or for anticipating that the right woman driver will make a trek over the mountains, or for the exact moment to kill Brady Long.

And it has been worth every second of the wait.

I have to remind myself to hold on to my patience as well as my temper in dealing with the detective. She has a way of rattling my nerves, making me edgy and unsure, sparking my temper into anger.

And that won't do.

Not yet.

I look at the door of her silent room again.

I feel my rage, but I'll keep it under rein.

For a little longer.

And then . . . ?

I crack the ice cube with my teeth.

And then, watch out.

Annette buzzed Jalicia just as she was packing up to go home for the evening. "Mr. Tinneman's on line one."

"All right," she said.

"Should I put him through?"

"Go ahead," the doctor said, frowning a bit. She'd hardly heard from anyone about Padgett Long and now Padgett's father's attorney had called three times in one day.

"Dr. Ramsby?" the lawyer said, sounding ruffled. "I'm glad I caught you before you left."

"Is there something I can help you with?" She glanced at the clock. It was late and getting later, and she wanted nothing more than to head home to a nice meal, a stir-fry she would make for herself.

"After I talked to you, I went over to visit Mr. Long, Padgett's father."

"How is he?" Jalicia asked.

There was the slightest hesitation on the line. "Not well. I'm not breaking any attorney/client confidentiality here. It's a known fact. The care-givers at Regal Oaks won't commit to a time line, you understand, but I wouldn't expect him to live out the week."

"I'm sorry." He'd said as much earlier.

"But there's been an unexpected complication. A tragedy. The real reason I called you. Hubert Long's only son, Brady, Padgett's brother, was killed today."

"Killed," she repeated, shocked, a protective hand

automatically covering her heart. "In some kind of accident?"

"I'm afraid it's a homicide, Dr. Ramsby. The police are being pretty tight-lipped in Grizzly Falls, but I have confirmed that Brady Long is dead."

Jalicia blinked, processing. "Homicide?"

"It would seem. It's all over the news in Montana."

"How? What . . . ? I'm sorry." She kept apologizing. For people she'd never met. But they were Padgett's family. Her only family? And within the week it was likely they would both be gone.

Her mind was already skipping ahead. She rolled her chair back to the file cabinet and unlocked it to find the paperwork on Padgett Long: three thick files.

"This tragedy has us all—boggled—a little."

"Yes."

"This is all a delicate subject as Mr. Long is still alive. But we have to plan for the inevitable, since it will affect Padgett's care somewhat."

"I understand."

"Hubert's been informed of Brady's death, and he has a request."

"About Padgett?"

"Yes."

Hauling all three manila-bound files, Jalicia rolled her chair back to the desk, opening the most recent information on her patient. She then clicked onto her computer to gather information in the database, where most of the intelligence was kept.

"Padgett Long will be Hubert Long's sole survivor now. His sole heir."

So there were no other living relatives to the estate, and Tinneman was sorting through an unexpected turn.

"There's a trust set up for Padgett, of course," he went on, "And as she's—infirm—the estate will always see that she's cared for. But there is another area that needs to be addressed . . ."

"What is that?" she asked when his pause stretched into uncomfortable silence.

"If you check through your files, the old ones, where it shows when Padgett was admitted, you'll see, I believe, that she spent a little time—just about four months—at another institution."

"Okay." She pushed the two most recent documents aside and concentrated on the one that was fifteen years old. Some of the pages had yellowed and had that musty smell of disuse. Cradling the phone between her shoulder and ear, she carefully turned through the pages in the oldest folders. "I've got her records in front of me."

"Good. That institution is Cahill House in San Francisco."

"I'm looking, Mr. Tinneman, but I don't see anything."

"I'm sure you have a copy."

"There are a lot of pages. I might need some time to peruse the file closely. Oh, wait . . ." She ran her finger down a yellowed page and there, in faded letters, she read: *Transfer from Cahill House*. The notation was buried deep in the first three typed pages of Padgett's admission form. Jalicia rechecked the computer and frowned. This same information had seemingly been omitted when it was transferred to the database. "I've got it. Cahill House in San Francisco?" The address was barely legible. "Is that a private hospital? I've never heard of it."

"No, not a hospital. Not really." His voice was a little strained, as if his collar were suddenly too tight. "It's owned by the Cahill family and has been for generations. It's a place where girls can stay who find themselves—in trouble."

Jalicia squinted at the phone. "You mean pregnant?" First she'd heard the strain of Brady Long's unexpected death in his voice, now he'd started tiptoeing through the words. Embarrassment over an unwanted pregnancy? Was he reflecting Hubert Long's viewpoint?

"Yes, she was pregnant."

"Did she go full term?" Dr. Ramsby asked, when Tinneman shut himself down again.

"She gave the child—a boy—up for adoption."

Jalicia leaned back in her chair, absorbing. Her gaze looked out the window to the pale winter sunlight filtering through the clouds, and she thought of the woman in room 126 with the blue, blue eyes, the hidden intelligence that lurked there. "Willingly?" she asked.

"Of course."

"The woman who hasn't spoken a word since she's been here, she agreed to give up her baby?"

"What are you suggesting, Dr. Ramsby?" he asked tersely.

"I haven't seen any indication that Padgett Long could make that kind of decision on her own."

"Padgett signed the adoption papers for her son and they were sealed," he stated flatly.

Had Padgett really ever been competent to sign away her child? Jalicia wondered. Then again, what

would she have done with a baby? "Let me understand what's happening here, Mr. Tinneman. Are
you afraid that Padgett's child is going to find out
that he or she was born into a very wealthy family
and will want his or her share of the inheritance?"

"I'm afraid it runs deeper than that," Tinneman
said, his voice tense.

"How so?"

"It's Mr. Long's wish that he meet his grandson
before he dies. He's obsessed with finding the boy.
Especially now, with Brady's death."

"And this boy, his grandson, has lived with another family for his entire life."

"I understand it may be a surprise to him, but I
doubt that the parents would object to their son
meeting his biological family, given the circumstances."

Dr. Ramsby didn't like the subtext: because the
Longs were a family of wealth. "What are you asking
me to do?"

"We just want help in finding the boy. Mr. Long is
willing to be extremely generous with him and his
family."

Jalicia thought she understood. "You plan to make
him an offer, maybe keep him from attempting to
make a claim on the estate?"

"Before you make assumptions, Dr. Ramsby, consider that the costs of raising a child through college are significant, even, in some cases, impossible.
And there are all kinds of other expenses in raising
a child as well, so, yes, there are monetary consider-
ations. And Mr. Long plans to be very generous.
Very." His unctuous tone sent a frisson down Jalicia's back. "And consider this: when found, the boy

will finally learn his biological family history, personal and medical. It will give him a sense of who he is in the world and help everyone concerned."

"What about his father?"

"What?"

"Padgett's son's biological father."

"He's out of the picture." Said quickly. Dismissively.

"Did he even know he was going to have a child?"

"I don't know."

"But you were a part of this adoption, or your firm was." She flipped through document after document on the Sargent, McGill, and Tinneman letterhead. "There are laws governing father's rights, Mr. Tinneman."

"I know the law."

"Who is he?"

"Padgett never named the father," he said tautly. "She's the only one who knows who he is."

"And she's not talking." Literally. Dr. Ramsby glanced at the picture of her own daughter, grinning into the camera near the bud vase. Clarice was fourteen, about the same age as Padgett's missing son.

"She's never mentioned anything in any of your sessions?" There was a note of hope in the attorney's voice.

"Now we're talking doctor/patient privilege."

"Finding this boy would be a big help. Hubert Long would be eternally grateful. To you. To Mountain View. If you could talk to Padgett for him . . . ?"

"I think you need to take this matter up with"—she glanced at her notes—"someone at Cahill House. They have the records."

"I already tried that," he said swiftly. "They won't

release any information about the case to anyone but Padgett."

So the oily lawyer was trying to come in through the back door.

"Doctor Ramsby—"

"I can't discuss this any further. If you, or anyone else, wants to come and visit Padgett, talk with her yourself, then you're welcome to do so. But I can't help you in that matter. Thank you for informing me of my patient's brother's death. I'll make certain she knows." Dr. Ramsby hung up, shaking her head. Families. Always a trial. And Tinneman . . . the lawyer knew better than to try to wrangle information from her, information she couldn't give him. Jalicia had never met Tinneman, but she didn't like him and decided he was a true snake in the grass.

And what did all this mean for Padgett Long?

Chapter Twenty

He was back.

The son of a bitch was in the next room, humming to himself, stoking the fire or cooking or doing . . . whatever the hell it was he did on the other side of the door. Regan watched his shadow move around the adjoining area that she'd only caught glimpses of when he opened the door and came into "her" quarters to leave her food, or water, or take the damned bucket he'd given her to relieve herself in, or to stoke the fire.

In those glimpses of his living area, she'd seen parts of a long table, and a heavy armoire and bookcases on the one wall that was in her line of vision. She wondered what kind of job, if any, he held and, of course, as she lay fighting the cold and the darkness, she always wondered who he was.

Why did she feel she knew him?

Holding the scratchy blanket tight to her chin as the fire burned ever lower, the scent of wood smoke strong, Pescoli had thought about all the criminals she'd busted over the years and she hadn't been able to come up with a name or face that she could place on this maniac.

None of them fit.

She'd arrested a number of thugs who'd threatened her or those she loved, but their taunts had proven idle, a spitting out of rage and trampled pride as the lowlifes had been hauled away to jail to contemplate their misdeeds and fester their hate of cops, the system, and her. But once they were released, to a one, they avoided her like the plague.

This mutt was different.

His rage was darker.

And leveled not only at her, but at other women as well, and authority. She'd felt his hostility like an entity in the room with them, sensed that he was sneering at her despite his sometimes smooth and cajoling tone. As if he cared about her.

She didn't believe the son of a bitch for a second.

And now that he was back and she couldn't keep at her futile attempts at escape, she had to unmask him. More importantly, she had to stop him.

Before he killed her.

A tall order.

One she couldn't fill handcuffed.

She saw shadows moving under the door and realized he'd walked toward her room only to stop on the other side of the threshold.

No doubt the depraved prick was even now peeking inside. What a perv! She forced her body to quit quivering, set her jaw, and glared up at the small peephole in the door, silently and defiantly daring him to come inside.

If she could talk to him some more, she might

learn who he was, where this damned lair was located, and what his plans were. If she didn't lose her temper and just kept him going on.

As if reading her mind, he clicked open the door and stepped into the dark room. A wedge of light illuminated her austere quarters and she caught a glimpse of her own clothing, folded neatly by the fire. Was her weapon there, too? What about her phone? All she could see were her jeans, sweater, jacket, and shoes.

"What?" he mocked.

Trying to make out the contours of his face, she squinted up at him, holding the blanket over her body. The fire had nearly died, the temperature in the room was not a lot of degrees above freezing, and the light was so weak, only brightening the area just skirting the stove, that she was thwarted. And those hideous goggles and ridiculous beard.

He kicked the door shut. It closed with a solid thud that jarred Pescoli, put her even more on edge. *Don't let him get to you, it's all part of his game. Play it cool.* But the door closing seemed the knell of death, reinforcing the fact that there was no escape, that she was locked in here, prey to whatever vile fantasies his sick mind concocted.

"So, Detective . . ." His voice was a raspy whisper that crawled across her skin. "Your escape plan isn't working."

Her pulse jumped. *He knows about that? Has he been secretly watching me? Filming me? Laughing at my impotent attempts to free myself?*

"You may as well give up. Whatever you've decided to do, it won't work." He was stepping closer to her, standing tall, trying to intimidate her as she was forced to lie or sit, naked on the cot.

He had a ski hat on with blond hair poking from it, but she thought even his hair might be fake. He was going to a lot of trouble not to be recognized.

"Hungry?" he asked.

As if he cared. The truth was her stomach was turned inside out with fear; she wouldn't be able to swallow a bite.

"No?"

She didn't respond and he cocked his head, studying her like a bird eyeing an interesting insect scuttling on the ground. "You know, Red, I expected more from you." Mock disappointment was audible in his raspy voice. "A little bit of fire. This passive-aggressive act isn't really working."

"I'm not acting."

"Ah. She speaks. At last." He seemed pleased and Pescoli mentally kicked herself for saying anything. *But you have to engage him, draw him out, make him say something that will trip him up or give you some clue as to his plans. Is there cell service up here, wherever this place is? An access road? Is it visible from the air? How far from town are you?*

"You don't know me," she stated flatly.

"Don't I?"

He was so smug, she felt a needle of doubt pierce her heart. Was he someone close to her? Who? "Then why don't you let me see your face?"

"Where's the fun in that?"

"This is fun?" she asked.

"Of course it is." Jesus, he was enjoying himself.

"Oh, sure. A riot," she mocked and moved to a sitting position, keeping the blanket covering her, her handcuffed right wrist holding her hand down by the cot's leg. Her left wrist, linked by the chain to her right, lay against her right thigh.

"You're modest," he said, obviously enjoying himself. "That surprises me. I thought you wouldn't be so shy."

You don't know the half of it, jerk-off.

He scratched at the back of his neck. Maybe his fake hair was itching. If she could just pull off his hat, wig, and goggles, get a good look at his eyes, she was certain she'd be able to place him.

What good will that do if you can't get free?

Pescoli wanted to deck the jerk-wad, to knock him flat and peel off his disguise. "Like I said, you don't know me at all."

"Really?" He placed a finger against his chin like a bad stage actor trying to portray being lost in thought. "I know that you've been married twice, to losers both of them. They both cheated on you, right? But you got Joe, your college sweetheart, back by sleeping with someone else."

Her blood was boiling, but she bit her tongue. Let him rant. Maybe if he gave up some bit of information he considered useless, she might glean something about him, something that would ultimately give her a clue to his identity.

"That's right . . . you were separated from Joe at the time, so that made it okay for you to act like the slut you really are."

He was enjoying her humiliation. Pacing from one side of the room to the other. Walking past her cot as she held the blanket over her. Coming closer with each pass. "What? No defense, Red?" And he seemed edgy. Good. This was better. Let him get agitated. Maybe he'd slip up.

She said nothing and she noticed, through the shadows, a tightening of his lips, not quite completely hidden by his beard.

"And now you're sleeping with another scumbag."

She felt the muscles in her back tighten. He could damned well leave Santana out of it. It was all she could do to remain quiet. Still. When she wanted to kill him.

"And you're supposed to be so smart, Red. Clever. Able to figure things out. Save lives." Again the clucking sound echoed through the chamber. He even chuckled, as if at her ineptitude. "But you're a failure. Your own life's a mess. Here you are, the captive rather than the captor. Pinewood County's finest. Handcuffed with your own set of cuffs. Ironic, don't you think?"

He was pissing her off but good, which sent adrenaline pouring through her veins. "Guess we're all a bit dull here in the Bitterroots, huh?" she drawled.

He stopped suddenly and bared his teeth, hands clenching. For a moment she thought he would lose the hold on his own control. She braced herself, but then, after a moment, he resumed pacing.

"It's a wonder you were ever hired," he shot back. "You're a miserable excuse for both a woman and a detective."

As she watched him stalk back and forth she had a vision of someone she'd seen before . . . someone walking down a hallway at the department, someone . . . she couldn't quite grab hold of the image. But she was certain she'd seen him while she'd been working. And then there were all of his disparaging remarks about cops. What was it about him and the sheriff's department? Something in his talk suggested that he had a personal axe to grind, that the Pinewood County Sheriff's Department was his personal source of ridicule.

Why?

Had he not been able to get help when he needed it? Had the department made a mistake and someone he cared about been hurt or killed? Had he been personally wounded so badly by the department or some other arm of the law that he was out to show up cops, specifically the cops of Pinewood County? Or was he just a criminal who hated all cops?

He sure as hell didn't like being needled.

Carefully, she observed him pace, getting closer, silently taunting her for being chained to the cot. His confidence had returned after her jab and he was almost swaggering as he passed and she wondered . . . if he got close enough . . . could she get the jump on him? He would have to be very close because her one wrist was secured low, but she had to try. She had no doubt that the son of a bitch was going to kill her.

"But you're not alone in your failure," he said. "Do you know that your esteemed team of crack deputies and even . . . yes," he was shaking his head now at the ineptitude of the police, "even the FBI were duped recently by a copycat?"

"A copycat?"

"Chandler and Halden, they flew up with Dan Grayson to Spokane."

This was a lie.

"They thought they were going to break the case wide open and make a big bust, take down the Star-Crossed Killer," he snarled. "And what did they get?" He stopped in front of her, staring at her through the amber lenses of the goggles. "Nothing! A big fat goose egg." He snorted in disdain. "They arrested a goddamned *woman* who was pretending to be me." He stared at her as Regan puzzled through his words.

"Oh, that's right. You didn't know, did you? After I shot your tire out, Grayson and the dynamic duo were chasing their tails in Spokane."

There had been a copycat killer? One good enough to fool the FBI and the sheriff's department? It didn't seem right and yet, her captor was so damned serious . . .

"I thought you'd like to know what your colleagues have been up to for the last day or so," he said, nearing her. She felt all of her muscles coil. One or two more steps. "Chasing around in circles like the idiots they are."

Her heart was pounding, but she tried to remain outwardly passive. If he would just step a little closer . . .

Her blanket slipped a fraction and she saw his attention tighten as he stopped right by her.

Close enough!

She shifted, swept her legs straight out from the cot and jammed him hard. White-hot pain ricocheted up her leg as he rocked on his feet. The blanket tangled his ankles and he lost his footing and fell.

"Ahhgg!" He hit hard, his chin slamming into the hard stones.

"Shit!"

Regan was on him in an instant, the short tether of her handcuffs keeping her close to the cot.

Before he could get to his feet, she yanked up on his hair, stretching his neck and wrapping the links of her handcuffs under his throat.

"Hey!"

She pulled harder, the chain digging into his soft flesh.

He made a strangled cry, tried to roll away.

Naked, riding his back, she pulled as hard as she could, trying desperately to cut off his air.

But he was writhing. Fighting her, his surprise giving way to fury. "You bitch!" he sputtered, rearing up, nearly pulling her arm out of its socket.

Pain bristled through her torso and she cried out.

Still she hung on his back.

He tried to get to his feet, but she drew her knee up, splitting his butt cheeks, trying to hit his testicles.

She kicked.

Her knee connected.

He let out a howl that echoed through the rooms. Reverberated through her mind.

"Bitch! Goddamned—" His words were cut off, his breath whistling and wet.

Die, you son of a bitch! Die!

Gasping and frantic, he dug wildly at the chain closing off his windpipe with his fingers.

Pescoli's arm felt as if it were being wrenched from her body.

He twisted and turned, his fingernails raking his skin as he tried to force them between the skin over his windpipe and the sharp, tiny loops of steel.

Gritting her teeth, she pulled harder, hoping to close his windpipe forever. Her shoulder screamed in pain. Was on fire. It was all she could do to hang on. *Don't let go. If you do, it's over! Hold on! For God's sake, pull!*

Again he reared, trying to get to his knees. Attempting to shake her off.

She clung like a burr.

He struggled.

And she saw the back of his neck.

Without thinking, she leaned forward, teeth bared. She bit down. Hard into the flesh where his shoulder and head connected. Tasted salt and sweat.

He shrieked in pain.

She bit harder. Closing her teeth.

If she could nick his jugular vein or carotid artery, he would bleed out. Her teeth ripped into his flesh.

He bucked hard.

She nearly flew off. Twisted. She heard something pop in her arm. A tendon give way.

Blood flowed. Metallic. Salty. Running from his body into her mouth.

Keep at it!

Don't let go!

He was sputtering now. Writhing and screaming. Determined to throw her off. He flipped over, so she was beneath him.

Bam!

The back of her head crashed against the stone floor. Her right wrist felt as if it were severed from her arm.

Pain exploded behind her eyes.

Her jaw slacked and he tossed his head away from her.

Using both arms, she ignored her pain and pulled even harder on her cuffs, determined to choke him.

He pressed his weight down hard, crushing her. Her spine popped, her bare skin rubbed raw by the bare, cold stones. God, he was heavy. So heavy. And strong. Her lungs felt as if they couldn't move, her bruised ribs ached. Her wrist . . . *Help me,* she thought, barely able to draw a breath.

No, no, no. Don't give up. You can't.

She bit into him again, blood streaming from her mouth.

She felt as if she were drowning. Her lungs burning, blood filling the back of her mouth, as he shoved her even harder into the floor.

She tried to keep up the fight, but her jaw loosened as she struggled for air.

He was gurgling, still trying to pull the chain from his neck. Then he switched tactics. He convulsed, crashing his elbow backward. The joint landed with bone-jarring accuracy against her ribs.

"Aaaawwww," she cried, sputtering blood. The blow felt as if it shattered two of her healing ribs.

Pain rocketed through her chest.

She nearly blacked out.

He threw his head back. *Crack!* His skull hit her forehead and crushed the bridge of her nose.

More pain. Agonizing and brutal.

More feeling of drowning in a sea of blood.

She gasped, sputtering and spitting, still holding to her cuffs as if for her life. But her strength was slipping away and he grabbed hard on the chain, pulling it away from his neck, gulping for breath.

No! She couldn't let him get the upper hand.

Oh, for the love of God . . .

She fought to hold on, but it was too late. Her muscles no longer obeyed her mind. Vainly, desperately, she tried to keep the chain looped around his neck tight, but he shifted and pulled against her arm, twisting until she yelled.

Don't give up, Regan, do not give up . . . Oh God, help me. Please, please, please! Like lightning, blinding pain sizzled up her arm and shoulder.

She felt the tide turning.

She had no strength left . . . not enough. Nor could she keep up the pressure as he slowly pressed his weight into her, crushing her bruised ribs, intent on breaking them all. He kept up his headbanging as well, hitting her over and over again with the back of his head, pulverizing her face.

Let go, Regan . . . give up . . . you can't do it . . .

She heard the hopelessness and despair in her own words even as her muscles let go. The blood on the chains was slick, and her grip loosened.

With an effort, he peeled her arms over his head and rolled away, the fake beard, now bloody, falling off. She caught a glimpse of his jaw in the semidarkness, the line of his nose. But she was gasping, breathing hard, her vision out of focus, her body shuddering. Lying on the cold sharp stones of the floor, feeling blood, hers and his, drying on her body, she couldn't move, couldn't raise her head.

She felt rather than saw him climb to his feet. Still breathing hard, he whispered, "You'll pay for this, you goddamned cunt." He spat on the floor, his promise still running painfully through her head. "And it starts now."

Fine, she thought. *End it. I'm done.* She was gasping, dragging in air, the taste and feel of him a revulsion. She loathed the man. Hated him. Wearing only his blood, she rolled her head to one side and tried to see him.

"You just sealed her fate."

What the hell was he talking about? *Her* fate? No, she must've misheard. He meant *your* fate. Pescoli was too tired, in too much pain to care about his stupid mind games. She'd tried to escape and had failed miserably. Now he planned on punishing her.

Was he planning to take her into the woods, to lash her to a tree and leave her to freeze to death?

Fine. Bring it on. She'd find a way to escape. If she could just get her strength back, quit hurting for a minute . . .

"You don't get it, do you?" he said as he stood in the shadows at the door.

She didn't care. Couldn't answer.

He cleared his throat, spat again, and swore under his breath. She couldn't be sure, but she thought he held one hand over the back of his neck where she'd nearly torn away his muscle . . .

If she just had been a little stronger.

"You think you're the only one? That there won't be consequences?"

She didn't know what he was talking about.

Didn't care.

She hurt all over. And he'd won.

For now.

"There was a chance she might have survived, but now it's over."

"She?" Did she speak aloud? Or, was it in her head?

He was talking nonsense. Trying to rattle Pescoli, but it wouldn't work. She wouldn't give him the satisfaction. *Just leave me alone,* she wanted to scream. *Leave me be.* She couldn't even muster the strength to try and determine his identity.

"You're just too dumb to understand, aren't you, *Detective.* Too self-centered to think that your actions would affect anyone else."

She was still having trouble breathing, her body starting to shiver almost convulsively with the cold.

"But I'll explain it to Elyssa. *She'll* get it."

Who's Elyssa . . . ? Her mind was shutting down.

"You're not curious?" he mocked. "Don't you want to know whose death sentence you just signed?"

This is a ploy. Only a ploy. Don't buy into it.

With an effort, she rolled an eye in his direction. Deep down, she wanted to call his bluff, to call him a friggin' liar, but something in the way he stood near the door, in the superior tone of his voice, gave her pause.

"Elyssa O'Leary . . . surely you have a missing persons report on her."

Oh, please God, no. The name *was* familiar.

She could almost feel the depravity of his smile crawl through the darkness. "Yes, I see you know her."

It was all making sense now. Sick, horrifying sense as she remembered thinking she'd heard a woman crying, softly sobbing. Pescoli had convinced herself that the woman's broken sobs were only the product of her imagination.

But how . . . ?

Her heart turned to ice.

Cold, horrifying dread pounded through her brain. *Elyssa O'Leary. Missing for several weeks . . . Only child . . . a student of some kind . . .*

"I wasn't sure it was her time. Not yet. I might have given her another week or so . . . let her live through the holidays . . . But you convinced me, Red. She's ready."

This wasn't a bluff. He couldn't know about the O'Leary girl . . . Pescoli licked her lips. Tasted his repugnant sweat and blood all over again. This was wrong. So wrong. "You're a liar," she accused him.

"Only when I have to be, and I certainly don't have to lie about this."

With a sick feeling, she knew he was telling the truth. The son of a bitch had picked this bleak moment for a stab at honesty.

"When the storm breaks tomorrow, she dies. Christmas Eve."

Denial tore through Pescoli's soul. She couldn't let this happen! Wouldn't! "Take me," she whispered.

"Oh, so you do believe me."

She closed her eyes and repeated hoarsely, "Take me." Where there was hope, there was life. If she could buy the girl a few more days, Alvarez and the rest of the department might be able to locate this lair.

"You need to think about what you just did. And there are others, before you . . ."

Others? Plural? Oh, Lord, he plans to harvest more and keep me alive, then taunt me with their deaths! He intends to tell me about each one, every innocent woman that I will be unable to save. This could take weeks, or months . . . or years.

Who knew how many women he planned to kill?

"Then punish me. Please." She hated to plead with him, to buy into his twisted game, but she couldn't have another woman's death on her hands.

"Oh, believe me, I am," he said, his voice smooth as snake oil. "I'm punishing you and tormenting you. Forever. Elyssa O'Leary's death. It will be your fault, Pescoli. Hers and the others. All your fault. Think about that. You signed their death sentences and you'll live knowing you sent them to their fates."

She felt battered inside. Stripped bare. How many did this sick, sick man plan to kill? How many would she know were going to be slaughtered? "You can't do this," she whispered.

"Who's going to stop me? You?"

"The police—"

"Grayson? That cocky buffoon? Or that shrewd

little partner of yours?" he taunted. "How about Nate Santana?"

"You better hope he never finds you."

"Oh. I'm scared. Shivering in my boots."

"You should be." Her voice cut like steel and for a second he actually quit treating her with contempt. "He'll make you wish you were never born."

"Right."

"You can't do this," she repeated and watched as his mouth twisted into a smile of pure evil.

"Watch me."

And then he was gone, the door opening and closing with a thud.

"No, oh . . . oh, please, no," she whispered, bleeding to her soul. Naked, shivering on the floor, Pescoli stared at the dark, closed door and knew with terrifying certainty that she'd just sent an innocent woman to her death.

As surely as if she'd stabbed Elyssa O'Leary in the heart.

Chapter Twenty-One

Screw playing by the rules!

Santana climbed out of his cabin desk chair and walked to the window. There was still a cop car at the main house on the Long estate, but as he watched, it, like all the other county-owned vehicles, pulled away and drove down the long lane, taillights reflecting red against the snow, blinking as the Jeep passed behind trees.

He wondered if he was being watched and found he didn't care. Regan was missing, a maniac was on the loose, and somehow Brady Long's death might be tied to the damned Star-Crossed Killer.

After leaving the police to look into the tire tracks running along the edge of the property, Santana had returned to his cabin with Nakita. The dog had taken up his favorite position near the fire and was snoring softly, but Santana was too keyed up to relax. He'd already taken care of the livestock, then pulled out several maps of the area, including one issued by the forest service, then on the Internet he'd checked the latest satellite and topographical maps.

"Where are you, you son of a bitch?" he muttered as he marked all the locations where the bodies and wrecked cars had been found and decided his map probably duplicated what the Pinewood County Sheriff's Department and FBI had already created. "And who are you?"

Someone who knew Brady Long.

Someone who lives nearby.

Someone who gets his rocks off by taunting the police.

Though the contents of the notes the police had received hadn't been made public, the fact that they existed was well known.

How did it make any sense?

Santana tossed another chunk of oak on the fire, then adjusted the logs with his poker. As he stared at the flames he thought of Regan. Was she alive? Injured? Or . . . was it already too late? His fingers clenched over the smooth metal of the poker and his shoulder muscles bunched.

Inside, he felt a vast hole. An emptiness borne of the unknown, and his own deepening fears.

Never had he felt so useless, so impotent.

"God *damn* it," he gritted through clenched teeth. He refused to let this beat him down. He would find her. One way or another.

Slamming away from the desk, he grabbed his jacket and gloves and headed outside into a clear night, the stars glimmering, tiny pinpoints against the velvety black sky. The first truly clear night in how long? He couldn't remember.

Brady Long's death was tied in with Star-Crossed somehow. If he knew why, he'd be a lot closer to learning who Star-Crossed was. A lot closer to finding Regan.

So why Brady? He'd worked for the man for quite a while; had known him for years. Brady was a privileged, selfish pain in the ass who used people to his own advantage. Clementine was a case in point, though she never disparaged her boss.

Brady had enemies in abundance: two ex-wives, jilted girlfriends, and a slew of business partners he'd screwed over. Any one of them could have wanted him dead. Were probably happy, if the news of his death had reached their ears. But would one of them actually carry out their wish? Pull the trigger and shoot the man in his shriveled heart?

A lot of hate for that.

Nate walked into the barn and turned on the light. The horses snorted and shifted in their stalls. He looked in on Lucifer, whose eyes showed the whites, and he soothed the horse with a soft chant of nonsensical words that calmed the beast enough to have him shuffle close to Nate and even head butt his proffered hand. Nate scratched the colt's head. Animal whisperer? Maybe. But right now all he felt like was a scared, insignificant, and ineffectual human being.

"Brady has two ex-wives," he said aloud.

Lucifer blew through his nose in disdain.

"One was his college sweetheart. A decent woman. He probably made a mistake letting her go, but then maybe she left him. The second one was a gold digger but she made no bones about it. She liked Brady a little, his money a lot. He left her well off when they split and everybody was supposedly happy."

Lucifer moved his lips as if he wanted to speak. Nate felt gripped by emotions and swallowed hard, tamping them down into the pit of his soul. If he wanted to help Regan, he needed a cool head.

"He's got a bunch of jilted girlfriends. And a fiancée, I think, who couldn't quite close the deal in time. Brady's dead. She woulda wanted him alive until after that ceremony.

"And his business partners..." Nate drew a breath. That was a list he didn't possess. "Somebody wanted him dead for some reason, and they wanted him to suffer. If it's Star-Crossed, what's with the women? Leaving them to freeze to death? What's the connection between them and Brady?"

His words echoed softly through the stables. Lucifer snorted and moved away from him, as if he were embarrassed by the last question. Nate reluctantly snapped off the light and walked back into the clear, frigid night.

And it didn't really matter about Brady's ex-wives and girlfriends anyway. A man had killed these women. The way they'd been left to die, freeze, brought back to health to be tortured anew—that wasn't the work of a woman.

Whoever had Regan was male. He could feel it.

And that bastard was one helluva marksman, which should have decisively narrowed the field, but in these parts of Montana, marksmen were thick on the ground.

Back inside the cabin, he felt time slipping away, time that could cost Regan her life. Shedding his jacket and gloves, he walked toward the fire. Nakita's eyes opened expectantly.

"William Aldridge," Nate said to the dog, continuing his dialogue, hoping something would shake loose, tumble from his own lips, provide a clue. "Sandi's ex. He killed most of the animals on display at Wild Will's with his own rifle. Kept the taxidermist fat and happy."

But Aldridge as Star-Crossed?

Nakita's chin rested on his paws, his eyes watching Nate steadily. Santana stopped talking and let his thoughts take over. Bob Simms lived near the canyon, where they found one of the womens' vehicles. The Asian victim. Wendy something-or-other. And Simms was as crazy as they came. A lunatic whose views on government and laws—there shouldn't be any—kinda said it all. He killed and trapped animals for their pelts and hides and meat—permits be damned. He'd run up against the authorities time and again, and Nate suspected his home was boobytrapped. If there was a stand-off, he wasn't sure he'd bet on the police . . .

Could it be Simms? He'd been married once, but that wife was dead. Died in childbirth in the throes of delivering their sixth son. And those boys were terrors, each and every one. Enough to send a sane man over the edge, and Simms's sanity wasn't rock solid as it was. Once upon a time the man had been more stable, less prone to conspiracy theories and boiling rage. Nate recalled that Simms had known Padgett Long, way back when, maybe even had a crush on her, but she, of course, hadn't shown him the least bit of interest. Before Padgett's accident, she'd been the "it" girl around these parts and Bob Simms wasn't even the faintest blip on her radar. And since then Simms had been on a downhill slide.

Who else? Nate asked himself, and came up with another name: Gordon Dobbs, also a marksman,

though he spent most of his time making chainsaw
art and was surprisingly adept at it. Nate was pretty
sure Gordon's wife had left him recently; there'd been
talk in town, though Nate purposely avoided listening to any gossip. Now, he wished he'd opened his
ears a bit more. Could Gordon be morose enough
to kill? To plan these vile deaths? Again, it seemed
unlikely.

Then what about someone on the police force?
Wasn't one of the deputies—Pete Watershed—once
a sniper for the army? Hadn't Santana read an article
last year in the local paper, the *Mountain Reporter*,
that Watershed had tranquilized a marauding black
bear with a perfect shot? And Cort Brewster was always entering some kind of sharpshooting contest
or another. Bragged about his skills. It was tough to
get away from the man and his stories if he caught
you around town. Another reason Santana had steered
clear of Grizzly Falls as much as possible.

But now he needed to get involved. Now he
needed to be in the center of this investigation. For
Regan.

He had to find her!

With renewed purpose, he called the sheriff's department, gave his name, and asked for Selena Alvarez. It was late, but he believed she would be there.
Regan was her partner and, with the little he knew
of Selena Alvarez, he was pretty sure she would still
be on the job.

He was right, for a few moments later she answered carefully, "This is Detective Alvarez. What can
I do for you, Mr. Santana?"

"Brady Long's killer is Star-Crossed. They're one
and the same man. Maybe it hasn't been deter-

mined yet, but it's true. You know it and I know it. Tell me you're working on that assumption."

"I have to work with facts. And that's not a fact."

"But it will be. I'm going on gut instinct, Detective. And I'm going to find this son of a bitch."

"You are not part of this investigation," she reminded him briskly.

"I could help you."

"You would just get in the way."

"You're wrong," he said tautly.

"Let us do our job, Mr. Santana."

He'd seen a bit of the press conference on television with Grayson ducking questions and answering in vague generalities. It had convinced him they were all scratching their heads and covering their asses.

"Go ahead, then. You do yours. I'll do mine."

"What does that mean?" she demanded sharply.

But Santana had already hung up in disgust. It had been a waste of time to call her. He thought for a moment, then took two strides to his desk area. He wasn't the most organized man, but he had a file or two that held important papers. He thumbed through them quickly, grabbing a small note tucked inside, memorizing its contents, then dialing another phone number.

If he was gonna do this, he was gonna need help.

Chris was being a butt! Flopped on her bed, texting like mad, Bianca was practically begging him to come over. Yeah, Dad's idea to have him over was lame, lame, lame, but there was *nothing* to do. *Nothing!* Even Jeremy, that loser, hadn't bothered calling or texting.

But he did escape here, didn't he? Figured that out, somehow.

Everyone in the house was going stir-crazy and the tension was as thick as Michelle's face makeup. Bianca tried not to think about that too much as she sent another text and hoped Chris responded.

He was kinda bugging her.

Did he know she needed him right now?

And what would be the excuse to blow her off this time? That he was playing video games with Zach and Kevin? He could do that anytime.

Sighing, she plucked at a piece of pink thread from the bedspread and looked out the window. The sky was dark, the snow wasn't falling anymore, and a moon was rising, reflecting silver on the trees and ground. "We're going to have a white Christmas," Michelle had told her a week ago.

Big deal. This was Montana. White Christmases happened almost every year, and Bianca was sick to death of them.

She stood up and stared outside, contemplated sneaking out, but knew that she couldn't get away with it. Plus, she didn't have any way to get around.

In the panes of glass, she saw her own watery reflection and she thought about Mom. Where *was* she?

Biting her lip, Bianca nearly jumped from her skin when the phone suddenly rang. Maybe Chris had called the house!

No way. He never phoned her at her dad's.

On the second ring, she heard Michelle, say, "Hello? . . . Yes . . . yes, he's here . . . just a sec," and then louder, "Luke! It's for you."

Bianca headed for her bedroom door but stopped short when she heard Michelle hiss in a whisper, "It's the sheriff's department."

Mom!

Bianca's heart froze.

Her father groaned and she imagined him rolling off the couch though the TV was still on. News, it sounded like, though it was late enough that it was probably on the DVR.

"Is it about Regan?" he asked soberly, and Bianca knew instinctively that she'd learn more if she didn't walk into the room, if she stayed eavesdropping.

"I don't know, but it's her partner," Michelle said. "Wanted to speak with you."

"Christ," he murmured, but he wasn't angry. He sounded as worried as Bianca felt and, just as she suspected, her dad did still care about her mom, if only a little.

"Always something!" Michelle said and in the mirror placed on the wall in the hallway outside the bathroom door, Bianca caught a reflected view of the living room. Her father, hair rumpled, was standing in stocking feet and sweats, blocking her view of the flickering television. Michelle, wearing skinny jeans, a sweater, high-heeled boots, and a frown, was facing him, her arms crossed over her chest and under her boobs so that more cleavage than usual was visible in the V-neck of her fuzzy red sweater.

"This is Luke Pescoli. Yeah . . . Hi . . . What? Jeremy? He did *what*?" Her father heaved an angry sigh and shook his head. "Great." She read the tension in his back. "Yeah . . . Okay . . . Listen, can't you cut the kid a break . . . His mom . . . Well, hell, do you know anything more about Regan?"

Bianca strained forward. The news hadn't been about Mom. Jeremy, somehow, had gotten himself into trouble again. It figured. He had dog food for brains! Cisco was smarter than he was by a long shot.

"Oh. All right. Thanks."

Dad hung up the phone and Michelle said, "What about Regan?"

"Nothing new," was the grim response.

Bianca clutched the jamb to her bedroom and slowly sank to the floor. *Mom, where are you?* She fought back an urge to cry and kept her eyes on the mirror's reflection of Dad and Michelle, whose pretty face had taken on a decidedly tense expression.

"Well, what did Jeremy do?" Michelle demanded.

"Got in a fistfight with Cort Brewster and is in the drunk tank."

"My God." She was annoyed. "Over Brewster's daughter? You're not going to go get him, are you?"

Dad was looking around, as if for his coat. "You think I should leave him there?"

"Yes! He needs to learn some things."

"In the drunk tank at the sheriff's department? With his mother missing, possibly kidnapped?"

"He could have thought of those things first, instead of adding to the problem."

"He could've. But he didn't." Dad was starting to get annoyed right back.

Michelle instantly switched tactics, reaching for him, one hand gently patting his chest. "Let him just think about a few things, that's all I'm saying. I don't want a big scene tonight, so let's put it off till tomorrow, hmm? Maybe we can pretend that we don't have your kids with us. Like it's supposed to be."

Bianca surfaced from her fear and misery to really look at her stepmother. Her dad was looking at her, too.

"What do you mean?" he demanded.

"I didn't mean anything," she said quickly. "I just—miss—having you all to myself, that's all. I don't want you chasing after Jeremy tonight."

Dad heaved a sigh. Bianca suddenly, urgently, wanted him to go get Jeremy, bring him back, bring him home, but Michelle had gotten to him. "It wouldn't kill him to spend a few hours in lockup," he growled.

Michelle wrapped her arms around his neck and kissed him in a way that made Bianca want to puke. She eased away from the door and back inside the bedroom. She felt angry and hurt. Michelle didn't want them around, her and Jer. It was all an act. It had always been an act, she realized now.

Oh, Mom, come and get me! she silently pleaded. *Hurry. I'm sorry. I don't want to live with them. Come home!*

Cisco trotted into the room. As if sensing her emotions, he came over to her and pressed his paws against her legs, looking up at her anxiously. She scooped him close and he licked her face, something that would've seemed gross before but now she welcomed.

"Oh, doggie," she said brokenly, burying her face into his fur.

Mom, please be okay. Please, please, please, be okay.

"Any word on finding Pescoli?" Brewster asked, sticking his head in Alvarez's office.

"No." Selena was terse.

The undersheriff nodded and looked grim. He'd cooled off a bit over Jeremy, and Selena had called

Lucky and told him where Jeremy was, but currently the kid was still in the drunk tank with Ivor Hicks. No one seemed to know what the next step should be, though Selena had made it clear she thought Jeremy should be released. She'd said as much to his stepfather, but Lucky hadn't said whether he was coming down to collect him, which was just as well, she supposed, since Brewster probably would have tried to stop him.

"You should go home," he said.

"I'll go home when the sheriff goes home." She was bugged that, after all his bad behavior, Cort Brewster felt he could tell her what she should do.

"Grayson's still here?"

We're all still here, Selena wanted to say. Nobody wanted to leave with Regan at the mercy of this monster.

As if hearing his name, Grayson appeared in the hallway and stopped beside Brewster. "Jeremy's stepdad coming to pick him up?" he asked Alvarez.

"That kid's not leaving tonight," Brewster cut in. He might have cooled off, but he sure as hell wasn't giving in.

Grayson gave him a long look. "That kid's mom is missing."

"He hit me," Brewster ground out.

"I've seen the tape," Grayson returned.

Brewster whipped around to glare at Selena, who he knew had to have requested the tape be given to the sheriff. She returned his gaze coolly. Let him try to shift blame to her. The tape told the truth of the story.

"He's going to be released," Grayson told the undersheriff. "Alvarez . . ."

"I'll get it done." She got up from her desk.

"That damn punk hit me first!" Brewster said again, more forcefully.

"He's being released, and you're not pressing charges." Grayson was immovable.

"Oh, yes, I am! I don't care whose kid he is! And I don't like his influence on my daughter. And I want him to know it."

"I suggest you give this some more thought," Grayson said pointedly.

Brewster bit back what he was going to say and Alvarez, hoping to defuse the situation, said, "Nate Santana called. Wanted to be part of the investigation. I told him to let us do our job, but he sounded unconvinced."

"Jesus, what a loser," Brewster muttered, and Selena wondered if he meant Santana or Jeremy. Didn't really matter.

She had to push Brewster out of the way of the door as she headed into the hall.

"And send Hicks home, too," Grayson said to both Brewster and Alvarez. "Call his son."

"I already left a message for Bill," Brewster said. "But the old guy's probably sober enough now to release on his own."

Grayson grunted. "Get 'em both out of the drunk tank and let's concentrate on what really matters: who this bastard is, and where he's keeping Pescoli."

"Are we staying here all night?" Brewster asked.

"Leave, if you want," Grayson said.

"I was just thinking we didn't need to pay out more overtime," he said lamely.

Alvarez turned down the hall, knowing she wouldn't

be heading to her apartment anytime soon. She couldn't. Not until she was beyond exhaustion and she felt there was nothing further she could do to help Pescoli.

Regan lay on the cot, beaten and battered. She hurt all over, but not as much as her mind told her she ought to. Maybe she was dying. Maybe the fight had ruptured something inside her that was slowly killing her.

No. No, she didn't believe that. There was something she had to do.

Save them.

She opened her eyes to almost total darkness. The fire was nothing but glimmering red coals. She was clutching the blanket with a death grip; she'd grabbed it for warmth in a twilight state of floating pain.

She had to save the other victims. Had to.

She couldn't let the bastard win.

Carefully, she lifted her right wrist, about all the energy she had left. It was scraped raw, through more layers of skin than she believed a human possessed. Blood was everywhere. Hers. His, too, undoubtedly.

But as much as she hurt, as injured as she was, she couldn't give up.

Setting her teeth, she slid to the edge of the cot and looked down at the weld. Her fight with her captor had taken a toll on it. An unexpected bonus for her. It looked very weak. Maybe weak enough to break?

Regan's heart started pounding a deep, painful

tattoo. If she could summon her strength, she might be able to free herself.

But would it be in time to save Elyssa and the others?

Determinedly, closing her eyes, clenching her teeth, she yanked hard on her right handcuff.

Chapter Twenty-Two

Jeremy gazed around the room, holding his breath. Two days until Christmas and he was stuck here in this drunk tank with an old man who smelled like a brewery and looked really crazy. The way his eyes, when he was awake, stared wide behind those huge glasses gave Jeremy the creeps.

And the cell itself was gross. Cement floor, cement walls, painted an ugly gray, harsh overhead light with a metal cage around it, and metal benches bolted into the wall. No window, just the front doors of the cage, which were thick bars of dull steel.

"It's all Crytor's fault," the old guy was mumbling again. "If that Reptilian son of a bitch hadn't teleported me up to the mothership from Mesa Rock, and then did all those experiments on me, none of this would be happening now."

None of what? Jeremy was tempted to ask, but he didn't. Engaging the old coot was a mistake he'd already made once. For the next forty minutes, he'd heard Ivor-the-Nut-Case's life story. For the love of God, the guy still wasn't over his dead wife. Lily or Linda or . . . no, Lila, that's what it was. One of the Kress girls who were all beautiful when they were young. So beautiful. She'd been dead for a really long time, it seemed, but Hicks still talked about her as if they'd been together just last week.

He was weird, weird, weird. Someone to avoid. But there was nowhere for Jeremy to hide, and since they were the only two people in the drunk tank, he was stuck listening to Ivor's stories.

It would be different if he had his iPod or cell phone, but the undersheriff had confiscated both. God only knew how he'd handle Heidi when he got home.

Shit, what a mess.

"I saw a Yeti today," Ivor said, then frowned. "Maybe it was today. Thought it was a wraith, but it was a Yeti. It killed Brady Long."

"Huh." Jeremy hoped he would just stop talking.

"It was white. All white. With a long club."

"I thought Yetis were brown and furry."

"That's a Sasquatch, not a Yeti!" He glared at Jeremy, who reminded himself again not to engage the old geezer. Ivor mumbled some more but Jeremy closed his eyes and ears.

He tried to sleep and failed, so he walked around the perimeter of the cage, hearing voices of cops when the door to this end of the jail opened, and eyeing the drain in the middle of the sloped floor. He didn't want to think what had gone down that hole with its dirty-looking cover.

"I bet they called my son," Ivor suddenly said, sounding more of this world than he had since Jeremy had been thrown in with him. Jeremy squinted at the old man. Maybe he'd just needed to sober up. "They always call him. They never believe me, and they always call him."

"Well, maybe he'll pick you up," Jeremy said hopefully. Had anyone called his stepdad? Or, had the undersheriff put a stop to that before it happened?

"I don't want to be a burden." Ivor dropped his chin to his chest and sighed. "It's not my fault. It's Crytor's. But nobody wants to believe me."

The old guy fell asleep just like that, snoring enough to make Jeremy go deaf. A burden. Well, yeah. He was a complete nutcase, so he was definitely a burden.

Thoughts of his mother crept in though Jeremy tried to keep them at bay. He didn't want to think about her. About what could be happening to her, if she wasn't dead already.

Nobody was saying that Mom might be in the hands of that sicko killer. Nobody wanted to tell him that. But he knew that's what they were thinking. God, he hoped they were wrong, but where was she? Where was she?

With an uncomfortable twinge of conscience, he reviewed his own actions the last few days. He'd been in police custody twice this damn week. And he'd been a jerk to everyone; his mother, for sure. If he could only take it back! He'd do everything different. He would. He *would*.

He just needed a chance. Another chance. With a look to the snoring old man, Jeremy walked to the bars and wrapped his hands around them. He wanted to cry. Could feel the burn at the back of his eyes and moisture collect in his nose.

Mom . . .

Swallowing, he fought back his emotions. If he

yelled, would someone come for him? He had to get out. Had to help his mom.

He was just getting ready to try when the locked door at the end of the hall clanked open and Mom's partner walked through, looking drawn and determined.

"Are you here for me?" he asked.

"I'm releasing you, yes."

"To my stepdad?"

"To your vehicle."

Jeremy wondered what that meant. "And Mom?"

"We're still trying to locate her. The sheriff has asked that the charges against you be dropped."

Relief flooded through him, tempered by deeper worries. He looked back at Ivor, still snoring. "Glad I don't have to listen to him being abducted by aliens anymore. Or all about his dead wife, one of the beautiful Kress women, or the fact that a Yeti killed Mr. Long."

He thought her lips might break into a faint smile, but it didn't quite happen. "Ivor's a colorful character."

"So, it wasn't a Yeti, huh?"

"Not as far as we can tell."

She unlocked the door and he slipped through. He wanted to ask her more about his mom, but it was clear there was nothing she would tell him. "So, I'm outta here."

"I would go home to your stepdad and stepmother and sister," she said.

"Yeah." But Jeremy was already making other plans. Maybe he'd go to Ty's. Do something.

"Go be with your family. We will find her," she assured him as she walked ahead of him and then unlocked the door at the end of the hall.

He nodded, hurrying through the door, then heading upstairs to collect his cell phone and keys.

Tydeus Melville Chilcoate didn't trust anyone.

Especially strangers who appeared at his remote cabin in the middle of the worst friggin' snowstorm in decades. And yet, here was this guy standing on his broken-down front stoop. He didn't unlatch the chain, which he knew wouldn't hold anyone who really wanted to get in, but the shotgun he had in the hand hidden behind the door casing would probably do the trick.

"Chilcoate?" the tall dude asked. His eyes were dark beneath the brim of a cowboy hat that was collecting snow. "I'm Nate Santana. I work . . . er, worked for Brady Long."

Chilcoate's hand tightened over the stock of the gun, but he kept his cool. "I heard what happened to him. Bummer."

"Yeah." The guy didn't seem to believe it. "I got your name from Zane MacGregor. He said you could help me."

That prick! MacGregor was supposed to keep his mouth shut about Chilcoate, that was part of the deal! "You talked to him recently?"

"Just did."

"Well, shit." Chilcoate reluctantly cracked open the door and Santana walked inside. "Stay right there," he ordered and the man stopped short. "What is it you want?"

"I need help finding out who killed Brady Long," Santana told him. He handed Chilcoate a rolled-up map, a list of names, and a scratched-out biography, of sorts, on the man in question. "I got as much stuff as I could think of. Names of marksmen. Maps of the area. What I know of Brady."

"You were a friend of his?"

"I knew him a long time."

"And you want to find his killer," Chilcoate reiterated.

"What I'm looking for is a connection between him and this damned Star-Crossed Killer. I think they're the same man." The man's eyes darkened and his jaw was granite.

"Just a minute," Chilcoate said, pointing Santana to his worn recliner, which he reluctantly sat in, looking as if he might jump up and attack someone given the least provocation.

Chilcoate then headed into the larger of his two bedrooms, an area designated for his office. He closed the door on the secondhand chairs, scarred cabinetry, and massive television that made up most of his living space. He didn't like having Santana sitting in the middle of it, but whatcha gonna do with friends like MacGregor?

Within the bedroom's walls were a desktop computer, several telephones, and radio equipment. This was all a front, containing basic home office equipment when Chilcoate needed so much more. The basement, down a narrow stairway, was where he had a whole intel room set up—his own "control central"—but the basement was an area he had no intention of sharing with anyone, least of all a stranger who knocked on his door late at night. Damn MacGregor! He, better than anyone, knew that Chilcoate needed privacy and secrecy. Chilcoate dealt in information, and it was imperative his world was kept private and under the radar of the general populace.

Muttering to himself, he impatiently dialed Mac-Gregor's cell phone, counting the rings, glancing toward the door as he waited for him to answer. Finally he picked up, his voice sounded distracted and rushed, which pissed Chilcoate off to no end, even though he understood the reason for it. "Hey, man," Chilcoate said without preamble. "You send this Santana fellow to me? What the hell are you thinkin'?"

Zane MacGregor was a boyhood friend of Chilcoate's, his one true friend. Chilcoate had helped Zane recently with that crazy copycat who'd gone after his girlfriend. The copycat they'd all thought was the Star-Crossed Killer.

MacGregor said, "Santana's after the real Star-Crossed Killer. Even though it turned out that Jillian wasn't one of his targets, the bastard's still out there, killing women. He's in your 'hood, Chilcoate. I thought you could join forces with Santana and bring him down."

"No one knows about me," he reminded him. "That's the deal. You know that."

"You gotta stop being so paranoid, Chilcoate. You gotta help Santana get the killer."

"The police are on it."

MacGregor laughed. "Like you believe any arm of the government is straightforward and capable! Sure, man. Let the police handle this."

Chilcoate ground his teeth. He was right, of course. Chilcoate had actually been in the military where he had honed his skills in electronic surveillance and computer hacking. He was considered a genius by some; a serious threat by others. His disillusionment with all things government was a by-product of his own paranoia and secretive nature. But that didn't make the government right!

"You want me to get involved?"

"Yes," MacGregor stated emphatically.

"You're putting a real strain on this friendship. It hasn't been a week since you were here," he grumbled.

"You want this bastard to keep killing women?"

"Hell, no. But I'm not a one-man army."

"Santana is."

Chilcoate thought that over. He glanced toward the closed door and thought about the man seated on the other side of it. "You know him well?"

"Well enough. You've probably made a judgment on him by now. What do you think?"

"I wouldn't want to be tracked by him."

He grunted in agreement. "Then help him out. Like you helped me."

"Okay, Chilcoate said reluctantly, clicking off and reaching in a pocket for his smokes. Lit one up, thought carefully. He opened the bedroom door and let Santana get an eyeful of the upstairs equipment. He couldn't afford for anyone to see what was in the basement. "All right," he told the intense stranger. "I'll get to work. I'll let you know when I have anything."

Santana nodded. "Got any kind of time line on when that might be?"

"Go home. Go to bed. Tomorrow's another day."

The tall man smiled faintly, a flinty movement of his lips that held no humor. "Make it fast." Then, "Please."

Chilcoate walked him to the door and as soon as it was closed behind him, he threw shut all of his special locks. He stubbed out his cigarette and waited, counting to ten, as he heard the engine of the man's truck fire, then heard the crunch of tires on snow as Santana turned the vehicle and left.

Chilcoate waited five more minutes before heading down the narrow stairway to the basement and his true operation, ducking under ductwork, aware of the hidden cameras he'd placed in the cobwebby corners himself. At the back wall, in an alcove ostensibly designed to hold firewood, he hit a switch and the wall swung open, revealing an array of sophisticated, state-of-the-art computer and photographic equipment, radios, and cameras.

He rubbed his hands together as he dropped into a rolling desk chair that groaned under his weight. Now that Santana was gone and he was safe, he was starting to look forward to the task at hand. Time to hack into government computers and find out as much as he could about Brady Long, that fucked-up killer they called Star-Crossed, and how the police were faring in catching him.

I can't believe that she duped me!

The damned detective nearly ruined everything!

Worse, the voice in my head keeps pounding at me: *The taunts you made were a mistake! You were too cocky!* I can hear *her* voice telling me that I'll never amount to anything, that I will end up like my father.

Fat chance, Mother!

And yet, I wasn't prepared for how clever the detective turned out to be, how unafraid.

That will never do . . .

I must regain control.

I glance at the door to the detective's room, but

she is quiet now. Maybe I should have given her more of the date-rape drug, kept her unconscious, but my supply is running low and besides, I wanted the fight. But not like this!

Moving to the mirror, I examine my face critically, minus my disguise. My nose is slightly swollen from getting smacked by her flailing hands, but it's the marks on my neck from those damn handcuffs that really give me away. In this weather, however, turtlenecks are the rule, so it won't be noticeable, but she should have never been able to touch me. Never!

I won't make that mistake again.

And the bite marks on the back of my neck? Those are painful and deep. I twist around and look and am satisfied that the turtleneck also covers them. But pulling down the back of the shirt reveals that the skin is ruptured, the teeth marks clear. The wounds continue to weep a little, but not enough to be noticeable for my purposes today, and by tomorrow, they should be forming scabs. Bitch! Forensically, if I were to be caught, even the morons at Pinewood County would be able to match them to Pescoli's strong jaw.

Fury rages through me. I look forward to killing her. But later. After the others. She will pay dearly for each and every wound she inflicted.

You're subdued now, though, aren't you, bitch? Not a sound. Hurts like hell, doesn't it? You're lucky you're still breathing.

With an effort I drag my attention from her and glance at the document Brady Long so kindly pulled from the safe for me. The will. It has specks of blood on it. Brady's blood. For a moment I relive the moment of the kill. The surprise in his face. The awe.

I will have to destroy the will, but later. After I visit one of my other guests: Elyssa. She's ready. Ripe. Tomorrow she will leave the haven I've made for her and begin her last walk on this earth.

So, tonight, I play the part of her loving savior.

There are no disguises needed for Elyssa. The only cover is my turtleneck, which hides Regan Pescoli's ill-advised attack.

I've made a pot of potato soup and I pour some into a bowl and place it on a tray along with a plate of bread, apple slices, and cheese. I add a cloth napkin and a spoon and then make my way through the tunnels that wind around these hills, bringing me finally to steps and higher ground, to the stone and log cabin where Elyssa waits. The cabin is almost directly above the rooms belowground, but it's a circuitous trek to get from one place to the other, a natural defense that keeps my guests unaware of each other even while they're in the same area.

I unlock the door to the cabin and Elyssa nearly jumps up from her bed. Yes, she is ready. Her injuries are all but gone.

"Liam!" she cries. "Where have you been? I was afraid you weren't coming back!"

"I've been clearing the roads, trying to make them passable for you. The storms have finally given us a break, and I've been able to cut some trees out of the way. The roads are slick, but tomorrow, when it's daylight, I'll get you back to safety."

I smile kindly as I set the tray on the table beside her bed. Tears jump to her eyes. She's overwhelmed. "Oh, thank you," she breathes. "Thank you."

"Still can't get cell service, but once we get going we should be able to pick up a signal. I'll make sure I get you to the nearest clinic."

"Oh, Liam . . ."

She tilts her head just a little and looks at me from beneath her lashes, like women do when they're interested. It's the same old ploy I've seen a thousand times. It would be so easy to take her, to make love to her, to fuck the living hell out of her. But I cannot. Everything has to be as planned, especially tonight, for there is still work to do.

"Don't worry. Everything's going to be fine," I soothe her.

She glances at the food. "It looks like you've made enough for two . . ."

"I'd better not," I say regretfully. "I've got a few more things to do. Make sure that we can get out of here early."

"Okay." She's disappointed. Then she gives me a look straight on. "Tomorrow," she says in a voice heavy with meaning.

I nod and close the door behind me, making sure it's locked. She believes I'm extra cautious, keeping her safe. She likes locked doors. They all do. Silly, silly bitches. As if a lock will save them.

I head back to my rooms and smile. Yes, there is still much to do, but I'm on task. Better yet, I have a surprise for those idiotic cops. Something that will really get their engines fired up! A little something extra from me.

I can hardly wait!

Chapter Twenty-Three

What was the link?

Selena lay on her bed and stared at the ceiling. She'd finally gone home but that didn't mean she'd quit working on the case. She'd tossed and turned most of the night and when she did sleep, her dreams were peppered with images of Brady Long's dead body, the frozen corpses of the women they'd found in the forest, and Regan Pescoli, locked away somewhere, knowing her fate, maybe already lashed to the bole of a tree in the icy forest.

There had to be a connection between them—a connection more than the bullet dug out from the back of Brady Long's desk chair and the blown-out tires of the victims found in the forest. Santana believed the same person was responsible for all the deaths.

If he was right, the killer knew all the women and Brady Long.

None of his victims were chosen at random.

And that meant the killer was close enough to Long to know that he was returning to Montana and had lain in wait for him. That information alone had absolved many suspects of the crime. As far as Alvarez knew, none of the victims had known anyone in the Long family.

Start with Brady Long's murder. His death is the oddity. And it, too, was planned with ultimate precision.

She flung off the covers and, in a pj top and underwear, walked to the window where she looked outside. It was still dark, a few stars visible over the security lamps glowing harshly on the parking lot where snow was piled high around the individual spaces. The asphalt was covered with a shimmering layer of ice.

Her headache had left in the night and the cold that had been settling in her lungs seemed to be breaking up, but she knew she wouldn't be able to sleep again. A glance at the clock told her it was barely four, but she walked into the kitchen, filled the teapot, then remade her Murphy bed and slid it back into the wall. By the time she was through a short shower, her hair still damp, her body now dressed in workout clothes, the teapot was whistling.

She poured herself a cup of steaming hot water, tossed in a once-used bag, and carried it to her desk where notes, pictures, statements, and reports were spread out. Sliding into her desk chair, she began writing on a yellow legal pad, naming all of the victims and making lines that showed how they were connected to each other and those who were, or had been, suspects. She added in the people who had found the bodies and cars as well. The only connections there were Nate Santana, who had found Brady Long, worked for him, and was involved with Regan

Pescoli, and Ivor Hicks, who had stumbled upon Wendy Ito's body and shown up minutes after Santana at Brady Long's house.

Tapping her pen against her chin, she frowned.

In kind of a six-degrees-of-separation thing, she did note that Clementine's son, Ross, went to school where Elyssa O'Leary had studied, and they'd shared an English professor, but not a class.

None of the victims had lived in Grizzly Falls. Unless she counted Brady Long, who had taken up part-time residence as a child. He and his sister had spent their summers at the Lazy L Ranch. And Padgett had nearly been killed with her brother in an accident where Brady had escaped any serious injury.

So, how had the killer found these people?

"He's relentless. A hunter," Grace Perchant had warned Pescoli at Wild Will's. There, surrounded by dead animal heads mounted on the walls, she had mentioned that the killer was a hunter. And Orion was the hunter in mythology and astronomy. Craig Halden, a Georgia country boy turned FBI agent and a hunter himself, was certain the stars located on the notes found at the various crime scenes were intentionally part of the Orion constellation.

The trouble was that nearly every male over the age of ten in this part of Montana considered himself a hunter. It was a way of life.

Alvarez flipped through the old police reports that she'd pulled and copied but hadn't had time yet to read. For the most part nothing leaped out at her. She came across the report of the Long boating accident and read it over with curiosity. Brady had reported the event and Fire and Rescue had responded, taking Padgett by ambulance to a local hospital. Her father, Hubert, had been doing business in Missoula at the time and her mother, Cherilyn, who was already divorced from Hubert by that time, was living in San Francisco.

Clementine DeGrazio and her then four-year-old son, Ross, lived on the property, and there were several ranch hands as well, some of them whose names she recognized. Henry Johansen, now around sixty, was one. Alvarez had been told that sometime in his late forties Henry had fallen off his tractor and never been the same. Now he sometimes showed up at the sheriff's department, offering his help on cases, though he barely knew his own name half the time. Another ranch hand had been Gordon Dobbs, the guy who now either made chainsaw art that he sold off his front porch, or put a few shifts in at the local bars.

Neither seemed a candidate for Star-Crossed. She was about to toss the file aside when she noticed the name of the responding officer: Cort Brewster.

Selena felt a tremor slide up her spine.

Brewster was an incredible marksman.

He'd lived in the area since childhood; his parents still lived in the original family homestead.

He was a hunter, cross-country skier.

He had access to all county records.

And he was the undersheriff.

Your boss.

She took a deep breath and expelled it slowly. No, that didn't make any sense. It was true that Brewster didn't clock the regular eight-to-five, but he had flexibility with his hours and was out of the office often. He was also a family man, an elder of his church.

But he's organized.

Knows first aid and how to survive in the wilderness.
He has a temper.
Is intolerant of others.
And is a hunter.

Her heart was racing and she told herself not to go there, to end this line of thinking right now. But Brewster's name, signed when he was a deputy, burned into her brain.

No one knew the exact time that the victims' vehicles' tires had been shot out. Nor did anyone know when the victims were being cared for or hauled into the woods.

"It can't be," she said as her tea cooled and her mind whirled with the possibilities. The killer was big; one shoe print had proved that. Cort Brewster had to be six-three and pushing two-thirty. Not fat. He worked out in the same gym where Selena did. But definitely big.

The back of her mouth went dry.

Cort Brewster, next in line for sheriff if anything should happen to Daniel Grayson.

The idea was repulsive.

Unthinkable.

She argued with herself as she walked into the bathroom. *Brewster's a cop. A good cop, no matter what you might think of him.*

Though his hair had started to silver, he wasn't yet forty. Still older than what she would have expected for a serial killer.

She made a mental note to find out what, if any, connection there was between Brady Long, the boating accident that put Padgett into a mental hospital, and Cort Brewster.

"You're barking up the wrong tree," she told herself, but settled into the computer, logged onto the

Internet, and spent the next two hours trying to find
out more information on the man who was her boss.
Wrong tree be damned. Right now it was the only
one she had.

Snap!
With a metallic crack, the weld gave way.
Regan's heart soared. She bit back a cry of tri-
umph.
It was quiet in her prison.
Cold.
No bit of morning light showed through that
window high overhead, though the fire was on its
last breath, the faintest glow of red allowing her just
enough illumination to make out objects in the room.
Every muscle in her body ached. To move was ex-
cruciating and yet she was pretty sure that, other
than a few cracked ribs, no bones were broken. Her
arm didn't work very well and her head thundered,
but she had refused to give up or give in.
She didn't stop to wonder where the bastard was.
He'd been gone for hours, probably back to his real
home. She did wonder if he had a wife. Maybe even
kids. The thought made her sick, but she was convinced by the length of time that he was gone, both
during the days as well as the nights, that he had a
regular job somewhere, and either a house or apartment. That this dungeon was his fantasy lair, the
place where he could let his sick persona run free.
She eased off the cot and, with her uninjured
shoulder, pushed up on its frame, fitting the frame
close to her neck as she teased the thin links of her
handcuffs free of the now unwelded leg. There wasn't
much room, the chain caught several times.

Give me strength, she thought, *and patience.*

Slowly the chain slipped through and she was free.

Take that, you son of a bitch, she thought, though her hands were still cuffed in front of her. She found the poker, the only weapon in the room, then once it was at her side, located her clothes. Fighting pain, she stepped into her jeans, socks, and boots, but she couldn't bother with her sweater, bra, or jacket. She had to keep her arms free.

Heart thudding irregularly, she made her way to the door. She thought she was alone, had heard him leave, and the fact that no light glowed from under the door told her that he'd let his fire die as well. There were no lanterns lit.

But he could be asleep.

You don't know what's on the other side.

Wishing for all she was worth that she had her sidearm rather than the poker, she held her breath and tried the door.

Unlocked.

The bastard truly believed she was no threat. And why not? She'd probably looked half dead after their fight. She'd certainly felt that way.

The door creaked open and she braced herself, half-expecting him to hurl himself at her.

But the room on the other side was dark, the fire nearly dead. It was larger than hers by three times and the fireplace was massive. Again, there were windows high overhead and she had the feeling most of this lair was built underground. Several doors opened from the main living area with its wide stone floor and huge table. The armoire stood against one wall and for the first time Regan no-

ticed that there was electricity—light switches near
the doors, outlets on the walls.

What was this place? The room she'd been imprisoned in, where she was certain others had been
kept before her, was cruder, as if it had once been
used as a storage area, the wood stove added later.

Not that she had time to worry about it. Quickly
she surveyed the area, looking for a weapon, or the
keys to the cuffs, even a bobby pin that she could
strip of its plastic coating and use to unlock the
handcuffs. There was nothing on the table.

But the armoire . . .

Without hesitation, she limped to the huge cabinet
and opened the double doors. Inside were papers.
Books on astronomy and astrology were slid into slots.
Along with boxes neatly stacked and drawings . . . It
was too dark to see, but . . .

Her stomach dropped as she recognized the
pages. Notes that had been left on the trees above
the victims' heads and more . . . Oh, God, so many
more.

Telling herself that she was running out of time,
shivering with the cold, she opened some of the
drawers and searched. *Come on, come on, please let
the keys be . . .*

She saw them then. A drawer of metal keys. Door
keys and car keys and . . . there were the tiny handcuff keys. Her hands shook as she worked the lock
with difficulty. Half-expecting a door to be flung
open at any second, she set her jaw and forced the
tiny key into the lock.

Click!

One cuff fell open.

She didn't waste a second and unlocked the second,

the right one. She needed to bandage that wrist but there was no time. She stuffed the key and handcuffs into her pockets. Oh, if she could turn the tables on this bastard, she'd love to force his hands behind his back and march him into the station! Maybe even give him an inkling of what police brutality really meant. She surveyed the room for a weapon, or phone, or computer, anything so that she could protect herself and get word to the outside world, but no luck.

Damn.

But she did uncover a flashlight, and when she cast its beam over the contents of the armoire one last time, she nearly jumped out of her skin. There, along with the neatly drawn notes with their cryptic messages and stars, were pictures. Of the women he'd captured. Each one naked, bound to a tree, still very much alive, terror in their eyes.

Pescoli's stomach quivered.

She had no choice but to leave the evidence where it was, and find a way of escape. For herself. For Elyssa. For the others he'd alluded to.

Where are they? Where is Elyssa?

Here somewhere?

Or already being forced through the forest to a lone tree where she is certain to die a lonely, brutal death?

Fury burning through her blood, Pescoli hurried back to her prison, grabbed the rest of her clothes, and carefully pulled them on, chafing at the extra time it took because of her injuries. She intended to find the other captives and kill the son of a bitch who had held them against their will.

The poker at the ready in one hand, flashlight in the other, her body still aching, she held her breath and slowly opened the door to freedom.

*   *   *

"I don't understand," Elyssa whispers, her eyes round with fear.

Oh, she understands, all right. All of her fears, the ones that have been hidden just beneath the surface of her consciousness, are rising to the surface, causing her heart to pound with dread, her hope to disintegrate.

I see it. Have witnessed it before in this very room with its twin bed draped in the hand-pieced quilt Mother created over half a century ago. It seems fitting, somehow, that some of my guests have slept under Mother's handiwork. Theresa had mentioned how "beautiful" it was, the detail "intricate." If Theresa had only known that those very hands that had so lovingly cut and pieced the tiny scraps together had also shown a great ability to slap, or flick a lit cigarette, with equal ease.

This room Elyssa has come to think of as hers belonged to me, and now, time is slipping past. It's been a busy morning already and it's not yet light. After taking care of my other business for the police, I returned for Elyssa. When I entered her room she played coy, as I knew she would. Mentioned that it was now "tomorrow."

For an answer, I ordered her to strip off her clothes.

Oh, the eager anticipation, the hope of some sort of sexual connection; her eyes sparked with it. But it was extinguished quickly when I drew my hunting knife from its sheath.

My expression, too, altered at the same time. I know there isn't a speck of kindness in my eyes now. No hint of interest. "Just do it," I tell her firmly and the knife in my hand, my favorite long-bladed weapon, one which can gut and skin a deer so smoothly and easily, convinces her not to balk.

Tears begin to sheen in her large eyes. "If this is a joke, it's not funny." Her voice tremors.

She knows.

I catch her first fleeting, furtive glance around her room, as she contemplates her odds of escape.

"No joke."

"But—"

"Get on with it!"

"Please, I don't understand what you're doing. You know I like you." She was supplicating now, her hands in front of her, fingers wide, offering herself like the sacrificial whore I've always known she is. "I could . . . we could . . ." She swallows hard and motions toward the small bed with its fading quilt in an awkward, desperate attempt at seduction.

I usually play along for a bit, but this morning her attempts to bed me are irritating. There is no time. Because of that bitch Pescoli I've stepped up my game, already put the gears into motion. I need to make a real statement, get the attention of the stupid dickwads at the sheriff's department.

"Strip, now, Elyssa." I waggle the knife a bit. Menacingly.

She gasps and throws a hand to her own throat.

"I don't want to use this," I assure her. Firmly. The knife blade glints with the light from the lantern I've set on the small bedside table.

This isn't a lie. Cutting her isn't part of my plan. But I will. If I have to.

Wild-eyed, she slowly begins to peel off her clothes, taking her time, trying and failing to appear seductive, as if unsure that this isn't some kind of sexual fantasy I'm playing out.

She tugs her sweater over her head and looks at me. Tosses her hair.

God, she is pathetic.

I point the tip of the knife at her bra. "Keep going."

Slowly, painstakingly, she reaches behind her back and unhooks it, letting the scrap of red lace fall to the floor. Then she cocks her head and looks at me that same, silly way, her lips curved into a little-girl pout as her breasts are finally exposed. As if she, naughtily, has given me what I want.

I've seen her breasts before, of course, and they are gorgeous. Big enough to be noticed; a "handful," I've heard others say. With dark areolas, darker than most.

I'm almost tempted.

Almost.

"You like?" she said, breathily. Proud of those big mounds with the dark nipples. Clumsily, she runs a finger over her stiff nipple, then drags it upward, over her throat to touch her lips. Her index finger disappears into her mouth and she makes a sucking sound.

So contrived. So predictable.

She glances at my crotch, expecting to see swelling.

There is none.

"Move it," I order.

"But, Liam," she protests, her voice cracking.

"There's not much time. Take off your pants. Now!"

"Oh, God." Her hand falls from her mouth, but she obediently unzips her ski pants and strips them off. Her thong is still in place. Red and green. A holiday thong. How nice.

"That, too."

Within seconds the thong is disposed of and she looks at me. "Now what?" she whispers.

"I think you know."

I reach into my pocket and find the handcuffs, dangling them in my free hand, the knife still brandished in the other. For a second she's confused. There's a hint here of a sexual game. "Put your wrists together. In front of you." I don't have to worry about her escape, don't have to bother with forcing her hands behind her.

Nervously she complies and I slap the cuffs on her.

"What is this?" she asks.

"You'll see." I gag her then, but don't blindfold her. I need her to be able to walk and see. This part of "the complex" as I've come to call it, is aboveground, three hundred yards away from my work area and the room where Regan Pescoli has been held underground. "Let's go." Prodding her with the knife, I urge her from her locked room, down the corridor of the cabin to the outside door. She hesitates when I open it, but my knife blade urges her forward, so she trudges barefoot through the snow. There's a path that leads to the truck, one I've created myself, a break in the snow that follows the tree line, just in case anyone flies over. I don't want to call attention to the cabin, the smoke from the fire will be enough.

Moaning a protest, Elyssa follows the broken trail. The sky is still black as night, dawn not yet appearing over the eastern hills. Stars wink high in the heavens and the moon offers a bit of silvery illumination.

She's already shivering, her smooth skin prick-

ling with goose bumps. She's ahead of me, so I can't
see her breasts, but I know her nipples are hard
with the cold, and beneath her gag, her teeth are
chattering.

Get used to it, I think, as we reach the lean-to where
the truck is parked, its cover already removed and
folded. I eye the snowmobile. I would prefer to use it
as it's so much faster and more agile, could cut the
distance down as I drive cross country. But it might
draw attention, again from the air, and I'd need the
stretcher.

And it's not big enough.

Not today.

Feeling a bit of anticipation, I open the canopy
and tailgate. I nudge Elyssa forward and shine the
flashlight inside. The beam catches on two glaring, reflective eyes and Elyssa visibly jumps and
shrieks.

"Get inside," I say, the tip of my knife pressing
against her back.

Elyssa jumps again.

My other captive, the one already lying in the truck
bed, is naked and bound. Writhing beneath the
canopy, as if she thinks she might escape, she hurls
insults through her gag. Then again, she always has
been a mouthy one. Not nearly as compliant as Elyssa.

Elyssa hesitates.

I cut her.

Just a tiny prick on her back.

But it's all it takes.

She leaps into the bed of the truck and I slam the
tailgate shut and lock the canopy.

"Two for the price of one," I say, pleased with myself, though there's still so much work to do. I climb

into the truck and start the engine, backing out slowly, testing the wheels as I turn around and head down the mountain lane.

He doesn't know it yet, but this is Sheriff Grayson's lucky day.

Chapter Twenty-Four

Run, run, run!

Pescoli's mind screamed at her, pushed her, kept her going to the point that she was out of breath.

And freaked.

Her lungs burning, fear sizzling through every inch of her.

Don't go there. Don't panic. Do not!

God, if she only had her sidearm!

Yeah, right . . . down here? In these friggin' tunnels?

Forcing back the terror that caused the edges of her sanity to fray, she kept moving, swinging the beam of her flashlight along the narrow tunnels. Her door to freedom had opened to this, a subterranean maze. But she had to keep searching, looking for the other hostages, looking for a way out. Dust was everywhere, spiderwebs abounded, and droppings of vermin littered the tunnel floor as she strove to find a way out of her prison. Pain jabbed her ribs with every breath, her joints throbbed, her wrist burned where it was flayed, her legs were still wobbly, and her heart pounding crazily as she strained to listen, squinted to see, hoped beyond hope that she wouldn't run into the bastard returning down one of these dark corridors.

Earlier, with no time to waste, she'd begun opening doors only to discover that she was trapped in some kind of intricate maze. Aside from the main room with the fireplace, big table, and the sicko's armoire filled with the evidence of his crimes, there were hallways dug into the earth, all angling off in different directions.

An old silver or gold mine.

How in the world would she ever find the other women? Save them?

These hills were riddled with mines from a bygone era; though few of the old shafts and tunnels, she thought, were so intricate and large as this one.

There had to be a way out.

She just had to be patient.

Think logically.

While her mind was yelling at her to run.

And her mouth was dry with the fear that she was too late to save Elyssa O'Leary or anyone else.

You perverted son of a bitch, she thought, her grip tightening on the poker even as her muscles screamed in protest.

Calm down.

Take a deep breath.

Get your damned bearings!

What would Santana do? He, with his military background, backpacking, and river-guide experience. He, who was at home in the most treacherous terrain.

Remain calm.

Think logically.

Remember where you've been.

His voice resonated in her ears and in her mind's eye she saw his visage: his dark eyes, set back well into his head, his bladed cheekbones that hinted at some Native American ancestor, and his lips, thin and hard, but easily teased into a smile.

Her heart twisted and she wondered if she would really ever see him again. If she'd ever really touch him.

And the kids.

God, she had to keep going for Bianca and Jeremy.

She kept the fading, yellow beam of the flashlight on the darkness ahead. Someone, probably the whack-job himself, had spent lots of time, money, and effort renovating the adjoining rooms for his twisted purposes.

Whoever the bastard was, he'd been planning his killing spree for a very long time. The depth of his plot was evident in the files he kept in the big armoire and this labyrinth of underground tunnels.

She'd taken a knife from the main room along with her flashlight and the poker she still carried, then she'd tried to find a way out of the maze.

She had no idea how long she'd been at it, but with every step she had the sinking, horrifying sensation that time was running out, that around any corner she might run into him, that he was already searching for her.

Just keep going, she told herself over the pounding of her pulse. But she was exhausted, only getting through this on adrenaline and fear. The women who had been found in the forest came to mind, all five victims who had been held hostage here, underground, never given a chance before being marched out into the frozen wilderness and roped to lone trees in the worst winter Regan could remember.

Was she walking in their footsteps?

Had they been forced down these dark, close tunnels where it was so hard to breathe? Then there was Elyssa . . . *God, please let her still be alive. And if there are others . . . all of them, please . . .*

As her lungs filled with the dust in the tunnel, she swung the beam of her flashlight over the walls and ceiling. Spurs ran off the main underground corridor, but most of them had been blocked, the entrances boarded over, and from the amount of dust and dirt that had accumulated, she assumed he didn't use them, that they weren't his escape route.

She had to work slowly, so as not to get lost, and she'd marked her path with a stone she'd found, scratching the floor with arrows, reminding her of which path she'd followed and all the while, she knew that time was her enemy, at any second the monster would return.

". . . and so this is Christmas," John Lennon's voice filled the interior of the car. "And what have you—"

Alvarez clicked the radio off. "Right on, John," she said without any enthusiasm. Streetlights and stoplights glowed red, green, and amber, while the brick buildings of "Old Grizz," the area of town near the river, were adorned in clear crystal-looking strands. She drove past the courthouse where a tree over twenty feet tall was festooned in colorful bulbs, and as she wound her way up the hill to Boxer Bluff, she passed the Baptist church where a snow-covered nativity scene was illuminated with spotlights. Hand-painted wooden figures of Mary, Joseph, and the manger were surrounded by sheep and the Magi.

Images of her own youth flashed behind her eyes. The life-size creche that her father and brothers dutifully resurrected each holiday season to stand in the front yard of the two-storied house in Woodburn, the small town in Oregon where she'd grown up with all of her brothers and sisters, eight children in all, a family, she thought now, with too little money and too much religion. Each year her parents had shepherded the kids to Mt. Angel, to the cathedral-like parish for midnight mass, then on Christmas morning, they would return to their home parish nearby. Her brother Pablo was always the jokester and getting into trouble.

There was a part of Alvarez that missed those early years and the closeness of her family, the noise of a house filled with voices rising in Spanish and English, the music that was so much a part of their family, the ever-present smells of her mother's cooking.

But that was a long time ago.

Before "the incident" when she'd grown up fast, her innocence stolen.

Now she was a different person. Far different.

At the top of the hill, she wound her way through the streets to the sheriff's department where only a few vehicles were parked. Cort Brewster's rig was missing.

Which wasn't unusual.

Shifts hadn't changed yet, the night crew still on duty for a couple of hours. Alvarez thought she'd use that time to do some more checking on Brewster, then drive to the Long ranch to interview, again, Clementine DeGrazio and her sharpshooting son. Not much was known about Ross; a couple of speeding tickets, an absentee father, and an over-protective mother.

She pulled into her usual space, locked the car, and headed inside where, this early, the office was quiet. It was her favorite time at work, before the ca-cophony of a regular day started: phones ringing off the hook; cops questioning witnesses and grilling suspects; the banter among the staff. Before Star-Crossed had begun to strike, the workload and job had been interesting, but usually not extreme. Since Theresa Charleton's body had been found, the amount of work had exploded.

Now Selena walked into the kitchen, saw the sludge in the coffeepot from the night before, and began fresh, rinsing out the glass pot before refilling it. There were a few pieces of Joelle's fruitcake on one table, and only the crumbs from her cookies on the other.

Leaving the coffee to brew, she walked to her desk and fired up her computer. She checked her e-mail, read some reports, made mental notes about tips that had come in, forwarded to her from the task force desk. Nothing new. Surreptitiously she checked the undersheriff's professional records, seeing how many shooting competitions he'd won, how many times he'd been cited for awards of excellence on the job, then read anything that was printed on the Internet on her boss. She still hadn't officially clocked in, was working on her own time, so she justified her investigation, such as it was.

And still he was the undersheriff, had never risen above that position. Why?

Don't go there, she warned herself again, just as

she heard boots ringing down the hallway. Looking up, she saw Grayson pass in a cloud of fury. His dog was at his heels as he strode into his office.

More bad news?

She waited until the computer monitor went into its screen-saver mode, walked down to the kitchen, grabbed two cups of coffee, and headed to Grayson's office. He was already on the phone, his expression hard. He glanced up at her and nodded at one of the steaming cups.

". . . yeah, I know, but I think it would be best if you got your facts straight first. We're trying to avoid a panic . . . What? I don't know when the next press conference will be. As soon as there's something to report." He slammed the phone down and said, "Seen the paper?"

She shook her head as she handed him the mug.

He hitched his chin at the paper he'd tossed onto the desk. "Take a look for yourself."

She sat in a side chair, next to the dog's bed where the black Lab had taken his spot, and opened the paper. Bold headlines reported: SHERIFF'S DEPARTMENT STYMIED BY STAR-CROSSED KILLER—DETECTIVE FEARED LATEST VICTIM.

"Oh, no." She thought about her partner for the hundredth time this morning and couldn't shake the sense of doom that had seeped through her insides.

"It gets better. Keep reading." Grayson's jaw was rock hard.

The next line, in smaller type, declared: *Copycat Killer Arrested.*

She read the remainder of the article by Manny Douglas, who reported that the "Pinewood County Sheriff's Department and the FBI had been fooled into believing they had captured the Star-Crossed Killer with the arrest in Spokane." With more innuendo than actual fact, Manny suggested the entire investigation was botched and that the local authorities were "lost" and "baffled."

"He may as well have asked for my damned resignation," Grayson said. He looked tired, the grooves in his cheeks more pronounced, dark circles beneath his eyes. "Journalism at its finest," he said, then raked stiff fingers through his hair. "For what it's worth, I lodged a complaint with his editor."

"Well, whatever you do, don't resign." Alvarez tossed the paper into his trash can. "Don't you know you're not supposed to believe your press, good or bad?"

"Not much good these days."

She couldn't argue the point.

He held up his cup. "Thanks for bringing me the coffee."

She nodded. "Merry Christmas Eve."

"Thanks."

"Don't get used to it. I only pull out my gofer skills on the holidays."

His lips almost smiled. "So, anything new?"

She couldn't mention Brewster, not until she had something concrete, some evidence that linked the undersheriff to the crime, and the truth was, she wasn't sure he was their guy. "I'm going out to talk to Clementine and Ross DeGrazio again. Clementine's one of the few people who knew that Brady Long was going to show up at the Lazy L."

"What about his fiancée? People he worked with?"

"Zoller's working on them and Halden told me that he's talking to the FBI's field agents in Denver. I haven't heard back yet."

"And your visit with Grace Perchant?" he asked, his eyes crinkling a bit. "You never said how that went."

"It was interesting."

"Uh-huh. She talk to any ghosts?"

"Many, I think. Wendy Ito warned her about Pescoli."

"Of course she did." He gave her a look.

Alvarez didn't feel like arguing with him and really couldn't back up her arguments with fact anyway. Alvarez was about to leave when Joelle Fisher, dressed in a festive holiday cape and laden with Tupperware filled with what looked like sweets, poked her head into the office.

"Any word on Detective Pescoli?" she asked hopefully. There was a tiny pipe-cleaner angel tucked into her blond hair.

If possible, Grayson's expression turned grimmer.

"Oh, I see . . . Well, I brought some . . . things . . . More cookies and julekake, that's a traditional Scandinavian bread, my husband's mother's from Norway, you know . . ." she said, then her voice trailed off. "Okay, I'm sorry, it *is* the Christmas season and when I'm upset I bake. I even have some dog biscuits for Sturgis—"

At the sound of his name, the big Lab thumped his tail and looked expectantly at Joelle.

"Yes, buddy . . ." she cooed. "Merry Christmas, Sturgis." She was halfway into the room now and through the open door behind her, the increasing activity of the department was audible: the thud of deputies' footsteps as they walked past the door; ringing phones; computer keyboards clicking; and over it all a light buzz of conversation.

Joelle left a small container on the corner of Grayson's desk. It had a bright red bow and a card that said: Sturgis.

Grayson watched her but didn't say a word.

"Well, I'd better get these goodies into the lunch room." She turned on a gold high heel as if to leave.

"Joelle," the sheriff said and she stopped. "When Undersheriff Brewster shows up, have him see me."

Alvarez stiffened, cast a look at Grayson. Did he have suspicions as well?

The sheriff continued, "I want to make sure he dropped the charges against Regan's boy. The kid's got enough on his plate with his mother missing and today's headline."

Joelle's pretty face puckered. "Oh, he told me yesterday that he's got meetings out of the office and will be in a little after nine. But I'll call him."

"Do that."

Grayson seemed surprised that his second-in-command hadn't informed him about showing up late.

Joelle bustled out.

It was true enough that the undersheriff had a lot of duties that required him to be out of the office and his time spent behind his desk was naturally flexible, though, since the realization that a serial killer was stalking the county, Brewster and the rest of the staff showed up early and met to discuss the day.

Not so this morning, it seemed.

Alvarez returned to her desk and decided she wasn't done yet looking into the undersheriff's activities.

Sure he was a dedicated cop.

By all accounts a devoted family man.

An elder in his church.

Someone people looked up to.

A handsome, straightforward man.

He looked good on the outside, but there was always the chance that Cort Brewster had a secret life.

Elyssa had never been so frightened in her life. Now she knew that Liam, the man she'd learned to trust, was a cold-blooded killer, the one that she'd heard about before leaving school. She'd been vaguely aware that a sicko was prowling this part of the Bitterroots and somehow leaving women in the forest to die. She hadn't paid any attention; she'd been so excited about going home for the holidays and she'd hoped that Cesar was going to propose.

That seemed so far away now.

Part of her other life.

Tears ran down her face as she lay in the bed of the truck, a bit of light visible through the canopy windows. The vehicle wasn't moving now. He'd stopped somewhere and cut the engine. She'd barely been able to breathe, she was so scared as he'd opened the back of the truck and with gloved hands, pulled the other girl roughly out the back. Morning sunlight had reflected upon the snow, nearly blinding Elyssa, but she'd seen that they were in a forest, all white and quiet, no doubt a remote location.

The other woman, a prisoner like her, had cried out as Liam had dragged her onto the ground. Elyssa caught a glimpse of his knife and saw that the blade had a bit of blood on it. Hers, she knew, from when he'd roughly prodded her into this truck.

She thought about throwing herself outside of the vehicle, rolling out and knocking him senseless and trying to run. She wouldn't get far, but maybe one of them, either the other victim or herself, would be able to get away.

Reach the police!

Find help!

But, as if he'd read her mind, he'd slammed the tailgate shut and locked the canopy.

Click.

The sound was soft, but it resonated through Elyssa's brain, reminding her that she was locked away.

Alone.

About to die.

The glimpse she had of the other woman had burned into her brain: a tall, thin woman with small breasts, brown hair, and eyes that were wide and frightened. She'd begun screaming behind her gag as she'd been dragged from the truck. Elyssa had heard her frightened, strangled cries as Liam, if that was really his name, paid no attention.

Now there was nothing—no noise other than the frantic beating of her own heart.

And the silence was deafening.

Crushing.

Shaking, she sent up a prayer. *Dear Lord in heaven, please help me. Help her . . . save us.*

Tears drizzled from her eyes as she thought of her parents, how her mother would be hanging the stockings on the mantel and her father would be sitting in his chair, reading a newspaper, the television turned to some sports channel. And Cesar. Was he missing her? With his children.

Oh, God, how she missed them all.

How she wished she'd told them all how much she loved them.

How—

Footsteps crunched through the snow outside.

For a split second she thought someone might have come for her. A bit of hope lightened her heart.

Until she heard the door lock click.

Felt the truck sink a bit as he climbed inside.

Then heard the engine cough and start, roaring to life. With a crunch of tires, the pickup began to roll forward.

Elyssa O'Leary closed her eyes and prayed.

These, she knew, were the final moments of her life.

Chapter Twenty-Five

It was as if something was in the air. Something intangible, dark and evil.

Nate had spent a restless night, hoping Chilcoate would call, knowing he wouldn't. His mind had spun with ideas and dead ends, going over the information about Regan's abduction and the other killings in his memory. He couldn't quiet the questions and images and when he had finally drifted off, his dreams had been splintered and sharp. One minute he was making love to Regan, his body slick with sweat, the scent of her enveloping him as he kissed her, ran his fingers along her long legs. He'd heard her voice, deep and smoky. "That's it, cowboy," she'd whispered into his ear. "Right there . . . yeah, yeah . . . oh, yeah . . ." and then she'd withered away from him, her face twisting in fear, and he was standing on the brink of a yawning, dark canyon, snow falling all around.

He'd awoken shouting her name and had finally given up on sleep, spending the next few hours swilling coffee, studying maps, trying to piece together how Brady Long had been connected to the other victims, or more importantly, the killer.

And why the hell had Ivor Hicks shown up?

While Long's body was still warm, his soul not yet admitted into hell?

Ivor had arrived, at least three miles from his own place, little more than a shack at the base of Mesa Rock.

None of it made any sense, he thought, as he tried and failed to get Lucifer to take the bit. "Come on, boy," he'd cajoled and tried to get into tune with the animal. Lucifer had let him pat his sleek black shoulders and hadn't so much as pawed or tossed his head as Santana had placed the straps of the bridle over his neck. He'd acted as gentlemanly as he had the night before.

But the bit had set him off and rather than battle with the big colt, Santana had backed off.

Truth to tell, he wasn't in the mood.

And Lucifer took advantage of it.

Giving up on the bridle, Santana went about his other chores, all the while thinking of Regan, wondering where she was, an icy fear that she might already be dead, tied to some lonesome tree in the middle of the forest cutting through his soul. Yesterday, when he'd visited Chilcoate, he'd felt in control, but after his scattered dreams a gnawing fear had taken hold.

Gritting his teeth, he shoved the image of Regan from his mind and began measuring oats for the horses. Once he was finished with his chores, then he'd check with Chilcoate.

Whether the sheriff liked it or not, Santana intended to run his own investigation.

Because Regan Pescoli's disappearance was personal.

I'm jangled.

As I always am after I've accomplished my mission. But it's too early and I'm not finished, I think, as I drive into the next storm. It's barely started, just a few snow flurries of thick flakes, but if the sky and the weather service can be believed, soon another blizzard will roll through.

I hear her crying.

Irritating moans emanating from the back of the truck. Despite her gag and the whine of the engine and the hum of the tires, I can hear her.

Because I'm rattled. My nerves on edge.

Never have I done two in one day.

"Two in one. Two in one. Two in one." This becomes my mantra and I say it aloud, in time with the wipers, but she just won't shut up. Elyssa's cries have a way of cutting through the noise and burrowing deep in my brain.

Yelling at her through the back window that opens to the canopy won't help. She'll just wail all the louder.

And I feel the bite marks on the back of my neck. Inflamed. Angry. Like my building rage.

"Maybe music," I say and snap on the radio with a flick of my wrist.

But I'm far from the radio towers, deep in the mountains, and all I can hear over the crackle of static is Burl Ives's voice lilting on and on about a holly, jolly Christmas.

Not this year, I think and click off the radio. I concentrate instead on the job I have yet to do.

I've already picked out the area, far from the other one.

Won't Grayson and his crew be surprised?

"Merry Christmas!"

I have to shift down as I turn a corner and start up the hill, the four-wheel-drive propelling the truck through the drifting snow.

Up, up, up. This one is not going to be left in a valley. I've picked this spot with great care. It's perfect.

She lets out another moan.

What a whiner!

She deserves to die.

And she turned so quickly from vowing her love to that loser boyfriend of hers, to wanting me. A slut.

The wipers strain as the storm increases and the engine whines, tires slipping a bit as I drive to the ridge. I should have started earlier, as I knew the blizzard was on its way. I don't have much time.

Come on, come on, I think, as the old truck fishtails just before I round a final corner on this abandoned road. I know the clearing is just on the other side of the ridge. With some difficulty, I manage to turn the truck around, backing up, then pulling forward several times, just enough to point the nose of the vehicle down the hill for a quick escape. I can't allow myself to become overconfident and get the truck stuck.

Not that the imbecilic cops would ever find it.

There is still another vehicle they haven't located and probably won't until the spring thaw, a white

Volkswagen Beetle, crumpled and buried deep in Stone Ridge Canyon. Idiots!

Once my truck is pointed in the right direction, I park, cut the engine, and set the emergency brake.

Then it's time.

She's shivering in the back, making protesting noises as I open the door and pull her out. She is already covered with goose pimples, yet nervous sweat is visible on her body.

"No," she attempts to yell through her gag and I hear the word, know the meaning though her voice is garbled and muted.

"Let's go."

She is crying now, pulling the limp dishrag routine on me, as if her legs won't work. Some do this. Others try to flee. One tried to fight. In the end it's all the same, and as I lift my knife again, she gets the idea.

I loop a length of rope around her wrists; there's no time for chasing after her in the woods, and with my backpack in place, I prod her forward.

She doesn't want to go.

As much of an idiot as she is, she realizes that this is the end: There is no escape.

She is shivering as she stumbles along, plowing through the unbroken snow, cutting her own death path.

I hurry her along.

There isn't a lot of time.

I have places I need to be.

"Move it," I say, as I know the cold has settled into her bones. Through the ice-draped thickets of saplings and over the top of a ridge, I force her to follow a deer trail I've used for hunting since childhood.

She's visibly shaking now, either from fear, the cold, or both. Not that it matters. Down we walk, over a fallen tree where the jagged stump is now softened by the inches of white powder over it. The sky is obscured with clouds and the wind is blustery, blowing in fits and starts.

She contemplates running, I sense it, but she's an obedient doe, one who has given in to the whims of men her whole life, the way she tells it. A domineering father and then a string of boyfriends who never were quite the Prince Charming she'd hoped for. She'd told me about all of them, including Cesar, the latest, the one she'd wanted to marry.

Elyssa, of all the women I've hand-picked, is by far the least confident, a mouse of a thing . . . I probably shouldn't have chosen her, but her name . . . so perfect.

That thought brings a smile to my face as I realize that already my gift for the police might have arrived. If so, the sheriff's department will be set on its ear.

Chaos is bound to erupt.

The news, today, will be much more interesting than that boring press conference Grayson held. Posed on the steps of the sheriff's department with his stern expression, trying to appear like a U.S. Marshal on some old T.V. or movie Western. Yeah, Grayson, you boring tool, get real.

"This way," I say as Elyssa stops at the icy remnants of the creek. I nudge her with the knife and she jumps, starts walking faster across the icy stream and up a rise on the far bank. We're close now, having hiked nearly a mile. And she's probably going numb, frostbite setting in.

I don't want to carry her, so I say, "Run!"

She's startled, nearly slips, but catches herself and with my knife within reach, she gallops awkwardly over the hill to the clearing, and there stands the lonely cedar tree. A perfect spot.

Her eyes round as she spies the tree.

She gets it.

She's shaking her head, denying the inevitable, but I won't hear any further protests and while she silently pleads with me, her eyes wide and beseeching, her cuffed hands reaching outward, I ignore her and without any trouble lash her to the tree, pulling her back tight against the rough bark, hearing the muffled cry as her skin makes contact.

I can't take any more time and she's failing anyway, her body leaning into her bindings, her hair stiff with the snow. As she whimpers, I reach into my backpack for my kit, then nail the appropriate note over her head and carve out the star in the perfect position with my knife.

She's weak.

Pathetic.

Deserves to die.

Bits of bark drop onto her scalp and shoulders and I let it stay.

She's not saying a word now, seemingly out of it, and that just won't do. Hurriedly I pack my things, swing the backpack over my shoulder, and walk to the edge of the clearing. Then I pull my camera out of my pocket. "Hey!" I yell as I focus.

Nothing.

Damn it, I took too long!

"Hey! Elyssa!" My voice booms across these canyons.

Finally, she looks up and I click off the shot.

Not my best, I see, the digital image distorted a bit, but it will have to do. At least I caught the image of pure terror in her eyes.

Good.

I'm out of time.

And nature will take care of the rest.

I leave her then, jogging back the way we came, snow already filling the trail that we so recently broke through the snow.

This experience wasn't the best. I like women with some fight in them, a little fire.

Like Padgett.

I wonder about her as I jog, my breath fogging the air, my skin breaking out in a sweat under my insulated clothing. Does she know about her brother? Has she heard? Finally she is free again.

And the demon is dead.

I cut across the creek, cracking the ice, seeing a trickle beneath it, then head up the hill, along the deer trail, almost slipping once, but catching myself.

Though Elyssa's sacrifice has been less than exhilarating, the next will be one of the best. Better than either of the last two. Regan Pescoli is a worthy adversary, and the pain I feel in my muscles, the bites on my neck, are constant reminders that I must not underestimate her.

That would be an irreversible, fatal flaw.

I'm breathing hard as I climb the hillside, following the trail and knowing that even now Elyssa is expiring, the first one probably already dead.

Perfect.

A tiny zing sizzles through my blood at the thought that I ended her life. I had that power. This, the way I kill them, is slow. Slightly impersonal. I never feel that surge of supreme ecstasy I imagine a killer might feel who wields a knife.

But knowing that I controlled another's destiny, a woman, I'm sure, who was put on this earth to fulfill my needs, suffices.

For now.

Over the final hillock, I spy my truck. Quickly I load up, toss my backpack and kit into the back. Despite my gloves, I feel the cold.

No time to waste!

I climb into my truck, spark the engine, then let off the emergency brake. Snow begins to fall as the tires grip and I work my way down the hill, easing down the steep slope, the snow tires digging deep, transmission whining.

It's slow going, but eventually, around a final corner, I spy the county road in the distance. A few vehicles are traveling at a slow speed through the curtain of snow and I smile.

Once on a level surface, I increase my speed, frown at the clock, and tell myself it'll all work out.

I need to take care of an errand or two, then return to the mine and make sure Pescoli is as broken and needy as she was when I left her last night.

My jaw tightens. It worries me a bit that the marks will be permanent; always a reminder that she almost got the better of me.

Almost.

Setting my jaw, I head home.

I need to clean up before I return to town, where, I anticipate, all hell is breaking loose.

It's a good feeling and I turn on the radio once more only to hear Burl Ives's voice and that irritating melody again. "Oh, by golly, have a—"

I push the button to a country-western station.

For the love of God, what's wrong with the DJs, playing that insipid song over and over again? Despite Randy Travis's deep voice, I can't get the whole holly jolly thing out of my mind.

As the windshield slaps at the snow I find myself humming to the catchy little melody.

It's a damned curse.

"All I know is that Mr. Long called and told me that he would be visiting the ranch," Clementine said.

"You mean Brady Long," Alvarez clarified. An easy assumption; according to all reports, Hubert was on his deathbed.

"Yes." Clementine's lower lip quivered and she wrung her hands nervously. Her son, Ross, a tall, sullen kid, looked like he would rather be anyplace else on earth than standing in the vestibule of the home of a dead man and talking to an officer of the law. His head was shaved, a straggly goatee decorated his chin, and a tattoo peeked out from the neck of his ski jacket. Snow had melted on the jacket's shoulders and Ross's jeans were wet at the top of his boots, as if he'd been walking through deep snowdrifts. His face was a little red. The cold? Exertion? He nearly sneered at Alvarez and carried the air about him that suggested he would have liked the words *Bad Ass* inked across his forehead.

"You didn't talk to Mr. Long?" she asked Ross.

He shook his head vigorously, losing a bit of the disinterested, cool-appearing demeanor he was trying so hard to convey.

"You've been outside this morning?"

"Yeah . . . I went . . . I was in town."

All the evidence from the crime had been collected, but the sheriff's department had roped off the den with crime scene tape, and the hallways and dining area were a mess—fingerprint powder blackening the walls and furniture, footprints tracked throughout the house.

"What can you tell me about that conversation?" she asked Clementine.

"As I told the other officers, it was nothing out of the ordinary. Every so often, Mr. Brady, he would call and tell me to stock the kitchen and bar because he was going to come back and spend a few days here to unwind. That's how he usually put it, 'unwind' or 'relax' or 'get away from the grind.'"

"Do you know what he was 'getting away' from?"

"He never confided in me."

Alvarez wasn't certain that was the truth. "You work for him, too?" she asked Ross.

"When I'm not in school. I help out Santana."

"He's like the foreman," Clementine ventured. "Ross is his helper."

"Along with some others?"

Clementine was nodding.

"You've worked for the Longs for quite a while."

"Over twenty years."

"And Ross's father?" Alvarez looked at the boy, who shifted from one foot to the other.

"He left us. Before Ross was born. I wasn't married and he . . . he didn't want a baby." She licked her lips and looked at the floor.

"His name is Alvin Schwartz and he's a real asshole. He's a cop, too," Ross added.

"Enough!" Clementine said, shushing her son.

"Al? Who works at the jail?" Alvarez pictured the jailor, a part-timer who was in his early forties. A big guy, ex-football-player type, who wore his hair clipped so short as to be nearly bald. Other than the hairstyle, there was little resemblance between father and son.

"Ross takes after my side of the family," Clementine commented, as if reading Alvarez's mind.

Ross snorted, "He's not in the family."

They talked for a little while about the Long family and Alvarez learned little more than she already knew. Then Clementine said, "Mr. Hubert, he's near death, I heard." She sketched a quick sign of the cross over her chest. "And now, Mr. Brady is gone. I'm wondering if I even have a job left. Who will own this place?" She lifted her hands in a sweeping gesture to take in all of the house and surrounding acres.

"I don't know, but I imagine someone will call and let you know." Alvarez turned her attention to Ross. "You go to community college, right? And work around here. Can you tell me what you were doing yesterday morning?"

He stared at her. "You think I popped Brady?"

"Ross!" Clementine hissed and looked like she might faint.

"That's what she's getting at." His eyes glittered, as if he had figured out Alvarez's game. "Isn't it?"

"Just keeping track of everyone he knew," Selena said.

"I was at school. You can check with Jamie."

"Who's she?"

"*He's* my friend. I pick him up."

She took down Jamie's number, made a note to give him a jingle.

"Either one of you know Regan Pescoli?"

"Another cop," Ross said derisively.

"My partner."

"She's missing, isn't she?" Clementine asked and shook her head. "I saw it on the news."

Ross lifted a shoulder. "I met her a couple of times. I know her kid. He's cool."

"Is he?" She asked a few more questions, but it seemed the connection between Ross DeGrazio and Jeremy Strand was a thin one at best. Acquaintances. Not friends. There were a couple of years between them.

"I heard she was doin' Santana."

"Oh, stop it!" Clementine looked about to die. "I'm so sorry," she apologized.

Alvarez leveled her gaze at the kid. "Seems as if Ross here has a problem with authority."

"I just don't like cops."

"Because of your old man?"

"Because I don't like 'em."

Alvarez asked a few more questions, didn't get any more information, and decided she'd learned all she could. Whether he knew it or not, Ross DeGrazio was still, in her mind, on the suspect list, along with Cort Brewster.

But the kid seemed too green to pull off something so intricate. It just didn't quite fit. Just like Brewster; as much as she disliked the man, and as much as some pieces of the Star-Crossed puzzle fit his profile, she couldn't quite see him as a cold-blooded killer who had spent years planning this series of brutal slayings. She supposed smart-ass Ross could be stupid enough to get caught in some kind of gang killing, but even then she didn't see him as the trigger man. He had a problem with authority, yeah, but Alvarez would bet that Ross DeGrazio would rather run from the police than provoke, taunt, or toy with them. He just didn't have the balls. As for Brewster, he might kill in the line of duty or as an act of passion, as was proven by his attack on Jeremy Strand.

But Alvarez couldn't believe either of them had the time, effort, or dedication to have plotted and carried out these killings. As much as she'd worried about Brewster earlier, it just didn't fit.

Besides, she couldn't prove that either man had means, motive, and opportunity.

And though she was relieved to knock Brewster off the suspect list, it only meant that Star-Crossed was someone else.

Someone who would love to see her chasing her tail or arresting the wrong suspect, someone who thought he was so much smarter than the police.

We'll see about that, bastard. Don't count me out yet.

Chapter Twenty-Six

Santana shut the stable door and eyed the sky warily. Another blizzard was bearing down on the Bitterroots. Another night had passed with no news of Pescoli.

And he still hadn't heard one damned word from Chilcoate. Not one.

The guy wasn't returning his calls, nor had he bothered to phone and give Santana an update.

It hasn't even been twelve hours and here you are jumping out of your skin. Give the guy some time, he told himself.

But that was the problem.

He felt like he had no time left, not a minute.

And he had to do something.

Couldn't just sit around and wait, for God's sake!

Turning his collar to the wind, with Nakita leaping and bounding in the fresh snow, he glanced down the lane to the main house where lights were glowing, lights that had been on ever since he'd discovered Brady Long's body.

Was it just yesterday?

Jesus H. Christ, it seemed like a lifetime had passed.

He noticed a car in the drive . . . no, a Jeep, and for a split second hope jumped in his heart. Until he saw Selena Alvarez leaving through the front door and striding swiftly to the Jeep, a government-issue vehicle that was almost identical to Pescoli's, the one that had been totaled in its horrific spiral from Horsebrier Ridge.

He started jogging toward the main house and Nakita, loving the acceleration, yipped excitedly, then ran in circles around Santana as he yelled, "Hey!" before Alvarez could slide behind the wheel.

She paused and he waved while slogging through the snow that was beginning to pile up along the lane that he'd plowed late last night. He was breathing hard by the time he reached her rig.

"Something up?" she asked, the door to her Jeep open.

"I just wanted to know if you've heard anything." He didn't bother trying to mask his emotions. "About Regan."

"No. Don't make me remind you that you're not part of the investigation."

He ignored her. "What about Ivor Hicks?"

"What about him?"

"Did anyone find out what he was doing here . . . I mean, besides that cock-and-bull story about being forced here by aliens and seeing a Yeti."

"Ivor was drunk. At ten in the morning. That was pretty obvious to both of us, I believe."

"Didn't he find another one of the victims?"

Alvarez nodded slowly, her lips tight, snow catching on the brim of her hat.

"Was he drunk then, too?"

She didn't respond and he looked away, to the house, where in the reflection of the windows, on the upper story he saw Ross, standing in the shadows, as if he were trying to hide, but observing the scene below.

Her cell phone rang and she said, "Excuse me."

But he wasn't done. Even though he hadn't expected to learn anything, he felt a needle of disappointment prick his heart. "She's important to me," he said flatly, looking away toward the stable and barns, his jaw tight. The law, it seemed, was always an obstacle. "I'd just like to know if you hear something."

"I have to take this call."

He nodded, then took off, heading back to his little house. Nakita, now that some of his energy had been burned, was staying close to Santana's heels.

He knew Alvarez wouldn't call him. She'd barely give him the time of day. Even if she wanted to, which she didn't, her hands were bound.

So, as an outsider, he would have to do things his own way.

First up, he thought, buy Ivor Hicks a Bloody Mary.

"I'm afraid I have some bad news," Dr. Ramsby said with a soft smile as she gazed across her desk to the wan-looking woman seated in front of her.

Padgett Long was staring at her intently, her face devoid of expression, her wide blue eyes never leaving the psychologist's as rain drizzled down the window of Ramsby's office. She wore no makeup but she was still a striking woman with a smooth complexion, her curly dark hair and intense blue eyes rimmed by sweeping black eyelashes. But she didn't respond. Long ago, Jalicia had learned that it was the quiet ones who were the most frightening. One was always wary of the psychotics prone to outbursts, but the silent ones, the ones who lived in their own private hellish worlds—they were the ones to watch closely, the ones who could lull a person into a false and deadly sense of security.

"This unfortunate news is actually twofold."

Still not so much as a glimmer of understanding.

"First, your father is in failing health. I know we've told you that before. He's been in a nursing facility and steadily declining."

Padgett waited. Patiently. As if in another world.

"I spoke with Mr. Tinneman, your father's attorney, and he told me it was your father's dying wish to see his grandson, your child. I initially declined to talk to you about it. I wanted a member of the family to ask for your help, if they wanted it."

Was there just the flicker of understanding, an involuntary narrowing of the corner of her eyes?

"But I decided you have every right to know what your family is intending. Your father wants to find your son. It's my understanding that you may have given him up for adoption through the Cahill House in San Francisco?"

Still nothing.

Dr. Ramsby waited, feeling the gray of the Seattle weather seep through her window. The morning had dawned rain-washed, the sky muddled with low-hanging clouds. Though this office was decorated with soft, ambient light, a cozy love seat and matching chair, and, to accompany her desk, several side chairs, the drab of the day permeated all of the decorator's best interests.

She held a pen over Padgett's file, intending to take notes, but she decided it might be an exercise in futility, so she folded the thick file and tucked it into a drawer.

"The other news is about your brother."

The blue eyes didn't waver.

"I'm afraid he was killed yesterday. At your family estate in Montana." Padgett's gaze was transfixed upon the doctor, as if she were listening intently. "The authorities believe it was homicide. After speaking with Mr. Tinneman, I called the Pinewood County Sheriff's Department this morning and spoke to a Detective Alvarez. The police don't know yet who shot your brother."

Padgett shifted slightly in her chair. Refolded her hands.

"I assume there will be a funeral. You will probably want to attend?" She asked it as a question and there was a hint of interest, a blink.

"Padgett? Do you understand what I'm telling you?"

"Perfectly," the woman said without a second's hesitation. "My brother is dead, so I can leave now."

Jalicia's jaw literally dropped. "What?" Padgett was already starting to get to her feet, as if the discussion were over after fifteen years of being mute. "Wait a minute. You haven't said a word since you entered this facility and now . . . you're . . . able to speak . . . and you want to leave?"

"I've always been able to talk."

"But you haven't."

"Not to you or any of those other ridiculous doctors my father hired. Ask Rosie or Toby or . . . or Scott."

"Who are they?"

"Other inmates."

"You mean patients . . . there is no Rosie or . . ."

"Rose Anne Weeks, Tobias Settlemeier, and Scott Dowd. They were all before your time. Inmates."

"Where are they now?"

"They're dead, Dr. Ramsby. Someone pulled me down here to this very room to tell me that they'd died. Rosie committed suicide—hanged herself at the next facility to which she was committed by her parents. Toby's in prison. No one told me that. They wouldn't. But I overheard Nurse Martha telling one of the aides all about it." She offered up a saccharine smile. "She gossips, you know, and eats the desserts of the ones who don't really know what she's up to. She's really into apple crisp and ice cream."

She turned toward the door.

"We're not finished here," Dr. Ramsby said.

"Sure we are. I know that I came here voluntarily and that no one ever bothered to set up a guardianship. Otherwise, I'm pretty sure that I would have been before a judge to determine my ability, or inability, to take care of myself. Since that didn't happen, I suspect my father thought that my brother would always see to my care." Her eyes darkened with a deep, simmering hatred. "As if he would." She reached for the door handle. "Now that he's dead, it's safe for me again, so I know you have the authority and some money set aside for me. Again, Nurse Martha, maybe she talks a little more freely than she should. What I need from you is a car to pick me up and take me to the airport. SeaTac isn't far from here. I see and hear the jets, so then I'll want to be on the next flight to San Francisco."

"You mean Denver, right?" Dr. Ramsby clarified. She was beginning to believe that the slim woman before her knew exactly what she wanted and that she had for a long, long time.

"San Francisco. As you said, that's where my son is, but I won't be taking him to see dear old Dad. The old man didn't want him fifteen years ago, he's not going to get to see him now, even if I can find him, which is going to be difficult." Her lips thinned. "Let's get the ball rolling, shall we?"

"Just like that? You want to leave just like that?"

"I've wanted to leave for a long time, Dr. Ramsby. But it just wasn't safe."

"And now it is?"

"If my brother is really dead? Yes."

"Don't you want to call someone?"

"Who? My brother's dead, and if he's currently married, I've never met my sister-in-law."

"He wasn't."

"My mother's dead, too, and my father, as you said, is about to die. So who would that leave?"

"I don't know. Maybe . . . Let's see." She picked up the file and flipped to the reports listing visitors. "How about Liam Kress?"

Something twitched in Padgett's face. "I haven't heard from Liam in a long while."

"Maybe he'd like to know you were able to speak and intent on leaving."

Padgett shook her head. "No, I'm sure not. Now, let's get on with it." She made a looping motion. "Just do whatever paperwork you have to and I'll sign myself out of here. ASAP. I don't see why we can't get all of it done within the hour and you can see that I'll have that car waiting for me at the front gates, just as I've seen other cars come and go over the years. It's the McMurray Service, I believe."

"There's more to it than that."

"Yes. I'll need access to funds. I'm sure I have a bank account somewhere."

"I don't know. I'll give you Mr. Tinneman's phone number."

"I'll need more than that. I assume that there's an account for me, here, at Mountain View. I'll need a check for the balance."

"That might take some time."

Padgett smiled. "It's my money, doctor."

"Along with the paperwork, you'll need to pack your things—"

"Oh. That's right. You're relatively new here," she said and folded her slim arms across her chest. "You probably didn't get the memo. I'm already packed. Everything I need is in my bag."

"Already?"

"Yes."

Ramsby was puzzled. Felt she was being played. "How did you know you'd be leaving today, that your brother had died?"

Padgett tossed her hair over one shoulder. "Because I pack up every week, and on Sunday, Farrell, the aide, unpacks my bag and washes the perfectly clean clothes. So, you see, Dr. Ramsby, I've been packed for fifteen years. My clothes are probably hideously out of style and faded, but they'll get me out of here and once I'm free I'll take care of buying a few things."

She walked to the door, intent on leaving. "The

way I figure it," Padgett said over her shoulder as she tugged the door open and stepped to the hallway, the psychologist right behind her, "I'll be able to afford some new things." With an enigmatic smile and a wave, she headed toward the elevator, the very area where Ramsby had thought she'd fled not that long ago.

Jalicia stared after her, thinking hard.

Padgett Long had anticipated that she would be leaving, as if she'd known her brother had been murdered before she'd crossed the carpeted threshold to Ramsby's office.

How the hell had she known?

The last person Dan Grayson wanted to see was Manny Douglas, but the weasel of a writer was on his way to the department.

Considering how things were going with the press in general, and the *Mountain Reporter* specifically, Grayson wanted to throttle the journalist, or at the very least tell Douglas to take a flying leap, but Manny had been insistent.

"I've got something you need to see," he'd said on the phone fifteen minutes earlier. "If it were up to me, I'd say 'screw you' and just do my thing, expose the damned serial killer and be a hero, but my editor has some twisted ethics."

"You can expose Star-Crossed?" Grayson asked, but inwardly thought, *What a crock.*

"I've got some evidence."

Grayson had doubted it. "What evidence?"

"It's something you need to see."

"What is it?"

"I'll come show it to you."

"If you've got evidence, Douglas, you'll be leaving it."

"We'll talk about it."

"I've got a busy day." Grayson wasn't buying the bold reporter's story. Manny had been known to brag and bluster on more than one occasion.

"Not too busy for this. I'll be there in half an hour." And Manny had hung up in his brusque I'm-so-important way that always bugged Grayson, but then anything Manny Douglas did tended to get under the sheriff's skin.

It wasn't as if he didn't have enough to do.

But if the guy had anything, any little shred of evidence or a clue to the killer, Grayson couldn't afford to turn him away.

Outside a mother of a storm was passing through again, though the weather service said that it should break up by late that afternoon. God, he hoped so.

Now, the television set in his office was turned low to the news. Again, the weather was the topic, the report nearly finished.

"And I've got good news for all the boys and girls," the perky blond weather girl at KBTR television noon edition predicted after showing a satellite view of the area. "It looks like Santa is going to get through after all! So put out a plate of cookies and a big cup of hot chocolate tonight. It's going to be a cold one." She grinned into the camera, the white ball of her Santa's hat bouncing near her cheek. "Back to you, Kelly and Darren."

"Thanks, Rhonda!" Kelly, the smiling anchor-woman, said as she stared straight into the studio camera. Her smile was wide, her hair streaked blond, her personality usually bright. Today, her grin slid from her face and her expression mirrored that of her more serious co-anchor, Darren Faust, a square-jawed newsman with thick dark hair and an easy, if fleeting, smile.

"On a more somber note," she said, glancing down at her notes, "last night Sheriff Dan Grayson of Pinewood County held a press conference on the steps of the sheriff's office to discuss the latest information on the serial killer known as the Star-Crossed Killer who has been terrorizing the greater area around Grizzly Falls for the past few months. Ever since the body of Theresa Charleton was discovered by hikers—"

Grayson aimed his remote like a gun and shot the television. He knew what he'd said in the press conference, the questions he'd answered about the killer. He didn't need another run-through.

Stretching, he walked into the hallway where a janitor was busily mopping down the floor where dozens of boots had left a trail of melting snow. The janitor was a big man who worked part-time, but lately, with the bad weather, the department had added hours to his shift.

"Never ends, does it, Seymore?" the sheriff said.

"You got that right!" Chuckling, he worked his way backward from the orange cone he'd placed near the reception area warning that the floor was wet.

Alvarez was at her desk; he'd seen her return a few minutes earlier. Now she was frowning thoughtfully at her monitor and the image of a forest service map of the rugged, mountainous terrain where the killer had shot out the tires of the vehicles of his victims.

"Learn anything from the DeGrazios?" he asked, stopping in the doorway.

She glanced up. "You mean other than that her kid needs to be taken down a peg or two or twenty?"

"That bad?"

"Overindulged only child raised by a single mother who—"

"Loves him too much."

"I was going to say 'makes excuses for him.' And no, I didn't find out anything useful. I did run into Santana, though, and he asked what Ivor Hicks was doing at the Lazy L, and since Ivor was already released, I couldn't ask him."

"I thought Crytor had sent him."

"Yeah, so he says . . ."

"Manny Douglas is on his way down."

"Really?"

"Says he has something I need to see, which is probably just bull, but I thought you might join me."

"To referee?"

"To make sure I don't kill him."

"Yeah, don't do that. It might ruin your chances for reelection. Has the undersheriff come in?"

"Brewster called. Got hung up in a meeting downtown. He'll be in shortly. Why?"

"Just wondering."

"Yeah, right, Alvarez. You never wonder about anything without a purpose."

"Okay, you caught me. I have a crush on him," she said and he almost laughed. He noticed the spark in her dark eyes, something he hadn't seen in a long while, not since the first victim had been discovered.

"Does Brewster know?"

"Sure, but it's a problem, him being married and all." She gave him a steady glance. "You do know that was a joke, right?"

"Uh, yeah."

"Good." She scooted her chair back and followed him to his office just as Joelle called Grayson to say Manny had arrived.

"Show him in," Grayson said and hung up. With a glance at Alvarez, who was leaning against the window casing, he said under his breath, "Showtime."

Seconds later Joelle clipped in, Manny at her side. Grayson forced a smile he didn't feel. "Manny." The sheriff stood and waved the smaller man into a side chair. "You know Detective Alvarez?"

"Detective." Manny nodded toward Alvarez as he took his seat. Dressed in his usual outfit, khaki pants, a plaid shirt, and sweater vest, straight out of Eddie Bauer, he could have been a spokesperson for the store. Even his all-weather jacket seemed a part of a planned outfit.

Grayson figured he should clear the air and let the jerk of a reporter know where he stood. "I talked to your editor this morning. Lodged a complaint about that headline piece you wrote this morning. There are laws against libel, you know."

Manny didn't so much as flinch. "I stand by everything I wrote, Sheriff, and that's why it galls me that I'm here. If it weren't for my editor—"

"What is it you think is so all-fired important?" Grayson cut in, still seething about the scathing article attacking him and his people.

"It's about Star-Crossed."

"And?" Alvarez said, leaning forward slightly.

"Seems he's decided to make me his pen pal."

Grayson thought he hadn't heard right. "What?"

Manny was already reaching into his jacket. He withdrew a large manila envelope, the front of which was addressed to him in the same block letters that were used in all of the notes left at the crime scene.

Manny tipped up the envelope and the contents spilled out—pages of white paper. Each page was slightly different, the notes shorter or longer. With the notes were pictures, colored photographs of all of the victims bound to the trees where they had died.

"Jesus," Alvarez whispered.

Grayson felt his throat tighten. "Where did you get this?"

"Compliments of the U.S. mail."

"Is Pescoli—?" Alvarez whispered.

"No." Manny was firm. "These are the originals I received, but I've kept copies of the notes and the pictures. Most of the women I've identified, and I've figured out their initials are part of the killer's note. But the last ones must be still out in the woods somewhere."

Grayson stared down at the longest note and felt only a little relief that the letters *R* and *P* for *Regan Pescoli* weren't a part of the message—at least, not yet.

"Last ones?" Alvarez repeated. Then, "Brandy Hooper," as, looking pale, she stared at the new message:

BEWAR   THE SC   I ON' H

"We're going to press with a special edition," Manny said.

"You can't print this!" Grayson declared.

The reporter shot back with, "The public has a right to know!"

"I'll decide what the public is allowed to know. First we need to locate these women, try to save them, if possible, notify next of kin, and we can't let out all the details of these notes." Grayson wanted to throttle the little weasel.

"This is my story, Grayson, and I'm going to run with it."

"Not without my say-so. I'll get a court order to see that this is kept under wraps until the appropriate time." Grayson was beyond angry now. He felt a tic throbbing at his temples and it was all he could do not to throw the smug little bastard into jail for the rest of his rotten life.

But Douglas wasn't intimidated. "Then, Sheriff, I want an exclusive."

"You can't have it."

"The killer contacted me. Chose me." Douglas hooked a thumb at his chest. "These photos and notes are my property. I'm just showing you as a good citizen who—"

"Who just wants to profit from all this tragedy!"

"I'm the people's voice! And your conscience!"

"Oh, Christ, Douglas, don't even try that bullshit with me." Grayson was on his feet now, leaning across the desk where the damning evidence was strewn.

"Don't you get it, Sheriff? You have to play ball with me. Star-Crossed, he's going to send me more information, maybe even call me. So I'm on the field whether you want me to be or not!"

"Give it to him," Alvarez said.

"What?"

"Who cares who breaks the story first? Give him

the exclusive, with guidelines . . . rules that he has to play by. He's right. Star-Crossed might contact him again, use him as a conduit."

Douglas was nodding and some of his smugness evaporated, if only sightly. "Trust me, I want this guy put away as much as you do."

Grayson doubted it.

Alvarez placed a hand on his arm, a reminder to keep his cool when all he wanted was to throw Douglas's skinny little ass in jail and throw away the key. God, he was frustrated. But even sitting around and talking about it, they were running out of time. There was a chance, albeit a slim one, that they could still find the women in the notes alive.

She was right.

Grayson knew it.

But he hated to give in to blackmail.

"Don't fuck with me, Douglas," he warned, pointing a finger in the reporter's face. "Don't you goddamned mess with me, you got that? You play by my rules."

"Let's go!" Alvarez said.

"Just so you know, I have copies of these," the reporter reminded him, leaving the scattered letters strewn across Grayson's desk. "And don't you fuck with me, either, Grayson. It wouldn't be smart."

Chapter Twenty-Seven

Keep going.
Don't stop.
You'll find your way out of here!

Regan was exhausted. She'd followed the length of two tunnels and found nothing, no exit, no other secret chamber where the bastard locked his victims away. Her legs threatened to give out and she could barely hold the handle of the poker as she made her way along the length of what appeared to be a main tunnel and each of the offshoots she'd explored until she was certain they would go nowhere.

Her task seemed impossible and she was certain she'd been at it for hours. The flashlight's beam was turning yellow, dying slowly. She couldn't get lost in these tunnels without any source of light.

Reviewing the marks she'd made on the floor, she inched her way backward to the room where the creep did his work, the one with the big table and armoire, the place where he kept his treasures, pictures of his kills, and the notes he planned to leave with his next victims. She couldn't be here, but she didn't know how to leave!

Ears straining, she made her way back to the doorway she'd entered into the tunnel and listened, barely letting out her breath, trying to determine if someone was on the other side. Unlike the door to her room, the one in which she'd been held captive, this door was snug in its frame, no shaft of light pierced the tunnel gloom.

She waited.

Heard nothing.

No footsteps of a big man walking across stone.

No crackle or hiss of a fire.

Biting her lip, flashlight tucked under one arm, poker raised to defend herself, knife tucked in her waistband, Pescoli slowly opened the door . . . to find the room where he worked cold and dark, only a few tiny embers giving off any light. Relieved, she surveyed her surroundings and listened hard, hoping to hear the other woman, the sobs that had whispered through this old mine, the muffled cries of a woman distraught and frightened.

Again she was met with silence.

She looked through the drawers of the armoire, searching for batteries, and as she did she saw the notes again, the horrible pictures of terrified women as they froze to death. Daughters, sisters, mothers. Her throat thickened. It had been her job to find them, to save them, to protect them. *To protect and serve.* And she'd done neither.

She rifled through the notes again. A whole stack of them, one atop the other, his message growing clearer with each new page, with each new set of initials.

Hers were there, she realized.

BEWAR   THE   SC   RPION'   H

Halden had been right about the whole "Beware the Scorpion" thing and when she looked at the final page, the entire note read:

BEWARE THE SCORPION'S WRATH

Yes, she was an intended victim, and certainly Elyssa O'Leary, but there were others as well. Were they all captured already, hidden in the tunnels of this old mine?

But where?

Or was he still planning to hunt them down?

She didn't have time to try and reason it out. She had to keep moving. Discovering one more battery in a drawer, she rummaged for another, needing two. Unable to find another, she switched the flashlight off, hoping, even with just one new battery, that it would offer enough light to lead her out of this crypt.

There was another door, she realized. Another exit to the tunnels? She tried it and looked down several steps to another dark passageway.

How many of these suckers are there?

Drawing a strengthening breath, she propelled herself forward into the musty-smelling corridor. She'd barely taken two steps when she heard something.

Movement.

Oh, no!

Flicking off the flashlight, shivering in the dark with the closeness of the cold earthen walls surrounding her, she strained to listen.

Heard it again.

A soft little noise . . .

"Elyssa?" she thought hopefully, then felt something brush across the back of her head.

She nearly screamed.

Dropped the flashlight.

It rolled wildly, illuminating the walls and the thousands of tiny eyes staring at her. A whisper of wings fluttered as she spied the colony of bats nesting in the crevices of the ceiling. "Oh, hell," she whispered, nearly undone, her heart thumping erratically. Bats? Frigging bats? That was a good sign, right? They had to find a way out, to hunt, to feed.

Reaching down, she grabbed her flashlight and wiped the detritus, dirt, and bat crap from its handle. Her nerves were shot, her body aching and tired, but she kept on as the beam slowly faded.

She didn't take any of the tunnel's spurs, just shined her feeble light down them because she couldn't risk getting lost. If she stayed on this main path, she would be able to return to the hidden room, find a lantern or some other means of illumination, and start over.

The light went out and plunged her into darkness. Regan reached her left hand to the tunnel wall and kept moving forward. One step in front of the other. The tunnel jogged, and jogged again, but she was certain she was still in the main one.

Her foot bumped into something hard and she fell forward onto a set of wooden stairs. And was that fresh air from above? Something different than the stale atmosphere she'd been wandering in?

She climbed on her hands and knees, holding on to the poker and flashlight as she worked her way forward. The bottom step was worn and wooden, the next a bit higher, curving upward.

Regan wanted to weep. This was it! Freedom!

Heart leaping, she ascended slowly. Trying to be patient, not clamber wildly as she sought freedom.

Go slowly.

Be careful.

He could be waiting.

Up, up, up.

More fresh air filtered down and she saw a bit of daylight through a hole in the ceiling high above, no doubt the entrance for the damned bats. It offered some light, enough for her to make out the rough-hewn walls around her.

Around a final bend, she spied the door.

Anticipation zipped through her blood. Setting down her flashlight, she climbed the final steps and gripped the door's metal lever.

God, please, don't let it be locked.

She paused.

Listened.

Mentally geared herself for whatever lay ahead.

Then slowly, teeth clenched, she twisted the handle. The door clicked open and swung inward, revealing a wide, interior room much like the one she'd last seen. There was a work area and fireplace here as well, embers cold and dark, but daylight was streaming in through the windows.

Her knees nearly gave way as she looked outside, the white, dazzling snow nearly blinding. She searched the room quickly for a weapon, anything stronger than the poker and she found some tools, a hammer, screwdriver, and pliers. She stuffed them in her pockets and wished like hell for her pistol. Any gun. But there were none in this room. Nor a phone or computer or any means of communication. She found a tiny bathroom and kitchen alcove in this stone and log cabin. There was a bedroom as well. With an old iron-frame bed and sagging mattress.

Where he stayed. She could smell him and it made her sick. She thought of him, how he'd attacked her.

His size.

His voice.

His walk.

All familiar. She knew that she should recognize him and an image teased at the edges of her mind, but never quite developed.

Keep moving. He could return at any second.

She opened another door, one that could be locked with a key.

Her heart dropped as she spied the small bed with its handmade quilt, the table next to it where a plate with remnants of food and a half-full water glass remained.

Elyssa.

This is where he kept her.

Healed her.

Tended to her.

Gave her hope.

And it's too late.

He's already taken her.

To leave her in the forest to freeze to death.

You failed.

Despair cut a deep swath through Pescoli's soul. She told herself that the girl was doomed from the get-go. Didn't the notes she'd found in his lair prove it? And yet, if she somehow could have saved her . . .

Don't think of it.

Get out.

Get out now.

Before the bastard returns.

You can nail him.

Save the others.

Save yourself.

Just get the hell out now!

She was already moving to the door that opened to the outside. Whatever the obstacles she had to face in the frozen wilderness, it was a helluva lot safer than staying here.

She could get help.

Lead them back here.

And arrest the son of a bitch.

If she didn't kill him first.

Carrying a cup of coffee, Alvarez walked into the task force room, where those on duty were gathering.

The notes that Manny Douglas left with them appeared to be authentic. Alvarez had checked, comparing them to the ones that had been placed with the victims. These new ones, when set directly over their older counterparts, looked as if they'd been traced, each letter perfectly positioned.

Of course, the new evidence would be scrutinized and tested, compared by experts, analyzed by the FBI, but it looked like there were two more Star-Crossed victims. Two more dead or dying in the forest, though not, it seemed, Regan Pescoli.

Yet . . .

She set her cup of coffee on the table already littered with half-full cups and notepads as others took seats, the sound of chair legs screeching across the floor accompanied by muted conversation.

Cort Brewster and Dan Grayson entered the room together and stood near the desk where Zoller was on phone detail. The meeting was informal, just a means to update as many as possible who were working the Star-Crossed Killer case.

Grayson said, "I'll make this quick as we're all busy. Manny Douglas from the *Mountain Reporter* showed up today."

The reporter's name elicited a catcall from Pete Watershed. "My favorite."

There were mumbled snorts of disgust, as everyone had read the searing article. Grayson continued, "It seems that Star-Crossed has decided to communicate through him."

"Douglas?" Watershed frowned.

"That guy doesn't know the meaning of the truth," Rebecca O'Day, a corporal deputy, said, shaking her head.

"Well, he's now our conduit," Alvarez said as she passed around copies of the notes Douglas had left at the station.

"So now the creep is runnin' to the press?" Brett Gage asked. He was the chief criminal deputy, whose easy smile belied a will of steel. "Damn."

"Two more," O'Day whispered.

They all examined the message:

BEWAR   THE   SC   ION'   H

"No *R* or *P* for *Pescoli*," Trilby Van Droz said slowly. "But if you add them in, the third word could be scorpion."

"There's an apostrophe," Alvarez pointed out. "A possessive."

"Then, what's this guy saying?" O'Day asked. "'Beware the scorpion's hell'? Or 'Beware the scorpion's hate'? Or 'Beware the scorpion's hiss'?"

"Scorpions don't hiss," Watershed pointed out.

Gage added, "It doesn't have to be 'scorpion.' We can't just guess and assume."

"Maybe." Grayson wasn't convinced.

"Isn't that why we turned this over to the FBI? So they can use their cryptologists?" Brewster said.

"We have a list of missing women. If their initials work into this puzzle, we might figure it out ourselves," Alvarez said.

Brewster looked ready to argue, but Gage intervened, "Let's not just get stuck on the notes. What else do we know about this mutt?"

"That he craves attention," Alvarez said. "He made sure we got this information. He wants to be the hot topic. It probably bothered him no end that the copycat stole his press for a while."

O'Day speculated, "Could be why he stepped up his game—two more, and bragging rights to the press."

"But to Manny Douglas?" Gage scowled and leaned back in his chair. "You informed the FBI?"

Grayson nodded. "They're on their way back from Denver and an interview with Hubert Long that went nowhere. The man's comatose, not expected to live more than a couple of days, if that."

There was a moment of silence as they were all lost in their own thoughts and ideas. Then Alvarez said, "Elyssa O'Leary and Brandy Hooper," reading from the missing persons report she'd printed from her computer. "They're the most likely candidates for Star-Crossed."

"We haven't found any vehicles registered to them," Van Droz remarked.

"We will," Watershed said. "Just a matter of time."

"Well, if it's Hooper and O'Leary, then it looks like Star-Crossed has been cozying up to medical students," Zoller pointed out. "Start with Ms. Hooper. Twenty-seven, a resident at OHSU in Portland, Oregon, reported missing nine days ago when she didn't show up at her parents' home in Missoula. Reports were filed in Oregon, Idaho, and Montana. She's the only girl we have on file with the initials *B* and *H*, which, when added to the *E* and *O* from Elyssa O'Leary's initials, who, by the way is a nursing student, would give more credence to the BEWARE THE SCORPION'S . . . something with an *H*."

"O'Leary has an apostrophe," Alvarez said.

Everyone looked at her. "You think he went that far? To even add in the apostrophe?" Grayson asked.

"He has that much attention to detail," she responded.

"Again. A lot of assumptions," Gage said. "There's always the chance that other girls with the same initials have been abducted. Someone who hasn't been reported, or, at least not reported in this jurisdiction."

"O'Leary's parents believe her boyfriend, Cesar Pelton, is involved in her disappearance," Zoller reminded them.

"Any confirmation on that?" Grayson asked.

Brewster shook his head. "Chandler was checking on that."

Gage said, "For now, we won't assume these women are dead. They could still be held captive by Star-Crossed, or just be unlucky enough to have the initials of some of the victims."

"Fat chance," Watershed stated. "We know he's got them."

"There's a possibility we've got the wrong girls," Alvarez said. "So we won't notify their families, nor are we going to assume they're dead. We're going to find them, and we're going to also find the girls these initials do represent."

Grayson nodded his agreement, but Brewster shook his head. "I'm with Watershed. We *know* these are the girls."

"What we need to do is find them," Grayson returned. "And until we have concrete evidence that either Brandy Hooper or Elyssa O'Leary is a Star-Crossed victim, there will be no talking to the press or the womens' families. For the moment Manny Douglas and the *Reporter* are keeping a lid on the contents of the notes, but they can't wait to spill. So let's go get this guy! Get the choppers in the air. Find them!"

He said it with fervor and everyone in the room quickly got to their feet. As they bustled out, Alvarez saw the worry in their eyes. They all believed that somewhere out in the Montana wilderness, two other women were already dead, their bodies blue and frozen.

Maybe three, if you counted Pescoli.

* * *

Jeremy felt like hell. He'd crashed on Tyler's mom's lumpy couch after taking off from the jail. Now his back felt like he'd been sleeping on a bowling ball.

He sighed and got himself into a sitting position. It was still better than the drunk tank. What a bad trip *that* had been, with the old guy yabbering on and on about aliens and old women and Yetis . . . and still no word on Mom.

If he could think of *anything* to do to help find her, he'd do it. But what could he do? Who could he call?

His cell phone was vibrating in his jeans pocket. He pulled it out, annoyed, and saw that Bianca had called him about a jillion times. And then there were her texts:

Where R U?
Come get me!
Call me!!!
I h8 it here!
Where's Mom?

Every text with a damned exclamation point, as if she were wired. Or on something. Though as far as he knew, she was straight. Just a pain in the butt.

Pushing his hair out of his eyes, he got to his feet, used the bathroom, then splashed water over his face to wake himself up. He poked his head into Tyler's room where Tyler was facedown on the bed in his clothes, his face buried in a pillow. He looked half dead, but then made a loud, smacking noise with his mouth as he shifted position.

Tyler's mom was still sleeping, too. Jeremy could hear the sound of snoring through the closed door to her room. She was sawing some serious logs.

He grabbed his keys, cell phone, and wallet, then

walked out of the second-floor apartment, down the stairs to the parking lot. It was snowing like crazy and there had to be four inches piled up on the hood of his truck. He started to put on his gloves, but only had one. Searching his pockets, he didn't find the other, so he headed inside again, searched the couch, and couldn't find it.

Great.

Outside again, he nearly slipped on the stairs, then walked through the snow to his truck.

Man, was he sick of the stuff.

When he moved out of the house, he figured he'd head to California, where there was hot sun and hotter chicks. He'd learn to surf and maybe work in a surf shop on the beach, or in a computer store, or something. He'd do anything, if he could just get out of this cold.

But first Mom had to come home. Had to. It just couldn't be any other way.

His phone buzzed again. This time it was Heidi.

"Yeah?" he said, as he reached his truck and began batting the snow from its windshield with his one glove.

"What's up?"

"Not Tyler."

"What?"

"Never mind."

"My dad said you were in the drunk tank."

"Guess who put me there?" He was still pissed as hell at Heidi's jerk of a dad.

"Well, he let you go," she reminded him, in that wheedling voice that used to turn him on but now bugged him.

" 'Cuz I shouldn't have been arrested!"

"He thinks I should break up with you."

"Not exactly a news flash, Heidi."

"Are you mad at me?" she demanded, getting pissed.

"How would you like to spend the night in a drunk tank with an old guy who thinks he was transported to some alien ship? Not fun."

"Where are you now?"

"Leaving Tyler's."

"Can you stop by and pick me up?"

"No!" Did she have any brains at all? "I'm not gonna go another round with your dad. I know he's probably at work. I don't care. I'll talk to you later."

He clicked off and climbed into the cab, then started heading toward the center of Grizzly Falls. He didn't know where he was going, who he could possibly see. Who might help him find his mom.

He just knew he couldn't count on the police.

The wipers slapped the snow aside but it kept coming down. Jeremy turned by the sheriff's department and got a little heebie-jeebie shiver down his spine. Didn't wanna go back there!

His cell phone buzzed again. *Damn it, Heidi.* But this time it was Bianca.

"I got your billion messages, okay? I'm just busy," he said impatiently, turning the wheel and heading down the hill into Old Grizz.

"Come and get me!" she wailed. "I can't stand it here. Where's Mom? Have you heard anything?"

"No! I—" Jeremy sucked in his breath sharply. There, just climbing out of his truck, was Nate Santana, his mom's lover. Maybe he was the bastard who'd kidnapped her. Maybe it was *his* fault!

"What?" Bianca demanded.

"Gotta go." He clicked off, tossed the cell onto the passenger seat, then parked his truck next to

Santana's. Hurriedly, he climbed out, following the dark-haired man down the slippery, snow-covered sidewalk. "Hey!" he yelled. "Santana!"

The man cocked his head, then slowly turned around. Behind him, the neon sign of the Spot Tavern glowed through the white haze. Seeing Jeremy, Santana frowned, his harsh features growing even harsher. Jeremy strode up to him and they stared at each other through the falling snow.

Looking at him, thinking about him with his mom, thinking about everything that had happened to all of them these last few days, Jeremy felt anger boil up inside him. He wanted to kill the bastard!

"I oughtta rip your fucking head off!" he yelled furiously. "What have you done with my *mom*!"

Chapter Twenty-Eight

What the hell?

It took Santana a second to recognize Jeremy Strand, Regan's son, with his tousled, didn't-bother-with-a-comb hair and wrinkled pants. But there the boy was, standing just yards from him, eyes blazing, bare fists curled, standing on the balls of his feet, looking like he was ready to lunge.

"You think I had something to do with your mom's disappearance?" Santana asked, stunned by the kid's nerve.

"I know you've been doin' her!"

"Hey!" Santana took a step toward the kid, pointing a gloved finger at Jeremy's face. "That's enough! I wish I did know where your mother was. I do. But I don't. I had nothing to do with her disappearance."

"Sure." Jeremy spat on the ground. He was itching to take a swing.

"I don't have time for this BS. Take your attitude

and go home." He felt the clock ticking, the seconds of Regan's life sliding away. In a lower voice, he added, "I know it's rough, man, but this isn't helping."

"Like you would know!" Jeremy's jaw was set. Hard. He didn't appear as if he were ready to back down, and now a couple of men who had been heading into the bar had paused near the parking meters, watching from beneath the brims of hats fast collecting snow.

Nate groaned inside.

Just what he needed: a crowd.

Next thing you knew a police cruiser would stop by.

"Just calm down," he said, opening up his palm in a conciliatory gesture.

"You're the only lowlife she hangs out with."

Santana gritted his teeth. The kid was spoiling for a fight and Santana thought it might be a good lesson to take him on. They were about the same height, though Santana probably had thirty pounds on the kid. But sometimes, he knew from his own experience, something physical, including a wrestling match or fistfight, was just what a testosterone-fired teenage boy needed to get his brain back. To think straight.

The guys near the meters weren't budging. Hoping for some action. The door to the bar opened for a second, the sounds of conversation and music tinkling out, and then Ole Olson, a regular who was as wide as he was tall, walked onto the street. He was zipping up his coat and stopped short just outside the door, fascinated by the hint of a fight. This was no good.

"Listen, Jeremy, you need to go find your sister and wait."

"My sister," Jeremy snorted. "She's a pain."

"That might just be a family trait."

"Hey! Don't go knocking my family!" Jeremy bristled.

"It's what your mother would want. For her kids to be together."

"How would you know what she'd want?"

"I want her back, too," he gritted. "And I'm trying to figure it out, so don't get in my way!"

"Don't take any shit, kid," Ole, never long on brains, said, still trying to work his zipper. "Go on, what're ya waitin' for?" His fat hand yanked on the zipper tab so hard it snapped off. "Oh, hell."

"Is that what you want? To knock me flat?" Santana asked.

"Yes." Jeremy was emphatic.

"Then, come on. Take your best shot." He figured Jeremy might take one swing, but he could duck it and pin the kid on the icy sidewalk, if he had to.

From the corner of his eye he noticed Ivor Hicks jaywalking from a parking lot across the street and making a beeline for the welcoming warmth of the Spot.

Jeremy saw the old guy, too. Watched Ivor walk through the door. If possible, his lips thinned more.

"I don't have time for this," Santana said, his attention on Ivor. Jeremy seized the moment, flinging himself through the air, throwing a punch that landed square on Santana's jaw.

Damn!

Pain exploded on the side of his face. Instinctively, Nate grabbed the boy and twisted him around, using a move he'd learned in the military, which sent the kid to his knees.

Leaning forward, the boy's arm twisted painfully, Santana gritted into his ear. "You do *not* want to mess with me. Got that? I'm doing everything I can to find your mom. I wasn't kidding when I say I care about her. I'm doing everything, every damned thing I can, to find her and make sure she's safe."

"She doesn't need you!"

"If you don't want your ass to land in jail, you'd better just walk away. Take care of your sister. This isn't the way to deal with it."

With that he released the boy and strode into the tavern, exercising his jaw. He knew the kid was just acting out. That his father was dead. That Regan and a half sister were all Jeremy Strand had in the world.

But the kid had better learn early on he couldn't just throw punches.

Inside the bar, Nate walked to one of the windows and watched Jeremy pick himself up. With a glowering look over his shoulder at the bar, he walked, shoulders hunched, down the street toward a dented Chevy truck that had to be twenty years old.

I'm going to find your mother, Nate promised silently, as Jeremy, still frowning, pulled away from the curb, nearly hitting a truck with a canopy that pulled around a corner too fast and gunned up the slick street. Jeremy's truck stopped just in time and Jeremy yelled something at the guy, but the truck was already speeding across the railroad tracks at the base of Boxer Bluff.

Drawing a breath, Santana turned from the window and considered Ivor Hicks, who'd parked himself on a stool at the bar in his usual spot.

*   *   *

I nearly hit the old truck!

Hell!

I have to be more careful!

Sweat breaks out over my body, but I tell myself it's all right. The accident was avoided.

Another close call averted.

It was bad enough spying Ivor walking into the tavern as I came out of the restroom. Thankfully, he didn't see me, was more interested in some altercation on the street, so I paid my bill and headed out the back door, something I do often enough not to bring any attention to me.

I just wanted to give myself an alibi, let some of the regulars get a glimpse of me.

But not Ivor.

No way.

Not that I thought for a second he could put two and two together and come up with four, but he was the idiot who saw me just after I sent good old Brady to his Maker and he might come out of his drunken stupor enough to realize it was me at the Lazy L, not a Yeti.

The old man is a definite problem.

Always showing up at the wrong time.

I glance in the rearview mirror and realize that the truck that had nearly pulled out in front of me belongs to Regan Pescoli's kid. I've seen him hauling ass in the old Chevrolet more times than I care to remember.

Ironic, I think, as I drive up Boxer Bluff and past the Pinewood County Sheriff's Department, set back from the road not far from the jail.

I wonder if Manny Douglas has shared his information with the cops yet. Maybe yes. Maybe no. I know a part of him will want to keep the information and publish it, try to "crack the case" himself. His ego is so big that he'll have the mistaken notion that his fame will spread and he'll be propelled to national stardom. He has grandiose ideas. I've heard him brag that he once turned down a job at the *Seattle Post-Intelligencer*. "The *Post*," as he calls it. Like there isn't any other. Not even the *New York Post* or closer still, the *Denver Post*, or others scattered across the continent. Oh, yeah, Manny, you're brilliant. Maybe losing you is why "The *Post*" is no longer printing, the reason it went fully digital. They lost out on that whip-sharp, ace reporter Manny Douglas, and things have just gone downhill ever since.

Hah.

I laugh aloud, then pull into my usual gas station to tank up, buy some coffee, and talk to the cashier, wish her a Merry Christmas. I'll be on camera, and she'll remember me, along with the waitress where I left a big tip for my breakfast.

Alibis, alibis, alibis.

If Manny has shared the contents of his mail, the sheriff's department is a madhouse.

And if he hasn't, they'll learn soon enough.

"Have a good one," I say with a wave as I carry my tall cup of coffee back to my truck.

"You, too. Merry Christmas!"

She's a pretty young thing and if her initials had been right for my purpose, she might have become a candidate. *No, no, no! Remember: No one local. No one who can be tied to you. Except for Pescoli. That was the deal.*

I fire up the truck and wonder about that. Maybe Pescoli was a mistake. But I couldn't help myself.

Not only did her name lend itself so well to the creation of my message, but how better to stick it to Dan Grayson than by taking one of his own?

But you shot Brady Long. He's local. The police will tie the bullet to the other killings.

That might have been a little bold; maybe even cocky, I acknowledge, as I roll out from under the overhang of the gas station where a black leg dangles from its eave, the booted foot of a stuffed Santa, trying to climb onto the roof of Bitterroot Gas and Mini Mart.

As I pull away, I see the rest of Santa's body lying facedown as he appears to cling to the roof, his sack of toys spilling over.

Everyone in this town is an imbecile except me. It's pathetic.

With a full tank and alibis all over the place, I turn on the road leading away from town and into the surrounding hills. I've had my fun, now it's time to deal with Regan Pescoli.

She hasn't been broken yet.

And even now is probably plotting her next escape.

Or is doing it right now.

My heart lurches.

You left her handcuffed and broken from the fight, but she's not one to give up easily. Did you lock the door?

Glancing in the rearview, I see the worry in my own eyes and I step on it. I'm less than half an hour from the mine.

Run!
Keep moving!
Run as fast as you can!

God, it was freezing.

But Regan kept going, flailing through the snow, panicked to the marrow of her bones.

Once she'd realized she was free, she'd snagged a jacket, thrown it on, left the cabin, and started running. Blindly. Crazily. Certain her assailant was on her tail. She had no idea where she was and the sun was blocked by the snow, so she didn't even know which direction she was heading.

She just ran.

As far and as fast as her battered body would allow.

But now the cabin was out of sight and she had to stop, dragging in deep, painful breaths, needing to get her bearings. She had to take stock and start thinking like a cop, not a frightened doe.

Squeezing her eyes shut tight, she grimaced, forcing the panic and pain to the back of her consciousness, trying like hell to find a calmness, the cold, calculating side of her brain, all of her training. She fought the urge to flee like a crazy person.

Sheer terror wouldn't help her find Elyssa O'Leary. *Think, Regan, think.*

She opened her eyes. Took another calming breath. Felt the snow melt upon her cheeks.

Already she'd made a mistake.

Her tracks would be visible for some time, even with the snowfall.

Whenever the son of a bitch returned, all he had to do was follow the broken trail of snow. It wouldn't take a seasoned tracker to find her.

Swearing under her breath, swiping the snow from her eyes and pulling up the hood of her jacket, she stared at her all-too-visible tracks miserably.

They might as well have been marked with a bright red sign: This way to Regan Pescoli.

Pull it together or else you'll die out here, if not from Star-Crossed, then from your own damned stupidity.

No way would it snow hard enough, or the wind blow fast enough, to cover her tracks.

But what about his?

She knew the sicko had taken Elyssa from the cabin. Recently. Surely there were other tracks? Maybe half buried, but tracks leading to a vehicle . . . the same damned truck that had brought her up here.

She had to go back. Circle around. Make it look like she was heading downhill, then double back around to the cabin and find his trail.

Shivering, her body aching, she hated to return.

But she had no choice, not really. To save herself. To save Elyssa. She had to track him down.

Santana straddled the stool next to Ivor's. They were at the bend in the bar, farthest from the door, only ten feet from the restrooms. Christmas music played on a loop of prerecorded songs that were competing for airspace with the rattle of glasses, fizz of the soda dispenser, clicks from the video poker machines, and hum of conversation. Ivor was nursing a beer and staring glumly into his near-empty glass.

"Merry Christmas," Santana said, shaking off the remnants of his fight with Regan's kid. He hitched his chin toward Ivor's drink. "What're ya havin'?"

"Coyote Creek Pale Ale."

"On Christmas Eve?" Santana looked at the bar-keep, a tall, lanky twenty-five-year-old who was prematurely balding. "Give him another. I'll have the same."

Ivor eyed Santana. "Wouldn't mind somethin' different . . . Well, you know, like you said, bein' as it's Christmas and all."

"Whatever the man wants," Santana said.

"Jack. On the rocks," Ivor said, quickly, then looked over the tops of his glasses as if he'd suddenly got wise that Santana might not be on the up-and-up. "You want somethin' from me?"

"Just conversation. I just saw you here and thought that after yesterday, you know, findin' Brady Long and all, we deserved to unwind."

"I'll drink to that!" Ivor said, some of his misgivings allayed as the barkeep sent a small glass his way and he immediately lifted it to his lips.

A glass of the pale ale appeared before Santana. "Helluva thing yesterday," he said, taking a sip. "About Brady Long."

"Oh, yeah." Ivor shuddered. Took another drink as the "God Rest Ye Merry Gentlemen" began to fight for airspace with the laughter and conversation. The bar began to fill up as men who had worked short shifts filtered in.

Dell Blight, sawdust in his hair, his suspenders stretched tight over his huge belly, swaggered in to a stool at the far end of the bar. Two other newcomers began racking balls at the pool table.

"What were you doing over at Long's?" Santana asked.

"Just takin' a walk."

"Kinda cold for that."

"I know, I know, but it's . . ." He looked from side to side, as if he were about to say something, then pushed his nose into the glass.

"It's what?"

"I ain't supposed to say. Billy, that's my son, he gets himself all worked up when I bring up the aliens." He raised his eyebrows over the tops of his thick lenses. "It embarrasses him. Got so I don't tell him nothin'. Well, I had to fess up about the Yeti. The one with the yellow laser eyes."

"Lasers?"

"Hell, yes!" He tossed back his drink and slid it toward the bartender, who in turn slid a glance toward Santana, who nodded. With a fresh drink, Ivor warmed up. "I thought I was a goner, fer sure, the way that beast looked at me. *Zzzzzzttt!* My ticker nearly gave out right then and there, that's why I came into the house. For help and then . . . I saw you and . . . you know the rest."

Santana nodded, took a drink.

"Don't tell Billy I said anything or he'll be mad at me. And . . . ya might not say anything about findin' me here, neither. He don't approve."

"I won't," Santana assured him. He rarely saw Billy Hicks, so it didn't matter. They'd known each other as kids, but that was a long, long time ago when all of them, Simms, Billy, and Santana himself, had been half in love with Padgett Long.

He thought about that. Brady and Padgett, the rich kids who only showed up in the summers.

"Good, good, 'cuz I don't want Billy to get mad. He has a temper, you know. Got it from his mother." He sighed. "Lila, rest her soul, was the most beautiful girl on God's green earth, I swear, but she had a mean streak in her. Oooowee." Staring across the bar, where colorful bottles were on display, glistening and shining in front of the mirror, Ivor said, "What was it she used to say whenever Bill got himself into trouble?" He rubbed his chin. "That she was a snake . . ." He shook his glass, the ice cubes rattling. "Or was it a rattler. Or cobra?" It was as if he were lost in time, not seeing the glass bottles or hearing Dell Blight snort in a fit of laughter.

"Oh, I got it . . . She would touch her belt, that was it, kind of a warning, 'cuz she would use it on the boy. And she would say, "Be careful or I'll . . . no . . ." Then Ivor's face lost all animation and he grimaced, his lips drawing back over his teeth. "She said, 'Beware the scorpion's wrath,' as she touched that thin little strap of leather, and she had a glint in her eye when she said it, daring the boy to defy her."

The song in the musical loop changed to "We Wish You a Merry Christmas," but Ivor didn't notice.

"But she was a beauty, Lila was. And rich once . . . or was supposed to be. Always thought the old silver mine would be worth a pretty penny, but she was wrong. Then, maybe, we all were."

"The silver mine, your house is on it."

"Old mining shack," Ivor agreed. "But yeah, it's home." He slid a glance at Santana. "Hasn't been the same since she died. Heart attack." He snapped his fingers again. "Just like that."

"Sorry."

"Ahh. Been years." He buried his nose in his glass again, looking for any bit of liquid solace he could find.

Santana felt as if he should make some kind of connection, that somewhere in all of Ivor's babbling there was something important, but before he could really piece it together his cell phone rang. Dropping some bills on the bar, he slapped Ivor on the back and walked outside.

Chilcoate's number flashed on the screen.

About damned time. "What have ya got for me?" he demanded, noticing the snow had stopped falling. Good. Clouds were breaking up to show patches of blue.

"We need to talk."

"We're talking."

"Not on a phone."

Chilcoate's fear of being wiretapped by the feds was something MacGregor had mentioned. Santana knew he wouldn't be able to budge him. "I can be at your place in twenty minutes," he said, already sprinting to his truck.

"Make it ten."

Teeth chattering, gasping for air, Regan rounded the stone and wood cabin as snow blew all around her and the wind played havoc with her hair. She spied the footprints leading from the door, her set that took off to the right, and to the left, those she'd ignored, half covered with snow, a second set of tracks. Made by two individuals. Large boot prints and next to them, much smaller tracks. Those, she realized, were created by feet bare of any covering.

Her heart sank.

Surely they belonged to Elyssa O'Leary.

True to the bastard's word, he'd already marched her away from the cabin and into the forest to spend her last few waking minutes or hours freezing to death. In her mind's eye, Regan pictured the other victims, all without a stitch of clothing on, their own footprints left in the snow leading to the trees where they had expired.

"You son of a bitch," she bit out, forcing her teeth not to chatter as she staggered toward the trees, keeping the tracks in view as she started down the steep slope. The snow was a curtain falling endlessly from the sky—a curtain she was afraid her pursuer would soon part.

There were no landmarks to give her some indication of where she was.

But you were in a mine, Regan. A gold or silver mine.

The hills were riddled with mines left over from a bygone era, but most of them were small and boarded over. Forgotten.

Not this one.

It was large.

Those tunnels weren't the work of one man. The bastard might have reinforced some; it had been obvious he'd spent hours there. But the original mine shafts were extensive.

She knew the history of the area, the names of those who had first laid claim to the land, become rich, but most of them had moved on, even Hubert Long, whose family's wealth came from copper . . .

But gold and silver . . .

She kept her eyes on the trail of footsteps, staying close, careful not to step over a drop off as the terrain was rough, rocks and boulders hidden beneath the snow.

A cold wind scuttled through the barren trees, cutting through her, slapping her face. She was shivering so badly, she had trouble thinking, and in the near whiteout the going was slow, treacherous, the path tracks becoming more and more obscured.

She had to keep moving, ignore the numbness in her fingers, the cold that bit at the back of her neck.

Her heart drummed.

What if he was coming back?

Somehow you've got to nail this guy.

She started down the hill again, rounding a corner and spying a lean-to of some sort.

Her heart nearly skipped a beat.

The tracks were leading directly to the open building and a road, obscured by snow, was visible. This was it! A way to civilization!

She half ran to the shelter.

There was an empty space where, judging from the tracks and some oil that had spilled, a car or truck had been parked.

The pickup with the canopy that brought you up here.

Better yet, parked close to the side, was a snowmobile.

"Oh, Jesus, please let there be keys," she whispered. "Please."

But before she could look, she heard a faint noise . . . a rumble that broke through the stillness of the forest. She stopped dead in her tracks.

The little hairs on the back of her arms lifted as the noise, the sound of an engine coupled with the whine of a four-wheel-drive, reached her ears.

"Oh, God," she whispered as the ghostly image of a truck appeared through the veil of snow. She had nowhere to run. Nowhere to hide.

The killer was back.

Chapter Twenty-Nine

Pescoli blinked snowflakes from her eyes.

Billy Hicks?

The man behind the wheel of the truck was Ivor's son, Billy?

She recognized his image as the big truck groaned up the hill, wipers tossing aside the diminishing snow, the driver staring straight at her through the glass.

Now he knows you can ID him.

Regan had been forced to drop the poker because it would impede her escape but her hand tightened over the hilt of her knife as their gazes locked. He was swearing. Angry. His eyes burning hellfire.

Well, she felt the same way!

She sprang from her useless hiding spot near the snowmobile. Before Billy's truck's engine died she started sprinting away from the lean-to, racing through the snow. She couldn't let him catch her! She had to find a way to save herself! To thwart him!

Knowing she didn't have a prayer of outrunning him, couldn't expect to elude him, she concentrated on outsmarting him. It was her only chance.

Keep moving.

She was halfway to the tree line when she heard the Jeep's engine die and the creak of a door opening. "You stupid bitch!" he screamed. *Thud!* The crunch of metal hinges. As if he'd pounded a fist into the side of his truck. She didn't look over her shoulder. Just ran. Putting distance between them.

Go, go! Faster, faster!

Her mind was whirling, her body protesting, but she kept running.

Billy Hicks?

A diabolical and well-organized killer?

She couldn't wrap her mind around it, but as she ran, hoping the snowfall dropping from the sky would become her cover, she remembered that his mother had been a descendent of a silver miner in the area, his grandfather a man who had owned the largest mine near Grizzly Falls. And Billy worked at his own carpentry shop; made his own hours by himself. There was no one keeping tabs on him and he would have the skills to make the mines safe and liveable. The large table, the hand-carved armoire, Billy had built them with his own hands.

Strong hands.

Brutal hands.

She heard the door of the truck slam and hazarded a quick glance back.

Oh, he was coming now. Moving to a jog behind her, but he'd taken time to grab some tools. A thick coil of rope was wrapped over his shoulder, a hunting knife, much larger than the one she'd pocketed, gripped in his strong fingers.

Terror cut to her core. He intended to lash her to a tree as soon as he caught her. He was upping his game! She nearly stumbled, saw a deer flash through the icy underbrush from the corner of her eye.

Don't do it, don't let him freak you out. Think, Regan, you can outplay this psycho.

If only she had a phone.

Or a damned gun!

Her mother's admonition, *If wishes were horses, then beggars would ride,* tore through her mind as she cut between the pine trees, darting behind them and over fallen logs, scrambling through the snow. *Keep running. For God's sake, keep running!* She was breathing hard, cold air blistering her lungs. Both legs ached and her right arm was a dead weight, still useless after her battle with him while still in handcuffs.

Don't think about the pain. Work through it! Run downhill! Eventually you'll reach a road or farmhouse . . .

But how long would it take? It could be miles. The Kress mine was in a remote area near Mesa Rock on a large tract of land. Her stamina was in short supply and—

Don't think about it! Keep the hell going!

Gripping the knife in her good hand, she angled around a tall spruce, between two bare aspens. Cutting around a rock, she twisted her ankle. Pain ricocheted along her shin. "Oh, God!" She landed wrong, her foot hitting a tree limb buried in the snow, throwing her forward. Her knees began to buckle. "Hell," she bit out, trying to catch herself. *No! Stay on your feet!*

But it was too late.

She fell, her feet giving out. Down she went, over

a steep embankment, into a wide gully, tumbling
faster and faster, free-falling along the steep hillside, out of control, the world spinning, snow everywhere.

Using her hands as best she could, she tried to
break her fall, digging her fingers into the snow,
creating drag, trying to slow her speed so she would
avoid the trees and rocks that loomed near the bottom of the draw.

On her back, head first, the sky shifting overhead, her arms out, hand grabbing.

Bam!

Her left hand smashed against something sharp.
The knife flew from her grasp.

Oh, no!

Dig in!

She tried to catch herself, to grab onto a root or
rock or limb—anything!—as she careened down
the wash. Then she saw him staring after her, running along the top of the ridge, keeping her in his
sites.

Bastard! she thought, *Goddamned sick bastard!*

She gave up trying to stop the free-fall. Whatever
lay below was infinitely safer than dealing with the
killer who now realized she knew his face and could
ID him.

Grayson turned off the wipers and guided his
Jeep into his reserved spot in the lot at the sheriff's
office. A few other vehicles were parked in the
heavy snow and two news vans had taken up residence on a side street.

If he could, he wanted to avoid the reporters.
Dealing with Manny Douglas earlier this morn-

ing was all Grayson figured he could handle. For the past four hours, he'd been on the road, coordinating with the rest of the search party, looking for any sign of the missing girls, driving the most desolate canyons and ridges in this sub-freezing weather, staying within the perimeters previously established. Checking and rechecking the areas where the two missing women were last seen, as well as the routes they most likely would have taken to get to their intended destinations.

But the search had been fruitless.

And even, he suspected, pointless.

So far, none of the search party had found anything. No bodies, dead or alive, had been located tied to stark trees in the lonely hills. Nor had either of the missing girls' vehicles been discovered in one of the myriad of canyons and ridges that rimmed the town.

But maybe a wild-goose chase, too.

Maybe someone close to the investigation was getting his rocks off by sending Manny Douglas the notes.

A stupid thought.

Desperate.

The notes were real. He could only hold out hope that the notes were premature—before the killings—or an attempt by the killer to throw them off track and embarrass the sheriff's department.

Except Brandy Hooper and Elyssa O'Leary are missing.

It all came back to that. God help them.

"Come on, boy," he said, shrugging off the weight of his job and whistling to Sturgis. The black Lab bounded out of the Jeep and, tail wagging, followed Grayson past a cluster of die-hard smokers battling the wind and cold on the department's front entryway.

He tore off his gloves, hat, and jacket as the inside of the office was sweltering, the thermostat hovering near eighty. "It's hotter'n hell in here."

"Don't look at me," Joelle said, her face red, beads of sweat dotting her forehead. "I called the repairman, but Rod isn't sure he can get anyone on Christmas Eve." She fanned herself with her hand. "I don't know what else to do."

"Don't worry about it." He had bigger fish to fry. The damned heat was nothing. He tossed his jacket onto a side chair as Sturgis settled onto his bed, but before he could round the desk, Grayson's cell phone rang.

Stephanie Chandler's number popped onto the screen. Grayson was surprised, as they'd talked earlier in the day when he'd called and explained about Manny Douglas's visit and the notes the reporter had received from Star-Crossed.

"Grayson," he said into his cell.

"Halden and I are on our way back to Montana, but I thought I'd give you a heads-up," the FBI agent said, though the connection was faint, as if she were outside and the wind was blowing. "Hubert Long died this morning."

"Natural causes?" He guessed as much, but who knew? Maybe someone couldn't wait and hurried him along. The same person who had killed his only son.

"Yes. He went into a coma early this morning just after midnight and his organs just started shutting down. Nothing suspicious. But we'd already dispatched a field agent in the Seattle office to contact Padgett because of her brother's homicide."

"Alvarez already talked to her doctor about Brady," Grayson confirmed.

"Well, if Padgett got that information, it's all she's going to get from us, because she checked herself out of the care facility and is catching a flight to San Francisco."

"What?"

"I know. It's strange. The staff was surprised, too. Our agent's meeting with the doctor in charge of Padgett's care. He'll be there soon."

"I thought she couldn't speak, was hardly able to dress herself."

"I don't know. We'll learn more when our agent gets to Mountain View. There's bound to be a dance around the whole doctor/patient privilege thing, but we've got a court order.

"Okay, the plane's here. I'll call when we touch down."

Hanging up, Grayson felt that same sensation he always experienced when things didn't make sense, when coincidence became the rule. He couldn't help but wonder about Hubert Long's death. Had the old man died before Brady, as expected, the younger man would have inherited the lion's share of the old man's money. Padgett would be cared for, yes, but Brady would be in charge. But now . . . Padgett was probably the sole heir to the entire estate.

A lot of money.

Left to a woman with supposedly diminished capacity.

Who checked herself out of the hospital as soon as she learned of her brother's death.

Grayson considered. Was it possible that Padgett Long, institutionalized for a decade and a half, had somehow masterminded or been involved in the death of her brother?

"Nah!" he said aloud as he made his way down the hallway to the lunchroom, searching for Alvarez. Something was off there, he thought, glancing out the window where the snow flurries were making it hell to get the choppers airborne. One minute the skies started to clear, the next the wind brought new clouds and more damned snow.

Padgett couldn't be involved in Brady's death. It was impossible. Right? But his thoughts wandered down that darkly cut path and, as he poured himself a cup of coffee and picked up one of Joelle's remaining sugar cookies, he thought about motive.

If anyone had one, it was surely Padgett Long, though she couldn't have pulled this off alone.

He remembered her accident, had recently looked it up in the files. Brady Long had been charged with reckless endangerment, but those charges, possibly because of Hubert's influence, or because Brady was underage at the time, or because somehow the investigation had been compromised, had been dropped almost immediately.

But the fact remained that Padgett was incapable.

But not incapable of checking herself out of the mental facility and hopping a plane?

He looked down at the half-eaten cookie in his hand, the rear end of a reindeer. He hadn't even noticed chomping off head, antlers, and forelegs. Finishing off the tasteless treat, he brushed his fingers together as he made his way to Alvarez's cubicle again.

* * *

"Okay, Chilcoate, what have you got?" Santana demanded, stepping into Chilcoate's isolated cabin.

Santana had driven like a maniac up the slippery, snow-laden back roads to the loner's house. Now, damn it, he wanted answers. For the entire duration of the trip he'd thought of nothing but Pescoli and what she might be going through.

If she's still alive.

That particular panic had been eating at him for the past two days, and now he needed action! He was through with waiting. If he had to tear these rocky, frozen hills apart piece by piece, he would. He had to do something to find her. The waiting game was over!

"Don't ask me how I got the information," Chilcoate warned, closing the door behind Santana, cutting off the cold. He hesitated a moment, clearly warring with himself.

"I don't give a damn where you got it, just give it to me," Santana snarled.

"Wait, wait. I shouldn't do this. Goddamn that MacGregor!"

"You said you'd help. You said—"

"I got your information," Chilcoate cut him off. "Damn it, that's not it." He made an impatient motion and headed toward a narrow stairway. "Come on. I've got everything downstairs."

He led Nate into a dusty basement that looked like it hadn't been used in decades, except for the nearly hidden cameras. Then he walked to the back wall and pushed a button. A panel slid open and a private arsenal of computers, printers, wifi systems, monitors, and spy-type equipment was revealed. It looked like some kind of command center for special ops. Jimi Hendrix was playing "All Along the Watchtower" from hidden speakers.

"You've never seen this," Chilcoate reminded him, as he motioned to his private area. "MacGregor said you were cool and I trust him."

"I was never here."

Chilcoate nodded curtly.

"There's not a lot," Chilcoate admitted, "but I think it's important. A writer at the *Mountain Reporter* received some kind of communication from the killer; Manny Douglas has already written a story and scanned copies of the letters, then sent everything to himself via e-mail."

"You hacked into the newspaper's computer?"

Chilcoate shook his head. "No questions."

"Fine."

"And you asked about Brady Long and his sister. I found out she left Seattle on a plane bound for San Francisco."

"No. She's in an institution."

"Not anymore."

"But she's mute. Hasn't said a word in fifteen years. How would she—?"

Chilcoate held up both hands. "I'm just tellin' ya. I've got her itinerary. She bought a ticket. Headed to the city."

"How? What does that mean?"

"You tell me." Chilcoate gazed at him steadily.

"You think she's a part of this?" Santana asked incredulously. There was a surreal quality to the equipment in the windowless basement room, lights glowing, all backdropped by Jimi's guitar licks.

"Don't know." Chilcoate wagged his head back and forth. "But it's interesting. I'm going to check into her stay at Mountain View. So far, it doesn't seem that she ever left before."

"But she may have had visitors?"

"And phone calls." He reached to his desk and pulled some papers from a printer. "Here's what I got from the newspaper files." He handed the sheaf to Santana. "These don't leave the premises, so I hope you're good at memorization."

Santana grunted, already lost in the article. The story, with a byline crediting Manny Douglas, was all about how Star-Crossed had contacted Douglas by sending him letters that were supposedly duplicates of those found by the police. According to Douglas's article, Star-Crossed, using the initials of the women he killed, was sending a message. The last one being:

BEWAR THE SC   ION'   H

Santana looked at the last note and in his mind he inserted Regan Pescoli's initials into the unfinished line. "Beware the scorpion's wrath," he whispered faintly, feeling the blood rush from his head as he repeated Ivor Hicks's weird phrase. He stared at the letters and the entire plot clicked together in his mind. Then he crushed the damned pages in his fist.

"Hey! What are you doing?"

"I heard that phrase just today." His voice was flat. Dead.

"From who?" Chilcoate demanded.

"The father of the killer." In that instant, Santana would stake his life on one clear fact:

Billy Hicks was the Star-Crossed Killer.

*   *   *

Alvarez still wasn't at her desk, but Grayson knew she had come in earlier.

A dozen unanswered questions pounding through his head, he tried the task room where the temperature, like the rest of the department, was hovering high in the stratosphere. Zoller had been replaced by Scott Earhardt, another junior detective, who was now manning the desk. A window had been cracked, yet Earhardt was sweating. The big table was still littered with gum wrappers and empty cups from the earlier meeting, but so far, the searches had turned up empty.

Standing near the far wall, Alvarez was studying the map. She caught a glimpse of Grayson and her face muscles tightened. "Oh, God," she whispered, paling slightly. "They found someone? O'Leary? Pescoli?"

"No." He shook his head. "But I did get a call from Chandler. Hubert Long died this morning and Padgett flew the coop," he said.

"What do you mean?"

He told her about Padgett leaving Mountain View Hospital and buying an airline ticket to San Francisco.

"I just spoke with the doctor today. She caught me when I was at the Lazy L, interviewing Clementine and Ross," Alvarez protested.

"She left sometime after she heard about Brady's death."

"Left . . ." Alvarez sniffed and shook her head. "I don't get it. You think she was faking her mental illness?"

"Seems unlikely."

"More like unbelievable."

"I know." He agreed. Had the same thoughts himself. "Fifteen years is a helluva long time."

"You don't think she's—involved—in her brother's homicide, do you?"

"How could she be?" Grayson asked, and they stared at each other.

"Well, then . . . why wait? If she knew a killer, why not hire him when she was first institutionalized?"

"Maybe she didn't know anyone then. Maybe she met him there and he ended up here . . . Hell, I don't know." He mopped the sweat from his forehead. "Jesus H. Christ, it's an oven in here." He looked at the map. "Forget Padgett for now. What've you got?"

"Something's been bothering me . . . well, not just one thing. Take a look at the map." She pointed to each of the spots where vehicles or bodies had been located. "We've never found a correlation between the killing grounds and the spots where he took the women and left them. But every spot on the map is within a ten-mile radius of Cougar Basin and Mesa Rock, both of which are pretty much in the middle of all the dumping grounds."

He was nodding. This wasn't a news flash. "We've scoured that area."

"Yeah, maybe."

"What are you getting at?"

"If you start here at Horsebrier Ridge, where we located Pescoli's Jeep," she said, pointing to a dot marked on the map and the pushpin stuck into it, "and head due north, you cross Mesa Rock, where good old Ivor claimed the Reptilians found him. Go on through and you end up at Wildfire Canyon, where Wendy Ito's body was discovered. And her Prius was located here." She moved her finger over the map to the spot where another pin was located. "Over here we have Nina Salvadore." Alvarez pointed to the area where Salvadore's body had been discovered.

Sweating, feeling like she was going over old ground, Grayson said, "So it's all near Mesa Rock where Ivor claimed the damned aliens took him. You trying to link them to Ivor Hick's 'abduction'?" He aimed for levity but heard the impatience in his own voice. "You don't think Ivor's involved. The man is generally drunk as a skunk. Incapable. Couldn't pull off the planning."

"I don't think it's Ivor," Alvarez assured him. "He is always drunk. We've taken him in so often he refuses to let us call his son to pick him up. But he isn't just an old man who hallucinates. Now he's the only person to have been on the scene where two of the bodies, Wendy Ito's and Brady Long's, were discovered."

"Nate Santana found Long."

"But Ivor was there," she said, pointing again to the map. "Mesa Rock abuts the Long property, right?"

Grayson gazed harder at the map and said slowly, "Yeah. There was a time when Hubert Sr., Brady's grandfather, tried to buy more land in the area. Mesa Rock is on government land, but there's an old mine of some sort there. Not copper, gold, I think, or silver, but the owner wouldn't sell."

"Who's the owner?"

"I'm not sure any longer." Grayson's eyes narrowed. "I think it was handed down through the Kress family. That's what it was called a hundred and fifty years ago or so. Silver. The Kress Silver

Mine." He met her gaze. "Ivor Hicks was married to Lila Kress."

"And still lives up on the property," she said.

"What are you thinking?"

"What about Ivor's son?" she asked.

Billy Hicks?

"No . . ." Grayson slowly wagged his head from side to side.

"Doesn't Billy own a place nearby, on the same tract of land? Didn't he know Padgett and Brady Long? Doesn't he work his own hours and volunteer at the Fire Hall? Maybe he used their computer to access ours. We're all tied in together. If he was smart enough, he might have been able to follow our investigation from the beginning."

"Billy Hicks isn't some stranger," Grayson argued. "He's lived here all his life!" But it was making a horrifying kind of sense, and the light in Selena's dark eyes, the tightness pulling at the corners of her lips, told him she already believed Billy Hicks was the killer.

"Just because a father isn't the brightest bulb in the strand doesn't mean that the son isn't smart."

"He's smart all right. I saw it on his application when he wanted a job." He rubbed a hand over his jaw.

"And you turned him down?"

"We weren't hiring. There was a freeze. Besides, Hicks had gotten into a couple of fights . . . God almighty . . ."

"We've got to pick him up," she said urgently.

"We'll go to his cabin. Interview him. Get evidence," Grayson warned. " 'Cause if you're wrong . . ."

"I'm not! He's got Regan."

"Shit," Grayson muttered, and they headed toward the door as one. His cell phone rang before he'd taken three steps. Glancing down, he said, "It's Kayan," then clicked on. "Grayson."

"Looks like we've got ourselves another one, Sheriff," Kyan Rule said without much emotion.

"Another one?" He and Alvarez exchanged tense glances. "Where?"

"In North Star Gulch. Tied to a tree. According to dispatch, a couple of kids out sledding in this mess found her."

"You make an ID?"

"No, sir, but it's not Pescoli, if that's what you're asking."

He was. He hadn't known it, but a guilty sense of relief slid through him. "Give me the exact location," Grayson commanded. "We're on our way."

"It's not . . ." Alvarez started.

"No. Not Pescoli."

Not yet.

Chapter Thirty

Frantic, his heart pounding, Santana left Chilcoate and ran to his truck. He punched out the numbers of Alvarez's cell phone and started the engine. "Come on, come on," he muttered, throwing his truck into reverse, backing up, then jamming the gears into drive and hitting the gas.

His call was sent straight to voicemail.

"Shit!" He left a quick message: "This is Nate Santana. Call me! I think the killer is up at the Kress Silver Mine. I think that's where he's got Regan!" Driving like a madman down the long, twisting road to Chilcoate's house, he turned north.

Ivor Hicks, that old nutcase, had spilled the beans. But he wasn't the culprit, he wasn't the one who had to fear the damned "scorpion's wrath." It was his son.

Hard to believe.

Billy Hicks was the killer?

It had to be! Had to!

"Damn, damn . . . damn," Santana said as the snow and gravel crunched beneath his tires as he wound through the thickets of drooping fir and stark, skeletal birch trees.

In his mind, over the ever-increasing frantic feeling of panic for Regan, he tried to roll back the years to when they were all kids—he and Billy, Padgett and Brady.

He flipped on the wipers and damned the falling snow, though patches of blue hinted that the storm was nearly over.

It had been true that Billy Hicks had felt proprietary toward Padgett Long, back in the day, like a number of others, as well. Santana had witnessed that need to possess her himself. All the horny high school boys had been hanging around her back then. She was beautiful, smart, and different from the girls they went to school with. Rich, sophisticated, and slightly naughty, Padgett only came around in the summer or at Christmas break.

"Fresh meat," one of the kids, Gerald Cartwright, had said, ribbing Billy once. "And, hell, in my book, she's USDA prime!"

Billy had knocked Cartwright flat. He'd ended up in the emergency room with a broken nose.

At the time, Santana had thought Cartwright had gotten off lucky. As a kid, Billy's temper had gotten the better of him, but as an adult, he'd seemed to keep it under control.

Santana pushed his truck onto the county road. Rising in the distance was Mesa Rock, a flat-topped mountain butting up to the abandoned Kress Silver Mine and Hubert Long's Lazy L, where Santana worked.

"Right under your goddamned nose," he said,

cutting a glance at his reflection in the rearview mirror. His jaw was set, his eyes dark as obsidian, the corners of his mouth pinched in disgust. If he'd pieced this together earlier, if he'd looked in the right places, Regan might never have been abducted.

He silently cursed himself as the road began a series of sharp switchbacks. Traffic was light; he hardly saw another vehicle. Good.

Shifting down, he thought of Brady Long. What a prick. He and Billy had been acquaintances, nothing more. But that had been a lifetime ago. What had set Billy off now?

Who the hell knew?

He had to call the police. Alvarez was out, so, with one hand, he punched in 9-1-1.

Before the second ring, the phone was picked up by a female operator. "Nine-one-one dispatch. What is the nature of your emergency?"

"This is Nate Santana. I'm looking for Detective Alvarez or anyone on the task force! Now."

"Sir, is there an emergency?"

"Hell, yes, there's an emergency. I know who the damned Star-Crossed Killer is and where he's located."

"Is anyone injured?"

"Five people have been killed already!"

"Sir—"

"Just get a message to Detective Selena Alvarez or Sheriff Dan Grayson of the Pinewood County Sheriff's Department! Tell them that I'm on my way to the Kress Silver Mine, out on the south side of Mesa Rock. I think that's where he's got them. His next victims are in the mine, and Billy Hicks, he's the damned Star-Crossed Killer!"

"If you'll stay on the line—"

Through the windshield he spied a minivan coming from the opposite direction and seeming out of control. The running lights were on dim, but they were heading right toward him. Damn!

He dropped the phone on the passenger seat.

The minivan's tires were gripping, trying and failing to gain traction, as the vehicle slid across a patch of ice.

"Shit."

Running lights bore down on him.

With both hands, Nate eased his truck toward the shoulder, keeping his speed steady.

"Don't do it," he warned. "Lady, don't hit me!"

The driver was worried, a woman with a van filled with kids. The nose of the van crossed the center line, if it could have been seen, her wheels bumping out of the twin set of ruts left by previous vehicles.

Santana didn't have time for an accident or anything slowing him down. He pushed his truck to the limit of the road, his right tire precariously close to where he knew there was a ditch. It was filled with snow now, the edge indistinguishable, but he had to get past her car!

He saw the minivan's fender heading straight for him.

He punched the accelerator, his truck fishtailing as he shot past the van. With an effort, he straightened out the wheels and jumped forward.

With one eye on the rearview mirror, he watched as the van wove across both lanes once, twice, then found its grip and lane. "Get home," he muttered under his breath and felt a fine sheen of nervous sweat between his shoulder blades. "It's Christmas Eve!"

The minivan disappeared from view and he

picked up the phone again, but he'd lost the call. His wipers scraped against the windshield, rubber screeching on dry glass. He snapped them off and pressed hard on the throttle.

There was still nearly ten miles of twisted, icy road before he reached the silver mine and Regan.

And what then? When you get to the mine, what will you do? How will you find her? There are miles upon miles of tunnels running beneath the acres that constitute the mine. How the hell will you locate Regan before it's too late?

He knew the answer to that one.

He'd start with Billy's house.

From there he might get a clue as to where the creep was holding his victims.

He might not tell you.

Wrong, he thought, his mind imagining just what he would do, if he had to.

Billy would spill his guts under the right kind of persuasion.

Usually, Santana was a nonviolent man, a person who could understand animals, commune with them with only touches. But when it came to humans, especially those who exacted their own torture and cruelty, Santana knew just what to do. Compliments of the U.S. Military.

The bitch isn't giving up.

I run after her, steady, barely breathing hard.

I've got her and she knows it.

I watch as she stumbles, then falls down the embankment. Stupid woman. Didn't she see that potential slide? She falls faster and faster down a ravine as I jog around the lip of the ridge, keeping her in my line of vision, staying on the deer trail that cuts along the edge of the hill.

She cries out and something flies from her hand. A stick . . . no, the bitch had a knife in her fist! One of mine! Now it's gone. Lost in the snow.

This is getting worse and worse.

More and more out of control.

Rage thunders through me.

She thinks she can steal from me?

Then cut me with my own blade?

She deserves everything I give her and more! While she tumbles toward the bottom, I find the path that angles deep into this depression and never once let her out of my sight.

She finally slows, stops, and forces herself to her feet, but she's unsteady. Dizzy. And I'm closing the distance as she staggers away.

For the first time I feel a bit of satisfaction.

She can't last forever.

And the snow has stopped falling, patches of blue above. I vault over a frozen log, and a weasel, a blur of white with a black-tipped tail, scurries away deeper into the undergrowth. I take that as a good sign.

Yes, in many ways, it's a perfect day for her to die.

Of course, I would prefer to break her spirit.

To make her depend upon me.

To have her think she's in love with me.

To want me.

To offer herself up sexually.

I would love to see the hope in her eyes as she imagines me mounting her the way that bastard Santana does.

Oh, I would make her forget him!

Fuck her within an inch of her life.

Leave her sweating and panting and hurting with the feel of me.

Not that I would do it. It's not part of my plan, and I've made no exceptions in that area. Yes, I left two in the forest in one day, Brandy earlier than Elyssa, which was a slight alteration, but I couldn't leave Brandy alone too long. She had too much fight in her, even as she turned to me.

As for breaking Pescoli's spirit, it would have taken too long, been too dangerous. This is better, in a way. This chase. I can be satisfied leaving her in the forest now. I have my camera in my jacket, along with a small hammer and the note. I keep a copy of them with me—in my killing jacket—always.

I shift the coil of rope on my shoulder and feel a little zing of anticipation in my blood, a rush of adrenaline that keeps me going, my legs striding easily, my lungs beginning to burn with the cold, dry air.

How will Grayson feel when they finally discover her?

Desperate?

Disheartened?

Furious?

All of the above?

Good!

Bring it on. I can't wait until the cops find one of their own, naked and dead. Then they'll get the message: Everyone's vulnerable. Even you, Grayson, you sanctimonious prick. Now do you think I'm not good enough? Just the pathetic son of an old lunatic and a whore of a woman who left them?

"Beware the scorpion's wrath," I say softly and

the warning seems to slither through the icy trees and across the frozen streams, making the forest shiver with anticipation.

How often did my bitch of a mother whisper those very words before she hit me across my bare buttocks with a slim belt that stung and bit into my flesh? How many times did she force me to stand waiting, trembling in the corner, without a stitch on? Oh, I quivered and cried, anticipating her attack. And as she struck, she told me about Orion and the sting of the scorpion which had killed the great hunter. Oh, yes, she repeated the story with great relish, savoring it, as much as the beating she inflicted.

Sick, horrid woman!

And I took it. All of her wickedness and wrath while dear old Dad turned a blind eye, then poured himself into a bottle so far and so deep that his sanity fled.

Oh, yes, Mother. You finally delivered your punishment until, at twelve, I turned the tables. I was as tall as you were, and as strong. I refused to strip. Grabbed that belt and swore I would kill her if she ever tried to hit me again!

But then, you had one more trick up your sleeve. One more humiliation in store for me.

You walked out of the house and died less than a week later. Got the last laugh by leaving me alone to live with a drunken old man who believed in aliens. And I got to suffer the pity and scorn of the community.

I've heard them talk behind my back all these years. Whisper to each other. Laugh about the old goat and his sorry boy.

My jaw aches now, thinking about you.

I surface as if from a dream. I've spent too much time thinking about the past while running after Regan. Caught in my reminiscence, I've run on instinct, following her, but not closing the distance.

No more!

Now, I focus.

Run faster.

Feel my heart beating and the coil of rope jostle with my strides. My grip on the hilt of my knife never lessens and I start closing the gap, running faster, dragging cold air between my teeth, my gaze as always, centered upon my prey:

Regan's athletic backside.

She's sexy in a very earthy, darkly feminine way.

But now she's really slowing. Laboring. Those long, athletic legs straining.

This, I realize with a deep sense of self-satisfaction, is going to be easy.

Brandy Hooper was already dead, her skin blue, the gouges in her flesh attesting to her struggle against the rope that bound her to the tall, lone fir tree. A star had been carved into the bark of the tree above her head, and with it a note had been nailed into the trunk. Alvarez read it as a gust of frigid wind caused the page in her hand to flap and moved the stiff, frozen strands of the dead girl's hair. As predicted, this message was identical to one Manny Douglas had received.

"God save us," Alvarez said, feeling a quiet rage simmering deep within. Instinctively, for the first time in a long, long while, she made the sign of the cross over her chest, an automatic response from her childhood. As soon as she realized what she'd done, she felt embarrassed, flushing even in the harsh cold.

What the hell was that all about?

It's Christmas and you're scared to death.

She cleared her throat as she observed the dead girl, a woman who had intended to become a doctor, whose life work was to be healing people. "This means that Elyssa O'Leary's dead, too," Alvarez said and heard the fatalistic note in her voice.

"We don't know that." Grayson's expression was hard and he shook his head slightly, as if denying what was so obvious.

And Pescoli, what about her? Alvarez couldn't stop thinking about her partner. Where was she? In what condition? Oh, Jesus. She had to stop herself from making the sign of the cross again. This case was eating at her, digging at her from the inside out.

The crime scene team was on its way, the area cordoned off by deputies.

"I've seen enough," she said, turning away, sensing the grains of sand slipping through the hourglass. There was nothing left to do for Brandy Hooper, but maybe they could still save Elyssa O'Leary. *Who are you kidding? You just said she's dead. You know it!*

But Regan Pescoli. She was still alive. Oh, God, she hoped so. And they had to find her.

"Billy Hicks did this," Alvarez said, knowing it deep in her heart, urgency propelling her. Hicks was upping his game. What if he decided to kill again? What was to stop him?

"We'll go to his cabin," Grayson said.

The skies had cleared enough that the helicopters were up and Grayson had ordered the pilots to search the area near the old Kress Silver Mine. But it wasn't enough for Alvarez.

"We need evidence," Grayson reminded her as they headed for her Jeep. "Linking Billy to the crime."

"We'll find it." She was already opening the driver's door. "Let's just get to his place."

"Make it fast," Grayson stated grimly.

Oh, God, oh, God, don't give up. Don't!

Regan was gasping for air, her mind racing as she tried to think of a way to save herself. Hicks was closing in on her; there wasn't much time.

The snow had stopped and she could see farther, though the sun against all the whiteness was blinding and she still didn't know where she was.

In a physical struggle with him, she would lose.

Since she'd lost the knife, she had no weapon aside from a screwdriver.

She had to outwit him.

Somehow.

But inside she was shredding.

The physical toll was too much, draining her mentally as well.

Gasping, her heart feeling as if it would burst, she slogged forward, downward to God only knew where. The trees had given way and she was in an open glen, it seemed, and ahead, an extremely flat area, rimmed by the forest.

What? Why was the ground so perfectly even?

A lake!

Frozen solid.

Snow covering the ice.

If she could reach the place before he caught her, the frozen water, maybe she could lure him out on it. He outweighed her by at least seventy pounds, and the rope was heavy, adding even more weight. There was a chance he would fall through first.

This is a crazy idea. You'll fall through the ice and drown.

But so will he.

And she was running out of options. Fast.

Better to try anything than let the son of a bitch kill her without a fight.

Bring it on, Billy. I'm ready!

Chapter Thirty-One

I shouldn't be surprised.

As I run after her, I know she's a cretin.

Pescoli, the supposedly smart detective, is just like the others in that inept sheriff's department that rejected my application. Well, take that, Grayson. How does it feel? To be the laughingstock of the whole damned country! That's right, asshole, the press, from as far away as Nashville and LA, are looking at you and your ridiculous force being made to look like imbeciles by me, someone not good enough. Well, put that in your pipe and smoke it!

What the hell is she doing running straight at the lake? Another stupid decision!

No doubt Regan Pescoli laughed at me, too, over and over again. All those times I came to pick up my loser of a father from the cell where he was held, "sleeping it off."

Yeah, she had some fun at my expense. Bitch! So

much like all the others. Common, brainless, cruel whores!

The only kind woman I ever met was Padgett.

My throat closes at the thought of her.

Beautiful.

Sophisticated.

With intelligent blue eyes and loving hands.

She hadn't laughed.

Hadn't avoided me because I was crazy Ivor Hicks's son.

Even when her father had banned us from seeing each other, she snuck out to be with me. At the time, so long ago, I wondered if her interest was only an act of defiance. But I hadn't cared. I'd won the prize! She was the only bright spot in my otherwise dreary, pathetic life.

I smile at the thought of her, sliding a bit, and I catch myself. I'm getting a little winded, my legs beginning to cramp. I have to end this soon.

For me.

For Padgett.

I promised her then, as we made love under the summer stars, that I would always keep her safe.

Of course, it had turned out to be a lie.

How was I to know that Brady followed us? Took pictures of us in each other's arms? Snapshots of Padgett's naked breasts, of me holding her as I came? Who would have thought he would have taken something so beautiful and made it so ugly and dirty, showing the photographs to Padgett's father?

The old man had been beside himself, had banned us from *ever* seeing each other again. If that hadn't been bad enough, Padgett had made the fatal mistake of going boating with her brother.

And she nearly died.

That brainless asshole had tried to kill her!

There's no doubt in my mind that Brady wanted her dead. Well, he's gone now, too.

Because of me. Because of my patience. There were plenty of other times in the past fifteen years that I was near enough to strangle him, or stick a knife right through his black heart. But I waited. The opportunities weren't right.

This time, however, everything fell perfectly into place.

And Brady bled out looking at me, knowing that I killed him, realizing that his sins were finally punished.

Everything I've planned for so long has worked out. Everything except for Pescoli, and that's only a matter of a few more minutes.

I watch her run straight at the frozen lake. Where does she think she'll go? Onto the ice? No way. So she's run out of places to hide. Good.

I push myself, getting close enough to see the panic in her eyes as the bitch takes a quick glance over her shoulder.

That's right, Detective, I'm coming.

Spurred onward, Regan headed straight for the huge expanse of even landscape, sunlight glancing off spots where ice still showed through the white blanket. It was her only chance for salvation.

She cast another quick look behind her.

God, he was so close. Maybe only fifteen or twenty yards!

He was smiling, but then, as if he suddenly understood her intention, shook his head. "Stop! You stupid—"

She didn't wait to hear the rest of his oath.

Over the pounding of her heart, the pulse throbbing in her brain, his voice faded.

Despite the pain searing through her body she ran onward. Hard. Plowing a trail that he could follow straight at the lake. Her feet slid a little as she hit the ice, the snow slipping over the frozen water.

"No!" Hicks's voice boomed across the wide expanse, and she just kept running, feeling nothing but solid ice beneath her, heading to the middle of the expansive lake. Cougar Basin, she thought as she spied Mesa Rock rising nearby. That's where she was.

If there were only some way to call someone. Tell them. But she was all alone. No one in sight, only her own ragged breathing making a sound.

I should have brought a gun.

The rifle or her damned pistol!

But in my hurry of unloading the truck, in my panic to chase her down, I left the weapons in the truck and grabbed the rope. I didn't want to use the guns, thought the crack of gunshot so close to my own home might attract attention I couldn't afford. And I didn't want to shoot her. What would be the fun of that—a distant taking of life? If a quick killing were what I needed, then I would have shot all the women in their cars, just taken them out as they were driving, then carrying them back to my place to nurture them, heal them, bring them to the brink of falling in love with me . . .

So I didn't bring a gun, not even to intimidate her, as I knew it wouldn't. And the damned truth of the matter is I thought catching her would be far easier than it has proved to be.

Now she's running onto the lake! God knows part of it is frozen solid, and even in the middle there has to be several inches of ice, but still, it's dangerous.

"Stop," I command again and the idiot just keeps on running, slipping and sliding through the pristine layer of snow covering the icy surface.

I follow. It's solid under my feet. Nothing shifting. It's probably safe.

Probably.

And I'll catch her.

But I have to be cautious. Listen for that cracking that spells death.

"There's nowhere to go," I yell, but she doesn't even break stride. I should have known she would be more trouble than I thought. Damn it, why have I underestimated her?

Fury burns through me.

It's time to end it. Now.

To hell with caution. I take off and run as if the hounds of hell are at my heels.

Santana drove as close as he dared to the house where Billy Hicks lived. The old cabin, over a hundred years old, had been built near the mine, in a clearing rimmed by trees. He parked behind a stand of pine, then, with an eye on the cabin, crept through the woods in its direction.

Nothing moved around the old house.

And no one showed in the dark windows.

A ruse?

He watched, mindfully aware of the seconds elapsing, spurred by the knowledge that Regan was somewhere nearby. But the house remained dark inside, no smoke curling from the chimney. It looked abandoned.

And there were tracks in the snow. Someone had recently been walking around outside, someone with a smaller shoe size than a six-foot-four man.

Regan?

His heart leaped.

He felt a sizzle of anticipation.

Had she escaped?

Nervously, he made his way to the front door, opened it, and stepped inside. But within minutes, he determined that she wasn't inside, though someone had been. The spare bedroom, complete with tiny bed, had recently been occupied.

Had this been where he'd kept her? Locked her inside? Surely she could have escaped this place?

In a further search, he found the other bedroom, a stark room rimmed in plank walls, with hooks for clothes and an ancient cast-iron bed, made with military precision.

Hicks's room.

He wondered if the bastard had brought Regan here? Stripped her down. Maybe tied her to the iron rails of the headboard while he . . .

No! He knew from the media reports that as demonic as the Star-Crossed Killer was, he didn't sexually abuse his victims.

Quickly, he returned to the main living area where the fire had grown cold and several doorways led to deep tunnels. Was Regan hidden inside them somewhere?

No—the footprints indicated otherwise.

Unless they were from some other woman, one of the other victims whose initials were part of Hicks's disturbed message to the police.

Still the entire house seemed unoccupied, recently vacated.

No sound emanated from the dark, subterranean hallways and he sensed that they, too, were empty.

And the footsteps outside.

Fresh.

Heart thudding, his mind conjuring up all kinds of horrible scenarios for Regan, he stood for a second in the middle of the house and closed his eyes.

He felt as if the place were dead inside, no living creature drawing a breath.

Damn. Opening all the doors to the tunnels, he bellowed, "Regan! Regan Pescoli?" He waited, his voice echoing back to him as he listened hard, hoping for some sound of response, the faintest reply.

Nothing.

Not the tiniest sigh.

Nor the cock of a gun if Hicks had heard him and were siting on him.

Again he tried. "Regan, it's Nate! Where the hell are you?" he yelled at the top of his lungs, his voice booming.

If Hicks was lying in wait somewhere, Santana had certainly blown any element of surprise.

But he felt nothing.

Sensed no stirring.

Just dead air.

For now he had to trust his gut instincts. He hurried back outside and running, followed the trail of small footsteps partially covered in snow.

* * *

Alvarez was driving as if the devil himself were chasing her, wheeling around corners, heading into the hills surrounding the Kress Silver Mine and the cabin Billy Hicks called home.

Her cell phone was vibrating like hell in her jacket pocket and she grabbed it and flipped it on when they reached a straight stretch.

Grayson, riding shotgun, was already talking to the 911 operator. He hung up and said, "Somehow Nate Santana figured out that Hicks is our boy."

"I just heard." Alvarez hit the redial button. "Let's find out what he knows." She braked for a corner, but the Jeep held as she headed north and suddenly Mesa Rock was looming over the surrounding hills.

Santana didn't pick up. "He's not answering," she said.

"Shit." Grayson muttered, "He's too busy playing the Lone Ranger. You'd better step on it."

She did.

Santana read the tracks all too well. At the shed where Billy Hicks's truck was parked there were suddenly two sets of prints, the smaller ones he assumed to be female, possibly Regan's, and now a larger set. Most likely belonging to Billy Hicks himself.

The killer was hunting her down.

Relentlessly.

Santana felt a deep jab of guilt. He'd known Billy all of his life, should have recognized that he was cold. Brutal. Merciless.

So, go get him.

Find Regan.

Two weapons were lying behind the seat of the truck. A rifle and a pistol.

He grabbed·them both.

Taking off at a dead run, feeling that he was already too late, he followed the tracks. His soul was heavy with dread.

What if she was already gone?

What if he reached her just to find her mercilessly lashed to a tree, her body frozen and blue?

Don't think about it. Just find her!

His cell phone jangled and he nearly dropped the damned thing as he tried, and failed, to answer it while wearing gloves. Still jogging, he recognized Alvarez's number and yanked off one glove, only to miss the call.

He kept running, the same long-distance pace he used in the military, his eyes moving from the trail to the area ahead as he hit the REDIAL button.

She answered after two rings. "Alvarez." Before he could ID himself, she said, "I got your message."

Thank God!

"We know about Hicks."

"I'm near his cabin now. The house is empty. But his truck was parked in a shed on the property, to the south of the house, beneath a rise. From the tracks at the vehicle, I can tell that two people are heading due north through the trees. My guess is Pescoli escaped, and he's tracking her down. I'm following."

"This is a police matter, Santana. I can't authorize you to—"

"Just get the hell out here. Fast! And send helicopters over the ridge, just south of Mesa Rock!" Before she could respond he gave her a quick rundown of what he knew, finishing with, "Get the damned dogs, snowmobiles, and choppers out here. I'm heading north." He clicked off and increased his pace.

He slid a bit, then saw where the tracks separated, where she'd apparently fallen down the steep incline, sliding and twisting in the snow. The hunter had bigger feet, and he skirted the edge of the drop-off. He followed the hunter's trail at a dead run. Tree branches slapped his face, snow dropping onto his shoulders and hair, but he sped through the forest with the agility learned from years of tracking game.

Running faster, he plowed across the clearing at its base, darting after the prints that looked fresher, no longer covered in snow.

He was getting close!

Into the woods he sprinted, still heading north, spying a hawk as it soared upward.

Where were they heading?

What the hell was at Cougar Basin besides the lake?

They're heading to her death. He's forcing her to the tree where he'll kill her.

Jaw rock hard, holding tight to both guns, Santana ran steadily through the wintry forest, closer to whatever hideous scenario the psycho had planned. He didn't know how much ground he had to cover, but whatever the expanse, it was too damned much!

Regan was halfway across the lake. Her lungs were on fire, her thighs and calves screaming in pain, her useless arm aching with each jarring step.

Hicks was only a few feet behind.

She hoped, prayed, for the ice to give way under his weight, but so far it held firm.

"Pescoli! It's over," he yelled, but he was breathing hard, struggling, too.

She kept moving.

"I mean it." In his hand was his knife, and he was close enough to her that he could throw it at her.

She kept running, zigzagging, keeping him off guard. Beneath the snow the ice was slick, her feet slipping as the sun shone bright, only a few clouds remaining, the air so crisp it was brittle.

It was as if they were the only two creatures in the universe: a wounded, failing woman and a gasping, looming man who was closing the gap between them. The shoreline surrounding the lake was far away, snow-laden trees glistening in the wintry sunlight.

"It's your time, Pescoli."

"Like hell." God, he was close. Her pulse pounded in her ears, her eyes burned with the cold.

"I said, 'It's your time,' now!" He lunged. Thrusting his body through the air, his knife raised, he threw himself at her.

She flinched, shifted quickly to one side. Sliding. Sliding . . .

Crash! He hit her hard, but she was still on her feet. "Shit!"

She kept running.

Sliding.

Putting icy distance between them.

She glanced around. Couldn't help herself.

Angry as a wounded bull, he'd pulled himself to his feet. "There's nowhere to run. You may as well give up!"

He was heading in her direction again, his face red, his eyes filled with a burning hatred. But she'd bought a little time.

Try to get him to fall again. And this time, jump on him. Use the damned screwdriver!

He was growing closer again. She heard his tortured breathing.

"Why? Why are you doing this, Billy?" she yelled, trying to catch him off guard, make his mind shift from its deadly purpose.

He was so near he could almost touch her.

Oh, no, no, no!

"Because it's what I do."

He propelled himself forward again, and this time, as she tried to duck away, she slipped, her feet shivering across the ice.

In a second she felt a big hand circle her ankle.

Oh, no!

"I told you," he said, sounding smug. "It's your time." But there was another noise as well—the deep, sharp sound of ice cracking and splitting.

"What the hell?" There, where his fingers clenched above her foot, nearly crushing her bones, was the first splintering web of deep cracks. He glared up at her, his face flushed with anger. "You stupid, stupid cunt."

"You're goin' down, Billy," she said, and kicked him hard, aiming for his head with her free foot.

Craaaaaaack!

The ice emitted a heart-stopping sound.

Beneath her, Regan felt the mass shift. Groan.

His fingers tightened over her ankle, twisting, and she cried out as tendons popped.

It was over, she knew, but if she was going to die, she was damned well taking this monster with her.

* * *

"The chopper's up!" Grayson said.

Alvarez stood on the brakes and her Jeep shuddered to a stop near Nate Santana's truck.

"Snowmobiles, too, heading to Cougar Basin. Deputies are on their way to cordon off the mine and this place." He opened the passenger door as Alvarez slid from behind the wheel. "I hope Santana knows what he's talking about."

"Santana wouldn't steer us wrong."

Weapons drawn, they stepped out quietly, carefully, silently, circling the house. Alvarez noticed the footprints, motioning to them as Grayson nodded.

They knocked on the door. "Billy Hicks? Police! Open up!"

Nothing.

They looked at each other.

Knew backup was still five minutes away.

Five minutes they didn't have.

They burst through the door, first Grayson, then Alvarez.

The place was empty.

A quick check of the rooms confirmed that if anyone was inside, they were hidden deep in the tunnels below.

"That son of a bitch," Grayson said, then called Brewster. "We need every entrance to the mine cut off and the tunnels explored. This guy's got himself the Roman catacombs up here."

Outside, they saw the tracks.

"Let's go!"

Together, they began to run.

* * *

The ice was splintering, breaking, water seeping upward.

It's over, Regan thought, knowing she was going to die a horrid, freezing death where her lungs would fill with water and she would never see her children again. Who would care for them? *Jeremy, oh, God, Joe, I'm so sorry. I should have been more careful and taken care of him.* Her son was already in trouble, and now with both parents gone . . .

And Bianca . . . Lucky, take care of her.

Hicks screamed as the ice gave way. He dropped the knife, tried to hold on to something, anything, his hand grappling wildly as he tumbled through the crevice, deep into the icy water. His grip on her leg didn't lessen and she, too, was dragged toward the ever-growing hole. She kicked and fought, her foot connecting with his head, but like a vise, his hand held fast.

Slowly but surely, he pulled her with him, down into the frigid, deadly depths.

"Regan!" She heard her name as she clung to the slippery surface. It was Nate's voice, but came from a distance, over the rumble of thunder. From a great, great distance . . .

Her leg was in the frigid water and Billy's weight inexorably pulled her downward, within the yawning hole where he was sinking, intent on taking her with him.

"Regan! Hold on!"

Santana? Oh, please . . .

With a last frantic tug, Billy yanked Regan into the lake's dark, icy depths . . .

* * *

"No!" Santana ran, slipped, slid, across the ice. He saw the struggle, watched in horror as Billy Hicks, holding fast to Regan's ankle, dragged her into the water. "Oh, God, no!" The ice was solid where he was, but as he ran toward the hole he saw the splinters, the deadly gashes spreading the snow apart, allowing water to surface.

He had to get to her. Had to save her.

Tossing down the useless guns, he stripped off his jacket and beelined toward the shifting, dark waters. Overhead a helicopter flew low.

The police! Thank God!

"Stand down, Santana!" he heard from overhead, the sound of a voice he didn't recognize on a bull horn, screaming over the *whomp, whomp, whomp* of rotors. "Nate Santana, stand down!"

He reached the edge of the hole and dived in.

She was drowning, thrashing, fighting the madman in the water. He struck her and she flung a hand at him, only to miss, to tangle her hand in the rope that was uncoiling in the darkness. Overhead there was light, distorted and broken through the ice. They'd been sucked away from the hole, were doomed to die.

Billy came close again and she took the screwdriver from her pocket. As if in slow motion, she swung, the Phillips head driving hard into his eye.

Blood spurted and plumed in the water.

Regan kicked away, her lungs on fire, the water a smear of blood. She couldn't hold on. Couldn't reach the surface no matter how hard she kicked.

It's over, she thought wildly. *Billy's prediction is*

true. Adrenaline caused her to kick hard, but her lungs, oh, God, her lungs were about to explode!

She thought of Bianca, on the cusp of womanhood. *Oh, baby, I didn't mean to abandon you . . . I love you . . .*

And Jeremy . . .

And Nate . . .

Her lungs were stretched to the limit, every air sac within feeling as if it would burst.

Pain, searing and hot, cut through her.

She let out a breath, air bubbles rising.

A bit of relief.

Don't give up! Don't! Fight. For your kids! For Santana! You have too much to live for.

But the pain . . .

More bubbles.

Billy, like an octopus in a sea of his own ink, was struggling wildly, but he was drifting away, from her, from the rope . . .

She let out another breath.

Felt light-headed.

This is it . . .

Her arm, the one twisted in the rope, was being pulled and her last grim thought was that Billy Hicks, the Star-Crossed Killer, had bound her with his deadly rope as surely as if he'd lashed her to a tree.

She let out her final breath and felt her lungs start to fill.

No!

Under the ice, Santana saw her give up.

Watched as the woman he loved let out her final, dying breath.

No, Regan, damn it, you're not going to die on me!

Tugging on the rope that had wound around her arm, he pulled hard, simultaneously swimming toward the surface, to the hole that was only a few feet away. His lungs burned, but he wouldn't give up, swimming hard, as hard as he had on the high school swim team. Reaching the surface, he broke through, gulping air, dragging her with him, cradling her head close to his chest as he hung on to the uncertain ice. The rescue team from the helicopter had lowered a man near them.

"Hold on," he whispered into her wet hair. "Damn it, Pescoli, don't you die on me. You got that?" His voice broke and he cursed himself for his weakness, but he kissed her head and said, "I love you, Detective. Damn it all to hell, I love you."

Chapter Thirty-Two

Freedom!
Finally.

After half her life spent in that miserable institution, Padgett Long would never again have to pretend. She stood at the railing of a small bistro in Sausalito. No one else was outside, the outdoor furniture bundled in a corner, the other patrons clustered at tables surrounding a huge gas fireplace in the center of the restaurant.

The night wind was brutal. Cold. Smelled of the Pacific as it tore at her hair. But she lifted a glass of champagne to her lips and stared across the dark, choppy waters of the bay to the lights of the city, glowing bright, towering toward the heavens. God, the taste of freedom was sweet.

And finally she could start the rest of her life.

Somewhere within the hilly slopes of San Francisco was Cahill House and within its secretive walls: answers. About her baby.

He would be a teenager now, lengthening out to become a man, probably growing whiskers, maybe fighting acne. Did he look like his father? She smiled to herself and shivered. No one but she knew the identity of the man; no one could guess. Everyone would probably think, if they knew, that her child had been sired by Billy Hicks who called himself Liam Kress.

Fool!

He'd been interesting. Intriguing with a cruel, guiltlessness to him that had intrigued her as a rebellious youth and had come in handy later on, when she'd found it necessary to use it for her freedom. A few infrequent references to the fact that as long as Brady was alive, she was imprisoned in the act she'd created.

Truly, she'd never really thought Billy would kill Brady. Not that her bully of an older brother hadn't deserved to die. A bullet had been too kind. In Padgett's opinion, Brady should have suffered. He'd tried to kill her when he'd found out she was pregnant, that there was another heir to their father and grandfather's fortune. But she'd survived, had her child and feigned her condition. Not that it hadn't existed, she thought now, as she felt the wind tear at her hair.

When she'd first been dragged from the water, near death, she'd barely been able to see or hear or connect the dots. She hardly remembered her son's birth and that still tore at her soul.

Well, Brady certainly got his.

Compliments of Billy Hicks and his belief that Padgett had loved him. Sorry. Billy was just a means to an end. And he, too, had suffered a well-deserved fate. To think he was a serial killer. A real whack job!

Jesus!

She had known he was twiggy; had seen his savage streak and even understood why it existed, but she'd never thought he would actually go out and hunt women in some bizarre scheme. It didn't make a lot of sense. Now, Brady's death, that had been necessary. Payback. But all those women . . .

She studied her champagne and frowned. A little sad. But mostly angry that she hadn't understood how vile Billy had been. Not that she could have done anything to alter things. Had she uttered one word or ever attempted escape, she was certain her brother, Brady, would have killed her. As long as Brady had thought she was out of it, mentally unable to pull a clear thought together and certainly not capable of speech, Brady hadn't worried about her.

Stupid, stupid man.

A real bastard.

All that blood is thicker than water talk was nonsense, perpetuated by ninnies who liked to stitch soothing quotes on pillows. Blood runs pretty damned thin when money is in the picture.

So now . . . Padgett was rich. And no longer hiding behind the walls of a sanitarium. She took in a long, chilling breath and held it in her lungs as she closed her eyes, then smiled as she exhaled. She could, finally, begin her life. And it started just across the cold, windswept bay.

To Cahill House.

Where she hoped to find answers.

She didn't have to be rash or in a hurry.

After all, she thought, tossing back the rest of her champagne, it was well known that Padgett Long was a very patient woman.

* · * · *

"I thought I told you guys to stay out of trouble," Pescoli said, eyeing her recalcitrant children as they stood at the side of her damned hospital bed. Jeremy in oversized everything including his ever-present stocking cap; Bianca in her ski jacket tossed over a turtleneck and jeans.

They'd never looked so good to Pescoli.

Tears burned behind her eyes, but she blinked them back, couldn't let them see her break down or give them any indication that she was suffering from nightmares of drowning with Billy Hicks's blue face looming in the water before her.

Fortunately, her injuries were relatively minor considering her ordeal. True, she'd almost died, but had been revived and, it seemed, examined by every doctor in the hospital. In the end she had more than her share of cuts and abrasions, bruised ribs, torn tendons in her shoulder that had been re-paired, but all in all, she would live.

"We're not in trouble," Bianca ventured. She tossed her curls over her shoulder defiantly, but her skin was pale and the shadows under her eyes were real. She'd been worried. Scared.

"You were an angel when you stayed with Dad?" Pescoli asked, trying to lighten the mood.

"Oh, Mom . . ." Bianca rolled her expressive Luke-like eyes. "I *tried.*"

"Well, I know how hard that can be," Pescoli admitted and scared up a smile on her daughter's face. "What about you, Jer. I heard you took on Cort Brewster."

"Maybe." Jeremy's gaze slid away.

"He *is* my boss," Pescoli reminded him.

"He's a prick!" Jeremy stuck to his guns.

"Jer!" Bianca cut in.

Pescoli tried and failed not to chuckle. "Let's keep that between us." She was a little light-headed, the results of pain medication.

"Do we have to go back to Luke's?" Jeremy tried to look as if staying with his stepfather was tantamount to sleeping in a den of hungry lions.

"Until I get out of here, yeah." Pescoli wasn't budging on this one.

Bianca said, "I don't know if I can take it."

"He's your father." Pescoli couldn't let them run free while she was laid up, no matter how much they complained.

"He's not mine," Jeremy pointed out.

"The doc says I'll be released in a couple of days. Until then, buck up. You can make a sacrifice for me, right?" When neither kid responded, Pescoli repeated, "Right?" again.

"I'm old enough to stay alone," Jeremy protested.

"Not by the law, my man. Not yet." Being a mother sometimes took more patience than Pescoli had. "And I don't think you've really proved a helluva lot of maturity in the past few days."

Jeremy stared at her hard. With eyes that reminded her of his father, Joe. "I was worried about you."

Pescoli's throat closed. "I know. I appreciate it. And now I'm going to be fine, so, please, for the next two days, hold tough, deal with Lucky and Michelle, and when I get out of here, we'll have Christmas in January."

He snorted his agreement.

"And Bianca," she said, "you're in charge of the snowman pancakes and flocking the tree pink."

"Ouch!" Jeremy said.

"Meeeow," Bianca responded and through the half-open door, Pescoli heard the sound of a doctor being paged. "Mo-om! That's so mean!"

"Must be the meds," Pescoli muttered but they all laughed. "Now, if you really want to get on my good side, go to Wild Will's, order a hamburger to go and smuggle it in here! Hey, what's that?" For the first time Pescoli noticed a small silver band around Bianca's left ring finger.

Her daughter flushed. "It's a Christmas gift from Chris. A promise ring."

Pescoli didn't like the sound of that. "Promise for what?"

Bianca twisted the ring. "Just, you know, 'cuz he likes me."

"Jer?" Pescoli glanced at her son. "What does it mean?"

"I don't know. Kinda like I promise to someday, like, get engaged to you."

Pescoli leveled her gaze at her daughter. "Is that so?"

Bianca was shaking her head. "No, not really." A lie.

"You're thirteen. There will be no promises."

"Mom, it was really sweet of him." Bianca wasn't going down without a fight.

"You heard me, Bianca." God, she had to get out of here. "You need to return it."

Sparks flared in her daughter's eyes. "But—"

"Okay, okay, we'll deal with this when I get home,

but trust me, you're waaaay too young for any kind of promises besides 'I'll go to the winter dance with you.' Even that's a stretch." She pushed herself up in bed, felt her IV connection pull at her wrist and wished to hell she could get someone to release her. "Look I'm going to find a way out of here, so you get the house ready, okay. We'll have Christmas." She saw the spark in Jeremy's eyes, "But until it's official and I call you, I'm afraid you're stuck with Lucky."

Her kids grumbled but left and she pushed the call button for a nurse. She was going to be released come hell or high water.

Within two minutes the door opened again and she said, "I need to get out of here ASAP," before she saw her partner striding into the room.

"You got that right!" Alvarez was shaking her head. Her hair was pulled tight into a bun at the base of her neck and she wore all black—sweater, slacks, boots, and jacket. Like she was going to a damned funeral. Only the hoops glinting from her ears broke up her somber attire. In one hand was a bouquet of white carnations and bright yellow daisies, in the other was a pack of Nicorette gum. "The Department's just falling to pieces without you. Anarchy reigns."

Pescoli grinned at the sarcasm. It wasn't like uptight Selena Alvarez to joke, but here she was, her lips twitching, relief on her sharp features.

"You know, Pescoli, you scared me to death." She set the flowers on the ledge of a window overlooking the parking lot. Snow was falling over the asphalt that had been plowed earlier in the day.

"Didn't mean to." She winced as she pushed the

lever on the bed to raise her head. "Have we located Hicks's body?"

"Not yet."

Then her nightmares wouldn't cease.

Alvarez dropped the gum onto Pescoli's table near her half-full glass of water. "Merry Christmas. I thought you might be wanting to smoke and I thought since you're in the hospital and all, and New Year's is right around the corner, maybe you should quit. Like for good. Besides I don't think the doctors would approve if I brought in a pack of cigs."

Pescoli eyed her partner. "I'll give it some thought."

"Meaning 'butt out'?"

"Something like that." But she picked up the pack of tasteless gum. "Seriously, how're things at the office?"

"Better. Since Star-Crossed is now officially over. Joelle wants us to have some kind of New Year's party, but everyone's dog tired and just wants to have some time with their families."

"You?" Pescoli asked and saw the shadow cross her partner's eyes.

"Nah. I don't have anyone around. I volunteered to cover some of the shifts."

"You could use a break."

"I'll get one." She nodded toward the bed. "Once my partner's back on her feet."

The door opened and a heavy-set nurse with apple cheeks swept in. "Can I get you something?" she asked as she hit a button to turn off the call light.

"Yeah, how about a release," Pescoli said. "The

doctor mentioned I might get out of here today and I need to get back to my kids and my job."

"Tomorrow, I think he said." Nurse Patterson wasn't easily bluffed. "But I'll check, Detective."

"Good."

The nurse backed out the door and Alvarez, her expression turning somber said, "Seriously, Pescoli, I know you and I, we're kind of oil and water, don't always get along, surely don't see eye to eye, but . . . what we do, it works."

"Yeah?"

"And there was a time when I knew that son of a bitch had you. I knew that your initials were part of his message and I thought that psycho had already killed you." Her eyes were dark as obsidian. "I was sure that we were going to find your body tied to a damned tree."

"It wasn't."

"Not quite. Christ, Pescoli, what the hell were you thinking? Taking off on your own? Letting that son of a bitch get the drop on you!" She was agitated now, her cheeks flushed, more flustered than Pescoli had ever seen Alvarez who was usually wound so tight, under so much control.

"I was just thinking about my kids. I didn't ask the creep to shoot out my tire!"

"I know, but he was playing you. Somehow he was playing you!"

"He was playing everyone."

"Well . . . yeah." Alvarez took a step toward the bed. "That's true, but listen, I'm not kidding, if you ever scare the hell out of me like this again, I might just have to shoot you myself!"

Pescoli nodded. "You can use my gun."

The storm in Alvarez's eyes broke and she let out a short, disbelieving laugh. "You're . . ."

"I know, I know. I'm everything you hate, but listen, we got him, didn't we?" Pescoli pointed out. "I'm alive and we got the mutt!"

"That we did, Partner." Alvarez, obviously unable to argue the point, let out a long sigh. "That we did."

Epilogue

"So, cowboy, what say we toast the New Year?" Pescoli said from the couch in her living room where the Christmas tree was already looking dead.

From the rocker on the other side of the coffee table, Santana raised a speculative eyebrow. "With what? Diet 7-Up?"

"I was thinking more in terms of champagne."

"You're still on pain pills."

"And you're no fun!" she teased, loving that she could goad him.

"Why don't we wait until you're 100 percent."

"That might take years."

"Maybe into next year."

"That's only an hour away." She shifted on the couch, felt pain in her shoulder and sighed. "I hate being laid up."

"Really?"

Regan half-smiled. She remembered nothing of the ordeal that had saved her life. They told her she'd "died." That she was blue and not breathing, that if not for Santana dragging her out of the frozen lake and administering CPR, she might never have come to.

It seemed impossible now. And though her fall into the ice and struggle for her life were only a week past, she felt as if it were a lifetime ago.

Billy Hicks's body had yet to be found.

Rescue attempts had failed.

Searches had turned up nothing.

But with the spring thaw, Pescoli and the rest of the Pinewood County Sheriff's Department were certain that what was left of the Star-Crossed Killer would rise to the surface. They would search again, when the weather broke, but for now, Hicks was floating in his own freezing, watery grave.

Which was just fine with Pescoli.

Elyssa O'Leary's body had been found, tied to a hemlock tree in the hills overlooking the basin. When Regan had learned of her passing, she'd felt a personal guilt, wishing so much that she could have saved her. So much. But Elyssa seemed to be the last victim that he'd captured.

The FBI and sheriff's department had searched the tunnels of the old mine and torn Hicks's lair upside down. Regan had told them about his files and boxes of pictures of potential victims and the public was breathing a sigh of relief. They'd found papers indicating that William Liam Hicks had sometimes used the alias of Liam Kress, taking his middle name and his mother's maiden name, including the times he'd visited Padgett Long.

Was Brady's sister involved in his death? That was a murky area that was still in question. No connection could be proven that she'd hired Billy Hicks/Liam Kress to rid her of her brother, but agents Chandler and Halden of the FBI weren't giving up. There was evidence that Billy had stolen a copy of Hubert's will from the Long estate; a corner of one page with Tinneman's firm's name and a spatter of Brady's blood had been found in the dead embers of Billy Hicks's cabin.

Ivor was broken-hearted.

Disbelieving.

Finding solace with Jack Daniel's and Jim Beam, even more entrenched in his fantasy about an alien abduction according to townspeople who'd run across him at the Spot.

Now that the reign of terror was over, and Regan was growing stronger, she was ready to deal with her personal issues. She'd been pleasantly surprised to learn that Lucky had given up his quest for full custody of the kids, and that Jeremy and Bianca seemed more than okay with the arrangement. Neither of her children had mentioned living with him and Michelle again. In fact, Pescoli had overheard them making fun of Michelle's Santa pancakes with blueberry eyes and whipped-cream beard.

It galled her that she felt an ounce of satisfaction in their attitude, but there it was. Both kids were out for the evening. Jeremy with Ty, his questionable friend, but Regan suspected somehow he'd find a way to hook up with Heidi Brewster. She'd warned him to take it slow and had even left a box of condoms in his bedroom, explaining they were for "when the day came," and that she was in no way condoning teenage sex.

But she'd been there.

As for Bianca, she was staying over at a friends as well. Regan had checked it out. Bianca had assured her that "absolutely" her boyfriend Chris wasn't going to show up. She also swore that she'd given back the "promise ring."

Well, maybe.

At least she wasn't wearing it in Regan's presence. But that didn't mean a lot.

"So," Santana said, reaching to the coffee table where the remnants of some of Joelle's "Special Christmas Bars" were scattered on a plate, "What do you think about moving in together?"

"What? Are you serious?" She was shaking her head. "I have kids to raise."

"And you, darlin', need a life of your own." He chewed on the cookie, then took a seat on the couch next to her, lifting her leg with its air cast on her ankle, onto his lap.

"You would be a lousy stepfather."

"I'd be a *great* stepfather," he said, pretending affront.

"Yeah?"

"Yeah."

She looked at him hard. "Is that what you want?"

A smile slid from one side of his mouth to the other. "I want you, and it's all part of the package. Besides, they're interesting to be around."

"Hah."

He rubbed her leg and she had trouble concentrating. "I liked things the way they were," she told him.

"Hmmm." There was disbelief in that syllable.

"What's wrong with a no-tell motel?"

"Nothing says we still can't do that."

She thought it over. "I think you and me living together might be the end of something wonderful."

He leaned down and kissed her bare leg. Damn it, she felt a tingle as his lips brushed over her skin. "Could be the start," he pointed out, kissing her a little higher and the tingle deep inside spread.

"You're bad," she said, having trouble concentrating.

"You have no idea."

"Oh, yeah, I think I do."

"Let's test that theory, shall we?" He shifted, lengthening out on the couch beside her and kissing her temple. "Tell me, Detective, what's your most secret fantasy?"

"You mean besides the one with you?"

"Naughty girl," he said, his voice low as he leaned over her.

She touched the side of his jaw and winked. "You have no idea."

Please turn the page for an exciting sneak peek of
Nancy Bush's newest thriller,
coming soon from Zebra Books!

Prologue

A blast of wind slammed against the old pickup and nearly wrenched the wheel from Rafe's hands. "Damn," he muttered. With an effort he kept the vehicle bouncing hard down the road. Night was thick and black and the keening wail of the wind kept Rafe's senses on high alert.

He glanced down at the crown of the blond angel snuggled up next to him. She was older than he was by six months, but she was so fragile that he felt manly and protective with her. He wanted to put an arm around her but needed both hands to wrangle this miserable old Dodge down the highway.

They were running away. Running away together. It scared him and thrilled him at the same time.

He saw her slide a hand over her protruding belly and it made him feel warm inside. His baby. Their baby. He wanted to crow with delight.

They'd gotten away!

But there was still danger.

She was silent as they continued to bounce and shake down the road. He hoped to hell the rough ride didn't hurt the baby. They were going for a new start, a new life.

Damn! It felt *good*!

Rafe gazed through the inky blackness and saw tree limbs bend toward the vehicle as he passed, as if they were trying to stop them. Nothing could stop them. He wouldn't let it.

He mused, "You know, they found that woman's body. The whore that called herself a witch? She'd been dead a while. Nothing but bones, really."

Rafe was much better at being a dope in love than a conversationalist. The woman beside him listened quietly, neither encouraging or discouraging him.

"Y'know I told you about the Blackburns?" he went on. "I do some work for them sometimes? They're that old couple who hide behind their curtains and spy on the other houses? They saw the fire across their field a few years back and thought the witch died then. Maybe she did. But the cops and stuff dug all around and didn't find her. Guess he hid her. But they found her now. Just a bag of bones."

They drove on for a while. The crying wind rose to a shriek as they passed through the mountains. The Coast Range. Rafe was taking them away from the beach and toward Portland though he didn't have the foggiest idea what they would do when they reached the city. But Tasha had told him where to go.

They passed a rest stop, one lonely light shining through the cold night air. Rafe had been feeling his bladder and with a grimace, stepped on the brakes and turned the Dodge back around.

"What are you doing?" she demanded sharply.

"Gotta drain the lizard, hon. I'm quick. You know how quick I am."

"They're coming."

"I know." He dared to touch her silken hair, comforting her. But she was tense and her blue eyes were shadowed and haunted as they looked up at him.

Rafe drove into the rest stop and parked in the handicap spot closest to the restrooms. The men's and women's signs were visible under the yellow light by the doors.

He started to get out and Tasha scrambled after him. Looking down at her awkward form with love, he observed, "Pretty soon that little bugger's gonna be here. What are you doing outta the truck?"

"I have to go, too," she said.

"You're peeing for two." He grinned in the darkness, his dark hair flying around his face.

He helped her toward the door and made sure the women's room was unlocked, then whistled as he strode toward the men's room. He couldn't believe his good fortune. She loved him. Loved. Him. They'd only made love a couple of times, of course, all under the cover of secrecy because she would be in deep, deep shit if anyone at the house found out. The first time they'd actually gone out to the graveyard and it had been a surprisingly warm May night. They'd made love right on top of one of her dead relatives. It had really made him feel weird, but she'd been so beautiful. White skin, blond hair, a kind of smile that made him want to throw her down and screw the hell out of her. Brand her as his. And he had, too. God, it had been something. She'd had to clap her hand over his mouth 'cause he'd wanted to howl and scream that he'd claimed her.

They made love the next night, too. This time just under her bedroom window. It had been a little chillier, and they'd had to be quicker. The danger was heightening. He'd come so fast he'd been a little embarrassed but she'd said it was okay. Had to be that way. Only way they could be together.

And then the people in the house had gotten stricter on her. He'd had trouble seeing her alone. But she loved him. She told him she loved him over and over again. And he loved her just as much.

So, they'd planned to run away and here they were.

Zipping up, Rafe strolled out of the bathroom. She wasn't out yet. Women never were. He glanced at a small field surrounded by the waving firs and decided to walk over and have a smoke.

Tasha leaned against the side of the stall, feeling cumbersome and fat. Her eyes were closed and she was mumbling encouragement to herself. She had set them on this path and now it was just a matter of timing.

Her head throbbed. Nothing new. She'd had the same trouble since she could remember. Migraines, or something like them. Pregnancy sure hadn't helped.

She heard the rumble of another vehicle pulling into the rest stop, the noise just barely discernible over the keen of the wind. Her heart clutched. She waited and then footsteps headed into the women's room, carefully measured treads.

Tasha's eyes flew open and her lips parted. The saliva dried in her mouth.

The footsteps slapped against the concrete floor, pausing a moment by Tasha's door. She was glad for the dim illumination; the lightbulbs barely worked at all. She dug her fingernails into her palms.

Whoever it was didn't bother going into another stall. They just turned around and headed back outside without using the facilities.

Shaking a little, Tasha carefully slipped her lock and tiptoed toward the outside door. She would be seen under the yellow light if she made a break for the pickup. Yet, she had no choice.

Silently cursing her ungainly shape, she drew a long breath then hurried as best she could into the night and to the passenger door. It was open, but there was no Rafe inside. Sidestepping the door, she slipped around the rear of the pickup. The vehicle three spots over was a dark sedan. Whoever had driven it here was not anywhere to be seen.

She thought she heard voices. A snatch on the wind.

". . . . baby. . . ."

". . . wasn't supposed . . ."

". . . get . . . away . . ."

". . . . you can't . . . !"

Tasha moved from the rear of the Dodge, back to the side, keeping the pickup between her and the grassy area where the voices seemed to be coming from. She couldn't discern who was talking. Wasn't sure Rafe was even one of them. But they were talking about a baby. They were talking about *her*.

Minutes passed. Eternities, it seemed.

She finally dared to leave the security of the pickup, but when her feet hit the muddy field grass she slipped and went down on one knee. She glanced around anxiously but there was no one. Nothing but the shrieking wind and rattling limbs and wet slap of water that flew off the branches.

She opened her mouth. "Rafe?" she called softly, sliding one clenched hand inside her coat pocket. "Rafe?"

The knife came swiftly. Slicing down on her. Cutting through her coat and piercing the skin at her left shoulder. Tasha screamed. Shocked. It pulled back and stabbed again and she stumbled away.

"Rafe!" she screamed and heard a moan.

Then her attacker was on her and she was rolling with them in the mud. Rolling and rolling. Fighting.

The last thing Tasha remembered was the knife-blade held high above her, glinting in the yellow light.

Denny had to take a whiz really bad. Damn, motherfuckin' coffee. Went through you like you had no pipes. He pulled into the rest stop as the faintest sign of daylight, more like just a little less of darkness, started moving over the hills.

He pulled his rig into a spot designed for RV's and big semis and leaped from the cab, race walking to the men's room. He was peeing by the time he got the damn zipper down and he let out a huge sigh of relief.

Finished, he looked at his reflection and ran a

hand through his thinning hair. "Fuckin' A," he said to his receding hairline. Making a face at his craggy mug, he headed back outside. A little lighter. Little better. He'd be in Astoria in an hour or so, depending on the snowpack in the Coast Range.

He was just about back to his rig when he heard something. Something like a groan. He glanced around. There was a beat-up Dodge pickup in the lot and he realized its passenger door was ajar.

"Hey," he called.

No answer.

Squinting at his watch he went to the door and pulled it wider. No one there.

The groan was louder.

Coming from beyond the pickup. Circling the vehicle, he checked the field opposite. Something there. Movement of sorts.

"Hey," he called again as he walked cautiously toward it. Wouldn't do to be some kind of wild animal searching for food scraps. He could do without that encounter.

Something on the ground.

Something with clothes on . . .

And then it rose to its feet, a bloodied figure, towering over the prone body on the ground.

Denny's heart nearly exploded from his chest. "Holy shit."

"The baby," the figure said, clutching its chest.

Denny stepped back; he couldn't help himself, as the figure before him staggered toward him then fell to its knees. A man. Now turning to once again bend over the limp mound on the ground.

"Hey. Hey, man," he said, reaching out a hand.

The mound on the muddy grass was a woman,

pregnant, her belly exposed like a white mound with black marks across its crest. Bloody marks. From knife wounds scored across the skin.

"Oh, Jesus." Denny pushed the man away who fell over without resistance, his eyes staring at the sky, blood dampening his chest.

Denny dragged his eyes back to the woman. She was breathing shallowly. Alive. Barely.

And the baby? Whoever had tried to cut the poor little thing out had not succeeded.

Sending a prayer to the man upstairs, he ran for his truck and cell phone.

Romantic Suspense from
Lisa Jackson

See How She Dies	0-8217-7605-3	$6.99US/$9.99CAN
Final Scream	0-8217-7712-2	$7.99US/$10.99CAN
Wishes	0-8217-6309-1	$5.99US/$7.99CAN
Whispers	0-8217-7603-7	$6.99US/$9.99CAN
Twice Kissed	0-8217-6038-6	$5.99US/$7.99CAN
Unspoken	0-8217-6402-0	$6.50US/$8.50CAN
If She Only Knew	0-8217-6708-9	$6.50US/$8.50CAN
Hot Blooded	0-8217-6841-7	$6.99US/$9.99CAN
Cold Blooded	0-8217-6934-0	$6.99US/$9.99CAN
The Night Before	0-8217-6936-7	$6.99US/$9.99CAN
The Morning After	0-8217-7295-3	$6.99US/$9.99CAN
Deep Freeze	0-8217-7296-1	$7.99US/$10.99CAN
Fatal Burn	0-8217-7577-4	$7.99US/$10.99CAN
Shiver	0-8217-7578-2	$7.99US/$10.99CAN
Most Likely to Die	0-8217-7576-6	$7.99US/$10.99CAN
Absolute Fear	0-8217-7936-2	$7.99US/$9.49CAN
Almost Dead	0-8217-7579-0	$7.99US/$10.99CAN
Lost Souls	0-8217-7938-9	$7.99US/$10.99CAN
Left to Die	1-4201-0276-1	$7.99US/$10.99CAN
Wicked Game	1-4201-0338-5	$7.99US/$9.99CAN
Malice	0-8217-7940-0	$7.99US/$9.49CAN

Available Wherever Books Are Sold!
Visit our website at **www.kensingtonbooks.com**

Thrilling Suspense from
Beverly Barton

__Every Move She Makes	0-8217-6838-7	$6.50US/$8.99CAN
__What She Doesn't Know	0-8217-7214-7	$6.50US/$8.99CAN
__After Dark	0-8217-7666-5	$6.50US/$8.99CAN
__The Fifth Victim	0-8217-7215-5	$6.50US/$8.99CAN
__The Last to Die	0-8217-7216-3	$6.50US/$8.99CAN
__As Good As Dead	0-8217-7219-8	$6.99US/$9.99CAN
__Killing Her Softly	0-8217-7687-8	$6.99US/$9.99CAN
__Close Enough to Kill	0-8217-7688-6	$6.99US/$9.99CAN
__The Dying Game	0-8217-7689-4	$6.99US/$9.99CAN

Available Wherever Books Are Sold!

Visit our website at **www.kensingtonbooks.com**